Anonymous

Archaeologia Cantiana: being Transactions of the Kent Aechaeological Society

Vol. II

Anatiposi

Anonymous

Archaeologia Cantiana: being Transactions of the Kent Aechaeological Society

Vol. II

Reprint of the original.

1st Edition 2023 | ISBN: 978-3-38230-227-6

Anatiposi Verlag is an imprint of Outlook Verlagsgesellschaft mbH.

Verlag (Publisher): Outlook Verlag GmbH, Zeilweg 44, 60439 Frankfurt, Deutschland
Vertretungsberechtigt (Authorized to represent): E. Roepke, Zeilweg 44, 60439 Frankfurt, Deutschland
Druck (Print): Books on Demand GmbH, In de Tarpen 42, 22848 Norderstedt, Deutschland

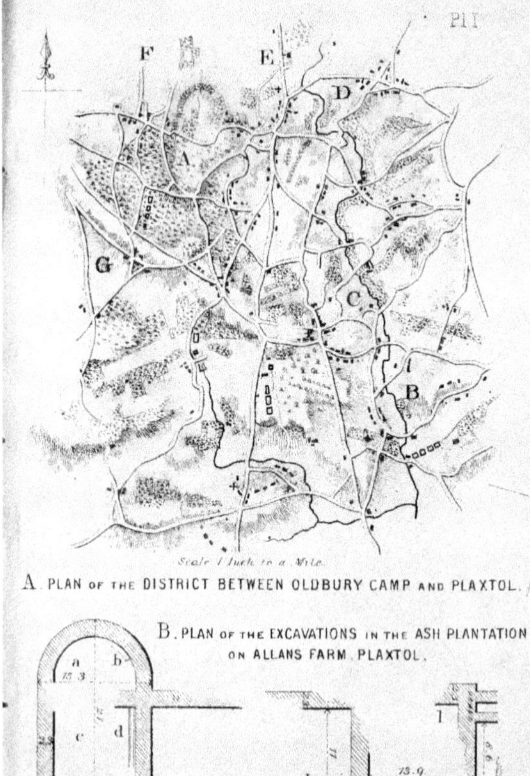

A. PLAN OF THE DISTRICT BETWEEN OLDBURY CAMP AND PLAXTOL.

B. PLAN OF THE EXCAVATIONS IN THE ASH PLANTATION ON ALLANS FARM, PLAXTOL.

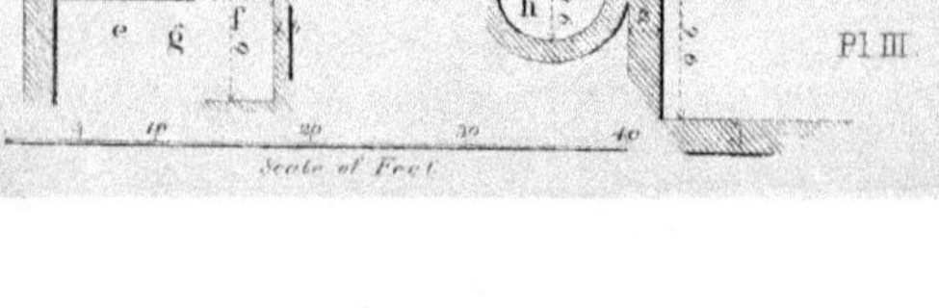

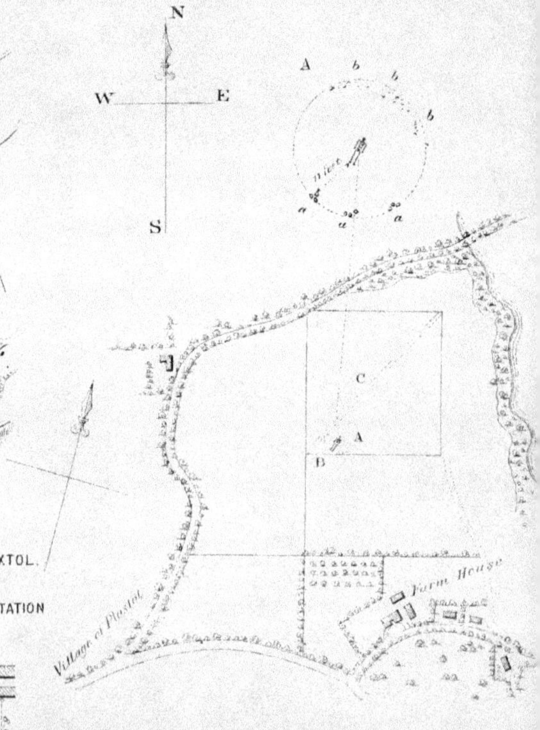

PLAN OF PART OF MR THOMPSONS FA

IN THE PARISH OF PLAXTOL.

Uniu'sis s'ce matris ecc'lie filiis. Will' fili' hetronis sal't. Reru' gestaru' memoria
ideo in scriptura' redigi't ne p' cessu te'por' in obliuione' labat'. Ideo notu' fieri desid'o
ta' p'sentib; q' futuris. q'd ego Will' fili' hetronis dedi 7 concessi d'o 7 eccl'ie S'ce Ma
rie Magdalene de Cubwelle 7 frib; ibide' d'o seruientib; in p'petua' elemosina'
ecc'liam beati petri de Aldurtunia. 7 hoc feci p' salute a'ie henrici regis 7
a'ie mee. 7 ancessor' meor'. his testib;. Willo de Ainesfordia 7 Rad' fr'e ei'. hug'
de Crrintunia. Eustacio de dikesmue. Joh' de berhes. Gileb'to capello. Barthol' ca
pello. heluulfo saluage. 7 Thoma fil' suo. Jacobo tunc diacono. Walt'o d' chanei
7 Multi Alii

PEDIGREE OF THE COHEIRS OF GRANDISSON,

As developed in Common Pleas Judgment Roll, Michaelmas Term, 6 Ric. II. (1382), *Roll* 508.

(See pp. 13 and 34.)

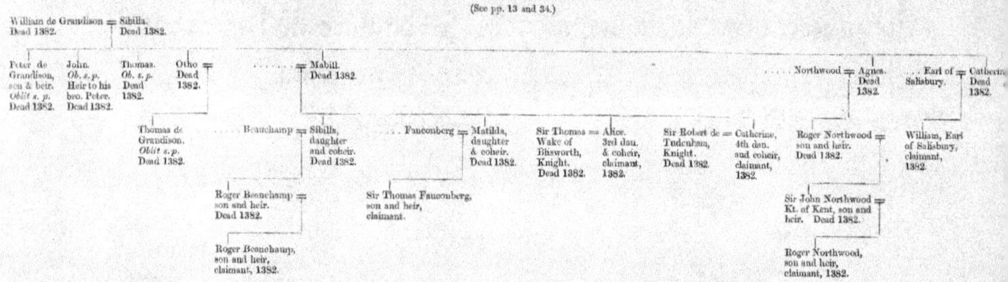

PEDIGREE OF THE COHEIRS IN GAVELKIND OF SIR JOHN DE NORTHWODE,

As developed in Common Pleas Judgment Roll, Michaelmas Term, 47 Ed. III. (1373), *Roll* 257.

(See pp. 14 and 36.)

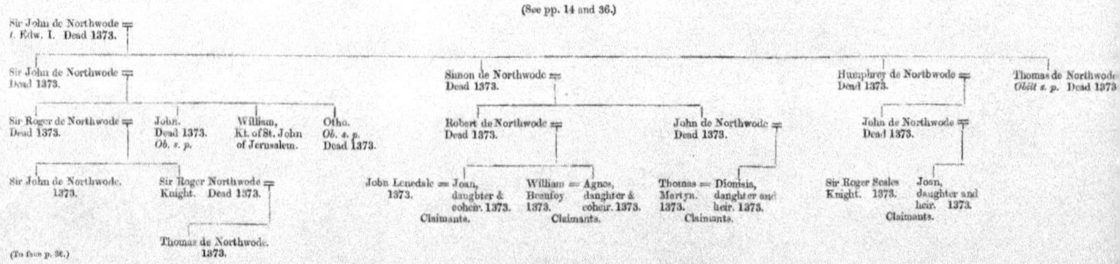

(To face p. 36.)

PEDIGREE DEDUCIBLE FROM THIS ROLL AND THE NOTES.

(Pages 9 to 42 inclusive.)

Sir Stephen de Northwode ╤

Henry de Wautham ╤
Dead 50 Hen. III., 1265.

Sir Roger de Northwode ╤ Bona Fitzbernard *alias* Bonafilia de Wautham,
41 Hen. III., 1257. heir to her brother, 50 Hen. III., 1265.
Ob. Nov. 9, 1285. See note 4, Appendix, p. 32.
13 Edw I.

John de Wautham.
Dead 50 Hen. III., 1265.

Sir John de Northwode ╤ Joan de Badlesmere.
Ob. May 26, 1319, *Ob.* June 2, 1319,
12 Edw. II. 12 Edw. II.

Sir John de Northwode ╤ Agnes, daughter of Sir William de Grandison, by Sibilla, his wife. *Ob.* Dec. 4, 1349.
Ob. v. p.

James. *Ob. s. p.* — Thomas. — Richard. — Simon. — Humphrey.

Agnes, relict of Sir John de Cobham. Her third husband was Christopher de Shukkburgh. ═ (5) 1356.

Joan, relict of Thomas de Faversham. *Ob.* May, 1356, 30 Edw. III. ═ (4) 1342.

Margery, relict of Sir Nicholas de Halgton. *Ob.* 1340. *s.p.* ═ (3) 1340.

Elizabeth, widow of Richard Foliot, and daughter of John de Seagrave. *Ob.* 1335. ═ (2) 1331.

Sir Roger de Northwode ╤ Juliana, daughter of Sir Geoffrey de Say, by Idonia, his wife. *Ob.* Feb. 20, 3 Edw. III. 1328-9.
Married under 15.
Æt. 12, 1319.
Ob. Nov. 6, 1361.

Sir John. — Otho. — Sir William, Knight of St. John of Jerusalem. — Thomas. — Robert.

Peter Rede of Dover. ═ Juliana de Northwode.

Stephen Pysinden. ═ Agnes.

Sir John de Northwode ╤ 1350. Joan, daughter of Robert Here, of Faversham.
Born 1321.
Ob. Feb. 27, 1379.
2 Rich. II.

Sir Roger ═ Margaret, daughter of Nicholas de Halgton, by Margery, afterwards third wife of his father, Sir Roger Northwode.

Geoffrey. *Ob. v. p. s. p.* — Agnes. *Ob. v. p. s. p.*

Sir Roger de Northwode ═ Alice. See notes to Seal 12, p. 42.
B. 1356. *Æt.* 23, 2 Rich. II.
Alive 17 Rich. II. *Ob. s. p.*

William ╤ — Elizabeth. Isabel.

James ╤ — Two sons.

John Digge ═ Juliana.

Sir John Dengeyne. ═ Joan.

(To face p. 42.)

SIDE VIEW _ OAKEN SHAFT.

12 Feet high.

Vases found inside Oaken Shaft.

Main-Cross Beam, Oaken-Shaft, 6 feet 6 inches

¼ inch scale

Cross Trees, 18 inches

1 inch scale.

Oaken Planking 3 ft 6 ins

1 inch scale.

F.G. Hetherclift lith. 17 Mill Stree[t]

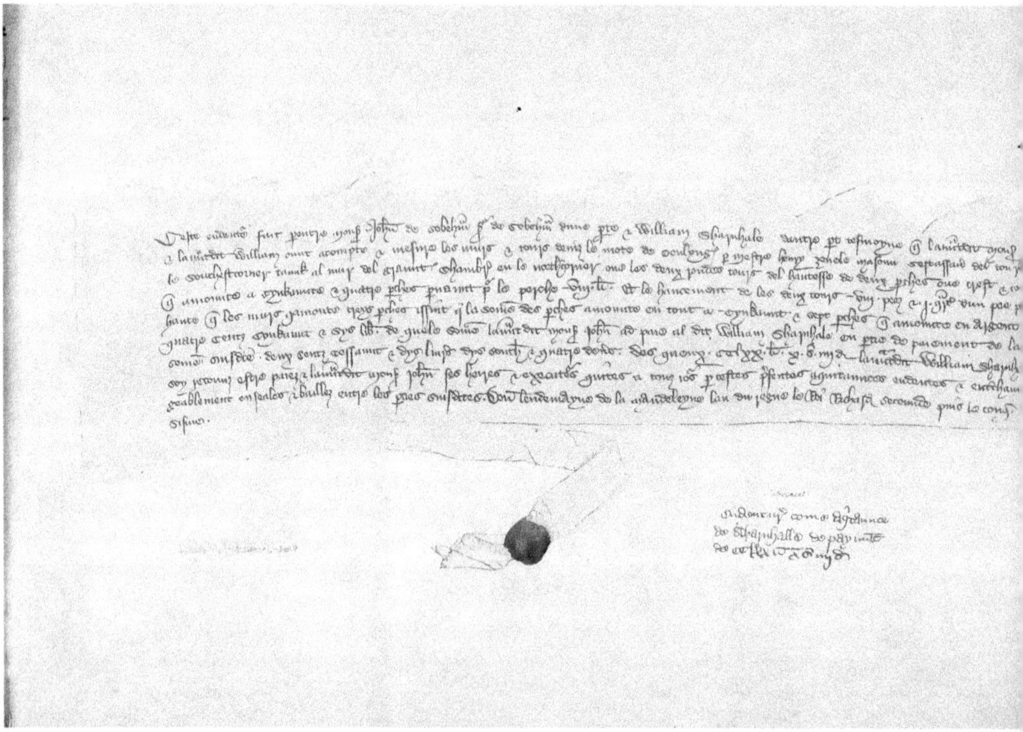

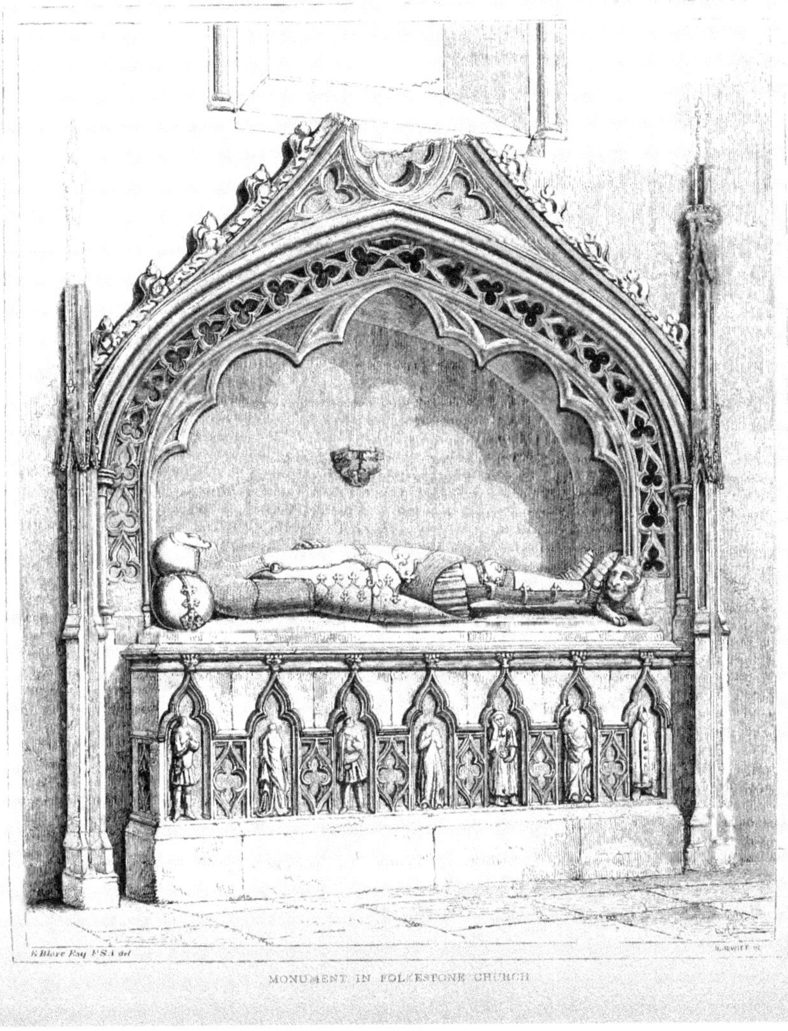

E Blore Esq F S A del — R. Sewitt sc

MONUMENT IN FOLKESTONE CHURCH

PEDIGREE COLLECTED FROM THE DIFFERENT RECORDS CITED

IN PAGES 133 TO 142 INCLUSIVE.

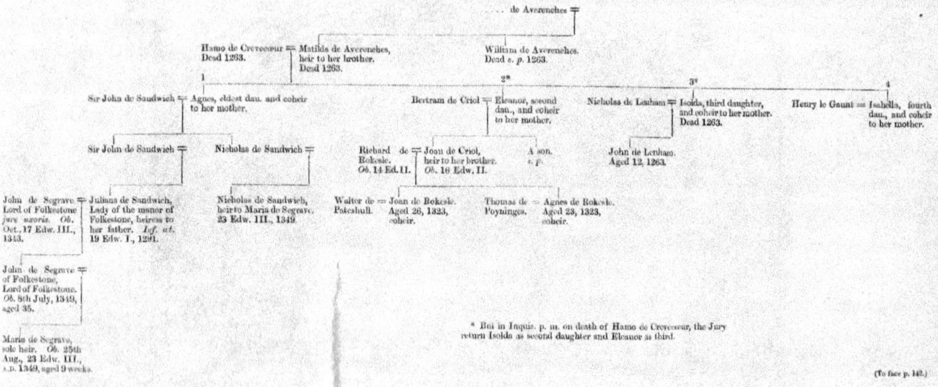

* But in Inquis. p. m. on death of Hamo de Crevecœur, the Jury return Isolda as second daughter and Eleanor as third.

(To face p. 142.)

Archæologia Cantiana.

Archæologia Cantiana;

BEING

TRANSACTIONS

OF THE

KENT ARCHÆOLOGICAL SOCIETY.

VOLUME II.

London:
PRINTED FOR THE SOCIETY
BY JOHN E. TAYLOR,
LITTLE QUEEN STREET, LINCOLN'S INN FIELDS.
1859.

"ANTIQUITATES SEU HISTORIARUM RELIQUIÆ SUNT TANQUAM TABULÆ NAUFRAGII, CUM DEFICIENTE ET FERE SUBMERSA RERUM MEMORIA; NIHILOMINUS HOMINES INDUSTRII ET SAGACES, PERTINACI QUADAM ET SCRUPULOSA DILIGENTIA, EX GENEALOGIIS, FASTIS, TITULIS, MONUMENTIS, NUMISMATIBUS, NOMINIBUS PROPRIIS ET STYLIS, VERBORUM ETYMOLOGIIS, PROVERBIIS, TRADITIONIBUS, ARCHIVIS, ET INSTRUMENTIS, TAM PUBLICIS QUAM PRIVATIS, HISTORIARUM FRAGMENTIS, LIBRORUM NEUTIQUAM HISTORICORUM LOCIS DISPERSIS,—EX HIS, INQUAM, OMNIBUS VEL ALIQUIBUS, NONNULLA A TEMPORIS DILUVIO ERIPIUNT ET CONSERVANT. RES SANE OPEROSA, SED MORTALIBUS GRATA ET CUM REVERENTIA QUADAM CONJUNCTA."

"ANTIQUITIES, OR REMNANTS OF HISTORY, ARE, AS WAS SAID, TANQUAM TABULÆ NAUFRAGII; WHEN INDUSTRIOUS PERSONS, BY AN EXACT AND SCRUPULOUS DILIGENCE AND OBSERVATION, OUT OF MONUMENTS, NAMES, WORDS, PROVERBS, TRADITIONS, PRIVATE RECORDS AND EVIDENCES, FRAGMENTS OF STORIES, PASSAGES OF BOOKS THAT CONCERN NOT STORY, AND THE LIKE, DO SAVE AND RECOVER SOMEWHAT FROM THE DELUGE OF TIME."—*Advancement of Learning*, ii.

The Council of the Kent Archæological Society are not answerable for any opinions that may be put forward in this Work. The Contributors of the different Papers are each responsible for their own remarks.

CONTENTS.

LIST OF ILLUSTRATIONS.

ADDENDA ET CORRIGENDA.

Page xliii., line 11, *for* J. J. Hayward, Esq., *read* J. J. Howard, Esq.

111, line 19. "Supervisoris et Contrarotulatoris" should have been printed, as in the original, "Supvis̃ et Conᵃ-rotul." William de Basyng and Gilbert Geldewene were, apparently, *both* of them Comptrollers and Surveyors of the Works, or, possibly, the former was Comptroller and the latter Surveyor. In the uncertainty caused by the contracted form of the original, the safest course will be to leave it so, without any attempt at extension.

125, line 13. The whole of these items of smiths' work should have been printed as in the original form. They are—"gumpħ, vertineƚƚ, cramponis, vincƚis, anulis, barr̃, boltis, hamis, stapuƚ, grossis clav̄ et minut̄, ferr̃ ꝑ tribuƚ et ligonibȝ, repacōe, batacōe et asceracōe secur̃ et aliorꝭ instrumentorꝭ cement̄."

125, line 14, *for* bands (*vinculis*), *read* chains.

128, line 2. "Plaster of Paris," in the original "plastr̄ ꝑis."

130, line 12, *dele* bolts.

130, last line but 3. "Grindstone, etc.," in original "j grindston cum j ferro ad idem, ij bolstrs ferr̃."

131, line 9. "Buckets, etc.," in original "ij situl̃ ferro ligat̄."

134, line 15, *for* her fourth daughter, *read* her fourth daughter, Isabella.

134, line 28, *for* domino, *read* domini.

138, line 1, *for* PAYNINGES, *read* POYNINGES.

141, line 15, *for* I, *read* We.

153, line 22, *for* Henn, *read* Hern.

191, line 35, *for* handed to T.'s charge, *read* handed to Tomlinson's charge.

203, 85th Section, at the note of reference to the word "Gentleman," *for* ¹ *read* ².

225, line 13, to "Michael et Robertus" this foot-note should have been given,—"*i.e.* Michael de Renstede and Robert Smyth de Cobham."

229, line 11, *for* Gudrid Creac, *read* Gudred Creac.

234, line 19, for the semicolon after "Londres" substitute a comma.

Kent Archæological Society.

President.

THE MARQUESS CAMDEN, K.G.

Vice-Presidents.

HIS GRACE THE ARCHBISHOP OF CANTERBURY.
THE LORD LIEUTENANT,—VISCOUNT SYDNEY.
THE EARL OF WINCHILSEA AND NOTTINGHAM.
THE EARL OF DARTMOUTH.
THE EARL STANHOPE, PRES. S.A., D.C.L.
THE EARL OF ABERGAVENNY.
THE EARL OF DARNLEY.
THE EARL AMHERST.
THE VISCOUNT FALMOUTH.
THE VISCOUNT HARDINGE.
THE LORD DE L'ISLE AND DUDLEY.
THE LORD CRANWORTH.
THE HONOURABLE J. M. BYNG.
THE HONOURABLE THOMAS E. LLOYD MOSTYN, M.P.
SIR E. C. DERING, BART.
SIR NORTON J. KNATCHBULL, BART., F.S.A.
SIR THOMAS MARYON WILSON, BART.
SIR EDMUND FILMER, BART., M.P.
SIR BROOK W. BRIDGES, BART., M.P.
THE VERY REV. THE DEAN OF CANTERBURY.
THE VERY REV. THE DEAN OF ROCHESTER.
THE VENERABLE THE ARCHDEACON OF MAIDSTONE.
WILLIAM ANGERSTEIN, ESQ., M.P.
JOHN MORGAN COBBETT, ESQ., M.P.
GEORGE CUBITT, ESQ., M.P.
WILLIAM DEEDES, ESQ., M.P.
GATHORNE HARDY, ESQ., M.P.
JAMES 'ESPINASSE, ESQ.
ALEXANDER J. B. BERESFORD HOPE, ESQ., F.S.A.
EDWARD KNATCHBULL HUGESSEN, ESQ., M.P.
W. A. MACKINNON, ESQ., M.P., M.A., F.R.S., F.S.A., F.G.S.
CHARLES WYKEHAM MARTIN, ESQ., F.S.A.
DAVID SALOMONS, ESQ., M.P.
MAJOR SCOTT.
J. A. WARRE, ESQ., M.P.
JAMES WHATMAN, ESQ., F.R.S., F.S.A.

Honorary Secretary.

THE REV. LAMBERT B. LARKING.

Assistant Secretary.

EDWARD PRETTY, ESQ., F.S.A.

Council.

Trustees.

Auditors.

Bankers.

Messrs. Randall, Mercer, and Co., *Maidstone.*
(London Correspondents, Messrs. Masterman and Co.)

Messrs. Hammond and Co., *Canterbury.*
(London Correspondents, Messrs. Glyn and Co.)

RULES

OF THE

Kent Archæological Society.

1. The Society shall consist of Ordinary Members and Honorary Members.

2. The affairs of the Society shall be conducted by a Council, consisting of the President of the Society, the Vice-Presidents, the Honorary Secretary, and twenty-four Members elected out of the general body of the Subscribers: one-fourth of the latter shall go out annually by rotation, but shall nevertheless be re-eligible. Five Members of the Council to constitute a quorum.

3. The Council shall meet to transact the business of the Society on the second Thursday in the months of March, June, September, and December, and at any other time that the Secretary may deem it expedient to call them together. The June Meeting shall always be held in London: those of March, September, and December, at Canterbury and Maidstone alternately.

4. At every Meeting of the Society or Council, the President, or, in his absence, the Chairman, shall have a casting vote, independently of his vote as a Member.

5. A General Meeting of the Society shall be held annually, in July, August, or September, at some place rendered interesting by its antiquities or historical associations, in the eastern and western divisions of the county alternately: the day and place thereof to be appointed by the Council. At the said General Meeting, antiquities shall be exhibited, and papers read on subjects of archæological interest. The accounts of the Society, having been previously allowed by the Auditors, shall be presented; the Council, through the Secretary, shall make a Report on the state of the Society; and the Auditors and the six new Members of the Council for the ensuing year shall be elected.

6. The Annual General Meeting shall have power to make such

alterations in the Rules as the majority of Members present may approve; provided, that notice of any contemplated alterations be given, in writing, to the Secretary, before the 1st June in the then current year, to be laid by him before the Council at their next Meeting; provided, also, that the said contemplated alterations be specifically set out in the notices summoning the Meeting, at least one month before the day appointed for it.

7. A Special General Meeting may be summoned, on the written requisition of seven Members, or of the President, or two Vice-Presidents, which must specify the subject intended to be brought forward at such Meeting; and such subject alone can then be considered.

8. Candidates for admission must be proposed by one Member of the Society, and seconded by another, and be balloted for, if required, at any Meeting of the Council, or at a General Meeting, one black ball in five to exclude.

9. Each Ordinary Member shall pay an Annual Subscription of 10*s*., to be due on the 1st of January in each year; or £5 may at any time be paid, in lieu of future subscriptions, as a composition for life. All subscriptions to be paid in advance.

10. All Subscriptions and Donations are to be paid to the Bankers of the Society, or to one of the Secretaries.

11. All Life Compositions shall be vested in Government Securities, in the names of four Trustees, to be elected by the Council. The interest only of such funds to be used for the ordinary purposes of the Society.

12. No cheque shall be drawn, except by order of the Council, and every cheque shall be signed by two Members of the Council, and the Secretary.

13. The President and Secretary, on any vacancy, shall be elected by a General Meeting of the Subscribers.

14. Members of either House of Parliament, who are landed proprietors of the county or residents therein, shall, on becoming Members of the Society, be placed on the list of Vice-Presidents, and with them such other persons as the Society may elect to that office.

15. The Council shall have power to elect, without ballot, on the nomination of two Members, any lady who may be desirous of becoming a Member of the Society.

16. The Council shall have power to appoint as Honorary Member, any person likely to promote the interests of the Society. Such Honorary Member not to pay any subscription, and not to have the right of voting at any Meetings of the Society; but to have all the other privileges of Members.

17. The Council shall have power to appoint any Member, Honorary Local Secretary, for the town or district wherein he may reside, in order to facilitate the collection of accurate information as to objects and discoveries of local interest, and for the receipt of subscriptions.

18. Meetings for the purpose of reading papers, the exhibition of antiquities, or the discussion of subjects connected therewith, shall be held at such times and places as the Council may appoint.

19. The Society shall avoid all subjects of religious or political controversy.

20. The Secretary shall keep a record of the proceedings of the Society, to be communicated to the Members at the General Meetings.

HONORARY LOCAL SECRETARIES.

London.

JAMES CROSBY, ESQ., F.S.A. . . . . *Adelphi Terrace, Strand*, W.C.
MR. SMALLFIELD . . . . 10, *Little Queen Street, Lincoln's Inn Fields*, W.C.

Blackheath District (part).

J. L. JAY, ESQ. . . . . *Greenwich Hospital*, S.E.
F. J. SCUDAMORE, ESQ. . . . . *Maize Hill, Greenwich*, S.E.
STACEY GRIMALDI, ESQ. . . . . *Maize Hill, Greenwich*, S.E.

Bromley District.

R. B. LATTER, ESQ. . . . . *Bromley*, S.E.

Cranbrook District.

REV. J. L. ALLAN . . . . *Cranbrook.*
REV. W. SMITH MARRIOTT . . . . . . *Horsmonden.*

Dartford District.

JOHN HAYWARD, ESQ. . . . . *Sutton Rectory.*

Gravesend District.

G. M. ARNOLD, ESQ. . . . . *Gravesend.*

Lewisham District, with part of Blackheath.

J. J. HOWARD, ESQ., LL.B., F.S.A. . . . *Lee Road, Blackheath*, S.E.
REV. J. S. CLARKE . . . . *Blackheath*, S.E.

Maidstone District.

G. WICKHAM, ESQ. . . . . *Maidstone.*
M. BULMER, ESQ. . . . . *Maidstone.*

Malling District.

MR. DOBELL . . . . *Malling.*

Rochester District.

G. B. Acworth, Esq. . . . . *Star Hill, Rochester.*

Westerham District.

J. Board, Esq. . . . . *Westerham.*

Tunbridge District.

Thomas Hallowes, Esq. . . . . *Tunbridge.*

Tenterden District.

Arthur Havers, Esq. . . . . *Tenterden.*

Tunbridge Wells District.

Rev. D. Winham . . . . *Tunbridge Wells.*

Ashford District.

Thomas Thurston, Esq. . . . . *Ashford.*

Canterbury District.

John Brent, Jun., Esq., F.S.A. . . . . . . *Canterbury.*

Dover District.

W. Clayton, Esq. . . . . *Dover.*

Eastry District.

Captain Belfield . . . . *Eastry.*

Faversham District.

F. F. Giraud, Esq. . . . . *South House, Faversham.*

Hythe District.

H. B. Mackeson, Esq. . . . . *Hythe.*

New Romney District.

John Humphery, Esq. . . . . *New Romney.*

Sittingbourne District.

W. Murton, Esq. . . . . *Tunstall.*

Isle of Sheppey District.

Rev. George Bryant . . . . *Sheerness.*

Isle of Thanet District.

Rev. S. Robins . . . . *St. Peter's, Thanet.*

SOCIETIES IN UNION,

For Interchange of Publications, etc.

The Architectural Museum, South Kensington Museum, W.
The Kilkenny and West of Ireland Archæological Society.
The Lincoln Diocesan Architectural Society.
The Sussex Archæological Society.
The London and Middlesex Archæological Society.
The Ecclesiological Society.
Société Archéologique de Dunquerque.

HONORARY MEMBERS.

William Henry Blaauw, Esq., M.A., M.R.G.S., *Beechland, Newick, Sussex.*

The Rev. J. Bosworth, D.D., F.R.S., F.S.A., Christ Church, Oxford; Professor of Anglo-Saxon, Univ. Oxford; PH.D. of Leyden, LL.D. of Aberdeen, Corresponding Member of the Royal Institute of the Netherlands, M.R.S. of Lit. London, Honorary F.R.S. of Sciences, Norway, F.S.A. Copenhagen, F. of Lit. S. Leyden, Utrecht, Rotterdam, Bristol, Newcastle-upon-Tyne, etc.

The Lord Braybrooke, F.S.A., 10, *New Burlington Street, and Audley End, Saffron Walden, Essex.*

Rev. J. S. Brewer, M.A., Professor of History, King's College, London, and Reader at the Rolls Chapel, *General Record Office, Fetter Lane, London,* E.C.

Rev. E. Cardwell, D.D., F.S.A., Principal of St. Alban Hall, and Camden Professor of Ancient History, *Oxford.*

Rev. Wm. Cureton, D.D., Canon of Westminster, *Dean's Yard, Westminster,* S.W.

Sir Henry Ellis, Kt., K.H., B.C.L., F.R.S., Hon. M.R.I.A., Hist. Scand. Holm. et Soc. Reg. Antiq. Hafn. Socius, Soc. Reg. Antiq. Franc. Corresp. et Acad. Reg. Sc. Brux., 24, *Bedford Square,* W.C.

Augustus Franks, Esq., F.S.A., Director of the Society of Antiquaries, *British Museum.*

Thomas Duffus Hardy, Esq., Assistant Keeper of the Records, *General Record Office,* E.C.

Edward Hawkins, Esq., Vice-President of the Society of Antiquaries, Keeper of the Antiquities, *British Museum,* W.C.

Rev. Joseph Hunter, Vice-President of the Society of Antiquaries, Assistant Keeper of the Records, *Record Office, Carlton Ride, and* 30, *Torrington Square,* W.C.

Thomas William King, Esq., F.S.A., York Herald, *Herald's College,* E.C.

Sir Frederick Madden, Kt., K.H., F.R.S., Hon. M.R.I.A., Hon. F.S.A. Edin., etc., Keeper of the MSS., *British Museum,* W.C.

Rev. Samuel Roffey Maitland, D.D., F.R.S., F.S.A., *Gloucester.*

Sir Francis Palgrave, K.H., F.R.S., F.G.S., Deputy-Keeper of the Records, *Rolls House, Chancery Lane,* W.C.

J. T. Quekett, Esq., Professor of Histology and Conservator of the Hunterian Museum, etc., *College of Surgeons, London,* W.C.

C. Roach Smith, Esq., F.S.A., Hon. Member of the Societies of Antiquaries, Newcastle-upon-Tyne, Scotland, France, Normandy, The Morini, Abbeville, Picardy, Copenhagen and Spain, *Temple Place, Strood.*

Rev. Arthur Penrhyn Stanley, M.A., F.S.A., Canon of Christ Church, and Regius Professor of Ecclesiastical History, Oxford, *Christ Church, Oxford.*

The Lord Talbot de Malahide, F.S.A., *Malahide Castle, Dublin.*

The Rev. Edward Trollope, F.S.A., *Leasingham, Sleaford. Lincolnshire.*

William Twopeny, Esq., 48, *Upper Grosvenor Street,* W.

The Rev. Robert Willis, M.A., F.R.S., F.G.S., Jacksonian Professor of Natural and Experimental Philosophy, *Cambridge.*

Sir Charles Young, Kt., Garter King of Arms, F.S.A., London and Edinburgh, and Hon. D.C.L., Oxon. *College of Arms, London,* E.C.

MEMBERS.

Corrected up to 20th June, 1860.

N.B.—THE * PREFIXED DENOTES LIFE COMPOUNDERS.

Abergavenny, The Earl of, *Birling Manor.*
Abergavenny, The Countess of, *ditto.*
Acworth, G. Brindley, Esq., *Star Hill, Rochester.*
Addison, C. G., Esq., *Inner Temple,* E.C.
Akers, George, Esq., *Malling Abbey.*
Akers, Mrs., *Malling Abbey.*
Akers, James R., Esq., *Tunbridge Wells.*
Alcock, Rev. John Price, *The College, Ashford.*
Alcock, John Price, Esq., *Ashford.*
Alford, The Very Rev. H., Dean of Canterbury, B.D., *Deanery, Canterbury.*
Allan, Rev. J. Lloyd, M.A., *Cranbrook.*
Allen, Rev. J. H., *Brockhull, Hythe.*
Alleyne, Sydney, Esq., *Tunbridge.*
Allfree, Rev. G., *Tunbridge Wells.*
Amherst, The Earl, *Montreal, Sevenoaks.*
Amherst, The Dowager Countess, *Knole.*
Andrews, Alfred Benjamin, Esq., *Canterbury.*
Angerstein, William, Esq., M.P., *Woodlands, Blackheath,* S.E.
Armytage, Col., *Broomhill Bank, Tunbridge Wells.*
Arnold, G. M., Esq., *Milton Lodge, Gravesend.*
Arnott, Rev. Samuel, M.A., *Chatham.*
Ash, Rev. Jarvis Holland, D.C.L., *Calverley Park, Tunbridge Wells.*
Ashpitel, Arthur, Esq., F.S.A., 2, *Poet's Corner, Westminster,* S.W.
Astley, Edward Ferrand, Esq., M.D., *Marine Parade, Dover.*
Atkins, J. P., Esq., *Halsted House, Sevenoaks.*
Austen, Rev. John Thomas, *Rectory, West Wickham, Kent.*
Austin, Henry George, Esq., M.R.I.B.A., *Precincts, Canterbury.*

Badeley, Henry, Esq., *Sevenoaks.*
*Bailey, Thomas T., Esq., *Hall Place, Leigh, Tunbridge.*
Baker, Thomas H., Esq., *Owletts, Cobham.*
Baker, Mrs. William, *Boley Hill, Rochester.*
Baldwin, Rev. F. St. Leger, M.A., *Bearsted Vicarage.*
Ball, Mr. John Howell, *Strood.*
Balston, W., Esq., *Springfield, Maidstone.*

Barling, Mr., *Maidstone.*
Barrow, Francis, Esq., 1, *Pump Court, Temple*, E.C.
Barry, John Milner, Esq., M.D., *Tunbridge Wells.*
Bartlett, Mr. Samuel John, *Maidstone.*
Batcheller, Miss, *Dover.*
Bayley, Francis, Esq., 66, *Cambridge Terrace, Hyde Park*, W.
Baverstock, James Hinton, Esq., *Fant Fields, Maidstone.*
Beale, Rev. S. C. Tresse, M.A., *Tenterden.*
Beale, William, Esq., *Maidstone.*
Beattie, Alexander, Esq., 25, *Warrior Square, St. Leonard's.*
Beckwith, William, Esq., *Seacox Heath, Flimwell, Sussex.*
Beeching, S., Esq., *Tunbridge Wells.*
Beeching, T., jun., Esq., *Tunbridge Wells.*
Beek, Charles, Esq., *Mauritius.*
Belfield, Captain, *Eastry House, Sandwich.*
Bell, Mr. James, *Cranbrook.*
Bell, Matthew, Esq., F.G.S., *Bourne Park, Canterbury.*
Bennett, Rev. Henry, B.A., *St. Nicholas-at-Wade, Thanet.*
Bennoch, Francis, Esq., F.S.A., *The Knoll, Blackheath*, S.E.
Bensted, William Harding, Esq., *Iguanodon Quarry, Maidstone.*
Berens, Henry Hulse, Esq., *Sidcup, Footscray*, S.E.
Berens, Mrs., *Kevington, St. Mary's Cray.*
Bertie, The Hon. and Rev. Frederick, *Albury, Wheatley, Oxon.*
Betts, Edward Ladd, Esq., *Preston Hall.*
Betts, Mrs., *ditto.*
Bingham, Lieut.-Colonel G. W. Poulett, *The Vines, Rochester.*
Bishop, William Henry, Esq., 2, *Woodville, Gravesend.*
Blackett, Walter, Esq., *Tovil, Maidstone.*
Bland, Rev. Miles, D.D., F.R.S., F.S.A., Prebendary of Wells, 5, *Royal Crescent, Ramsgate.*
Bland, William, Esq., *Hartlip Place, Sittingbourne.*
Blandford, Henry, Esq., *Maidstone.*
Blencowe, Robert, Esq., M.A., *The Hook, Lewes.*
Bligh, The Lady Isabel, *Rotherfield Rectory.*
Bligh, The Hon. Sir John, K.C.B., *Enbrook, Sandgate.*
Blunt, Rev. Walter, *Bicknor.*
Board, John, Esq., *Westerham, Edenbridge.*
Bodkin, William Henry, Esq., Recorder of Dover, and Assistant Judge of the County of Middlesex, *West Hill, Highgate, London*, N.
Bolton, Mr. Joseph, *King Street, Dover.*
Boscawen, The Hon. James, *The Grove, Sevenoaks.*
Boteler, William, Esq., *Eastry.*
*Botfield, Beriah, Esq., M.P., *Norton, Daventry.*
Bottle, Mr. Alexander, *Dover.*
Boys, Rev. E. G., Vicar of River.
Boys, Major Henry, *New Road House, Rochester.*
Boys, J. Harvey, Esq., *Margate.*
Boys, Rev. Thomas, 50, *Herbert Street, Hoxton*, N.
*Brabazon, Rev. W. J. Moore, M.A., *Sarratt, Rickmansworth.*

Brackett, Mr. William, *Tunbridge Wells.*
Bradstreet, Rev. William, *Lower Hardres, Canterbury.*
Bradstreet, Mrs., *ditto.*
Brecknock, The Earl of, *Wildernesse Park, Sevenoaks.*
Brenchley, T. Harman, Esq., *Wombwell Hall, Gravesend.*
Brent, Algernon, Esq., 7, *Albert Street, Gloucester Gate, Regent's Park, London,* N.W.
Brent, Cecil, Esq., 7, *Albert Street, Gloucester Gate, Regent's Park, London.*
Brent, John, jun., Esq., F.S.A., *Dane John Grove, Canterbury.*
Bridges, Sir Brook W., Bart., M.P., *Goodnestone Park.*
Brine, Mr. James, 10, *Week Street, Maidstone.*
Brockman, Col. George, East Kent Militia, *Canterbury.*
Brockman, Rev. Tatton, M.A., *Beachborough, Hythe.*
Brooke, F. C., Esq., *Ufford, Woodbridge, Suffolk.*
Brown, Mr. Joseph, *Week Street, Maidstone.*
Brown, William, Esq., *Wateringbury Place.*
*Bruce, John, Esq., Vice-President of the Society of Antiquaries, 5, *Upper Gloucester Street, Dorset Square, London,* N.W.
Bryant, Rev. George, M.A., *Sheerness.*
Bullard, Mr. John Simpson, *Strood.*
Bulmer, Martin, Esq., *Maidstone.*
Burney, The Venerable Charles Parr, D.D., F.R.S., F.S.A., Archdeacon of Colchester, *Rectory House, Wickham Bishop's, Witham, Essex.*
Burney, Rev. Edward Kaye, *Thornham Vicarage, Maidstone.*
Burnside, Rev. A., *Vicarage, Farningham.*
Butler, Rev. D., M.A., *St. Thomas Hill, Canterbury.*
Buttanshaw, Rev. Francis, M.A., *Maidstone.*
Buttanshaw, Rev. John, Fellow of Corpus Christi College, Oxford, *C. C. C., Oxford, and Eastry.*
Butterworth, J. W., Esq., F.S.A., *Upper Tooting,* S., *and* 7, *Fleet Street,* E.C.
Byass, R. B., Esq., *Nevill Park, Tunbridge Wells.*
Byng, The Honourable James, *Shipbourne.*

Camden, The Marquess, K.G., *Wildernesse Park, Sevenoaks.*
Campion, William, Esq., *Denny, Hurstperpoint, Sussex.*
Canterbury, His Grace the Archbishop of, D.D., F.R.S., F.S.A., *Lambeth Palace,* S.
Carnell, George F., Esq., *Sevenoaks.*
Carr, Rev. T. A., Vicar of Cranbrook.
Carr, William, Esq., *Little Park, Tunbridge.*
Carus-Wilson, Rev. C., *Eastry.*
Cator, Major-General, R.A., 6, *Eaton Place, Belgrave Square,* S.W.
Cator, Lieut.-Colonel, *Pickhurst, Bromley,* S.E.
Cator, Peter, Esq., *Beckenham,* S.E.
Chapman, James, Esq., *Paul's Cray Hill,* S.E.
Chatterton, Lady, 47, *York Street, Portman Square,* W.
Cheere, Captain, R.N., *Aylesford.*
Child, Coles, Esq., *Bromley,* S.E.

Chivers, Mr. H., *Palace Street, Canterbury.*
Clabon, John Moxon, Esq., F.G.S., 21, *Gt. George Street, Westminster*, S.W.
Clark, Thomas, Esq., *Farncomb, Godalming.*
Clarke, Rev. James S., M.A., *Blackheath*, S.E.
Clarke, Joseph, Esq., F.S.A., Diocesan Architect, 13, *Stratford Place, London*, W.
Clayton, Rev. Augustus, *Combe Bank, Sevenoaks.*
Clayton, W., Esq., *Town Wall Street, Dover.*
Clements, Mr. Thomas, Capitular Surveyor, *Rochester.*
Clifford, Mr. James, *Maidstone.*
Coates, Rev. R. P., M.A., *Precincts, Rochester.*
Cobb, Rev. Benjamin, M.A., *Vicarage, Lydd.*
Cobb, Rev. Robert, M.A., *Detling Vicarage.*
Cobb, Rev. William Francis, *Rectory, Nettlested.*
Cobbett, John Morgan, Esq., M.P., *Skeynes, Edenbridge.*
Cole, George Calverley, Esq., *Sevenoaks.*
Colquhoun, John Campbell, Esq., *Chartwell, Westerham.*
Cook, William, Esq., *Roydon Hall, Tunbridge.*
Cooke, Mr. C. J., *Maidstone.*
Cooke, George Nethercoat, Esq., *The Croft, Detling.*
Corner, G. R., Esq., F.S.A., *The Paragon, New Kent Road, London*, S.E.
*Cornthwaite, The Rev. Tullie, *The Forest, Walthamstow*, E.
Cotton, H. P., Esq., *Quex Park, Isle of Thanet.*
Cottrell, Mr. Henry C., 70, *London Street, Reading.*
Courthope, George, Esq., *Whiligh, Hurst Green.*
Cox, Captain C. I., Q.G., *Fordwich.*
Cranworth, The Lord, *Holwood, Bromley*, S.E.
Croft, The Venerable James, Archdeacon of Canterbury, *Saltwood, Hythe, and Precincts, Canterbury.*
Crofton, Anthony, Esq., *St. Laurence, Ramsgate.*
Crofts, Rev. C., *School House, Sevenoaks.*
Crosby, James, Esq., F.S.A., *Adelphi Terrace, London*, W.C.
Cruttenden, Mr., Honorary Photographer, *Week Street, Maidstone.*
*Cubitt, George, Esq., *Denbies, Dorking.*
Curteis, T. W., Esq., *Charlton Park, Canterbury.*

Dale, Rev. C., *Ringwould, Deal.*
Dalison, M. D. D., Esq., *Hamptons.*
Darnley, The Earl of, *Cobham Hall, Gravesend.*
Dartmouth, The Earl of, 40, *Grosvenor Square*, W.
Darwall, Mrs., *Hubert Terrace, Dover.*
Dashwood, Francis, Esq., *Hallcot, Bexley*, S.E.
Dashwood, Rev. George Henry, M.A., F.S.A., *Stow Bardolph, Downham Market, Norfolk.*
Dawson, Mr. F. J., *Rochester.*
Day, T. H., Esq., *Frindsbury, Rochester.*
Deedes, William, Esq., M.P., *Sandling Park, Hythe, and* 18, *Eaton Square*, S.W.
De L'Isle and Dudley, The Lord, *Penshurst.*

Delmar, William, Esq., *The Elms, Canterbury.*
Denne, Denne, Esq., *Elbridge, Canterbury.*
Denne, Mrs. Denne, *ditto.*
Denne, Henry, Esq., *Canterbury.*
Dennett, Mr. J. T., *Cranbrook,*
Dering, Mrs. Cholmeley Edward, 47, *York Street, Portman Square.*
Dering, Sir E. C., Bart., *Surrenden Dering, Ashford.*
Dering, George, Esq., *Barham Court.*
De Wilde, George James, Esq., *Northampton.*
Diamond, Hugh Welsh, Esq., M.D., F.S.A., Honorary Photographer, *Twickenham House, Twickenham.*
*Digby, Kenelm, Esq., *Shaftesbury House, Kensington,* W.
Digby, Richard Wingfield, Esq., *Coleshill, Warwickshire.*
Dobell, Mr. William, *West Malling.*
Dobson, William Henry, Esq., *Woodville Terrace, Gravesend.*
*Douglas, James Stoddart, Esq., *Chilston Park.*
*Drake, Rev. R., *Stourmouth Rectory, Wingham.*
Dudlow, J. N., Esq., *West Malling.*
Dunkin, A. J., Esq., *Dartford.*
Dyke, Sir Perceval Hart, Bart., *Lullingstone Castle.*

Eardley, E. G. Culling, Esq., F.R.G.S., Hon. M.R.I.B.A., *Belvidere, Erith,* S.E., *and Bedwell Park, Hatfield, Herts.*
Eastes, James, Esq., *Ashford.*
Eden, Rev. Arthur, *Ticehurst, Hurst Green, Sussex.*
Edge, Rev. William John, M.A., *Vicarage, Benenden.*
Edmeades, Rev. William Henry, *Nurstead Court, Gravesend.*
Elliott, James, Esq., *New Hall, Dymchurch.*
Elliott, Mr. Robert, *Tunbridge Wells.*
Ellis, Charles, Esq., *Ulcombe Place.*
Ellis, William Smith, Esq., *Hydecroft, Charlwood, Surrey.*
Elsted, W. Philpot, Esq., *Dover.*
Elwes, Valentine D. H. Cary, Esq., *Tongswood, Hawkhurst.*
Elwin, J. W., Esq., *Terenure, Dublin.*
Elyard, S. Herbert, Esq., 15, *Devonshire Road, Balham,* S.
*'Espinasse, James, Esq., Recorder of Rochester, and one of the Judges of the County Court of Kent, *Boxley Lodge.*
Essell, George, Esq., *Precincts, Rochester.*
Essell, George Ketchley, Esq., *Rochester.*
Eveleigh, Rev. James, M.A., *Alkham, Dover.*
Everest, Henry, Esq., *Temple, Strood.*
Ewart, Major C. B., R.E., *Hythe Barracks, and Army and Navy Club, Pall Mall,* S.W.

Fagge, Charles, Esq., *Hythe.*
*Falmouth, The Viscount, *Mereworth Castle.*
*Falmouth, The Viscountess, (Baroness Le Despencer,) *ditto.*
Farrar, Henry Jeffreys, Esq., *Cranbrook.*
Ffinch, Rev. B. D., M.A., Rector of St. Paul's, *Deptford,* S.E.

Faussett, Thomas Godfrey, Esq., F.S.A., Fellow of Corpus Christi College, Oxford, *C.C.C., Oxford, and* 16, *South Audley Street, Grosvenor Square.*
Field, George, Esq., *Ashurst Park, Tunbridge Wells.*
Field, John, Esq., *Dornden, Tunbridge Wells.*
Filkin, R., Esq., M.D., 5, *Ormond Terrace, Richmond, Surrey.*
Filmer, The Dowager Lady, *Eaton Square*, S.W.
Filmer, Sir Edmund, Bart., *East Sutton Place.*
Finch, The Honourable Daniel, *Precincts, Canterbury.*
Finch, Lieut.-General the Honourable John, *Berkhampstead, Herts.*
Fisher, Cuthbert J., Esq., *Huntly, Tunbridge Wells.*
Flaherty, W. E., Esq., 4, *Manor Villas, Manor Road, South Hackney*, N.E.
Fletcher, J. F., Esq., *St. Margaret's Villa, Rochester.*
Fletcher, Lieut.-Colonel, *Kenward, Yalding.*
Forman, Robert Henry, Esq., *Well Hall House, Eltham*, S.E.
Foss, Edward, Esq., F.S.A., *Churchill House, Dover.*
Foster, Samuel, Esq., *South End Hall, Sydenham*, S.E.
Fox, John, Esq., 3, *Constitution Crescent, Gravesend.*
Fox, Robert, Esq., *Falconhurst, Cowden.*
Fraser, Rev. Robert, M.A., *Cheriton Rectory, Hythe.*
Frend, Edwin, Esq., 1, *Brick Court, Temple*, E.C.
Frend, Mr. G. R., *St. George's, Canterbury.*
Fry, Frederick, Esq., *Maidstone.*
Fry, Miss, *Plashet, Essex*, E.
Furley, Edward, Esq., *West Malling.*
Furley, George, Esq., *Canterbury.*
Furley, Robert, Esq., *Ashford.*
Furrell, George, Esq., *Rochester.*

Gale, Rev. T. H., *Godmersham.*
Gape, George, Esq., *Charlton House, East Sutton, Staplehurst.*
Geary, Lady, *Oxenhoath.*
Gibbs, Edwin Mackie, Esq., *Clarendon Cottage, Gravesend.*
Gibbs, William, Esq., *East Street, Faversham.*
*Gidley, Gustavus, Esq., M.D., *Sandgate.*
Gilbert, W. B., Esq., Mus. Bac. Oxon., *Maidstone.*
Gilder, Rev. Horace, *St. Peter's Rectory, Sandwich.*
Giraud, Francis, Esq., *Preston Street, Faversham.*
Giraud, F. F., Esq., *Faversham.*
Glasgow, The Right Rev. the Lord Bishop of, *Tunbridge Wells.*
Godefroy, John, Esq., *Church End House, Little Hadham, Herts.*
Godfrey, John, Esq., *Brook House, Ash, Sandwich.*
Golding, Mr. Charles, *Harrow Road, Paddington*, W.
Gore, Frederick R., Esq., *Barne Hawe, Edenbridge.*
Gore, Mr. George, jun., *Darnley Road, Gravesend.*
Gould, H. M., Esq., *Wateringbury.*
Gower, W. Leveson, Esq., *Titsey Place, Surrey.*
Graham, Allen, Esq., 76, *Westbourne Terrace, Hyde Park*, W.
Grant, Colonel E. F., R.A., *Southend, Eltham*, S.E.

Green, Rev. William, M.A., *Penshurst Rectory.*
Green, Mr. James, *St. Margaret's Street, Canterbury.*
Gregory, J. S., Esq., *Shoreham.*
Griffiths, Rev. John, Keeper of the Archives, *Oxford.*
Grimaldi, Rev. Henry Beaufort, *Maize Hill, Greenwich.*
Grimaldi, Stacey, Esq., F.S.A., *Maize Hill, Greenwich Park.*
Grimaldi, Wynford Beaufort, Esq., 6, *Gray's Inn Square, London,* W.C.

Hallet, Rev. James Hughes, *Petham, Canterbury.*
Hallowes, Thomas, Esq., *Tunbridge.*
Hammond, Col., *Lauriston, Dover.*
Hammond, William Osmond, Esq., *St. Alban's Court, Wingham.*
Hammond, William Oxenden, Esq., *St. Alban's Court, Wingham.*
Hampson, Sir George F., Bart., *Detling.*
Hannam, George Emilius, Esq., *Bramston House, Ramsgate.*
Harbin, Rev. Charles, *Teston Rectory, Maidstone.*
Hardinge, Viscount, *South Park, Penshurst.*
Hardy, Gathorne, Esq., M.P., *Hemsted, Cranbrook.*
Harris, Thomas Noel, Esq., *Ileden, Canterbury.*
Harrison, The Venerable Benjamin, M.A., F.S.A., Archdeacon of Maidstone and Canon of Canterbury, *Precincts, Canterbury.*
Harrison, Rev. Henry, *Kiln Down, Goudhurst.*
Harrison, Rev. J. B., *Walmer Rectory, Deal.*
Harrison, Rev. Thomas, M.A., *Rectory, Newchurch, New Romney.*
Hart, William Henry, Esq., F.S.A., *Folkestone House, Roupell Park, Streatham Hill, Surrey,* S.
Harwood, Henry Hansard, Esq., *Tunbridge Wells.*
Hatch, Benjamin, Esq., *Tenterden.*
Havers, Arthur, Esq., *Tenterden.*
Hawkins, Rev. E., D.D., Canon of Rochester, and Provost of Oriel College, Oxford, *The Vines, Rochester.*
Hawley, Sir Joseph Henry, Bart., *Leybourne Grange, Malling.*
Hawley, Rev. Charles, *Leybourne Rectory, Malling.*
Haynes, Mr. William, *Maidstone.*
Hayward, John, Esq., *Sutton Rectory, Dartford.*
Hayward, William Webb, Esq., *The Gleanings, Rochester.*
Hilder, Edward Augustus, Esq., Coroner of Gravesend, *Gravesend.*
Hill, Henry, Esq., F.S.A., 2, *Curzon Street, Mayfair,* W.
Hillier, Frederick, Esq., *Park Place, Sydenham,* S.E.
Hilton, Edward Jones, Esq., *Faversham.*
Hilton, S. Musgrave, Esq., *Bramling, Wingham.*
Hilton, Captain Thomas, *Nackington, Canterbury.*
Hodsoll, J. H., Esq., *Loose Court, Staplehurst.*
Holmes, Rev. W. R., *Tunbridge Wells.*
Holttum, Edward, Esq., *Canterbury.*
Hooper, William Edward Parry, Esq., *Cresswell Park, Blackheath,* S.E.
Hooper, Rev. J., M.A., *Meopham Vicarage, Gravesend.*
Hope, A. James B. Beresford, Esq., F.S.A., *Bedgebury Park, Goudhurst.*
Hope, The Lady Mildred, *Bedgebury Park, Goudhurst.*

Horne, Rev. W., M.A., *Barming Rectory, Maidstone.*
Hoskins, Rev. W. E., *Rectory, Chiddingstone, Edenbridge.*
Howard, Joseph Jackson, Esq., LL.D., F.S.A., *Lee Road, Lee,* S.E.
Hudson, Mr. A., *Cranbrook.*
Hugessen, Edward Knatchbull, Esq., M.P., *The Paddock, Smeeth, Ashford.*
Hughes, Henry, Esq., *Bradbourn, Sevenoaks.*
Humphery, John, Esq., *New Romney.*
Hunt, Rev. Robert Shapland, *Edells, Edenbridge.*
Hussey, Rev. Arthur, *Rottingdean, Brighton.*
Hussey, Edward, Esq., *Scotney Castle, Lamberhurst.*
Hussey, Edward, Esq., F.R.C.S., Surgeon to the Radcliffe Infirmary, *Oxford.*
Hussey, Henry Law, Esq., 10, *New Square, Lincoln's Inn,* W.C.
Hussey, Henry, Esq., 7, *Hyde Park Square, London,* W.
Hussey, Richard, Esq., F.S.A., 16, *King William Street, Strand,* W.C.
Huxley, J. E., Esq., *Devonshire Cottage, Tunbridge Wells.*

Jackson, John Flower, Esq., *Martin's Grove, Crayford.*
James, Edward Woodford, Esq., *Croom's Hill, Greenwich,* S.E.
James, Sir Walter, Bart., *Betshanger, Sandwich.*
Jay, J. Livingstone, Esq., *Greenwich Hospital.*
Jemmett, George Elwick, Esq., *Ashford.*
Jenkins, Rev. Robert C., *Lyminge Rectory, Hythe.*
Johnstone, Hon. H. Butler, M.P., 21, *Park Street, Grosvenor Square,* W.
Jones, Rev. Edward, *West Peckham Vicarage.*
Jones, Miss, *Hayle Place.*
Joy, Henry Winkles, Esq., *Maidstone.*
Joyce, Rev. William Henry, Vicar of Dorking, *Surrey.*
Judkins, Benjamin, Esq., *Tooley Street, Southwark,* S.E.

Kadwell, Mr. Charles, 15, *Royal Circus Street, Greenwich,* S.E.
Keddell, J. S., Esq., F.R.C.S., *Sheerness.*
Keene, Alfred Thomas, Esq., 1, *Lincoln's Inn, London,* W.C., *and Tunbridge Wells.*
Keith, Rev. William A., *Burham, Rochester.*
Kelcey, Stephen, Esq., *Stone Hall, Canterbury.*
Kenrick, Miss Elizabeth, *Stone House, Canterbury.*
Kenrick, John Brydges, Esq., *Eastry.*
Kibble, Thomas, Esq., *Green Trees, Tunbridge.*
King, David, Esq., M.D., *Eltham,* S.E.
King, General, *Hythe.*
King, Knowles, Esq., *Maidstone.*
King, Mr. T. S., *Rochester.*
Kingsford, Henry, Esq., *Littlebourne.*
Kingsford, Montague, Esq., *Ashford.*
Kirkpatrick, John, Esq., *Horton Park, Hythe.*
Knatchbull, Sir Norton J., Bart., F.S.A., *Mersham Hatch, Ashford.*
Knatchbull, Lady, *ditto.*
Knatchbull, Rev. Wyndham, D.D., *Smeeth Rectory, Ashford.*
Knocker, Edward, Esq., Town Clerk of Dover, *Castle Hill, Dover.*

Knox, Rev. J., Chaplain to the Hon. Artillery Company, *Greenwich*, S.E.
*Knyvett, Felix, Esq., *Lambeth Palace*, S.

Lake, Henry, Esq., 10, *New Square, Lincoln's Inn, London*, W.C.
Lambarde, William, Esq., *Beechmont, Sevenoaks.*
Lane, H. Murray, Esq., Blue Mantle Pursuivant, 39, *Queen Anne Street, Cavendish Square*, W.
Langley, John Inwood, Esq., *Gloucester Place, Greenwich*, S.E.
Larking, John Wingfield, Esq., *Athenæum Club, Pall Mall*, S.W.
Larking, Miss, *Headington, Oxford.*
Larking, Rev. Lambert B., M.A., *Ryarsh Vicarage, Malling, Maidstone.*
Larking, Mrs. Lambert, *ditto.*
Latham, Mrs., *Dover.*
Latham, Rev. John, M.A., *East Malling.*
La Trobe, Charles Joseph, Esq., C.B., F.R.G.S., *Athenæum Club, Pall Mall*, S.W.
Latter, Robert Booth, Esq., *Pixfield, Bromley*, S.E.
Laurence, William, Esq., *Maidstone.*
Lee, Rev. Edward Henry, B.A., Curate of Cliffe, *Cliffe Parsonage, Rochester.*
Lees, Rev. William, *Tunbridge Wells.*
Leggat, Richard, Esq., *Eastry.*
Leitch, A. M., Esq., *Folkestone.*
Lester, Mr. Edward, *Bostal, Rochester.*
Lewin, Thomas, Esq., *Eltham*, S.E.
Lightfoot, Mr. W. J., *Sandhurst, Staplehurst.*
Lindsay, Rev. Henry, *Ide Hill, Sevenoaks.*
Little, William Robert, Esq., *Oriel College, Oxford.*
Lochée, Alfred, M.D., *Canterbury.*
*Locock, Sir Charles, Bart., *Holmwood, Speldhurst.*
*Long, Lieutenant-Colonel, *Bromley Hill*, S.E.
Lower, Mark-Antony, Esq., *St. Anne's, Lewes.*
*Lowndes, G. Alan, Esq., *Gladwyns, Harlow, Essex.*
Lowry, Thomas, Esq., M.D., *Malling.*
Luard, Major, *The Mote, Ightham.*
*Lubbock, Sir J. W., Bart., F.R.S., *High Elms, Farnborough.*
*Lubbock, John, Esq., *High Elms, Farnborough.*
Lucas, S. Lancaster, Esq., *Wateringbury.*
Lutwidge, C. R. F., Esq., 22, *Calverley Park, Tunbridge Wells.*
Lyall, Rev. Alfred, *Harbledown.*

Mackarness, Rev. Henry, *Ash Vicarage, Sandwich.*
Mackay, T. H. Esq., *Petham House, Canterbury.*
Mackeson, H. B., Esq., F.G.S., *Hythe.*
Mackinnon, W. A., Esq., M.P., M.A., F.R.S., F.G.S., *Belvidere, Broadstairs.*
Mac Lachlan, Rev. E. H., M.A., *Tudely, Tunbridge.*
Mahon, Viscount, *Chevening, Sevenoaks.*
Majendie, Lewis A. Esq., *Hedingham Castle, Halstead, Essex.*
*Malcolm, John, Esq., *Lamorby.*
Manclark, W., Esq., *Rochester.*

Mansel, Lady, *Wrotham Heath, Sevenoaks.*
*Marriott, Rev. W. M. Smith, M.A., *Horsmonden Rectory.*
Marsh, Rev. E. G., M.A., Canon of Southwell, Vicar of Aylesford, *Aylesford Vicarage.*
Marsh, Mr. John, *Maidstone.*
Marsh, Richard, Esq., *Sandwich.*
Marsham, Rev. J. Jacob, M.A., *Shorne Vicarage.*
Marsham, Admiral Jones, *Loose.*
Martin, Charles Wykeham, Esq., F.S.A., *Leeds Castle.*
Martin, George White, Esq., *St. Margaret's Bank, Rochester.*
Martin, Rev. Richard Wykeham, M.A., *Elsfield Lodge, Leeds.*
Martin, John, Esq., *Ensinge, Chilham.*
Martin, John Francis, Esq., *Hurst Lodge, High Road, Lee,* S.E.
Masters, William, Esq., Alderman of Canterbury, *High Street, Canterbury.*
Masters, William, Esq., *Romney Place, Maidstone.*
*Mercer, Charles, Esq., *Maidstone.*
Mercer, Richard, Esq., *Maidstone.*
Mercer, Samuel, Esq. *Maidstone.*
Mesham, Rev. Arthur B., B.D., *Wootton Rectory, Canterbury.*
Milligan, Rev. H. M., M.A., *Sutton Valence.*
Milne, Alexander, Esq., *Eltham,* S.E.
Minet, Charles W., Esq., *Dover.*
Mitchinson, Rev. J., *King's School, Canterbury.*
Molyneux, Hon. Francis George, *Tunbridge Wells.*
Monckton, John, Esq., *Maidstone.*
Monckton, S., Esq., M.D., *Brenchley.*
Monro, Major, *Tower House, East Sutton.*
Moor, Rev. A. P., M.A., M.R.A.S., F.R.G.S., Sub-Warden of St. Augustine's College, *Canterbury.*
*Moore, Rev. Edward, M.A., *Frittenden House.*
*Moore, Rev. Edward, *Boughton Malherbe.*
*Moore, Rev. George B., M.A., *Tunstall Rectory, Sittingbourne.*
*Moore, Henry T., Esq., *Southborough, Tunbridge Wells.*
Moore, John Allden, Esq., *Woodlands Terrace, Blackheath,* S.E.
Moore, Stuart A., Esq., *General Record Office, Rolls Yard, Chancery Lane,* W.C.
Moore, William, Esq., *Wierton, Staplehurst.*
Moreland, William Courtney, Esq., *The Court Lodge, Lamberhurst.*
Morgan, Charles Octavius, Esq., M.P., V.P.S.A., 9, *Pall Mall,* S.W.
Morley, William Hook, Esq., 35, *St. Michael's Place, Brompton,* S.W.
Mosse, Rev. Samuel Tenison, *Buckland, Dover.*
Mostyn, The Honourable Thomas E. Lloyd, M.P., *Gloddaeth, Carnarvonshire.*
Mostyn, The Lady Augusta, *ditto.*
Mudford, Mr. Frederick, *St. George's Canterbury.*
Mummery, J. R., Esq., F.L.S., 10, *Cavendish Place, Cavendish Square,* W.
Munn, Joseph, Esq., *Tenterden.*
*Munn, William Augustus, Esq., *Throwley House, Faversham.*
Murton, William, Esq. *Tunstall, Sittingbourne.*

Nares, Rev. Edward Robert, M.A., Rural Dean, *Wittersham Rectory.*
*Neame, Frederick, Esq., *Macknade, Faversham.*
Neve, W. T., Esq., *Cranbrook.*
Nevill, The Viscount, *Hope Hall, Tadcaster.*
Nevill, The Lady Caroline, *Birling Manor, Malling.*
Nevill, The Honourable Ralph, *ditto.*
*Norman, Charles Loyd, Esq., *Bromley,* S.E.
*Norman, George Warde, Esq., *Bromley,* S.E.
*Norman, Henry, Esq., F.S.A., *Oakley, Bromley,* S.E.
Norwood, Edward, Esq., *Charing.*
Norwood, John Dobree, Esq., *Ashford.*

Oakden, Ralph, Esq., *Ladham House, Goudhurst.*
Oakley, Rev. John, 60, *Doughty Street, Mecklenburgh Square, London,* W.C.
Oakley, William, Esq., *ditto,* W.C.
O'Neill, William, Esq., *Lawn Cottages, Eltham Road,* S.E.
Onslow, Rev. Middleton, M.A., Rural Dean, *East Peckham Vicarage, Tunbridge.*
Orger, Rev. E. R., *St. Augustine's College, Canterbury.*
Osmotherly, Mr. John, *Cliffe.*
Ottaway, James Cuthbert, Esq., Mayor of Dover, *Dover.*
*Ouvry, Frederic, Esq., Treasurer of the Society of Antiquaries, M.R.S.L., F.Z.S., etc., 29, *Upper Gower Street, London,* W.C.
Oxenden, Rev. Ashton, M.A., *Pluckley Rectory, Ashford.*
Oxenden, Rev. Charles, M.A., *Barham Rectory, Canterbury.*

Palmer, Rev. Francis, M.A., *Cambridge Terrace, Dover.*
Papillon, Philip O., Esq., M.P., *Crowhurst, Battle.*
Parker, Rev. Charles, *Vicarage, Bodiam, Hurst Green, Sussex.*
Parker, Thomas, Esq., *The Brook, Lamberhurst.*
Parkes, Mr. George T., *Church Street, Dover.*
Parkin, Rev. Charles, M.A., *Vicarage, Lenham.*
Pearman, Rev. A. J., *Vicarage, Bethersden.*
Pearman, Rev. M. T., M.A., *Cranbrook.*
Pearson, Rev. G. C., M.A., *Hopebourne, Canterbury.*
Pearson, Rev. William, *Thanington, Canterbury.*
Pearson, W., Esq., *Harbledown.*
Penn, John, Esq., *The Cedars, Lee,* S.E.
*Perkins, Frederick, Esq., F.S.A., F.L.S., F.G.S., *Chipstead Place, Sevenoaks.*
Petley, C. R. C., Esq., *Riverhead, Sevenoaks.*
Philips, Henry, Esq., *Faversham.*
Phillips, James, jun., Esq., *Ryarsh.*
Philpot, Mr., *Tunbridge Wells.*
Philpott, John, Esq., *West Farleigh.*
Pickering, Mrs. *Addington Vale, Malling.*
Plomley, Francis, Esq., M.D., *Maidstone.*
*Plowes, John Henry, Esq., *York Terrace, Regent's Park,* N.W.
Plummer, Stephen, Esq., *Canterbury.*
Pollard, James P., Esq., 51, *Upper John Street, Fitzroy Square,* W.

Pool, Mr. William, 49, *High Street, Canterbury.*
Pope, Rev. W. L., *Tunbridge Wells.*
Poste, Rev. Beale, M.A., *Bydews House, Maidstone.*
Pott, Arthur, Esq., *Bentham Hill, Tunbridge Wells.*
Pout, Augustus, Esq., *Yalding.*
Pout, Mr. Edward, *High Street, Canterbury.*
Powell, Charles, Esq., *Speldhurst.*
Powell, William, Esq., *East Lenham, Maidstone.*
*Poynder, Thomas Henry Allen, Esq., *Hartham Court, Chippenham, Wilts, and* 21, *Upper Brook Street,* W.
*Poynder, Mrs., *ditto.*
Poynter, Ambrose, Esq., *Marine Place, Dover.*
Pratt, Rev. Jermyn, *Campsea Ashe, Woodbridge.*
Pratt, The Lady Caroline, *Wildernesse Park, Sevenoaks.*
Pratt, The Lady Frances, *Wildernesse Park, Sevenoaks.*
Prentis, George, Esq., *Dover.*
Preston, Rev. J. D'Arcy, M.A., *Sandgate.*
Pretty, Edward, Esq., F.S.A., *Charles Museum, Maidstone.*
Pryer, Mr. Alfred, *White Heath, Hollingbourne.*
Puckle, Rev. John, M.A., *Dover.*
Punnett, P. S., Esq., *Chart, Sutton.*

*Randall, Alexander, Esq., *Foley House, Maidstone.*
Randolph, Rev. C., *Riverhead.*
Rashleigh, Rev. George, M.A., *Horton Kirby, Dartford.*
Reader, Edward Francis Stratton, Esq., *Sandwich.*
Reid, James, Esq., *St. George's, Canterbury.*
Rice, Edward, Esq., *Dane Court, Sandwich.*
Richardson, Edward, Esq., *Melbury House, Harewood Square,* N.W.
Richardson, Mr. Henry Samuel, *Greenwich,* S.E.
Richardson, Mr. J. M., *Tunbridge Wells.*
*Riddell, Rev. J. C. B., *Harrietsham Rectory.*
Riddell, Sir W. B., Bart., M.A., Recorder of Maidstone, Judge of the County Court, North Staffordshire, Member of the Council of King's College, London, *Palace, Maidstone.*
Ridgway, Joseph, Esq., *Fairlawn, Tunbridge.*
Ridgway, Mrs., *ditto.*
Rivers, Rev. H. T., B.A., *St. Paul's, Chatham.*
Roberts, Thomas Walton, Esq., *Glassenbury, Cranbrook,*
Robertson, Rev. Canon, M.A., *Precincts, Canterbury.*
Robins, Rev. Sanderson, M.A., *St. Peter's Vicarage, Thanet.*
Robinson, Rev. T., D.D., Master of the Temple, and Canon of Rochester.
*Rogers, John, Esq., F.R.S., *River Hill, Sevenoaks.*
Rosher, Charles, Esq., *Rosherville, Northfleet.*
Ross, Thomas, Esq., *Claremont, Hastings.*
Rouch, Rev. F., M.A., *Precincts, Canterbury.*
Rugg, John Salmon, Esq., *East Court, Detling.*
Rugg, Robert, Esq., *Maidstone.*
Russell, Rev. John Fuller, B.C.L., F.S.A., *Greenhithe.*

*Russell, John, Esq., *New Romney.*
Rycroft, Lady, *Everland, Sevenoaks.*
Rycroft, Nelson, Esq., *ditto.*
Rye, W. B., Esq., Assistant-Keeper of the Printed Books, *British Museum,* W.C.

Sadler, Rev. Henry, *Ulcomb.*
Saint, Rev. J. J., M.A., Rural Dean, *Speldhurst Rectory, Tunbridge Wells.*
Saint, Miss, *Groombridge Place, Tunbridge Wells.*
*Salomons, David, Esq., M.P., Alderman of London, *Broom Hill, Tunbridge Wells.*
Sandilands, Edward Vincent, Esq., *Hythe.*
Sankey, H. T., Esq., *Canterbury.*
Sankey, Robert, Esq., *Canterbury.*
Sankey, W., Esq., *Dover.*
Sass, H. W., Esq., 45, *Connaught Terrace, Hyde Park, London,* W.
Savage, John, Esq., *St. Leonard's, West Malling.*
Savage, Mrs., *St. Leonard's, West Malling.*
Savage, Captain, *Goddington House, Frindsbury.*
Savage, Mrs. *ditto.*
Schreiber, John Charles, Esq., *Woodchurch.*
Scoones, Major, *Tunbridge.*
Scott, Major, *Maidstone.*
Scott, Rev. F. T., *Vicarage, Sibbertswold.*
Scott, John, Esq., *Blackheath,* S.E.
Scratton, John, Esq., *Tenterden.*
Scudamore, Frank Ives, Esq., *Maize Hill, Greenwich,* S.E.
Scudamore, Frederick, Esq., *Maidstone.*
Segurs, Mr. William, *Gas Office, Rochester.*
Selwyn, Rev. E. J., M.A., *Lee Park, Lee,* S.E.
Sharland, George Edward, Esq., *Constitution Crescent, Gravesend.*
Shepherd, Rev. E. J., M.A., *Trosley Rectory, Malling.*
Sheringham, Rev. J. W., *Vicarage, Strood.*
Sicard, ~~Andrew~~, Esq., *Bridge.*
Sikes, Rev. Thomas, M.A., *Chevening Rectory, Sevenoaks.*
Silver, Miss, *De Crespigny Park, Camberwell,* S.
Simmonds, Clifton, Esq., *Brookland.*
Simmonds, Henry, Esq., *The Friars, Aylesford.*
Simmonds, William Clarence, Esq., *The Friars, Aylesford.*
Simmons, Captain Chestney, R.N., *Dover.*
Skinner, George Tucker, Esq., *Rochester.*
*Sladen, Rev. Edward Henry Mainwaring, *Alton Barnes Rectory, Pewsey, Wilts.*
Slark, Captain William, *Herne Bay.*
Smallfield, Mr., 43, *St. Paul's Road, Camden Square,* N.W.
Smallfield, Mr. George, *Cranbrook, Auckland, New Zealand.*
Smith, Arthur, Esq., *The Shrubbery, Walmer.*
Smith, Rev. B. F., *Rusthall, Tunbridge Wells.*
Smith, Charles Augustin, Esq., F.R.S.L., *Croom's Hill, Greenwich,* S.E.

Smith, Rev. Harry, *Crundall Rectory, Canterbury.*
Smith, Herbert, Esq., 2, *Sloane Terrace, Sloane Street, London*, S.W.
Smith, Miss, *St. Aubyn's, Tunbridge Wells.*
Smith, Rev. Richard, B.D., *New Romney.*
Smith, Robert H. S., Esq., *Museum of Science and Art, Kensington*, W.
Smith, J. Russell, Esq., 36, *Soho Square, London*, W.
Smith, William Masters, Esq., *Camer, Gravesend.*
Smythe, Mr. John, *Maidstone.*
Soames, Rev. W. A., Vicar of Greenwich, S.E.
Sondes, Lord, *Lees Court, Faversham.*
Sorsbie, Rev. Robert, M.A., Fellow of Durham University, *Precincts, Rochester.*
South, John Flint, Esq., *Blackheath Park*, S.E.
Southgate, Francis, Esq., *Denton Court, Gravesend.*
Southgate, Rev. Frederick, *Vicarage, Northfleet.*
Spurrell, Flaxman, Esq., F.R.C.S., *Bexley Heath, Kent.*
Stanhope, The Earl, D.C.L., F.R.S., President of the Society of Antiquaries, Trustee of the British Museum, *Chevening Place, Sevenoaks.*
Stanhope, The Hon. Edward, *Chevening, Sevenoaks.*
Stanton, Lieutenant-Colonel, *Barming House, Maidstone.*
Stapleton, The Hon. and Rev. Sir Francis J., Bart., *Mereworth Rectory.*
Starling, R. J. Esq., *Tunbridge Wells.*
Startin, Mrs. *Hammerwood, East Grinstead.*
Stedman, Mr. R. B., *West Malling.*
Steele, Stephen, Esq., *Strood.*
Stevens, The Very Rev. Robert, D.D., Dean of Rochester, *Deanery, Rochester.*
Stevens, Rev. Henry, *Wateringbury Vicarage.*
Stevens, N. E., Esq., *Tunbridge Wells.*
Stewart, Alexander J. R., Esq., 13, *Belgrave Square, London*, S.W.
Stewart, The Lady Isabella, 13, *Belgrave Square, London*, S.W.
Stewart, Captain Thomas Dilnot, *Sandwich.*
Stilwell, James, Esq., *Dover.*
Stirling, Sir Walter, Bart., F.R.S., *Burr's Wood, Tunbridge Wells.*
Stokoe, Paul Henry, Esq., *Maidstone.*
Stone, Rev. Canon, *Precincts, Canterbury.*
Stone, John Graham, Esq., *Rochester.*
Stratford, John Wingfield, Esq., *Addington Place, Malling.*
Stratton, Rev. John Young, *Rectory, Ditton, Maidstone.*
Stratton, Rev. Joshua, Precentor, *Precincts, Canterbury.*
Streatfeild, H. D., Esq., *Chiddingstone, Edenbridge.*
Streatfeild, Mrs., *Chart's Edge, Westerham.*
*Streatfeild, J. Fremlyn, Esq., 15, *Upper Brook Street, Grosvenor Square, London*, W.
Streatfeild, William Champion, Esq., *Chart's Edge, Westerham.*
Stride, Lewis, Esq., *Dover.*
Stringer, W., Esq., *New Romney.*
Strong, Mrs., *Hayes, Kent.*
Sutton, Peter, Esq., *West Malling.*

Sutton, John, Esq., *Blackheath.*
Swaun, F. D., Esq., *Lee Priory, Canterbury.*
Sydney, Sir William Robert, *The Bourne, Maidenhead.*
Sydney, The Viscount, (Lord Lieutenant,) *Frognall.*
Sykes, Rev. Thomas Burr, *St. Peter's, Maidstone.*

Talbot, John G., Esq., *New Falconhurst, Edenbridge.*
Tanner, Edward Russell, Esq., *Maidstone.*
Tarbutt, W., Esq., *Cranbrook.*
Tassell, Thomas, Esq., *Maidstone.*
Taswell, G. W., Esq., *St. Martin's, Canterbury.*
Taswell, Rev. George, *Bekesbourne.*
Taylor, Rev. Edward Stuart, *Chiddingstone.*
Taylor, John Edward, Esq., *Weybridge, Surrey.*
Taylor, R. C., Esq., *Boughton Place, Staplehurst.*
Temple, Rev. W., Rector of St. Alphage, Canterbury, *Eastbridge Hospital, Canterbury.*
Terry, James, Esq., 8, *Woodlands Terrace, Blackheath,* S.E.
Thomas, Jesse, Esq., *Rochester.*
Thomas, R., Esq., *Eyhorne House, Hollingbourne.*
Thomas, Mr. John, *Rochester.*
Thompson, G. T., Esq., *Dover.*
Thompson, Richard, Esq., *Kenfield, Canterbury.*
Thompson, Robert, Esq., *Westerham, Edenbridge.*
Thoms, W. J., Esq., F.S.A., 40, *St. George's Square, Belgrave Road,* S.W.
Thomson, H. U., Esq., M.D., *Dover.*
Thomson, Major, *Updowne, Sandwich.*
Thorpe, Rev. John Frederick, *Maidstone.*
Thurston, Thomas, Esq., *Ashford.*
Tilleard, John, jun., Esq., *Upper Tooting,* S.
Timins, Rev. J. H., *West Malling.*
Toke, Rev. Nicholas, *Godington, Ashford.*
Tomlin, F. A., Esq., *Sandwich.*
Tooth, Robert, Esq., *Swifts, Cranbrook.*
Trimnell, Mr. William Charles, *Parade, Canterbury.*
Tufton, Sir Richard, Bart., *Hothfield.*
Turner, Francis, Esq., 15, *Queen Square, Westminster,* S.W.
*Twisden, Thomas, Esq., F.S.A., *Bradbourne Park, East Malling.*
Twopeny, Rev. David, *Stockbury.*
Twopeny, Edward, Esq., *Woodstock Park, Sittingbourne.*
*Tyssen, John Robert Daniel, Esq., F.S.A., 9, *Lower Rock Garden, Brighton.*

Umfreville, Samuel T., Esq., *Ingress Park, Greenhithe.*
Utting, R. B., Esq., 9, *Cornwall Terrace, Camden Town,* N.W.

Vallance, Rev. William, M.A., *Southchurch Rectory, Essex.*
Vincent, Rev. Richard, M.A., *Woodlands Manor, Sevenoaks.*

Waddington, Rev. Herbert, B.A., *Newington, Hythe.*

Walker, Henry Bachelor, Esq., *New Romney.*
Walker, William Dering, Esq., *New Romney.*
Wallace, Rev. George, *Precincts, Canterbury.*
Waller, Edmund, Esq., *Farmington Lodge, North Leach, Gloucestershire.*
Walter, Rev. Frank, *Boughton, Staplehurst.*
Walter, William, Esq., *East Farleigh.*
Walter, William, Esq., *Rainham.*
Warde, Charles, Esq., *Squerryes Court, Westerham.*
Warre, J. A., Esq., M.P., *West Cliffe, Ramsgate.*
Warton, Charles, Esq., *Kemsdale, Hernhill, Harbledown.*
Wates, Edward, Esq., *Gravesend.*
*Way, Albert, Esq., *Wonham Manor, Reigate.*
Webster, Thomas, Esq., R.A., *Cranbrook.*
Welldon, Rev. J., D.D., *Tunbridge School.*
Welldon, Rev. Edward I., M.A., *Tunbridge.*
Weston, Lambert, Esq., *Waterloo Crescent, Dover.*
Whatman, James, Esq., F.R.S., F.S.A., *Vinter's, Maidstone.*
Wheelwright, J. Esq., *Meopham Court, Gravesend.*
Whichcord, John, Esq., *Maidstone.*
White, Rev. John, *St. Stephen's Vicarage, Canterbury.*
White, Thomas, Esq., *Wateringbury.*
White, Mrs. Thomas, *Wateringbury.*
Whitehead, John, Esq., *Barnjet, Maidstone.*
Whitehead, Thomas Miller, Esq., 8, *Duke Street, St. James's, London,* S.W.
Whitelock, Rev. B., *Groombridge.*
Whitmore, William, Esq., *Beckenham,* S.E.
Whittaker, Charles Gustavus, Esq., *Barming.*
Whittaker, Charles Gustavus, jun., Esq., *Coldrum Lodge, Addington, Malling.*
Whittle, John, Esq., *Star Hill, Rochester.*
Wickham, George, Esq., *Maidstone.*
Wickham, Humphrey, Esq., *Strood.*
Wigan, Rev. Alfred, M.A., *Luddesdown Rectory, Gravesend.*
Wigan, Frederick, Esq., *Hibernia Chambers, London Bridge,* S.E.
Wigan, J. A., Esq., *Clare House, East Malling.*
Wigan, Mrs., *ditto.*
Wigan, James, Esq., *Mortlake, Surrey,* S.W.
Wigan, L. D., Esq., *Rock House, Maidstone.*
Wigan, Rev. Septimus, *Ticehurst, Sussex.*
Wigan, Rev., W. L., M.A., *East Malling.*
Wightwick, T. N., Esq., *Canterbury.*
Wild, Thomas M., Esq., *Branbridges, East Peckham.*
Wildes, Henry Dudlow, Esq., *West Malling.*
Wilkinson, Charles, Esq., *Sandfield, Tunbridge Wells.*
Wilkinson, F. Eachus, Esq., F.R.G.S., *Sydenham,* S.E.
*Willement, Thomas, Esq., F.S.A., *Davington Priory, Faversham.*
Williams, Charles, Esq., *Cranbrook Lodge.*
*Wilson, Cornelius Lea, Esq., *Beckenham,* S.E.
Wilson, J. E., Esq., *Cranbrook.*

*Wilson, Samuel, Esq., Alderman of London, *Beckenham*, S.E.
*Wilson, Sir Thomas Maryon, Bart., *Charlton House*, S.E.
Winch, Richard, Esq., *Rochester*.
Winchilsea and Nottingham, The Earl of, *Eastwell Park*.
Winham, Rev. Daniel, *Tunbridge Wells*.
Wodehouse, Rev. Walker, *Elham Vicarage, Canterbury*.
Wood, Mr. George, *High Street, Canterbury*.
*Wood, Western, Esq., *North Cray Place*, S.E.
Woods, Rev. G. H., *Shopwyke House, Chichester*.
Woodfall, J. W., Esq., M.D., *Maidstone*.
Woodruff, Rev. John, M.A., *Upchurch Vicarage, Sittingbourne*.
Wrench, Rev. Frederick, M.A., *Stowting Rectory*.
Wright, Rev. Adolphus, *Ickham Rectory, Wingham*.

*Young, John, Esq., F.S.A., *Vanbrugh Fields, Blackheath*.
Young, John, Esq., *Lincoln's Inn Fields*, W.C.

*** Should any errors or omissions of honorary distinctions, etc., be found in this list, it is requested that notice thereof may be given to the Secretary.

The

Kent Archæological Society.

THE introductory pages of this, our second Volume, are purposely compressed into as small a compass as the necessary Report of our proceedings since our last publication will allow.

Narratives of periodical gatherings and festivities are more suited to the columns of a newspaper than to a work devoted to Archæological records and antiquarian research. For these we require all the space which our pages can afford.

If, therefore, our acknowledgments of the hearty welcome with which our Society was received at Rochester, by the Cathedral Chapter, the Corporation, and inhabitants of that ancient city, be brief, they are not the less gratefully offered; nor shall we be accused of insufficiently appreciating the munificent hospitalities of Cobham, and Cowling, and the Deanery, if we confine ourselves to a simple expression of cordial thanks. With these acknowledgments, then, pass we at once to a brief record of this the principal event that has occurred since our last publication, viz. the Second Annual General Meeting of the Society, held at Rochester, on the 3rd of August, 1859.

It was attended by,—The Marquess Camden, K.G., President; The Earl and Countess Stanhope; The Earl and Countess Amherst; The Earl and Countess of Darnley; The Earl of Brecknock; Lady Frances Pratt; Lady Caroline Pratt; A. J. B. Beresford-Hope, Esq., and Lady Mildred Hope; Lady Caroline Nevill; Lady Augusta Mostyn; Lady Isabel Bligh; The Hon. Ralph Nevill; The Hon. T. Lloyd Mostyn; The Hon. James Byng; The Hon. Mrs. Byng; Sir Percival Hart Dyke, Bart.; Lady Dyke; Lieutenant-Colonel Bingham; Sir Walter James, Bart.; Sir Walter Stirling, Bart.; Sir Charles Locock, Bart., and party; Sir Brook Bridges, Bart.; Admiral Jones Marsham and party; The Rev. The Provost of Oriel and Mrs. Hawkins; The Rev. Canon Robertson and party; The Mayor of Rochester (William Manclark, Esq.); The Recorder of Rochester (J. 'Espinasse, Esq.); James Whatman, Esq., Mrs. Whatman, and party; G. W. Norman, Esq., and party; C. Wykeham Martin, Esq.; J. Savage, Esq., Mrs. Savage, and party; J. Crosby, Esq., F.S.A., and Miss Crosby; Lancaster Lucas, Esq., and party; J. G. Talbot, Esq.; Rev. J. Riddell; Rev. C. Hawley; Rev. T. Hugo; Rev. Joshua Stratton; Rev. H. Stevens and party; Rev. Jacob Marsham; Rev. C. Randolph; Rev. Beale Poste and party; Rev. J. F. Cobb; Rev. W. A. Keith; Rev. R. P. Coates; Rev. J. P. Russell; Rev. E. Trollope; Rev. J. Woodruffe; Rev. W. Horne and party; G. B. Acworth, Esq., and party; W. Brown, Esq., and party; J. Thurston, Esq.; Dr. Plomley and party; W. W. Hayward, Esq., Mrs. Hayward, and party; Major Luard, Mrs. Luard, and party; M. Bell, Esq.; Captain Cator; Peter Cator, Esq., and party; W. Norwood, Esq.; Major Munn; S. Steele, Esq., and party; H. Farrar, Esq.; Colonel Stanton, Mrs. Stanton, and party; Captain and Mrs. Cheere; R. Thomas, Esq., and party; T. H. Day, Esq., and party; Jesse Thomas, Esq., and party; Humphrey Wickham, Esq., and party; G. R. Corner, Esq.; C. Roach Smith, Esq.; F. Fry, Esq.; W. H. Bensted, Esq.; H. Wickham, Esq.; E. Pretty, Esq., F.S.A.; Arthur Ashpitel, Esq., F.S.A.; Richard Hussey, Esq., F.S.A.; H. B. Mackeson, Esq.; W. Clayton, Esq., and party; A. J. Dunkin, Esq., and party; Rev. L. B. Larking; and above three hundred others, whose names we could not obtain.

The MARQUESS CAMDEN, K.G., President of the Society, took the Chair, in the Corn Exchange, at twelve o'clock, and commenced the business of the day by calling on the Honorary Secretary to read—

The Report.

"The Report of the state and progress of our Society which I have this day the pleasure of presenting, is one on which we may well congratulate ourselves.

"On the morning of our Meeting at Canterbury, last year, our Society numbered 561 members. Since then, 89 candidates have been elected, and I shall this day have the honour of submitting to you the names of 46 more. Should you elect them, the total number of those who have joined the Society since its institution in September, 1857, not yet two years ago, will be 696; a significant reply to the question somewhat tauntingly mooted at the time, 'Is Kent able to institute an Archæological Society?'

"But the most gratifying part of this day's Report, and one which immeasurably adds to the force of our reply, is the announcement of the publication of our first Volume. It is, we hope, already in the hands of all our members, and we trust has given them satisfaction. It has met with much commendation from literary men of eminence, and we shall be much disappointed if the general opinion be not in its favour.

"At our Bankers' we have a balance of £161. We have also funded £233 in Three-per-cent. Stock. A sum of nearly £200 is due to us from our members. Our available assets for current expenses should be £365. From these assets a competent sum for the expenses of this day must be deducted. Nearly half a year's salary is due to our Assistant Secretary. A very few small sums are due to other parties. On payment of all these demands, the balance will be entirely absorbed in discharging the costs of printing our first Volume.

"It is to the question of this £200 arrears, that we wish specially to call the attention of our members. We cannot for one moment doubt their ultimate payment; but it will be palpably impossible to carry on the ordinary business of the Society, much less to publish a Volume, with anything like regularity, if the promised payments be not duly and regularly made. We would urge our Local Secretaries to give their special attention to this point. If members would have the kindness to furnish their bankers with a general order for the annual payment of their subscription, all further trouble would be removed. It is the smallness of the sum, 10*s.*, that causes it to escape the memory and makes it difficult of transmission. The best remedy is a general order upon a banker. But, whatever mode of payment be adopted, we press it most earnestly upon our members to make their remittances regularly; otherwise, disappointment in the operations of the Society must be the result.

"We would also draw the attention of the wealthier members of the Society, who have not yet contributed to the Illustration Fund, to the great service they will render by giving their aid in that department to the regular production of a fully and richly illustrated Volume.

"If all join, heart and hand, in the work, there is no doubt that our Society will be established on a permanent basis, and will continue to carry on its labours as energetically and successfully as it hitherto has done, during the short period of its existence."

The Society then proceeded to the election of officers, members, etc.; when—

James 'Espinasse, Esq., Recorder of Rochester, was elected a Vice-President.

Our rules requiring that six members of the Council retire by annual rotation, it was resolved that those who had attended the fewest meetings of the Council, during the last year, should be selected for retirement. Two vacancies having occurred, by the lamented death of Canon Chesshyre and the appointment of the Recorder of Rochester to the office of Vice-President, the number of actually necessary retirements was reduced to four, viz. E. Hussey, Esq.; T. Wightwick, Esq.; J. Rogers, Esq.; and G. Wickham, Esq. The following were the six elected to supply the vacancies:—

E. Hussey, Esq., re-elected;
J. Rogers, Esq., re-elected;
Major Luard;
Thomas Godfrey Faussett, Esq.;
The Rev. R. Drake;
Sir Walter Stirling, Bart.

Forty-six candidates were then admitted as members of the Society.

In pursuance of notice of the intended alteration of Rule 9, it was resolved that for "the 19th of September in each year," as it stands in the said Rule, the following words be substituted: "The 1st of January in each year." The result of this alteration will be that the subscriptions for the third year will not become due till the 1st of January, 1860; and, thenceforward, will be payable on the 1st of January in every succeeding year.

The thanks of the Society were then voted—

To the Mayor and Corporation of Rochester, and to J. Lewis, Esq., the Town Clerk, for the facilities afforded to the Society in the inspection of the archives of the city; in allowing the use of the Corn Exchange; and for the welcome given to the Society;

To the Dean of Rochester, for the hospitality kindly tendered to the Society and their friends at the Deanery, and for allowing the formation of a temporary museum there;

To the Dean and Chapter, for their kindness in throwing open the Cathedral and the adjoining monastic remains to the free inspection of the Society, and to G. Essell, Esq., the Chapter Clerk, for the kind facilities rendered to them in their survey, and in the inspection of ancient Records;

To E. Hayward, Esq., for his courtesy in giving free access to the Castle, and in allowing the dinner-tent to be erected in his garden;

To the Directors and Managers of the South-eastern Railway, for the liberal accommodation rendered to the Society in conveying the members to and from the meeting.

After voting the thanks of the meeting to their noble Chairman, the party adjourned to the Cathedral, where Richard Hussey, Esq., explained the peculiarities of the structure, and pointed out the periods at which its different portions were erected.

Mr. Beresford-Hope then delivered a most luminous lecture on the Rise and Progress and Peculiarities of Ecclesiastical Architecture, in its different periods.

The Rev. the Provost of Oriel conducted the members over the remains of the conventual buildings, giving descriptions of their various uses as he passed along.

The company then divided,

A. Ashpitel, Esq., gratifying one party with a most interesting lecture on the Castle and its various chambers, and on the origin, rise, and uses of Norman castles in general;

The Rev. Beale Poste and S. Steele, Esq., leading other parties round the ancient walls, and delivering learned dissertations on the remains thereof.

Soon after three o'clock, afternoon service was performed in the Cathedral, which was thronged throughout; and the choir, assisted by members of the choirs of Windsor and the Temple, under the superintendence of the Rev. R. Sorsbie, the Precentor, furnished an exquisite choral service, selected from Kentish composers.

At five o'clock, dinner was served, in a marquee in the Castle garden, to a party of about two hundred and fifty; the Marquess Camden occupying the chair.

After dinner, the party adjourned to the Deanery, where they were hospitably entertained by the Rev. H. Stevens and his sisters; the Dean himself, to the regret of all, being compelled by his infirmities to absent himself.

He had kindly permitted the Society the use of one of the apartments on the ground-floor of the Deanery for the reception of exhibitions, and the Rev. R. P. Coates very obligingly acted on the occasion as Curator. The result of his exertions, and the good feeling of several members and their friends, was a large collection, chiefly consisting of local antiquities, which completely filled the room. The attendance here at the appointed hour, eight o'clock, was very numerous.

THE EXHIBITION OF ANTIQUITIES AT THE DEANERY.

Mr. Roach Smith undertook the explanation of the various collections, which were arranged in groups as exhibited by the several proprietors. He commenced an extemporaneous address by a review of the general state of Kent under the Romans; its towns, roads, military stations, and those great establishments situated between the chief towns, which served as resting-places for the troops, and as inns for merchants and travellers,—places, the names of some of which are recorded, and their distances from well-known towns; but their remains had wholly disappeared, and respecting the very sites of some there had consequently been much discussion. These subordinate stations, termed *mansiones* and *mutationes*, formed unbroken lines from all parts of the Roman empire, and converged at Rome. The almost total absence, in Kent, of monumental inscriptions, such as are found so frequently in the north of England, and are so justly prized by the historian, though it deprives the county of an interesting source of archæological inquiry, affords strong negative evidence of its tranquillity under the Roman rule. Lapidary inscriptions usually spring from long military occupation, to which Cantium was never subjected; but, on the contrary, its situation and the character of its population fitted it for that superior civilization under which commerce and the industrial arts flourish, contributing in peace and quietude to the comfort and prosperity of the tillers of the fields and the artisans and traders of the towns and villages. The silence of the historian, whose pen was seldom employed but to chronicle invasion and conquest; and the character of those remains which yet abound, and which were represented upon the tables in the Society's temporary museum, significantly reflected the flourishing condition of the county; and this although a high state of cultivation is necessarily unfavourable to the preservation of the fragile and perishable works of art.

The vestiges of splendid villas, such as are met with here and there in more remote parts of this country, are not at the present day to be traced in Kent; but neither the vicissitudes of time, nor the constant operations of the spade and the plough, have effaced the foundations of numerous buildings,—the habitations of the agriculturist, of the artisan, and of the general body of the industrious classes. Almost daily, the cemeteries of the Romano-British population are met with, not only near the towns and villages, but in retired spots; and it is not unusual to discover that land now uncultivated must have been tilled by the Romans. This is proved when we find villas and extensive burial-places in the midst of woods and copses.[1]

The exhibition of the antiquities discovered at Hartlip by Mr. Bland, afforded a good example of the miscellaneous contents of a Roman villa of such considerable size that Mr. Roach Smith said it was not improbable it might have been one of the *mansiones* between Durovernum and Durobrivis. Its existence had long been known; but until Mr. Bland undertook its exhumation, it had never been explored. The foundations of the building were very extensive,[2] including one large semi-detatched apartment supported by buttresses, which was sufficiently capa-

[1] The discoveries made in Lockham wood, near Maidstone, by Mr. Charles and Mr. Clement T. Smythe, remain unpublished. The latter gentleman has left a MS. account of the excavations; and the antiquities discovered are in the Charles Museum. The glass vessels are rare and elegant. Amphoræ, in which were funeral urns in glass, and the other objects, are luckily preserved; but they remain unengraved, and the antiquarian world has not yet enjoyed the benefit of this discovery.

[2] A ground plan, with numerous plates and woodcuts, will be found in Mr. Roach Smith's 'Collectanea Antiqua,' vol. ii.

cious for the reception of a considerable body of troops. Baths of two kinds, admirably constructed and in excellent preservation, heated, as well as some of the rooms, by a hypocaust, illustrated the domestic manners of the Romano-Britons; and the general contents and fittings of a Roman country building of the better kind were well reflected in the Hartlip villa, and the miscellaneous objects discovered. The latter have now become the property of the Society, and are deposited in the Charles Museum. A selection was made by Mr. Pretty for this occasion.

From the Upchurch marshes the Rev. J. Woodruffe exhibited a large collection of fictile ware, which gave Mr. Roach Smith an opportunity of describing the peculiarities of the workmanship of the various kinds of vessels, and the nature of the locality in which they had been found. It is now marsh land, almost impassable from the encroachments of the sea; but in the time of the Romans it was covered with the works of potters, for several miles at least; and what are now found (such as the vessels exhibited) are the *débris* and rejected vases. Many of them are of elegant forms, and none positively ugly, like much of the modern pottery. Although comprising hundreds of patterns, they are all marked by certain leading and general features, which, Mr. Roach Smith said, had enabled those who had closely studied them to recognize the chief kinds made on the Medway wherever they may be met with; and it appears that the potters there established must have carried on an extensive trade with the interior parts of Britain. No evidence of the red, shining pottery, called 'Samian,' having been made there occurs; but, on the contrary, it is now well understood that it was imported from Gaul and Germany. The clay of the Upchurch marshes is particularly fine, and is capable of making very superior pottery, equal, as regards quality, to the Roman. Mr. Humphrey Wickham, who owns a considerable tract of this land, has had the clay tested by one of the chief Staffordshire potters. It is pronounced of the best description, showing the good judgment of the Romans in selecting the site for a manufactory.

Mr. Humphrey Wickham exhibited his collection of Roman and Saxon remains discovered on the Temple estate, adjoining Strood, some years since. It consists of sepulchral vessels, personal ornaments, coins, and weapons, the last being Saxon. The whole of these were brought to light by excavations for brick earth, which laid open a very extensive Roman and Saxon cemetery, for it appears the Saxons had interred their dead alongside of their predecessors. Among the ornaments exhibited were some *armillæ*, in what is called Kimmeridge shale, an inferior kind of jet; and a *bulla*, in pure jet, bearing a well-executed representation of Medusa's head. Upwards of six hundred coins were found.[1]

Mr. Wickham also exhibited a gold British coin, a new variety of the COMI . F . type, found in excavating the new railway between Chatham and Rainham; and some Saxon remains very recently dug up midway between the Temple Farm and Cuxton. They included an example of the *angon*, which the lecturer said was the *first* ever discovered in a grave in this country, this weapon being peculiarly Frankish, and not Saxon. It is described rather minutely by the historian Agathias. This formidable weapon, when entire with its shaft, was probably six or seven feet in length. Its point was quadrilateral, below which were barbs turning inwards. If a thrust from the angon failed to i flict a mortal wound instantaneously, it usually was propelled with force sufficient to penetrate the enemy's shield. The barbs hindered its being withdrawn; and the Frankish soldier, treading his foot upon the shaft, bore down his adversary's shield, and despatched him with another weapon. With it was a spear, a knife, and an earthen vessel resembling those discovered near Canterbury by the Rev. Bryan Faussett, and figured in his 'Inventorium Sepulchrale.'

The Roman remains exhibited derived additional interest from the collections, forwarded by Mr. Biggs and Major Luard, from the neighbourhood of Ightham. They contained examples of the 'Samian' ware, and other varieties of fictile vessels differing in mode of manufacture and in ornamentation from those made on the banks of the Medway. Major Luard's collections comprised also a very remarkable example of a Roman flue-tile, covered with a stamp, reading CABRIABANTI[VS], and a bronze statuette of Pallas, of exquisite workmanship, found at Plaxtol, an engraving of which is given in this Volume.

Mr. Rolfe, of Sandwich, exhibited two leaden seals of the Emperor Constantine, recently found at Richborough. They bear on one side the head, name, and titles of Constantine, as they appear upon his coins, but in somewhat higher relief. The

[1] A detailed and illustrated account of the discovery is printed in the first volume of the 'Collectanea Antiqua.'

reverse is plain and slightly convex. They had evidently been attached by means of a string to documents or to other objects sent from Rome to Rutupiæ. Mr. Roach Smith observed that the only other examples of Roman leaden seals he had known to be found in England were discovered at Felixstow, in Suffolk, and at Broughton Stannore, in Westmoreland; but none of these were marked with an Imperial impress.[1]

The department of Kentish Saxon antiquities received an unexpected accession in additional discoveries made in the King's Field, at Faversham, which on this occasion were first made known to the Society by Mr. Gibbs, whose former acquisitions from the same site are already made known to the Society. The fibulæ, pendants, and buckles, are mostly in the precious metals, and comprise novel varieties. One of the graves contained a quantity of the teeth of horses ground down as if to adapt them to be used in some game.

Lord Amherst exhibited his splendid gold Saxon brooch, found at Sarr, in Thanet, in 1843. The face of this jewel, upwards of two inches in diameter, is divided into four compartments by concentric circles, which are subdivided into cells of triangular and other forms. Some of these are filled with a triple range of ornaments, formed of gold wire twisted like cord or laid on in little circles. Other cells contain garnets, turquoises, and a white cretaceous substance, apparently mother-of-pearl decomposed. The reverse is plain, except at the head of the acus which fastened it, where a single square garnet is inserted. Lord Amherst having accidentally dropped this fibula, the jar of the fall displaced the hinder part, when it was discovered that the interior was filled with a substance resembling, if not identical with, plaster of Paris.

Mr. Clayton contributed some bronze enamelled ornaments, found near Dover. They may be assigned to the British epoch under the Roman rule; and are similar in character to some found in a barrow in Derbyshire, and engraved in Mr. Bateman's 'Vestiges of the Antiquities of Derbyshire,' p. 25. Others, chiefly found in the northern and central counties, are preserved in the British Museum.

At the conclusion of his address and description of the foregoing antiquities (which occupied two hours), a vote of thanks,

[1] A plate of these rare seals will be found in vol. iii. of the 'Collectanea Antiqua.'

proposed by Mr. Steele and seconded by Mr. Dunkin, was given to Mr. Roach Smith.

There were also exhibited—

Collections from Utica, Carthage, Athens, and Nolo. By Mr. Flenley.

Early carved ivories and paintings. Rev. J. Russell.

A beautiful Saxon processional cross, in bronze, from West Farleigh; and a pair of gloves, said to have belonged to James I. The Dean of Rochester.

Ancient deeds, and impressions of seals, including that of the Earl of Warwick, the King-maker. J. J. Hayward, Esq., F.S.A., and E. Gibbs, Esq., of Gravesend.

A large collection of the seals of Rochester and the Cinque Ports. Mr. King.

Rubbings from monumental brasses in Kent. The Recorder of Rochester and Mr. Kadwell.

The Recognizances of Kent, *temp.* James I.; and a large collection of various documents relating to the county. Mr. Dunkin.

Pedigrees of Kentish families. Mr. Mackrell.

Powder-horns of the fifteenth century. The Rev. G. Faussett.

Drawings of churches and mansions in Kent. Mr. G. R. Corner.

Monumental brasses; Irish Celts; seals. The Recorder.

Wood carving from a house near the Cathedral gateway. Mr. G. P. Acworth.

Stained glass window, with armorial bearings, of the sixteenth century. Mr. H. Wickham.

Greek picture, with chased silver frame, sixteenth century. Rev. D. Ash.

A processional spur. Mr. Skinner.

Bronze cock of a fountain (?), in the form of an animal's head, fifteenth century. Mr. E. L. Betts.

A rapier and long processional sword. The Recorder.

Circular bronze fibula, of the fifteenth century, inscribed "*Ave Regina Cœlorum. Ave Do*[*mina?*]." Major Luard.

A most enjoyable day was concluded by a full choral service in the Cathedral, at ten o'clock, P.M.

4TH AUGUST, 1859.

At ten o'clock, A.M., a large party assembled in the Corn Exchange, where the Marquess CAMDEN again presided. Very interesting and learned papers were read by—

Rev. Thomas Hugo,—On Bishops Gundulph and Ernulph, and their works in the Cathedral and Castle.

Rev. E. Trollope,—On the passages of John, King of France, through Kent, as one of the prisoners of Poictiers.

Major Luard,—On Roman Remains found at Plaxtol.

A paper on the siege of Rochester Castle, by King John, kindly prepared by G. R. Corner, Esq., was deferred for want of time; the excursions to Cowling Cliff, Cobham, etc., requiring an early departure.

The thanks of the Society having been duly voted to the contributors of papers and the noble Chairman, the party started on their excursion.

The Honorary Secretary apologized for his inability, from great fatigue, to accompany the excursion, stating that he held in his hand some very curious documents from the collection at Surrenden, being the builders' and workmen's receipts for the erection of Cowling Castle, early in the reign of Richard II. He would not detain the company by reading them; but handed over to the Rev. R. P. Coates transcripts thereof, made by himself, for the use and amusement of the company when they should arrive at Cowling.

Thither large numbers proceeded, where they were most hospitably entertained by the occupier, J. Morton, Esq.; S. Steele, Esq., kindly explaining all the peculiarities of the building.

Thence they proceeded to inspect Cliffe Church, where its curiosities, including a very early paten, were exhibited and elucidated by the Curate, the Rev. E. H. Lee, and a cordial welcome given by the parishioners.

From thence they passed to Cobham Hall, where again a cordial and hospitable reception awaited them from the Earl and Countess of Darnley. After partaking of a cold collation, the noble Earl, aided by Earl Stanhope and Mr. Beresford Hope, took the company in successive parties round the house and gardens, most courteously exhibiting and explaining all the objects of interest in the picture gallery and other parts of this noble and ancient mansion.

The business of the Meeting was concluded by a visit to Cobham Church, to inspect the numerous ancient brasses and monuments, where a most lucid and interesting lecture was given by Mr. Beresford Hope.

Thus ended the second and last day of our Second Annual Meeting, which may well be pronounced to have been most gratifying and satisfactory.

At the Quarterly Council, held at Maidstone, 8th September, 1859, twenty-five new members were elected, and the following Honorary Local Secretaries appointed:—

John Brent, jun., Esq., Canterbury, *vice* T. Wightwick, Esq.

F. F. Geraud, Esq., Faversham, *vice* Major Munn.

W. Murton, Esq., Tunstall, for Sittingbourne district.

Mr. Smallfield, 10, Little Queen Street, Lincoln's Inn Fields, for London and places out of Kent.

At the Quarterly Council, held at Canterbury, 36 new members were elected, making the total number admitted since the foundation of the Society in 1857, 759.

The Rev. Professor Willis, and C. Roach Smith, Esq., were elected Honorary Members.

G. Carnell, Esq., of Sevenoaks, and
Stacey Grimaldi, Esq., of Greenwich,
were appointed Honorary Local Secretaries.

The limits of our Volume preclude the possibility of our printing at one time all the learned and interesting papers which were read at Rochester, yet our readers must not be deprived of the gratification of seeing them on record. We therefore purpose, with the kind consent of the writers, to print them consecutively in our future Volumes, commencing this year with that of Mr. Beale Poste on the Walls of Rochester.

With the Report of the Council we close the narrative of our year's proceedings, which we are fully justified in designating as one of continued and successful progress.

KENT ARCHÆOLOGICAL SOCIETY.

Balance Sheet of Accounts from 19th September, 1858, to 31st December, 1859.

Dr.

Date		£.	s.	d.	£.	s.	d.
1858. Sept. 19th.	Balance at Bankers				105	10	11
1859. April.	Dividend for one year on £212. 2*s.* 10*d.*				6	4	8
October.	Dividend for half-year on £233. 5*s.* 8*d.*				3	6	2
Dec. 31st.	Subscriptions, Life Compositions, Contributions to Illustration Fund, Payments for Royal 8vo, etc. etc., viz.—						
	Randall and Co.	424	15	2			
	Hammond and Co.	85	15	0			
	London Agents	7	6	6			
					517	16	8
					£632	18	5

Cr.

Date		£	s.	d.	£.	s.	d.
1859. April 20th.	Purchase of £21. 2*s.* 10*d.* new Three per Cent. Stock, being four Life Compositions				20	0	0
Nov. 3rd.	Purchase of £19. 4*s.* 4*d.* new Three per Cent. Stock, being four Life Compositions				18	6	2
Dec. 31st.	Postage and Porterage, $1\frac{1}{4}$ year				11	14	5
	Stationery, ditto				5	1	$5\frac{1}{2}$
	Advertising				1	1	0
	Annual Meeting at Rochester				32	2	1
	Local Secretaries' Disbursements, Travelling Expenses, Hire of Rooms, etc., $1\frac{1}{4}$ year				40	4	$2\frac{1}{4}$
	Salary of Assistant Secretary, $1\frac{1}{2}$ year				37	10	0
	Repairs				0	4	6
	Cost of 'Archæologia Cantiana'				367	5	2
	Miscellaneous Printing, Circulars, etc.				3	0	6
	Balance at Bankers:—						
	Randall and Co.	72	12	2			
	Hammond and Co.	27	2	8			
		£99	14	10			
	Deduct Balance due to Secretary	3	5	$10\frac{3}{4}$			
					96	8	$11\frac{1}{4}$
					£632	18	5

Audited and allowed,

JOHN SAVAGE, } *Auditors.*
J. N. DUDLOW, }

CONTRIBUTIONS

To the Fund for supplying Illustrations to the Society's Volumes.

		£.	s.	d.
Abergavenny, The Earl of		5	0	0
Acworth, G. B., Esq.		1	0	0
Allan, The Rev. G.		1	0	0
Amherst, The Earl		5	0	0
Beresford-Hope, A. J. B., Esq.		5	0	0
Blencowe, R. W., Esq., 1859, 1860		6	0	0
Bridges, Sir Brook, Bart.		3	0	0
Burney, The Venerable Archdeacon		0	10	0
Camden, The Marquess		5	5	0
Cardwell, Rev. Dr.		5	0	0
Cheshire, The Rev. Canon		1	0	0
Crosby, James, Esq.		1	0	0
Ditto (1860)	A	0	10	0
Culling-Eardley, E. G., Esq.		5	5	0
Dashwood, Rev. G. H.		0	10	0
Devon, Charles, Esq.		1	0	0
Ellis, C., Esq.		0	10	0
'Espinasse, James, Esq.		2	0	0
Falmouth, The Viscount		5	0	0
Foss, E., Esq.		1	0	0
Godefroy, J. N., Esq.	A	0	5	0
Golding, Mr. Charles	A	0	5	0
Hawkins, The Rev. Canon		1	0	0
Hawley, Sir Joseph H., Bart.		5	0	0
Hooper, W. E. P., Esq.		1	0	0
Hussey, E., Esq., *Oxford*		0	10	0
Ditto (1860)		0	3	0
Hussey, H., Esq.		0	10	0
Hussey, H., Esq., *Hyde Park Square*		0	10	0
Hussey, R., Esq.		1	0	0
Ditto (1860)		0	6	6
James, E., Esq., *Greenwich*		0	10	0
James, Sir Walter, Bart.		0	10	0
King, Knowles, Esq.		0	10	0
Knatchbull, Sir Norton, Bart.		2	0	0
Knatchbull, Lady		2	0	0
Larking, J. Wingfield, Esq.	A	0	10	0
Larking, The Rev. L. B.	A	1	1	0
Leeks, Edward F., Esq.	A	0	5	0

		£.	s.	d.
Luard, Major		0	10	0
Mackesson, H. B., Esq.		1	0	0
Maidstone, The Venerable the Archdeacon of		2	0	0
Martin, C. Wykeham, Esq.		5	0	0
Marriott, The Rev. W. Smith		1	0	0
Mesham, The Rev. A.		1	0	0
Norman, G. W., Esq.		5	0	0
Norman, H., Esq.		2	0	0
Oakley, W., Esq.		0	5	0
Onslow, The Rev. M.		1	0	0
Pollard, J. P., Esq.		0	5	0
Poste, The Rev. Beale		2	2	0
Pretty, Edward, Esq.		2	2	0
Randall, Alexander, Esq.		2	0	0
Rashleigh, The Rev. G.		1	0	0
Robertson, The Rev. J. C.		2	0	0
Rye, W. B., Esq.		0	10	0
Smallfield, Mr.	A	0	5	0
Smallfield, Mr. George		0	5	0
Smith, Arthur, Esq.		1	0	0
Stanhope, The Earl		2	0	0
Stanton, Lieutenant-Colonel		1	1	0
Stratford, J. Wingfield, Esq.		1	0	0
Taylor, J. E., Esq.	A	0	5	0
Twopeny, E., Esq.	A	0	5	0
Whatman, James, Esq.		5	0	0
Willement, T., Esq.		1	0	0
Wilson, Sir Thomas Maryon, Bart.		3	0	0
Wrench, The Rev. F.		1	0	0

The Designing and Engraving of the Society's Badge was defrayed by—

The Lady Caroline Nevill.
The Lady Augusta Mostyn.
The Lady Isabel Bligh.

To the Fund for enlarging the Museum and Library.

		£.	s.	d.
Golding, Mr. Charles	A	0	5	0
Larking, Rev. L. B. (two years)		0	10	0
Pretty, E., Esq. (two years)		0	10	0
Smallfield, Mr.	A	0	5	0
Smallfield, Mr. G.	A	0	5	0
Taylor, J. E., Esq.	A	0	5	0

Members willing to contribute to these Funds are requested to signify their intentions to the Honorary Secretary, or to the London Local Secretary.

BOOKS AND PAPERS PRESENTED

TO THE

KENT ARCHÆOLOGICAL SOCIETY.

By C. Roach Smith, Esq., F.S.A.

Report on the Excavations at Pevensey. By C. R. Smith, F.S.A.

On the Lake Dwellings of the Early Periods. Communicated to the Society of Antiquaries by W. M. Wylie, Esq., F.S.A.

On the so-called Anglo-Saxon Antiquities discovered near Kertch. By C. R. Smith, F.S.A.

By Thomas Willement, Esq., F.S.A.

Ancient Grant of Land, from Hamo Bovier to Christ Church, Canterbury: from the 'Archæologia,' vol. xxv.

Heraldic Notices of Canterbury Cathedral. By T. Willement, F.S.A.

By J. J. Howard, Esq., D.C.L., F.S.A.

Remarks on Four Deeds, with Seals appended; and a Memoir of Sir William Oldhalle, Knt. Communicated to the Society of Antiquaries by Weston Styleman Walford, Esq., F.S.A., 1858.

Observations on a Grant of an Advowson of a Chantry to a Guild in 34 Hen. VI. Communicated to the Society of Antiquaries by Weston Styleman Walford, Esq., F.S.A., 1859.

Armorial Bearings of Kentish Families. By J. J. Howard, Esq., D.C.L., F.S.A.

By A. W. Dunkin, Esq.

A Proposal for establishing a Society for Promoting Useful Knowledge in the County of Kent. By W. Shipley, Maidstone.

Improvements for ditto.

Desiderata. Three papers.

By W. J. Thoms, Esq., F.S.A.

Olaf den helliges Saga, ved Snorre Sturlasson.

Olaf Tryggvessöns Saga, ved Odd Munk.

By Mr. Smallfield.

Dr. Packe's Chorographical Chart of East Kent.

Specimens and Parts (containing a History of the County of Kent, and a Dissertation on the Laws, from the Reign of Edward the Confessor to Edward the First) of a Topographical, Commercial, Civil, and Nautical History of South Britain, etc. By Samuel Henshall, Clerk, M.A.

By M. Caumont, Directeur de la Société Française d'Archéologie, Membre correspondant de l'Institut de France, etc.

Congrès Archéologique de France.—Séances Générales tenues à Strasbourg, à Rouen, à Saint-Lo et à Vire, en 1859, par la Société Française d'Archéologie pour la Conservation de Monuments Historiques ; xxvie session.

Histoire de l'Architecture Religieuse au Moyen Age. Par M. Caumont. 1 vol. and an atlas of plates.

Proceedings of the Kilkenny Archæological Society, vols. i. and ii., new series, and part 1, vol. iii.

Transactions of the London and Middlesex Archæological Society, vol. i. parts 1 and 2.

Reports and Papers read at the Meetings of the Architectural Societies of the County of York, Diocese of Lincoln, Archdeaconry of Northampton, County of Bedford, Diocese of Worcester, and County of Leicester, during the years 1857, 1858, and 1859.

Transactions of the Cambridge Camden Society, 1841.

The Ecclesiologist, Nos. 136, 137, 138, 139, and Report, 1859.

Sussex Archæological Collections, vol. x., 1858.

Mémoires de la Société Dunkerquoise, sixième volume, 1858, 1859.

Newton's History of Maidstone, with MS. additions. *Presented by the* Archdeacon of Maidstone.

Robinson on Gavelkind. By J. D. Norwood, Esq. *Presented by* J. D. Norwood, Esq.

A Prospectus of the Tomb of Childeric I. By M. l'Abbé Cochet.

Wetton's Guide to Northampton and its Vicinity. *Presented by the Author*, E. PRETTY, F.S.A.

Willard's Memoir and Willard's Address, 2 vols. *Presented by* "JOSEPH WILLARD, of Kentish ancestry."

Musæum Tradescantianum: transcribed from the original edition of 1656. *Presented by* C. KADWELL, Esq.

Diary of a Month's Tour in the South of France. *Presented by the Author*, JOHN ADKINS BARTON, Esq.

Sigilla Antiqua: Engravings from Ancient Seals attached to Deeds and Charters in the Muniment Room of Sir Thomas Hare, Bart., of Stowe-Bardolph. *Presented by the* Rev. G. H. DASHWOOD, M.A., F.S.A.

Bibliotheca Cantiana: a Bibliographical Account of what has been published on the History, Topography, Antiquities, Customs, and Family History of the County of Kent. By JOHN RUSSELL SMITH. *Large Paper. Presented by the Author.*

DRAWINGS, BRASSES, &c.

By E. TWOPENY, Esq.

Hour-glass Stand on the Pulpit of East Langdon Church.

Ruins of St. Augustine's, Canterbury.

By Mrs. SANKEY, *Dover.*

St. Nicholas's Tower, formerly standing in Beach Street, Dover.

Crypt of St. Nicholas Church, formerly under the carriageway in Beach Street, Dover.

Refectory of St. Martin's Priory, Dover.

By E. PRETTY, Esq., F.S.A.

View of the Interior of Aylesford Church, showing the Cossington Chapel and Monuments. Engraved by W. W. Wilkinson, from a drawing by E. P.

Exterior View of Aylesford Church. Etched by E. P.

Poor's Box at Smarden. Etched by E. P.

And the following Etchings of Churches, by a Lady, from sketches by E. P.:—Allington, Aylesford, Detling, East Farleigh, Linton, Otham, Snodland, and Wouldham.

Stone figure, found at Sibbertswold. *Presented by the* Rev. F. T. SCOTT.

Rubbings of Brasses, from the Churches of Cudham, Dover, Orpington, Cobham, and Wittersham. *Presented by* Mr. C. KADWELL.

Etching of a Brass in Capel Church. *Presented by* E. M. GIBBS, Esq.

Lithograph facsimile of the Patent for crenellating Allington Castle, with the Great Seal of Edward I. *Presented by the* Rev. L. B. LARKING.

A Rubbing of the Brass of John de Grofhurst, *c.* A.D. 1330, in Horsmonden Church; and Drawings of Encaustic Tiles in Sandhurst Church; also some Local Tokens of the eighteenth century. *Presented by* W. J. LIGHTFOOT, Esq.

ANTIQUITIES.

Collection from Hartlip, of which a detailed Catalogue will be given in our next Volume. *Presented by* WILLIAM BLAND, Esq.

Saxon Antiquities, excavated in Harrietsham Churchyard. *Presented by the* Rev. J. C. B. RIDDELL.

Two Anglo-Saxon Glass Cups, with fragments of antiquities, dug up at Westwell. *Purchased by the Society.*

Archæologia Cantiana.

ON THE RECENT DISCOVERIES OF ROMAN REMAINS AT PLAXTOL, IN KENT.

BY MAJOR LUARD, R.A.

THOUGH the sites of most of the principal cities and stations of Roman Britain are pretty clearly defined, there are some the position of which is still a matter of dispute.

Such is the station called Vagniacæ. The only datum we have for the position of this place is to be found in the second Iter of Antoninus, who there tells us, that from London to Noviomagus was ten miles, Noviomagus to Vagniacæ eighteen miles, and Vagniacæ to Durobrivis nine miles; and though from these distances (Noviomagus being at Hollwood Park, and Durobrivis at Rochester) we may infer that it stood not very far to the south of that part of the Watling Street that lies between London and Rochester, antiquarians are not agreed as to its exact locality.

Gale places it at Maidstone; Horsley finds it at Northfleet. Latterly Southfleet seems to have been generally received as the site of Vagniacæ, and were I now arguing in favour of the latter place, I might advance that the road from Hollwood Park to Southfleet, at the present day, probably on the line of a British way, as it is not very straight, would pass near Farthing Street, near or through Green Street Green, on the London and Sevenoaks road, through Clement Street, and Green Street Green, near Darent. The term 'street' being generally looked upon as evidence of an ancient way, might not Green Street be considered still stronger evidence?

But such is not my present object, especially now that numerous evidences of Roman occupation have come to light in the parishes of Ightham and Plaxtol. By being allowed a little latitude as to distance, we might bring Vagniacæ nearer to those localities: the decision of this point, however, I must leave to those possessed of more antiquarian research than I can pretend to.

Plate I. is a copy from the Ordnance map of the district in question, and I append it, not only to point out to the reader the exact spots of these discoveries, B, C, D, E, F, G, but to show their relative bearing to the Camp at Oldbury, A, which from its size (enclosing an area of 127 acres*) and highly commanding position, must have been a station of some importance amongst the Romans; and we may infer that their occupancy of the Plaxtol valley was the result of the security afforded by the proximity of the strong garrison at Oldbury Camp.

I do not moot the question of its Roman origin; it is probable that it may have been a British earthwork, and the Romans, seeing the advantage of the position, established themselves there.

Allen's Farm, B, in the parish of Plaxtol, is the property of Mr. Martin, a respectable farmer of that village, who has taken great interest in these discoveries on his land, and is most anxious to preserve them. He is an antiquary at heart, well deserving the thanks of the Society, and mine in particular, for the kind and liberal way in which he has allowed me to go to and fro over his land, and dig when and where I pleased; and I am as-

* The area of Silchester (*Calleva*) is but 102 acres.

sured that we shall find in him and Mrs. Martin able co-operators in our future proceedings.

On that farm there is a small field of about two acres, now in hops. It is bounded to the east and south by arable fields, and to the west by an ash-plantation, which divides it from a stream that, rising in the parish of Kemsing, to the north-west, after running through the parishes of Ightham and Plaxtol, pursues a south-easterly course till it joins the Medway near Little Mill, in the parish of East Peckham. The ground falls gradually from the north-east corner towards the west and south till it meets the stream, and it must have been a pleasant site for a residence in former days, when the valley was better wooded, and the stream unpolluted by paper-mills. This piece of ground had been arable for some years, and in ploughing, the labourers had constantly turned up bricks and tiles, and fragments of pottery; but they saw no difference between these and the rubbish of the present day, that finds its way to the dung-hill and from thence to the field, and no notice was ever taken of the circumstance. At length (1857) Mr. Martin determined to plant hops, and the land had to undergo a process of deep ploughing; when not only was the plough obstructed by stone foundations upwards of two feet thick and four feet deep, but the beautiful bronze statuette of Minerva Victrix, that through Mr. Martin's kindness was exhibited at the local Museum at Rochester, at the last meeting of the Society there, and an inscribed tile, were turned up. Then curiosity was awakened, and in process of time I heard of it, but too late to watch proceedings and take a plan of the foundations, for by the time that I visited the place they had been dug up, and were lying in heaps by the side of the village road awaiting the hammer of the stone-breaker. Still, from the description of the labourers, I was led to believe that the form of the buildings had been rectangular, and their direction parallel to the building subsequently discovered in the adjacent plantation.

I found the ground covered with fragments of Roman tile and pottery of every description. The various materials for making hypocausts* strewed the ground in every direction, and were in such quantities that the use of hypocausts in the buildings that once covered that field must have been very general. Amongst the fragments of pottery were some highly ornamented, of Samian ware: one with the usual subject of a gladiatorial combat, and the moulding so common to that ware. On one spot was found a considerable deposit of remains of bones of animals.

My impression, founded on the information I collected from the labourers, combined with my own personal observation is, that the field had been covered with buildings, either of Roman occupation or of a Roman type.

Of the statuette a lithographic drawing, from a photogram kindly furnished by J. Mitford, Esq., is given in Plate VII. The goddess appears to have been armed with a spear and shield. The height of the figure is 8 inches. The tile, inscribed with the letters CABRIABANTI, is represented in Plate VI. and Mr. Roach Smith's remark in his interesting work on the Roman Castrum at Lymne, when speaking of stamped tiles found there, is applicable here, for the formula of all the fragments—and they were many—which we found was unvarying. His observations are well worth perusal, and may help to elucidate the tile before us.

Last spring, on grubbing up some of the ash-stubs in the adjacent ash plantation, Mr. Martin came to more foundations, of which he has kindly allowed me to superintend the excavation. Our progress has been necessarily slow from the closeness of the stubs. I trust,

* For a clear explanation of the construction of tessellated pavements and hypocausts, vide Professor Buckman's 'Corinium,' p. 63.

Pl. VII.

Plate VI.

Inscribed Tile. Found at Allen's Farm.

Full Size.

however, with Mr. Martin's goodwill and assistance, that by the next annual meeting of the Society, I shall be able to lay before them a perfect plan of the building, or rather, I should say, of the foundations, and possibly, by analogy, of the construction of the floors. More we cannot hope for, as from the ruthless way in which all aboveground seems to have been destroyed, and the rooms filled up, the hypocausts are all compressed into a confused mass of solid *débris.*

Plate III. shows a plan of the present state of these excavations. The walls are of strong masonry, varying from 1 foot 6 inches to 2 feet 3 inches in thickness.

In the semicircular room, *a*, *b* is a step or seat 1 foot wide, of tile laid in concrete; *c* is paved with stone on the solid; *d* appears to be a drain, it is 1 foot wide, and made of flanged tile; *f* is a room 5 feet 6 inches by 9 feet, paved and faced with tile, the facing being laid in a 6-inch coating of concrete; the floor of this room is 2 feet below the surface of the drain, *d*. May it not have been a bath, and *d* the drain for conducting the water to it? *e* is a mass of brickwork laid in concrete; I conjecture it to have been steps; there has also been brickwork at *g*. The semicircular wall at *h* is built in alternate courses of Roman tile and stone; its present depth is 3 feet 6 inches. On its flat side the wall is of solid stone for 18 inches from the angles and for a foot from the bottom; the remaining space is filled up with concrete, in the centre of which a flue, made of tile, passes through the wall into the room *k*. On opening the flue I found it full of soot, that smelt as if a fire had been but recently burning there. The room *g* is still a heap of rubbish, with the exception of the south-west corner. There are here indications of a hypocaust, and at *i* I came to a paved floor of tile, 32 inches below the present surface; which floor I conceive was for the support of the pilæ. At *l* there were wood-ashes and charcoal, also several broken 8-inch bricks, flanged tiles, and concrete. At *m* I found a mass of brickwork, consisting of four layers of tiles, the surface of which is 18 inches from the present surface. Of the arrangement of the walls at the south-east corner I am still in the dark.

Soon after these discoveries in 1857, a cemetery was found on a farm rented by Mr. Thompson, of Plaxtol, and belonging to Mr. Golding, of East Peckham. Mr. Thompson's labourers, being employed in removing the ragstone that cropped out near the surface, dug up a large urn, 10 inches in height by 38 in circumference, containing a skull. They broke it to pieces, expecting to find gold; what became of the skull I know not, but the fragments of the urn we carried home, and by means of cement have partly restored it. I have several fictilia in the same condition, especially a beautiful bottle made of a kind of biscuit-ware (see Plate IV.). The sight of this induced us to search further, and the result of our labours is shown in Plate No. V., and from the description of one of the labourers belonging to the farm, that there had been a shaw partly covering the place where we were digging, and a large hillock at the very spot, which hillock was levelled when the shaw was removed, it was evident that we had been working on the base of a tumulus, the skeleton being at the centre, and the groups of pottery round the circumference. The body had been carefully laid out, with the head to the north-by-east. There was not a vestige of arms or ornament, and from the length of the tibia, which I measured at the time (but my note of which I have mislaid), it must have been a person of short stature, possibly a female. A large, rude, semicircular stone was laid across the breast. The deposits at *a*, *a*, *a*, were either entire, or the respective fragments were found together; not so on the other side, at *b*, *b*, *b*, where they were broken and dispersed. Doubtless the shaw, having covered the groups on the south

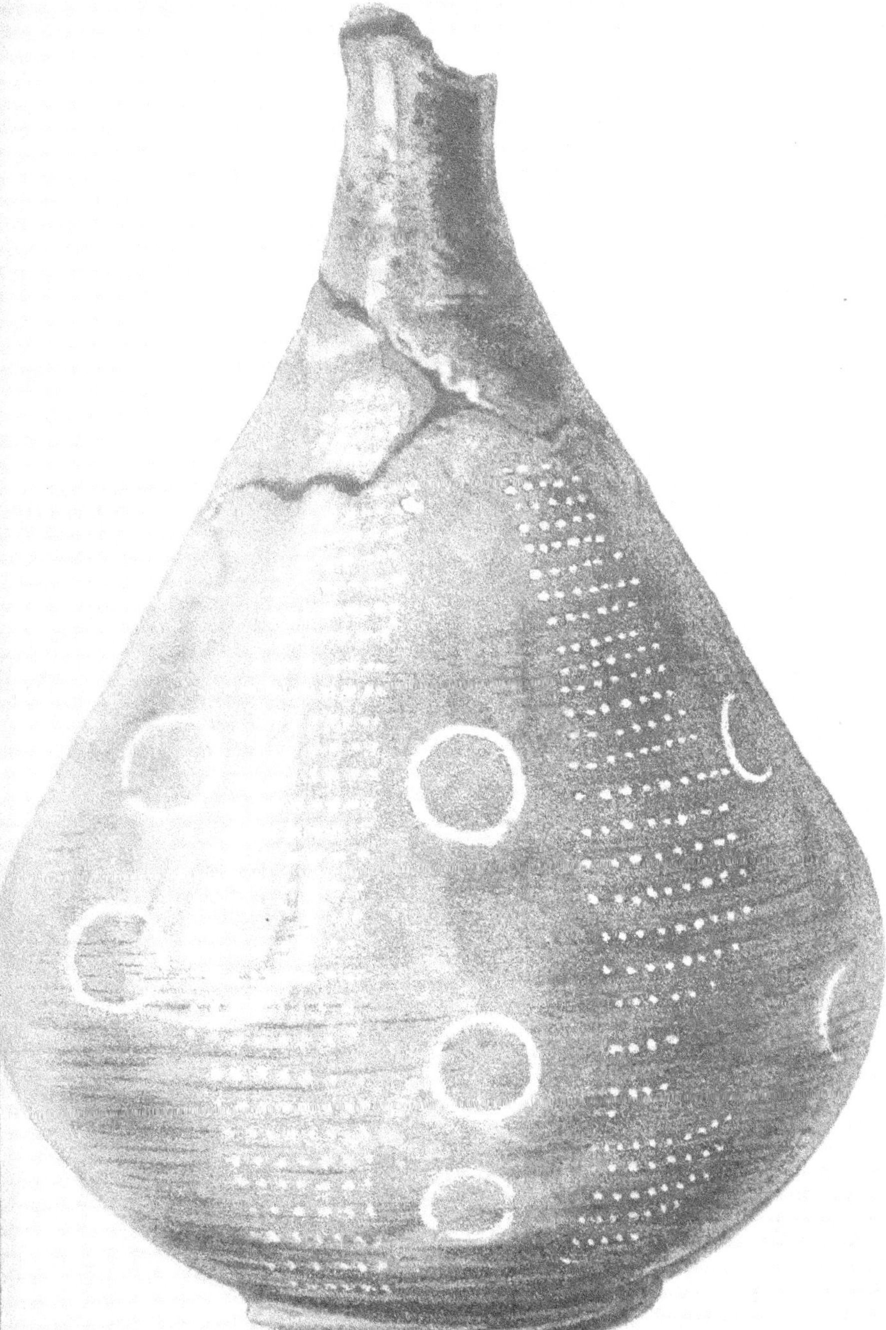

FULL SIZE.

BOTTLE FROM THOMPSONS FIELD.

Pl V.

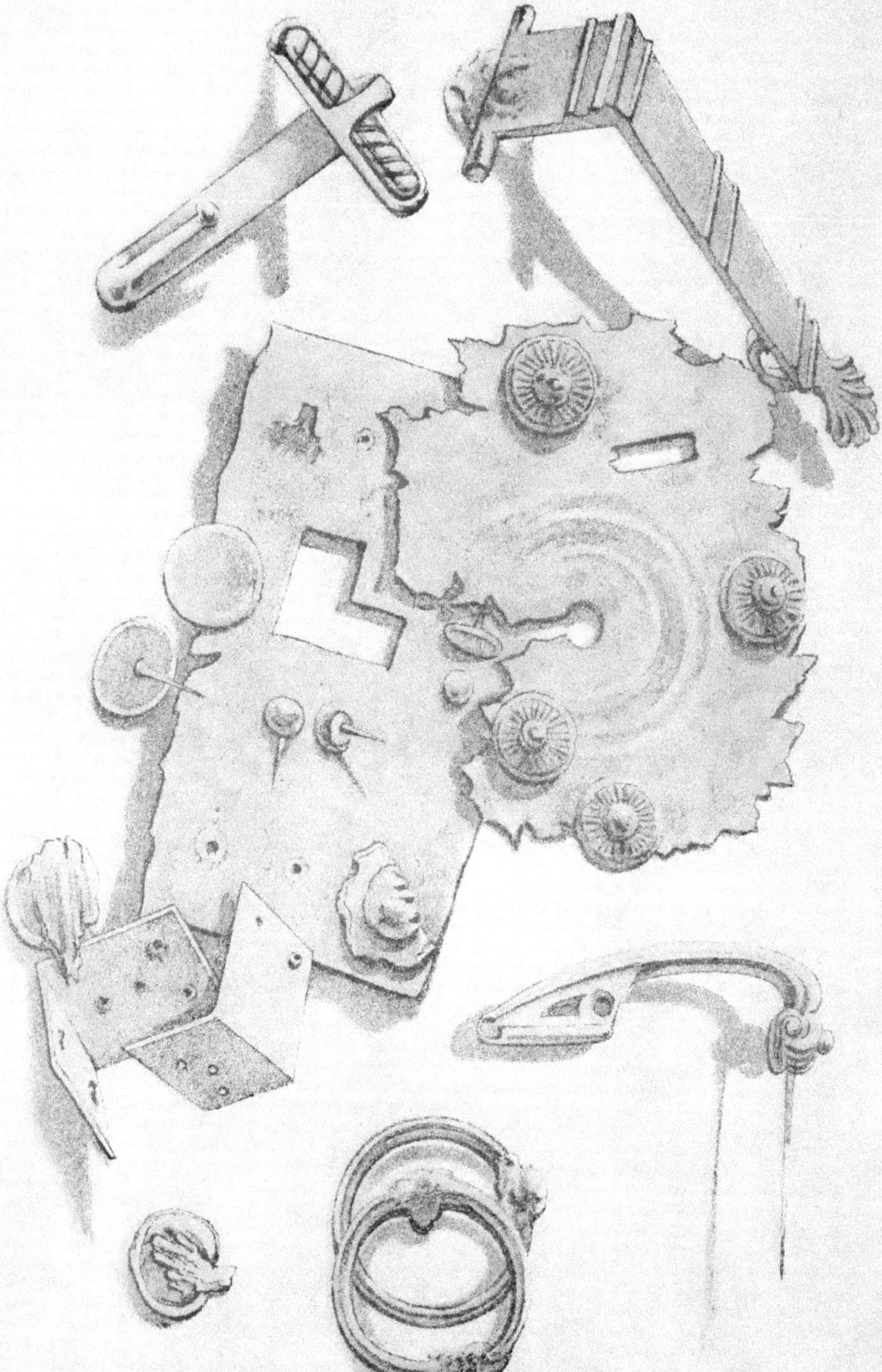

FIBULÆ, FOUND IN THOMPSONS FARM.

side, was the means of preserving them; whereas the rest, extending further into the field, came more under the action of the plough, and suffered accordingly. The articles found consisted of Samian ware of various shapes, black, brown, and red pottery, a glass lachrymatory, two bronze fibulæ, two bronze locks, hinges, clamps, studs, nails, fragments of wood, leather, chipped flints, pieces of glass, etc.

The vases, urns, and Samian vessels, were filled with bones, burnt and unburnt, some apparently of birds and animals.

On digging to the west of the cemetery, we came to the foundations of a wall (Plate II.–B), so close to the deposits of pottery that we concluded the cemetery had been surrounded by one.

We were told that about twenty years ago a paved road (Plate II.–C), about 4 feet wide, or thereabouts, was found running from the tumulus across the field in a diagonal direction towards the north-east.

Fragments of "crocks" were described as having been found in or near the sides of this roadway. The hedges have now all been removed, but by pacing, I estimated the original field in which this cemetery was found to have been a square of 100 yards. It is marked C on the Map (Plate I.).

On the spot marked D, Plate I., which is on a farm in the occupation of Mr. Biggs, of Borough Green, about twenty years ago some labourers came to a cinerary deposit. Many of the urns are now in the possession of Mr. Biggs, of Strood, and I was glad to see them at the local Museum, at the late annual meeting of the Society.

An old man at work on the spot at the time of this discovery carried home some of the urns. This act being succeeded by bad luck or ill health, his conscience either pricked him, or he came to the conclusion that it was "no cannie" to have such things in his possession;

he buried them in his garden, and died soon afterwards, and the spot of their re-interment is now lost.

At E, Plate I., near Ightham Court Lodge, a cinerary urn, about 8 inches in height, was dug up. It was filled with burnt bone and ashes, and had a Samian patera reversed over the mouth. The stamp on the patera is DIVIXI.

Nearer to Ightham church several Roman copper coins have been found. They are now in the possession of Mr. Benjamin Harrison, Jun., of Ightham.

At F, Plate I., is a field belonging to the St. Clere estate. Some years since, Mr. Children, who then held the farm, broke it up to plant hops, when groups of pottery, equidistant, each deposit being accompanied by a glass vessel (lachrymatory), were discovered extending diagonally across the field from the south-east to the north-west corner. Some of this pottery went into the possession of Mr. Evelyn, of Wootton, the possessor of the soil, some to the British Museum, and some Mr. Children took home, where they were converted into toys for the children, and feeding-vessels for the chickens, and between children and chickens but two are now left!

I stated at the beginning of this paper, my conviction that these several spots which I have now pointed out had a relative bearing to the Camp at Oldbury. I trust the reader will consider that opinion not lightly advanced, but rather borne out by the evidence adduced. That there must have been considerable occupation of these parts by the Romans is evident; whether it is sufficient to rob Maidstone of its honour and bring Vagniacæ into the Plaxtol valley, I must leave to the learned in antiquarian lore to determine.

GENEALOGICAL NOTICES OF THE NORTHWOODS.

(FROM THE SURRENDEN COLLECTION.)

A GENUINE Roll, devoted to the biographical and genealogical records of a distinguished family, and bearing date as early as the fourteenth century, is of rare occurrence. We have the gr tification of presenting our readers with the transcript of one, written between the years 1385 and 1405, as is evidenced by the handwriting and by its own statements. It seems to have been the work of some one in the service of the family whose history it relates—probably Thomas Brumpston, who is mentioned at the close of this paper—and it can hardly fail to be of great interest to all lovers of genealogical research, especially as it contains most circumstantial details of the descent of a baronial family of great wealth and importance in the county, whose representatives at this moment are among the coheirs to the baronies of Thurnham, Grandison, Northwood, etc. etc. There are little biographical sketches and touches of character thrown in here and there, relating to more than one knightly family in this county, which we cannot doubt will be considered sufficient to warrant the insertion of this Record. There is moreover one circumstance attaching to this Roll, that adds greatly to its value. It cites undeniable authority for most of its statements, many of them to this day of easy reference, being still among the records of the different Courts. Other facts are quoted from the lips of then living witnesses, and with very few exceptions the authenticity of its statements is unquestionably satisfactory.

The Roll itself, as stated above, is in the handwriting of the latter part of the fourteenth century; it is 7½ inches wide, and consists of several membranes stitched together. It was found in the Surrenden collection, in a box containing the ancient muniments relating to the manor of Thurnham. This manor being still the property of Sir Edward Dering, the contents of this box are actually legal evidence, being, as the language of the Courts has it, in "right custody." These muniments continue in almost unbroken series from the time of Henry II. to the present day. They commence with the original grant of the Church of Aldington,[1]* in Thurnham, by William Fitz-Helte to the Priory of Combwell, temp. Hen. II. They then continue through the De Thurnhams (one of whose coheirs[2] seems to have brought the estate into the family of Northwood), the Northwoods, and the Wottons, (to whom the Northwoods alienated) down to Catherine, Lady Stanhope, (the daughter and coheiress of Thomas, Lord Wotton), who in the middle of the seventeenth century alienated to Godden; and onward thence to the present day.

In the earlier part of these muniments, the descent of the baronial family of De Thurnham to its extinction in coheirs is fully developed, and among them we have their grants of the Church of Thurnham, etc. etc. etc., to the Priory of Combwell; but this portion must be deferred to a future paper, the present one being confined to the subject-matter of the Roll before us, viz. the descent of the Northwoods, or Northwodes.

It begins with the following introduction:—

"Quia ad sertam et rectam veritatis agnicionem quis, si quod transactum tempus fuerit a facto cujuscunque rei per humanam memoriam, que labilis est et inserta, nequaquam, aut raro,

* For the Notes to which the figures refer, see p. 29 *et seq.*

potest pervenire, huic est quod ea que veraciter in parto per diversa recorda, et in parte per informacionem quorundam fidelium materiam subscriptam limpide cognoscentium, cum maxima diligencia et sumptuosa investigacione approbatur ad perpetuam memoriam omnium hanc paginam inspicientium, ut subsequitur, redigitur in scriptis ut magis ambiguitas si qua de dicta subscripta materia imposterum evenerit proculdubio amputaretur et clarius ad serenandam cujuscumque conscienciam interponentis de eadem sertitudinalius potuit apparere."

Then commences the chronicle of the Northwodes, written in Latin, which we render into English; and to secure ourselves from error, we make the translation a servilely literal one:—

"In the first place, Sir Stephen de Northwode, Knight, was seized of 310 acres of land, 500 acres of marsh in the Isle of Shepeye, and four score and ten acres of marsh with their pertinencies in Upcherche, and of other manors, lands, and tenements in the county of Kent. And he had a son, by name Sir Roger, who succeeded by inheritance to those manors, lands, and tenements, after the death of the said Sir Stephen his father, as in fact appears by the letters patent of the Lord Henry, late King of England, son of King John, the date whereof is 8th January, in the forty-first year of his reign, by which the said late King granted, that those tenements in Shepeye and Upcherche (contained in the said letters patent), which are now called Northwode Scepeye, which were formerly held of the said late King, as of his manor of Myddelton,[3] in Gavelkind, should henceforth be held, by the said Sir Roger, of the said late King and his heirs, by service of the twentieth part of one knight's-fee, and by certain services also annually to be rendered. Which Sir Roger married Bona Fitzbernard,[4] and on account of the great affection which the same Sir Roger bore to the monastery of St. Sixburge, in the same island,—considering that the said monastery, owing to defect of right government, had fallen to ruin,—he, with no sparing bounty, relieved it from the greatest penury; wherefore, among the servants of God there, he is to this day called the restorer of that house. Of which Sir Roger and Bona issued Sir John de Northwode. The said Roger died the 9th day of November, in the year of our Lord 1286, and the fifteenth[5] year of the reign of Edward, son of the aforesaid King, and he and the said Bona are buried before the altar of the parish church of Menstre, in Shepeye. And the said Sir John succeeded him as son and heir, and did homage and relief to the said Lord Edward, late King of England, for his lands coming to him by inheritance after the death of the said Sir Roger, as appears among the Records[6] of the Exchequer, in Easter Term, the eighteenth year of the foresaid Lord Edward. Which Sir John married the Lady Joan de Badlesmere, lady of the manors of Horton near Canterbury, and Beausfelde near Dover in the county of Kent; she possessed also certain tenements in Southwerke, in the county of Surrey, and rents in the city of London. Of which Sir John and Joan issued Sir John, the eldest son, James, Thomas, Richard, Simon, and Humphrey. The said James died without heir of his body. Sir John, the eldest son,[7] married Agnes, one of the daughters of Sir William de Grandisson and Sibilla his wife, and, with the consent of the said Sir John, his father, endowed the said Agnes with the manor of Northwode Chasteners at the door of the church.[8] And of the said Sir John the son and Agnes issued Sir Roger, Sir John de Northwode, Otho, Sir William, Knight of the Order of St. John of Jerusalem in England, Thomas, and Robert. The said Sir John, the eldest son, died during his father's lifetime; and, that the said Sir John son of Sir John, and Agnes daughter of Sir William de Grandisson, were married, and that the said Sir Roger was their issue, is evident by the Records of a plea in the Common Bench, in Michaelmas Term, 6 Rich. II., Roll 508, on a certain writ[9] of '*forme donacionis*' prosecuted in the county of Berks against John Eastbury and others, at the suit of Roger Beauchamp and others, seeking by that writ the manor of Lamborne, with its pertinencies, in the said county; and by the judgment of the Court of the said Lord the King they obtained it. And the said Sir John the father and Joan his wife died, viz. the said Sir John[10] on the vigil of Pentecost, which then happened on the 26th day of May, in the twelfth year of King Edward son of King Edward, and the said Joan died on the vigil of the Holy Trinity next following, which then happened on the 2nd day of June, in the same twelfth year, as appears by an Indenture of the goods of the said Sir John, and by the offices[11] taken by the Escheator after their death and returned into the Chancery of the said Lord the King, by pretext of writs of *diem clausit extremum*, directed to the said Escheator in the county of Kent; and by office taken at Sydyngborne, on Friday next before the feast of St. John the Baptist, in the twelfth year of the reign of King Edward son of King Edward. After the death of the said Sir John, it was found that he died seized of many manors, lands, and tenements with their pertinencies, in the said county, held of the Lord the King *in capite*, without any mention that he held any freehold in the foresaid manors of Horton and Beausfelde. And it was also found that the foresaid Sir Roger, son of Sir John, the elder son of the said Sir John deceased, was of the age of twelve years at the feast of Easter next before the taking of the said Inquisition, and was his heir as to the manors, lands, and tenements with their pertinencies, held by knight's service. And as to the rest of the tenements of the tenure of gavelkind, the said Roger, Thomas, Richard, Simon, and Humphrey, uncles of the said Roger, and

Sir John, Sir William, Thomas, and Robert, brothers of the said Roger, were heirs according to the custom of gavelkind; making no mention of the foresaid Otho, brother of the foresaid Roger, in the foresaid office. And that there were so many coheirs to the said inheritance of gavelkind, appears, as well by the foresaid offices, as by the record of a certain plea in the Common Bench, in Michaelmas Term, 47 Edw. III., Roll 257, on a certain writ of consanguinity, at the suit of Roger de Scalis and others, against Sir Richard atte Leese, Knight, and others, prosecuted in the county of Kent.[12] And, by the office taken at Sydyngborne, on the Friday and year aforesaid, after the death of the said Joan, it was found that she died seized in her demesne as of fee, in the said manors of Horton and Beauesfeld, with their pertinencies; and also that the said Roger, then twelve years old, son of Sir John, the elder son of the said Joan, was heir to the foresaid manors with their pertinencies, and so those manors only were the inheritance of the said Joan. And, forasmuch as the manors of the said late Sir John, grandfather of the said Roger, were held of the Lord the King *in capite;* by reason of the minority of the said Roger, the said Lord the King Edward, son of King Edward, seised all the manors, lands, and tenements pertaining to the said Roger the heir into his own hands, and so they remained till the 20th day of June in the thirteenth year of his reign, on which day, by his letters patent he committed the custody of the foresaid lands and tenements, together with the marriage[13] of the said heir, to Sir Bartholomew de Badlesmere, Knight, to hold till the legal age of the said heir; who sold that marriage to the Lady Idonia de Leybourne, late wife of Sir Geoffrey de Say the elder; which Sir Geoffrey begat of the foresaid Idonia, Sir Geoffrey de Say, Sir Roger de Say, Juliana de Say, and Isabella de Say, as I have been told by many; among them, by John Wantynge, who was the

Esquire and Secretary of the said Sir Geoffrey the son, and knew them all personally.[14] Which Idonia, to whom the marriage of the foresaid heir belonged, by virtue of the grant of the said Sir Bartholomew, committed the said Juliana, one of her daughters, to wife to the said Roger, the foresaid heir, between the fourteenth and fifteenth year of his age. And the said Sir Geoffrey the son delivered over the foresaid Isabella, another of his sisters, to John Chaumpayne, lord of Norton and Newenham, to wife; and by pretext thereof, the said John Chaumpayne, by fine in the Court of the Lord the King Edward III., on the morrow of St. Martin, in the eighteenth year of his reign, acknowledged the foresaid manors, with their pertinencies, to be the right of Ralph, Parson of the church of Cudham; and for that acknowledgment, the said Ralph granted that the foresaid manors, with their pertinencies, which Alice, widow of Sir William Dages, Knight, and Robert Newelond, held for the life of Margery, widow of Sir John Chaumpayne, Knight, of the heirs of the foresaid Ralph, and which, after the decease of the said Margery, ought to revert to the foresaid Ralph or his heirs, should entirely remain, after the death of the said Margery, to the foresaid John and Isabella, and the heirs of the said John of his body begotten; and if it should happen that the said John should die without heirs of his body begotten, the said manors, with their pertinencies, should remain to the said Sir Geoffrey de Say, to hold to him and his heirs for ever. Of which Roger and Juliana de Say his wife, issued Sir John de Norwode, Roger, Geoffrey, and Agnes; which Roger the father, at the time of the baptism of the said Sir John,

[14] Sir Geoffrey de Say = Idonia de Leyborne (daughter of Sir William de Leyborne).

Sir Geoffrey de Say.	Sir Roger	Sir Roger Northwood. æt. vix 15. = Juliana	John Chaumpayne. = Isabella

his eldest son, had not completed the age of fifteen years, as we receive for truth from the information of Sir Richard Sheme, late chaplain of the foresaid Roger the father, and afterwards Vicar of Eastcherche, in Shepey,—and also of Agnes, the last wife of the said Roger, now[15] wife of Christopher de Shukkeburgh; and of Thomas Chicche of Balnerle, late his esquire, who often heard it stated by the said Roger himself. After their marriage they lived together for nine years and more; and he sued for his writ *de ætate probanda* after the feast of Easter, in the first year of the reign of Edward III.; and about the feast of the translation of St. Thomas, he obtained livery of his inheritance out of the hands of the Lord the King. And the said Juliana died the 20th of February, in the third year of the foresaid Lord the King Edward III. And also the foresaid Geoffrey and Agnes, their children, died, without issue, in the lifetime of their father, the said Roger. And a little before the feast of St. Peter ad Vincula, in the fifth year of the said Lord the King Edward III., late King of England, he contracted a second marriage, viz. with Elizabeth, late wife of Richard Ffoliot, Esq., and daughter of Sir John de Segrave, late lord of Folkstane;[16] and to obtain that marriage he gave the foresaid manors of Beauesfeld and Horton, near Canterbury, in the county of Kent, and a rent of nine marks in the parish of St. Olave's, in Southwerk, in the county of Surrey, by deed sealed with his seal of arms, dated at Ffolkstane, on Tuesday on the morrow of St. John the Baptist, in the fifth year of the reign of the Lord the King Edward III., to Durandus de Wydmerpole and John de Bykenore, son and heir of Sir John de Bykenore, Knight, and their heirs for ever.

16 Sir John de Segrave =
Lord of Folkstone.

Richard de Foliot = (1) Elizabeth de Segrave = (2) Sir Roger de Northwode.
Esquire, dead 1331. — 1331.

Moreover, to the said Durandus and his heirs a rent of £15. 6*s*. 8*d*., with its pertinencies, in the city of London, by his deed, dated at London, on Thursday next before the feast of the translation of St. Thomas the Martyr, in the fifth year of the reign of the said Lord the King Edward III., in like manner sealed with his seal of arms, and enrolled in the Husting Court of London of pleas of land, held on Monday in the feast of St. Mary Magdalene, in the said fifth year,—that they, when in full seizin, should grant the said manors and rents, with their pertinencies, to the foresaid Roger the father, and Elizabeth, and the heirs of their bodies legally issuing; and, if they should die without heirs of their body issuing, the manors and rents afores id should remain for ever to the right heirs of the said Sir Roger for ever. Which Durandus, and John son of John de Bykenore, by fine levied in the said Court of the said Lord the King Edward III., viz. in the quindain of Michaelmas, in his said fifth year, granted and rendered the manors and rents aforesaid in the counties of Kent and Surrey to the said Sir Roger and Elizabeth, and the heirs of their bodies issuing; so that on failure of issue begotten between them, those manors and rents should remain to the right heirs of the said Sir Roger for ever. And afterwards, viz. on the 11th day of December, in the ninth year of the said Lord the King Edward III., and the year of our Lord 1335, the said Elizabeth died without issue of her body, and is buried at Shepeye, nearly at the head of Sir Roger de Northwode, the restorer aforesaid. But, it is sculptured on the stone laid over the said Elizabeth:—

Icy gist Elizabeth Segrave file mons[r] Johan Segrave, iadysz femme Richard Ffoliot, et a Roger de Norwode le secunde, q transpassa le xi jo[r] de Decembr lan de grace mill cccxxxv[te].

"So that, in the superscription of the said stone, one hundred years are omitted from the date of our Lord. But consideration being had to the date of the deeds executed on effecting the said marriage, and to the date of the foresaid fine, by which the said manors of Horton and Beauesfeld were granted to the said Sir Roger and Elizabeth, and to the superscription of the said stone, by which it is supposed that the said Elizabeth was the daughter of Sir John de Segrave and the wife of Richard Ffoliot, who were surviving in the time of King Edward, son of King Henry, as appears among the Records of the Exchequer, in a book of fees of the county of Kent; and it being supposed afterwards, that she was the second wife of the said Sir Roger; and chiefly by the information of certain who saw her, and knew, that she died at Canterbury, under the care of a certain physician who pledged himself to her to cure her of the infirmity of which she died; and by a certain acquittance of Brother John Ryngemere, Prior of the order of brothers Preachers of Canterbury, by which he acknowledged that he had received of Sir Roger de Northwode twelve marks, which the said Sir Roger had ordained for the soul of Elizabeth, formerly his wife, the date of which is Thursday next after the feast of the Annunciation of the blessed Mary, in the year of our Lord 1342; and consideration also being had, that before this there had only been one Sir Roger, who was the son of Sir Stephen de Northwode, whose wife was named Bona, and who died in the fifteenth year of King Edward, son of King Henry, as is aforesaid, and who lived within fifty years before the ninth year of the reign of King Edward III., in which year, as is aforesaid, the said Elizabeth died,—it clearly appears that the omission of the foresaid hundred years in the sculpture of the said stone was done by the negligence of the workmen. So that if the said hundred years be added to the sculpture of the said stone, they will show the true year of the death of the said Elizabeth. And that the said Elizabeth died without issue of her body truly appears, inasmuch as after the death of Maria, daughter of Sir John de Segrave, late lord of Folkestane, brother of the foresaid Elizabeth, by virtue of the writ of our Lord the King of *diem clausit extremum*, directed to William de Langele, late Escheator of Kent, it was found by Inquisition taken before the said late Escheator, at Lymynge, 16th day of December, in the twenty-third year of the reign of Edward III., that the said Maria died seized of the manor of Folkstane, with its pertinencies, in her demesne as of fee; and that she died without heir of her body, by which the right to the said manor reverted to Mr. Nicholas de Sandwych, as kinsman and heir of the said Maria de Segrave,[17] viz. son of Nicholas, brother of John de Sandwich, father of Juliana, mother of John de Segrave and Elizabeth, father of foresaid Maria; who after a while sold the said manor to Sir William de Clynton, Earl of Huntingdon; so that, if the said Elizabeth, aunt of the said Maria, had had issue, the manor of Folkstane, without any hesitation, would have fallen to the said issue. And, afterwards, viz. in the month of January, in the thirteenth year of the reign of King Edward III., the same Sir Roger contracted a third marriage, viz. with Margaret, relict of Sir Nicholas de Halglton,[18] Knight, lord of Wokyndon in the county of Essex,[19] who had two daughters, Beatrice, now the wife of Sir Ralph Seyntleger,[20] Knight, and Margaret, who was married to Sir Roger de Northwode, son of the said Sir Roger and

18 Sir Roger de Northwode =(1) Margery =(2) Sir Nicholas de Halglton, Knight, of Wokyndon.
1340.

Sir Ralph St. Leger = Beatrice. Sir Roger de Northwode = Margaret.
son of Sir Roger, who married her mother.

Juliana his first wife. And afterwards, a little before the feast of the Nativity of our Lord, in the same fourteenth year,[21] in digging out a fox which was in an earth near Bengebery, the said Margaret was smothered, but not killed on the spot; because, after that accident, viz. on Thursday in the feast of the Holy Innocents, in the year of our Lord 1340, she made her will, by permission of the said Sir Roger; and, on the last day of December next following, in the said fourteenth year, died without issue. And immediately after the feast of Easter in the sixteenth year of the said lord the king Edward III., he contracted a fourth marriage, viz. with Joan, relict of Thomas de Ffaversham, lord of Gravene; and because Sir John de Northwode, first-born son of the said Sir Roger and Juliana his first wife, as is aforesaid, then being twenty years old, wanted more for his establishment than formerly, at the instance of Mr. Otho de Northwode, brother of the said Sir Roger, he, by a certain deed, dated at Ewelle in Faversham, the 4th day of October, in the said sixteenth year of King Edward III., granted to the said Sir John his son a certain annual rent of ten marks, to be received from his manors of Bykenore and Wychelyng, at the four terms of the year, in equal portions, to him and his heirs for ever; and he gave to Sir Roger de Northwode, his other son, and brother of the said Sir John, his manor of Beausfeld, to him and his heirs for ever, to the value of ten marks of land by the year.

"And afterwards, the said Lady Agnes, mother of the said Sir Roger de Northwode, died, viz. on the 4th day of December, in the year of our Lord 1349, by which the manor of Northwode Chasteners came to the hands of the said Sir Roger, as to the party to whom the reversion thereof belonged. And, in the following year, viz. in the year of our Lord 1350, John, son of the said Sir Roger and Juliana his first wife, against the will of his father, married Joan, one of the daughters of Robert Here, of Faversham, Sir Ralph Spigurnell marrying Elizabeth, the other daughter of the said Robert;[22] for which, the said Sir Roger was thinking of disinheriting the said Sir John, because that marriage seemed to him to be manifestly in disparagement of his blood; but, with the greatest difficulty, and by the mediation of Sir Arnald Savage, Knight, that thought of the said Sir Roger was prevented. Yet he was unwilling to interfere any further about the said Sir John with respect to the said marriage; but to exonerate himself from supporting them, more for honour than love, he gave the said Sir John the foresaid manor of Northwode Chasteners to him and his heirs; and lest the said Dame Joan should obtain any profit of dower from the said manor, if the said Sir John should die during the life of the said Sir Roger, he reserved to himself an annuity therefrom of £50 for the term of his life; but nothing was exacted or paid therefrom in his lifetime. And, afterward, in the month of May, in the thirtieth year of the reign of King Edward III., the said Dame Joan, the fourth wife of the said Sir Roger, departed from this life to the Lord. And, afterwards, on the feast of St. Peter ad Vincula then next following, the said Sir Roger, took a fifth wife, viz. the Lady Agnes relict of Sir John de Cobeham, as she herself tells us; and, in order to obtain the effecting of that marriage, before the espousals were celebrated between them, he gave to Sir John Sholdone, Rector of the church of Coulynge, and John Barny, nine marks rent in Suthewerke, in the parish of St. Olave, in the county of Surrey; and a rent

[22] Robert Here =
of Faversham.

John Northwode = Joan Here.
son and heir of 1350.
Sir Roger.

Sir Ralph = Elizabeth Here.
Spigurnell.

of fifteen pounds, six shillings, and eightpence in the city of London, which he had before given to Dame Elizabeth, his second wife; that they should give those rents to the said Roger and Agnes, and the heirs male begotten between them, and, in default of heirs male, as is aforesaid, that they should remain to the right heirs of the said Sir Roger for ever; which gift they afterwards completed. And, for the very great affection which he continuously bore to the foresaid Dame Agnes, afterwards, viz. in the quindain of Michaelmas, in the thirty-third year of the Lord Edward, late[23] King of England, by fine raised in the Court of the Lord the King, he acknowledged the manor of Horton, with its pertinencies, to be the right of Richard Sheme, Vicar of the church of Eastcherche, as that which the said Richard and Peter Hadland had of the gift and grant of the said Sir Roger; and, for this acknowledgment and agreement, the said Richard and Peter granted to the said Sir Roger and Agnes the foresaid manor, with its pertinencies, and rendered it to them in the same Court, to hold to them and the heirs of the said Sir Roger for ever. Of which Sir Roger and Agnes[24] there issued Juliana, the wife of Peter Rede, of Dover; and Agnes, the wife of Stephen Pysinden; and, as the same Dame Agnes tells us, he caused his foresaid first-born daughter to be called Juliana, in memory of the name of Juliana his first wife.

"And afterwards, viz. on the 6th day of November, on the vigil of St. Leonard, in the year of our Lord 1361, and in the thirty-fifth year of King Edward III., the said Sir Roger made his will, and appointed the foresaid

[24] Sir Roger de Northwode = Agnes, relict of Sir John de Cobham.

Peter Rede of Dover. = Juliana de Northwode.

Stephen de Pysinden. = Agnes de Northwode.

Agnes, and Richard Blore, and Fulco Payfrere, executors, and died;[25] as appears by the office taken before John Tye, then Escheator of the said King in the county of Kent, at Newenton, on the 7th day of December, in the said thirty-fifth year, by pretext of the writ of the Lord the King of *diem clausit extremum*, directed to the said Escheator; by which it was found that he died on the day and year aforesaid, seised of many lands and tenements in the aforesaid county; and that of the foresaid manor of Horton, he died seised conjointly with Agnes his wife, by pretext of the foresaid fine, as is aforesaid. And that John de Northwode was his son and heir, and of the age of thirty years and more, and justly more, because he had then nearly completed forty years; for by computing from the fifteenth year of King Edward, son of King Edward, in which year the said John was born, to the day of the death of the foresaid Sir Roger, forty years passed, and so in this that they said "more," they told the truth. And if, perchance, any one should say that he was the son of Elizabeth, it appears expressly false in this, that by computing from the feast of St. Peter ad Vincula in the fifth year of King Edward III., at which time the said Sir Roger and Elizabeth were married, to the vigil of St. Leonard's in the thirty-fifth year, as is aforesaid, on which day the said Sir Roger died, thirty years elapsed, and as much more as the distance from the feast of St. Peter ad Vincula to the vigil of St. Leonard; and thirty years being deducted from the age of the foresaid John, at the time of the death of his foresaid father, as was found by the said Inquisition taken after the death of his said father, there then remains only as much as there is between the feast of St. Peter ad Vincula, and the vigil of St. Leonard then next following. So that if by any means there must be a begetting between the foresaid Roger and Elizabeth, and a birth, from this it follows, that he must have been begotten and born within thirteen weeks, which is unintelligible to any one who examines the case justly and impartially. On the return of which office, the said Dame Agnes sued to have her dower out of the tenements whereof the said Sir Roger died seised, and had a writ directed to the said John Tye, the Escheator, to deliver to her her dower; which said John Tye, with the assent of Sir John de Northwode, heir of the foresaid Sir Roger, on the 20th day of December, in the said thirty-fifth year, assigned to the said Dame Agnes the manors of Shorne, Heriettesham, Yoke, and Wychelyng, with their pertinencies, to hold in the name of her foresaid dower. And because in the said manors there were many lands and tenements in gavelkind, it was agreed between them that although the said Agnes should marry,[26] yet she should hold those tenements for the term of her life, rendering to the said John and his heirs fourteen marks a year, to be levied by distress in the said manors, if, after she be married, that rent should happen to be in arrear at any term, and this by indenture between them signed.

"And afterwards, the said Agnes, Fulco Payfrere, and Richard Blore, as executors of the said Sir Roger, prosecuted against the said Sir John a writ of debt, by reason of the arrears of £50 rent reserved by the foresaid Sir Roger upon the grant of the manor of Northwode Chasteners, as is aforesaid, demanding of him, by the foresaid writ, £600, as appears among the Records of the Common Bench, in the thirty-seventh and thirty-eighth years of King Edward III., and, pending that undecided plea, by the mediation of Sir Arnald Savage, they entirely set it at rest in the house of the *fratres minores* at Canterbury; viz. that the same Sir John should satisfy the said executors with £250, which in fact he had paid to the said Agnes, without obtaining any favour for it; and the same executors remitted the residue of the foresaid debt.

"And afterwards, the said Dame Agnes married Christopher Shukkeburgh; and the foresaid Sir John, thinking how he might avenge himself on the foresaid Dame Agnes for the receipt of the foresaid £250, searched out the ways and means by which he might annoy her; at length, finding the foresaid deed of ten marks rent made to him by his father, in the 16th of Edward III., as is aforesaid, (to receive from the manors of Bykenore and Wychelyng ten marks a year, as is aforesaid,) he prosecuted, after the death of the foresaid Fulco Payfrere, one of the executors of his father, a writ of debt against the foresaid Richard de Blore, (executor of the will of the said Sir Roger,) and Christopher Shukkeburgh, and Agnes his wife, co-executors of the foresaid will of the said Sir Roger, to have by the foresaid writ two hundred marks; stating that the foresaid annual rent was in arrear for twenty years before the death of his foresaid father; and because those tenements whereon that rent arose had fallen to him by inheritance; therefore an action by writ of debt accrued to him, as appears in Easter Term in the forty-ninth year; at length, perceiving that the jury in the foresaid plea would go against him, by the mediation of Sir John Barri, at Canterbury, they compromised it; viz. that the said Christopher and Agnes should pay to the said Sir John £10, and the foresaid Sir John should deliver to her the foresaid annual rent of ten marks; and so he gladly ceased from his action.

"Of which Sir John and Joan issued Sir Roger de Norwode, William de Northwode, James de Norwode, Juliana de Norwode, now wife of John Digge, and Joan, now wife of Sir John Dengeyne, knight, of the county of Cambridge; and he caused his said first-born daughter to be called Juliana, in memory of the name of Juliana his mother. And he died on the 27th day of February, in the second year of the reign of King Richard,[27] as appears by the office returned into the Chancery of the King.

taken after the death of the said Sir John, at Sidyngborne, before John Brode, then Escheator of our said lord the King, on the Wednesday next after the feast of St. George, in the said second year; and it appears thereby that the said Roger, then of the age of twenty-three years, was son and heir of the said Sir John, as to the manors, lands, and tenements held by knight's-service; and as to the tenements in gavelkind, his co-heirs were the foresaid William and James. And because the said manor of Horton was of the tenure of knight's-service, the reversion of the said manor fell to Sir Roger, which Sir Roger granted that reversion, on the 13th of December, in the eighth year, to Thomas Chicche of Balnerle, Gilbert Manfeld, citizen of London, Nicholas Potyn, John Dreylond, William Emery, and William de Makenade, and the heirs of the said William Makenade, by a certain deed of his, enrolled on the dorse of the Chancery Close Roll, in the eighth year of King Richard II., and the month of February; under pretext of which the foresaid Christopher de Shukkebergh, and Agnes his wife, attorned to the said Thomas and the others aforesaid, by a certain deed of theirs, enrolled on the dorse of the Chancery Close Roll of the aforesaid King, in the month of February, in the year aforesaid."

Thus ends the Roll before us; but there is a transcript of it upon a paper, in a hand apparently of the time of Henry VII., in which the descent of the manor of Thurnham is continued from the close of this Roll to the alienation of it to the Wottons, temp. Hen. IV. This must be deferred to a future paper, as the genealogical descent of the Northwodes (with which we have been chiefly concerned in our present paper) is not continued in it. But there is another Roll, which it may be well to print here, as adding a few notes to the pedigree. The title to the Thurnham estate had evidently been questioned; and among the muniments we find the following case prepared for counsel, in a handwriting of the time of Henry IV. It is in itself a curious document, which will justify us in printing it entire, although the greater part of it is only a recapitulation of the pedigree which we have already obtained.

Le cas est tiel.

Rog̃ Northwode f^t s̃s de la man̄ de Thornch^am en son de^ne come de fee, ⁊ p^ist a fe^e Julian un dez filez le s^r de Say, ⁊ av̄ issu John̄ ⁊ Rog̃; ⁊ Julian m^rust; ⁊ a ap̄s Rog̃ p^ist a fe^e Elizab̄t iadɋ la fe^e Ric̃ Foliot, file le s^r de Seg^aue; ⁊ Elizab̄t m^rust s^aunz issu ent^e eux; ⁊ p^s le d^t Rog̃ p^ist un M^ggie a fe^e, iadɋ fe^e Nicolas s^r de Haghton lez qux̄ aū issu Beatrice ⁊ M^agrete ⁊ p^s Rog̃ enfeffa de mesme la man̄ John̄ Colne, clerk, ⁊ Bartholomew Bawdewyn, clerk, a eux ⁊ lo^r heirz en fee, et p^s lez ditz John̄ Colne ⁊ Bertholomew, lan xiiij le R. E. ti ree, leuer un fin de (m) la man̄ a lez ditz Rog̃ le pier ⁊ Marg̃ie, a eux ⁊ a lez heirz le d^t Rog̃; et M^gg̃ m̄ m^rust s^aunz issu; et p^s le d^t Rog̃ p^ist a fe^e Joh^ane iadz fe^e Thom̄ de Feuars^am, le s^r de G^aueney; ⁊ Joh^ane m^rust; et p^s Rog̃ p^ist a fe^e Agnes, iadz fe^e sire John̄ de Cobeh^am, ⁊ aū issu Julian ⁊ Agnes; et p^s Rog̃ m^rust s̃s de (m) la man̄ &c. ap̄s qy mort le d^t man̄ discendist a le d^t John̄, come fitz ⁊ heir. Le quel John̄ Northwode enfeffa de (m) man̄ Ric̃ atte Lese, ⁊ autrez; ⁊ p^s le d^t John̄ p^ist a fe^e Johne lez qux av̄ issu Rog̃ Northwode chr, Will̄ ⁊ James; et p^s le d^t Ric̃ ⁊ autrez lesser̃ (m) la man̄ a lez ditz John̄ Northwode ⁊ Joh^ane sa fe^e, a t̃me de lo^r deux viez; ⁊ John̄ baron Joh^ane m^rust; et p^s le d^t Ric̃ ate Lese g^aunta la reū de (m) le man̄ a le d^t Rog̃ Northwode chr, fitz le d^t John̄, p force de quel le d^t Joh^ane attorna; et p^s le d^t Rog̃, fitz le d^t John̄, relessa t^t le droit qil aū &c., a le d^t Joh^ane mier̃ le d^t Rog̃; et p^s le d^t Joh^ane leua un fin ou garr̃ a certez psons qu estat lez ten^antz du d^t man̄ ore ount &c.; ⁊ Rog̃ fitz John̄ m^rust sanz issu; ⁊ Will̄ fitz John̄ p^ist a fe^e &c.; ⁊ av̄ issu Elyzab^t ⁊ Isabell ⁊ m^rust; ⁊ p^s James av̄ issu ij fitz &c.

Lun question est, si le dit man̄ soit taille a le dit Rog̃ ⁊ cez heirs de son corps engendrez; si lez ij fitȝ du dit James s̃r barr̃ p la garr̃ Joh^ane de la moite del gauelkende de (m) la man̄e, ou noū; ⁊ si Rog̃ av̄ fee simple, si lez ditz fitz s̃r barr̃ de tierce ptie de (m) la man̄ p le d^t garr̃, ou noū. En aut^r s^r un cudentc̃ quer̃.

[*In dorso.*]

Evidencie ad cognoscendum demisum manerii de Thornham, ⁊ que terre dicti manerii sunt terre de gavelkendes.

Cause qerlle. J. Martin ⁊ Northwode.

A fit conclusion to this paper will be an original list of memoranda, drawn up in a hand of about *f.* Hen. IV. or *init.* Hen. V., which seem to have been put together by Nicholas Wotton, in order to collect evidence as to the title of his recent purchase of Thurnham from the Northwodes. It is worth preserving, because of its specific reference to our first Roll, and its notice of parties and circumstances therein described.

M^d ad inquirend evidenc cum Th. Brumpston[28] p le pe. de crew[29] de Northwode, et est una longa rotulus.

It. est la oue luy i relese collaterell p^r le taille de Horton, Bengbery, ⁊ Thornham.

It. m^d quod Ricardus Blore fuit dudum senescallus domini Johannis de Northwode, ⁊ Thomas Reyner de Strode habuit evidencias predicti Ricardi.

Dominus Adam, vicarius de Bredherst, fuit executor predicti Ricardi, vel Thome vel Johannis Wakhirst.

It. ad loquendum cum Th. Brumpston ad videndam cartam per quam manerium de Bengbery distringetur pro 5 marcis debitis collegio de Cobham.

It. ad inquirendum si aliqua mulier de sanguine de Northwode fuit maritata alicui de sanguine de Selinger; vel si aliqua mulier de sanguine de Silinger fuit maritata alicui de sanguine de Northwode.

It. ad inquirendum in patria per quem titulum J. Selinger[30] vult prosequi me pro Thornham.

It. ad loquendum cum Willelmo Einton quod loquatur Hoking de Maidston.

M^d quod dicitur quod Radulfus Selinger ultimus, et dominus Rogerus pater domini Johannis Northwode habuerunt 2 sorores, ad loquendum cum Johanne Hunt.

APPENDIX.

(1.) Aldington and Thurnham were formerly distinct parishes.—Among our muniments of the Manor of Thurnham is the original instrument, by Archbishop Chichele, A.D. 1433, for their ecclesiastical union; and another, by Archbishop Kempe, A.D. 1453, ratifying the same.

In the document, of which we have given a facsimile, we have William fitz Helte, as Lord of the manor of Aldington, granting the Church to the Priory of Combwell in these words (see Post Note, p. 40):—

"Universis sancte matris ecclesie filiis, Willelmus filius Heltonis salutem. Rerum gestarum memoria ideirco in scriptura redigitur, ne processu temporum in oblivionem labatur. Ideo notum fieri desidero, tam presentibus quam futuris, quod ego Willelmus filius Heltonis dedi et concessi Deo et ecclesie Sancte Marie Magdalene de Cumbwelle, et fratribus ibidem Deo servientibus, in perpetuam elemosinam, ecclesiam beati Petri de Aldintunia, et hoc feci pro salute anime Henrici Regis, et anime mee et antecessorum meorum. His testibus,—Willelmo de Ainesfordia et Radulfo fratre ejus, Hugone de Cirintunia, Eustacio de Dikesmue, Johanne de Berkes, Gileberto Capellano, Bartholomeo Capellano, Helnulfo Salvage et Thoma filio suo, Jacobo tunc Diacono, Waltero de Chanci, et multis aliis."

Whether Fitz Helte held the advowson as appendant to the entire manor of Aldinton, or merely to the moiety afterwards called Aldinton Septvans does not distinctly appear. He died shortly before 26 Hen. II., 1180, for on the Pipe Roll of that year, for Kent, under the heading "De placitis Curie," we have this entry:—

"Willelmus de Cyreton, et Amfridus de Canci, et Emma de Setuans reddiderunt compotum de c marcis, pro habenda terra Willelmi filii Helte."

In the next year, viz. 27 Hen. II., 1181, we have—

"Willelmus de Cyreton et Amfridus de Canci et Emma de Setuans reddiderunt compotum de lv^{li} vj^{s} viij^{d}, pro habenda terra Willelmi filii Helte. In thesauro lxv^{s} ij^{d} de Willelmo de Cyreton, et vij^{li} vj^{s} viij^{d} de Amfrido de Canci; et lxx^{s} de Johanne Monaco et Emma de Setuans. Et debent xlj^{li} iiij^{s} x^{d}. De quibus xv^{li} xij^{s} viij^{d} stant super

Willelmum de Cyreton, et viij^{li} iiij^{s} v^{d} super Amfridum de Canci, et xvij^{li} vij^{s} ix^{d} super Johannem et Emmam uxorem ejus."

In this year there is also the following entry, under heading "Nova Placita et Nove Conventiones de Placitis Curie:"—

"Willelmus de Haya reddit compotum de v marcis, ut inquiratur per legales mulieres si Emma de Setuans, que dicitur peperisse haberet puerum, annon. In thesauro xxij^{s} et debet xliiij^{s} et viij^{d}.

28 Hen. II., 1182. Under heading "De Placitis Curie," William de Haya is again entered as paying 44*s*. 8*d*., "ut inquiratur per legales mulieres, etc.," as before. This inquiry would seem to indicate that she had had a son by a first husband, Setvans, whose heirship it was necessary to prove and place on record, in order to secure its own and the king's rights.

Thus far, then, it would appear that William fitz Helte's lands were inherited by William de Cyriton, Amfrid de Canci, and Emma de Setvans, as his three coheirs; but there is no evidence by which we can at present determine what the precise relationship was, in which each of these parties stood towards him.

In 31 Hen. II., 1185, it is evident that a division of his estates had been made among his coheirs,—Aldinton (or rather, as the subsequent history of the manor indicates, a moiety of Aldinton) falling to the share of Emma de Setvans; for we have this entry, under the heading "De oblatis Curie,"—

"Idem Vicecomes reddit compotum de lxxj^{s} v^{d} de Aldinton, terra Emme de Setvans. Et de lx^{s} de Mapelescamps terra ejusdem."

In the next year, Emma seems to have been dead, and the lands in the King's hands, for the Sheriff enters charges for stocking it, etc.; and in 33 Hen. II., 1187, we have it positively entered—

"Idem Vicecomes reddit compotum de iiij^{li} xiij^{s} iiij^{d} de Aldinton, cujus heres est in custodia Regis:"

and a similar entry as to Mapelscomb."

We may conclude therefore that the Jury of Matrons returned her as having borne a son, by Setvans, who was now a minor, and his estates, as such, in the King's wardship. This moiety of the manor was accordingly afterwards called Aldington Setvans, or West Court. It was still held by her representatives in the time of Edward III., for in the "Probatio Ætatis" of William de Septvans ('Archæologia Cantiana,' Vol. I. p. 128), the Jury return that he held, "inter alia," the mediety of the manor of Aldington.

In Domesday it stands thus,—"Ansgotus de Roucestre tenet de episcopo Audinton," etc. etc., and "Godwinus et Aluuinus tenuerunt de Rege Eduardo pro duobus maneriis," which would indicate that it had been in two moieties in the time of the Confessor, but on the taking of the Survey consisted of only one manor. And here arises the question with which we started, Did this state continue, and was William Fitz Helte owner of the whole as one manor, or did he possess merely the moiety afterwards called Aldington Septvans? If the former, which most probably was the case, the division must have taken place, at his death, by apportionment among his coheirs, the eldest, of course, taking the franchises and jurisdiction. In that case, the Cobhams, who seem to have held one portion, viz. "Aldington Cobham *alias* East Court," must have obtained it by inheritance from William de Cyriton or Amfrid de Canci, and the manor was thus again held in two moieties, one by the family of Cobham, the other by that of Septvans, as coheirs of Fitz Helte, for many generations. We should not have entered into this discussion but that it involves a question of some importance as affecting the genealogy of the Cobhams. We must, however, wait for further evidence before we can speak decisively on the subject.

(2.) See note (4), on the descent of Bona Fitzbernard.

(3.) *i.e.* Milton.

(4.) By the Pipe Roll, 4 & 6 Hen. III., and the Fine Roll, 3 & 7 Hen. III., it is evidenced that Ralph Fitzbernard married Alianora, the second daughter and coheir of Stephen de Thurnham.

Now, among our Thurnham muniments, there is a Roll on which it is recorded that Mabil de Gatton was the eldest of the daughters and coheirs of Stephen de Thurnham, and that, on her death without issue, this Alianora, the second daughter, succeeded to the franchises of the manor, because, being held by knight-service, however the lands themselves might have been appropriated, the "caput manerii," its franchises and jurisdiction were indivisible; and, in conformity with this statement, we have a lease for six years of the manor of Thurnham granted by Ralph Fitzbernard, A.D. 1230, to Osbert, Vicar of Thurnham.

Had it not been, therefore, for a record on the Patent Roll, that Bona, the wife of Sir Roger Northwood, was the daughter of Henry de Wautham, we should very reasonably have concluded that she was the daughter and heir of Ralph Fitzbernard by Alianore de Thurnham, and that, as such, she brought the manor of Thurnham, as her inheritance, to her husband. The entry on the Patent Roll is as follows :—

[Rot. Pat. 50 Hen. III. m. 46.]

"Rex omnibus ad quos, etc., salutem. Dimissionem et concessionem quas Johannes filius Jollani de Nevill, anno regni nostri xlv, fecit Johanni filio Henrici de Wautham, nuper defuncto, de manerio de Shorne cum pertinenciis habendo eidem Johanni et heredibus vel assignatis suis, scilicet a festo Ascenscionis Domini anno predicto, usque ad finem novem annorum proximo sequencium completorum, ratas habentes et gratas, dilecto et fideli nostro Rogero de Nortwode et Bonefilie uxori sue, sorori et heredi predicti Johannis filii Henrici, pro nobis et heredibus nostris, concedimus et confirmavimus, sicut instrumentum inter predictos Johannem et Johannem inde confectum rationabiliter testatur. In cujus, etc.

"Teste Rege apud Cantuariam, xxx die Octobris, etc. etc."

It was however by no means an uncommon practice, in these early times, to designate an heiress, not by her paternal name, but by that of the party whose estates, or Barony, she had eventually inherited. We have an instance of this practice in the "Inquisitio post mortem," cited note (17) *infra,* wherein Agnes, the wife of John de Sandwico, is called Agnes Daverenches, whereas she was the eldest daughter of Hamo de Crevecœur, by Matilda Daverenches, whose coheiress she was in the estates and Barony of Daverenches; and so it may have been in the case of Bona de Wautham *alias* Fitz Bernard.

In Testa de Nevill we have—

"John de Waltham holds in Thurnham one-fifth of a knight's-fee of the heir of Fitz Bernard, and he of William de Say.

"Reginald de Cobham holds in Thurnham one-fifth of a knight's-fee of Alice de Bending, and she of William de Say."

[N.B.—This Alice de Bending was another of the five daughters and coheirs of Stephen de Thurnham.]

Among the Pedes Finium, 32 Hen. III., 1248, is an Assise of Mortdancestor, in which Sir John de Cobham is plaintiff and Sir John de Waltham deforciant, who acknowledges one carucate in Thurnham to Sir John de Cobham, and he, at the instance of Sir John de Waltham, grants it to Sir Roger de Northwode and Bona his wife, and the heirs of their bodies.

From these combined evidences it can hardly be doubted that Bona brought Thurnham to her husband, as heir of Ralph Fitzbernard. Either, then, her mother, the wife of Henry de Waltham, was daughter and heir, or Henry De Waltham himself was son, of Ralph Fitzbernard, and called "De Waltham" from his place of residence.

It is difficult in any other way to reconcile the discrepancies of the various evidences which we have cited.

(5.) Our chronicler is in error here. By a reference to the Escheats, we find the "Inquisitio post mortem" of this Roger Northwode was taken on Friday, on St. Andrew's day, 14 Ed. I., *i.e.* 30th November, 1285. It returns that he died on Monday before St. Martin's day, 13 Ed. I., *i.e.* 9th November, 1285; that John, his son, aged 31, was his next heir; that he held Thurnham of Sir William de Say, by half a knight's-fee and 15*s.* per annum to ward of Dover Castle, and five marks per annum to Sir John de Cobham. A very full extent of the manor is given.

It is hardly necessary to notice the further error of our scribe, in calling 9th November, 1286, the 15th of Ed. I.; it was the 14th.

(6.) *i.e.* "the Memoranda Rolls."

(7.) "Antenatus filius."

(8.) By the Common Law of England, the widow had a right to one-third of her husband's possessions for dower, and by the custom of Kent one-half. But there was another kind of dower, called "ad ostium ecclesie." This was made by the husband immediately after the marriage, and therein he specifically named the particular lands with which his wife was to be endowed. By this species of dower he could not settle upon his wife more than one-third of his possessions, but he might endow her with less. The advantage of this method was that the particular portion of the property to which the widow was entitled was immediately known, being specifically declared by the husband, so that, after his death, she could at once enter on that particular land, without any further claim for dower.

(9.) The Pleadings in this case are so important, as evidencing the successive steps in the descent of the coheirs of the Barony of Grandison, that we do not hesitate to transcribe the greater part of the Record.

"Berks.

"Roger de Beauchamp; Sir Thomas Fauconberge, Knight; Alice, widow of Sir Thomas Wake, of Blisworth, Knight; Katherine, widow of Sir Robert de Tudenham, Knight; Roger, son of Sir John de Northwode, Knight, of Kent; and William, Earl of Salisbury, by Thomas de Brokhampton, his attorney,—petunt versus—

"John Estbury; John Langer, Capellan; and William Person,—

"The manor of Lamborn, with its pertinencies, which John Tregoz and Mabil his wife gave to William de Grandisson and Sibilla his wife and the heirs of the bodies of the said William and Sibilla, and which, after the death of the said William de Grandisson and Sibilla, and Peter son and heir of the said William de Grandisson and Sibilla, and John brother and heir of the said Peter, and Thomas brother of the said John brother of Peter, and Otho brother of the said Thomas brother of John, and Thomas son of the said Otho, and Mabill, Agnes, and Katherine, sisters of the said John brother of Peter, and Sibilla and Matilda, the two daughters of the said Mabill sister of John, and Roger son of the said Sibilla daughter of Mabill, and Roger son of the said Agnes, and John son of said Roger son of Agnes, ought to descend by form of the said gift to the said Roger de Beauchamp, son of the said Roger son of Sibill, Thomas Fauconberge, son of the said Matilda, Alice third,[1] and Katherine, fourth daughter of the said Mabill sister of John, Roger Northwode, son of said John son of Roger son of Agnes, and the Earl, son of said Katherine sister of John, and the cousins[2] and heirs of the said John brother of Peter.

"And thereupon they say—

"That the said John Tregoz and Mabill his wife gave the said manor with its pertinencies to the said William de Grandisson and

[1] In the "Inquisitio post mortem" of Thomas Grandison, 19th November, 49 Ed. III., we have "prefata Alicia ut tertia, et dicta Katerina ut quarta filiarum prefate Mabilla."

[2] It is hardly necessary to remind the reader that, in ancient records, "cousin" does not imply necessarily the relationship which we now designate by that title, but that it is simply the literal translation of the word "consanguineus,"—"kinsman."

Sibilla his wife, in the foresaid form. By which gift, the said William de Grandisson and Sibilla his wife, were seised thereof in their demesne as of fee and right by the form, etc., in time of peace, in the time of King Edward, son of King Henry, cousin[2] of the King that now is, etc.

"And from the said William de Grandisson and Sibilla, his wife, the right descended by the form, etc., to one Peter, as son and heir, etc.; and from the said Peter, because he died without heir of his body, the right descended by the form, etc., to one John, as brother and heir, etc.; and from the said John, because he died without heir of his body, the right descended by the form, etc., to one Thomas, as brother and heir; and from the said Thomas, because he died without heir of his body, the right descended by the form, etc., to one Otho, as brother and heir; and from the said Otho, the right descended by the form, etc., to one Thomas, as son and heir, etc.; and from the said Thomas, because he died without heir of his body, the right reverted [*resorciebatur*] by the form, etc., to certain Mabill, Agnes, and Katherine, aunts and heirs, etc., viz. sisters of Otho, father of the said Thomas; and from the said Mabill, sister of Otho, the right of her purpart descended by the form, etc., to the said Alice and Katherine, the wife of Robert, who now claim, together with, etc., and to certain Sibill and Matilda, as daughters and heirs, etc.; and from the said Sibill, daughter of Mabill, the right of her purpart descended by the form, etc., to one Roger, as son and heir; and from the said Roger the right descended by the form, etc., to that Roger Beauchamp who now claims together with, etc., as son and heir, etc.; and from the said Matilda the right of her purpart descended by the form, etc., to that Thomas Fauconberge who now claims together with, etc., as son and heir, etc.; and from the said Agnes, the right of her purpart descended by the form, etc., to one Roger, as son and heir, etc.; and from the said Roger the right descended by the form, etc., to one John, as son and heir, etc.; and from the said John the right descended by the form, etc., to that Roger son of John, who now claims together with, etc., as son and heir, etc.; and from the said Katherine, sister of John, the right of her purpart descended by the form, etc., to that Earl who now claims together with, etc., as son and heir, etc., and that after the death, etc."

[Vide Common Pleas Judgment Roll, 6 Rich. II., Roll 508.]

It will be unnecessary to transcribe the remainder of the pleadings, our object being only to place on record the pedigree which it educes.

(10.) This Sir John de Northwode had Writ of Summons

8th June, 22 Ed. I. (see Rot. Vascon.), and again, 8th January and 23rd May, 6 Ed. II.; again, 26th July, 7 Ed. II., and again, 7, 8, 9, 11, and 12 Ed. II. (see Rot. Claus.).

(11.) Officia. The proceedings and return of the Escheator and Jury in "Inquisitiones post mortem" were called "Offices."

(12.) In these pleadings there is so much additional elucidation of the Northwode pedigree, that we feel it incumbent upon us to furnish an abstract.

"Kent.

"Sir Roger Scales, Knight, and Joan his wife; Thomas Martyn and Dionisia his wife; John Leuedale and Joan his wife; and William Beaufoy and Agnes his wife, by Nicholas de Massyngham, attorney of the said Roger and guardian of the said Joan wife of Roger; and John de Bretton, attorney of all the others, seeking against Sir Richard atte Lese, Knight, Stephen Note, William Topelyve, William Frogenhale, Thomas Badecok of Upcherche, and Thomas Bean, two parts of two messuages, two mills, and a thousand acres and a half of land, 40 acres of meadow, 100 acres of wood, 1000 acres of marsh, 10 pounds rent, and a rent of 50 cocks, 200 hens, and 1050 eggs, with their pertinencies, in Menstre, Estcherche, Wardon and Leysdon in the Isle of Shepeye, Wade, Middelton, Upcherche, Halgesto, Thurnham, Lenham, Wychelyng, Frensted, Bikenor, Newenton next Sidyngborn, Aldynton next Holyngbourn; and against Christopher Shukkeburgh and Agnes his wife, two parts of 60 acres of land, with their pertinencies, in the said villes of Lenham, Wychelyng, Frensted, Bikenore and Heriettsham, Shorne and Horton next Chartham. Of the entire of which tenements John de Northwode, great-grandfather of the said Joan, Dionisia, Joan, and Agnes, and of one Sir John de Northwode, Knight, and kinsman of one Thomas, son of Sir Roger de Northwode, Knight, whose heirs they are, was seised in his demesne as of fee on the day of his death, etc.

"And be it known, that one-third part of the said tenements is excepted, because the said Sir John de Northwode, Knight, and Thomas, son of Roger, etc., coplaintiffs, etc., were summoned to be here this day, viz. the octaves of St. Michael, to prosecute together, etc., and now do not prosecute, wherefore it is adjudged that the said Roger Scales, Joan, Thomas Martyn, Dionisia, John Leuedale, Joan, and William Beaufoy, and Agnes, shall prosecute without, etc., as to two parts of the said tenements, etc.

"Whereupon they say that the said John de Northwode, great-grandfather and kinsman, etc., was seised of the entirety of the said tenements in his demesne as of fee, in time of peace, in the time of King Edward, grandfather of the King that now is, and from

), *Roll* 508.

. . . . . Northwood = Agnes. Dead 1382.

. . . Earl of Salisbury. = Catherine. Dead 1382.

[R]obert de [...]am, [1]382. = Catherine, 4th dau. and coheir, claimant, 1382.

Roger Northwood = son and heir. Dead 1382.

William, Earl of Salisbury, claimant, 1382.

Sir John Northwood = Kt. of Kent, son and heir. Dead 1382.

Roger Northwood, son and heir, claimant, 1382.

[N]ORTHWODE,

), *Roll* 257.

Humphrey de Northwode = Dead 1373.

Thomas de Northwode. *Obiit s. p.* Dead 1373.

John de Northwode = Dead 1373.

Sir Roger Scales Knight. 1373.

Joan, daughter and heir. 1373.

Claimants.

the said John, the great-grandfather, etc., the fee, etc., descended to John, Simon, Humphrey, and Thomas, as sons and heirs, etc., because the said tenements are of the tenure of Gavelkynd, and partible among the male heirs, etc.; and from the said Thomas, because he died without heirs of his body, the fee of his purpart descended to the said John, Simon, and Humphrey, as his brothers and heirs, etc., because, etc.; and from the said John the fee of his purpart descended to Roger, John, William, and Otho, as his sons and heirs according to the custom of Gavelkynd, because, etc.; and from the said Otho, because he died without heir of his body, the fee of his purpart descended to the said John, Roger, and William, as brothers and heirs, according to the foresaid tenure, etc.; and from the said William, because he assumed the religious habit in the order of the brothers of the hospital of St. John of Jerusalem at Clerkenwell, in which order he took the vows, the fee of his purpart descended to the said Roger and John as his brothers and heirs, etc.; and from the said John, because he died without heirs of his body, the fee of his purpart descended to the said Roger as his brother and heir, etc.; and from the said Roger the fee of his purpart descended to John de Northwode, who does not now prosecute, and to one Roger, as sons and heirs, according to the tenure of Gavelkynd; and from the said Roger the fee of his purpart descended to the said Thomas, son of Roger, who does not now prosecute, as his son and heir; and from the said Simon, the fee of his purpart descended to Robert and John as his sons and heirs, etc., according to the foresaid tenure; and from the said Robert the fee of his purpart descended to the foresaid Joan, wife of John Leuedale, and Agnes, who now together prosecute, etc., as his daughters and heirs, etc.; and from the said John, brother of Robert, the fee of his purpart descended to said Dionisia, who now prosecutes, etc., as his daughter and heir, etc.; and from the said Humphrey the fee of his purpart descended to one John, as his son and heir, etc.; and from the said John the fee of his purpart descended to the said Joan, wife of Roger, who now prosecutes, etc., as his daughter and heir, etc. etc.

"Richard atte Lese and the others ask for a view. A day is given, etc."

[Vide Common Pleas Judgment Roll, Michaelmas Term, 47 Ed. III., Roll 257.]

(13.) Maritagium. This was one of the incidents to knight-service. During the nonage of the heir, the right of "maritagium" accrued to the King over his tenants *in capite*. While the infant was in ward, he had the power of tendering him or her a suitable match, without disparagement or inequality, which if the infants refused, they forfeited the value of the marriage; that is, so much as a jury would assess, or any one would *bonâ fide* give for such an alliance; and, if the infants married without the King's consent, they forfeited double the value. And the same rights which the King had in this respect over his tenants *in capite,* belonged also to all feudal lords over their tenants who held by knight-service.

The wardship and marriage of the heir were fruitful sources of revenue to the Lord. They were saleable as ordinary chattels, and were so treated.

(15.) The "Inquisitio post mortem" of this Agnes was taken 1405-6, 6 Hen. IV., and Sir Roger died in 1361, 35 Ed. III.; our Roll therefore must have been written between 1361 and 1406.

(17.) On referring to this Inquisition we find the Jury returning as follows:—

"Item dicunt quod dicta Maria obiit die Martis proximo post festum Sancti Bartholomei anno predicto. Item dicunt quod Nicholaus de Sandwico est consanguineus et propinquior heres ejusdem Marie, de manerio predicto, eo quod quedam Agnes Daverenges, que de manerio predicto fuit seisita in dominico suo ut de feodo et jure, nupsit se Johanni de Sandwico, et de eisdem Johanne et Agnete exierunt Johannes et Nicholaus. De eadem Agnete descendit manerium predictum eidem Johanni, ut filio et heredi. De eodem Johanne filio Agnetis descendebat manerium predictum cuidam Juliane ut filie et heredi ipsius Johannis filii Agnetis, que quidem Juliana nupsit se Johanni de Segrave. De eadem Juliana descendit manerium predictum cuidam Johanni de Segrave, ut filio et heredi predicte Juliane. De eodem Johanne de Seagrave, filio Juliane, descendit manerium predictum Marie filie et heredi ejusdem Johannis filii Juliane, que quidem Maria obiit sine herede de corpore suo exeunte, per quod revertebatur jus manerii predicto Nicholao de Sandwico, filio predicte Agnetis, avunculo predicte Juliane avee predicte Marie. De eodem Nicholao descendit jus predicti manerii isti Nicholao de Sandwico, ut filio et heredi ejusdem Nicholai et consanguineo et heredi predicte Marie, filio Nicholai, filii Agnetis, matris Johannis, patris Juliane, matris Johannis de Segrave, patris Marie. Dicunt eciam quod predicta Maria nullas habuit terras seu tenementa in comitatu predicto de hereditate Johannis de Segrave avi sui, et quod predictus Nicholaus est etatis quadraginta annorum et amplius." (See Inq. p. m., 23 Ed. III., pt. 2, No. 44.)

From this Inquisition and our Text, we are furnished with the following pedigree :—

Sir John de Sandwich = Agnes Daverenches, Domina de manerio de Folkstone.

Sir John de Sandwich = | Nicholas de Sandwich =

Sir John de Segrave. = Juliana de Sandwich. | Nicholas de Sandwich, heir to Maria de Segrave.

Sir John de Segrave. = | Sir Roger de Northwode. 1331. =[2] Elizabeth de Segrave =[1] Richard Foliot, Esq.

Maria de Segrave, sole heir, *ob. s. p.* 25th August, 1349.

(19.) Essex. In the more modern transcript of this roll this is written "Sussex."

(20.) Sir Ralph St. Leger was Sheriff of Kent, 10 Ric. II.

(21.) *i.e.* in the same year of our Lord, viz. 1340. She was married, it is stated, in the thirteenth year, therefore the marriage must have taken place in 1340, before the 25th of January, to bring it into 13 Ed. III., and the same year of our Lord, after the 25th of January, would be 14 Ed. III.

(23.) "The late King Edward III.;" therefore this Roll must have been written after 1377, the last year of that monarch.

(25.) This Sir Roger de Northwode had his summons to Parliament 3rd April, 1360, 34 Ed. III. (Rot. Claus.).

(26.) By the custom of Gavelkind, the wife is endowed for life with half the land of which her husband died seised, if it be not otherwise settled by deed or will ; but her estate therein ceases if she contract a second marriage. This clause, therefore, was to secure the estate for life to Agnes, without any forfeiture on a second marriage.

(27.) He had summonses to Parliament, 37, 38, 39, 42, 43, 44, 46, 47, and 49 Ed. III. (see Rot. Claus.).

(28.) This reference almost determines that Thomas Brumpston was the writer of our Roll.

(29.) *i.e.* "pedigree." This is doubtless the Roll which we have printed.

(30.) This would appear as if the questioner of the title to the estate was Selinger; but among our other muniments there is strong indication that James, the brother of the last Sir Roger, was the chief promoter of the dispute.

POST NOTE.

Among the Surrenden muniments, there is also the Confirmation of this Charter, granted by the Pope's Legate, Richard, Archbishop of Canterbury, to William Fitz Helte, on his petition for the same. We refer to our illustrations for an engraving of the archiepiscopal seal attached to this instrument. Richard Monachus was Archbishop of Canterbury from A.D. 1171 to A.D. 1184, and was acting as Legate A.D. 1174. Fitz Helte was dead, as we have seen, in A.D. 1180. We may therefore fix the date of his grant as between 1170 and 1180.

His own father, Helto, may possibly have succeeded the Ansgotus of Domesday, as owner of the manor. That survey was completed A.D. 1086, *i.e.* about ninety years before the date of our grant. Under ordinary circumstances, the interval of two owners between Ansgotus and himself would suffice to supply this gap; but, in this instance, we do not necessarily require more than one. Fitz Helte *seems* to have been succeeded by grandchildren; and, if so, was probably old at the time of his death. Even if he were then no older than seventy, he was not born after 1110. This will readily allow for one owner only between himself and Ansgotus, and that one may have been his father, Helto. Be this as it may, we have, at all events, an unbroken series of evidence, from the present day up to A.D. 1170, incontestably proving the ownership of Aldington during the whole of that period, a space of nearly seven hundred years.

One word more as to the coheirs of William Fitz Helte. It will be observed that, among the witnesses to his grant of Aldington Church, are HUGH DE CIRINTUNIA, and WALTER DE CHANCI. May not these two have been husbands of two of his daughters, and, by them, fathers of his coheirs, WILLIAM DE CYRETON and AMFRID DE CANCI; and may not his other coheir, EMMA, the wife of SETVANS, have been also his daughter? We advance these conjectures merely as suggestive queries.

L. B. L.

1.

2.

3.

4.

6.

5.

7.

7. (Counterseal.)

The Seals engraved in the three following pages are from the Thurnham muniments. They are those of—

1. JOAN DE NORTHWODE, widow of Sir John de Northwode, and daughter of Robert Here.—Affixed to her grant of the manor of THURNHAM to Trustees. Dated 28th January, 21 Ric. II., 1397–8.

Legend:—"S DNE JOHNE DE NORWODE."

2. SIR ROGER DE NORTHWODE.—Affixed to his release and quitclaim to his mother, Joan de Northwode, her heirs and assigns, of all his right in the manor of THURNHAM, and dated 20th August, 14 Ric. II., 1390.

Legend:—"SIGILLUM ROGERI NORTHWODE."

3. STEPHEN DE THORNEHAM.—Affixed to a Charter, wherein he grants to the Church of St. Mary Magdalen, Combwell, "septem solidos et octo denarios et obolum de decima Redditus mei de THORNEHAM percipiendos ad quatuor anni terminos;" and to the Vicar of Thorneham half a mark annually, "de decima ejusdem Redditus;" also to another Charter, wherein he grants to the same Priory a messuage and garden near the Church of Thorneham, pasturage for sheep, etc. The date is *temp.* Jo., about A.D. 1212.

Legend:—"SIGILL STEPHANI DE THORNEHAM."

4. Counterseal of No. 3.

Legend:—"DEUS SALVET CUI MITOR" (*sic*).

5. SIR THOMAS DE BIKENORE, Kt.—Affixed to his grant of the manor of BREDHURST to Henry Nasard of London (probably a mortgage). It is without date, but from collateral evidence we conjecture it to be late Edw. I., or early Edw. II., about A.D. 1300.

6. This Seal is affixed to a copy of an ancient Charter of Elianora de Leyborne, granting land, etc., to the Priory of Leeds. It is folded and sealed as a letter, and the following words added at the foot of the copy:—"Supplico vobis quatinus ista copia non discedat a manibus vestris, quia ignotum est quomodo ista terra et redditus alienantur nisi per negligenciam;" as though it had been made by the Prior or some official of Leeds Priory, to aid an investigation of Title. By the handwriting, it seems to have been made late Ric. II., or perhaps *temp.* Hen. IV., about the time of the alienation of Thurnham to the Wottons. Its principal interest is in the Seal, which, unless we much mistake it, is a riven heart, confirming Mr. Streatfeild's conjecture ('Excerpta Cantiana,' p. 8) that this was the punning device of the Crevecœurs. If we are correct, it would seem that this badge was adopted by the Priors of Leeds as their Priory seal, in honour of their founders, the Crevequers.

The Legend is unfortunately too much defaced for us to attempt anything like a representation of it. As a link in the chain of evidence relating to this device of the Crevecœurs, we have deemed this seal worthy a place among our engravings.

7. RICHARD (MONACHUS), ARCHBISHOP OF CANTERBURY.—Seal and counterseal affixed to his confirmation of the grant of the Church of Aldington, by William Fitz Helte, to the Priory of Combwell. Its date is *inter* A.D. 1170 and A.D. 1180.

Legend of Seal:—"SIGILLUM RICARDI DEI GRATIA CANTUARIENSIS ARCHIEPISCOPI."

Counterseal:—"RICARDUS DEI GRATIA TOTIUS ANGLIE PRIMAS."

8. ROGER DYGGE.—Affixed, with the seals of his co-trustees, to a lease of the manors of Northwode Chasteners, etc., to Sir John de Northwode, Kt., and Joan his wife, for life. Dated 24th August, 42 Edw. III., 1368.

Legend:—"SIGILLUM ROGERI DYGGE."

9. SIR RICHARD ATTE LESE, Kt.—Affixed to the same Charter as No. 8.

Legend:—"SIGILLUM RICARDI ATE LESE."

The charge in dexter chief is too much defaced for us to attempt a statement of what it may be.

10. HAMO, son of ETARD DE CRIEUEQUOER [CREVECŒUR].—Affixed to a Charter by which he confirms to Rodbert, son of Eilmer Bedellus, a part of his land in NORTHBLEAN, called UOXHOLE, for one acre of Warland "ad servicium domini Regis." It is without date; but the character of the writing would fix it as very early in the thirteenth century, *circiter temp.* Johan.

Legend:—"S. GILL. HA.... CRVEPVER."

11. JAMES DE BOURNE.—Affixed, with the seals of his co-trustees, to a grant of the manor of Northwode Chasteners to Joan de Northwode, widow, for life, with remainders successively to her sons, Sir Roger de Northwode, Kt., and James de Northwode. It is dated 20th May, 20 Ric. II., 1397.

Legend:—"SIGILLUM JACOB . . E BOURNE."

12. RICHARD CHEYNE.—Affixed to a deed of entail of the manors of Northwode Shepey, Northwode Chasteners, Thurnham, etc., made by Joan de Northwode (widow of Sir John) and her son Roger de Northwode: viz. that of Northwode Shepey to the said Roger and his wife Alice and their heirs; remainder in default to William, brother of the said Roger, etc. etc. —the other manors being differently entailed. It is dated 24th October, 17 Ric. II., 1393.

Legend:—"SIGILLUM RICARDI CHEYNE."

The Coats, 6 Lioncels, 3-2-1, a Canton Ermine, is that of Shurland. The heiress of Shurland married the grandfather of Sir Richard Cheney, who thus seems to have adopted the coat instead of his own.

13. Seal of the Priory of Combwell, affixed to their lease of the Parsonage of Thurnham, for twenty years, to Sir Edward Nevyle of Southfryth, Kt. It is dated 25th February, 26 Hen. VIII., 1534–5.

Legend:—"SIGILL ECCLESIE SANCTE MARIE MAGDALENE DE COMBWELL."

On the Table:—"MARIA FIDES TUA TE SALVAM FECIT."

14. Counterseal of No. 13.

Legend:—"FACTUM ANNO GRAC. MCXXX. TERCIO MENSE NOVEMBR . . ."

By the kind courtesy of Mr. Ready we have been shown an impression of this counterseal, in which the date has been changed to MCCXXX.

N.B.—Among the seals here engraved, we have, in some instances, supplied defective parts from others in the same collection.

8.

9.

10.

11.

12.

13.

14. (Counterseal.)

TES.

Henry de Wautham
Dead 50 Hen. III., 1265.

afilia de Wautham,
III., 1265.

John de Wautham.
Dead 50 Hen. III., 1265.

James. *Ob. s. p.* — Thomas. — Richard. — Simon. — Humphrey.

Sir John. — Otho. — Sir William, Knight of St. John of Jerusalem. — Thomas. — Robert.

Sir Roger = Margaret, daughter of Nicholas de Halgton, by Margery, afterwards third wife of his father, Sir Roger Northwode. — Geoffrey. *Ob. v. p. s. p.* — Agnes. *Ob. v. p. s. p.*

James = — John Digge = Juliana. — Sir John Dengeyne = Joan.

Isabel. — Two sons.

ANCIENT SEPULCHRAL SHAFT AT BEKESBOURN.

BY JOHN BRENT, JUN., ESQ., F.S.A.

TOWARDS the end of October last, the workmen of the "London, Chatham, and Dover Railway," in forming a cutting upon Bekesbourn Hill, three miles from Canterbury, came upon a large wooden structure, about thirteen feet below the surface of the soil.

Oaken beams, a foot square, first appeared, and then the planking of a quadrilateral oaken shaft, to the depth of six feet; then heavy crossbeams, then planking again, terminated by four crossbeams as at the top. These lay twenty-five feet below the surface.

The crossbeams were six feet six inches in length, firmly mortised together; the planks were mortised or rabbeted together, and let into the beams, each plank being pierced by transverse ties, crossing the corners of the shaft inside, and giving to the entire structure the appearance of having a flight of steps or stays within.

The ties projected two or three inches on the outside, as shown in the illustration.

There was no appearance of iron, or any other metal, having been used in the construction of the shaft, but the whole fabric was closely and skilfully knit together by the mortises and ties, while the weight of the materials themselves, and the pressure of the soil around, prevented any of the parts becoming displaced.

The entire fabric was of oak; the crossbeams evidencing by their grain that they were the product of large trees. The wood had become jet-black by age; but, although somewhat soft on the surface, was hard and compact at a short distance within.

The interior quadrature of the shaft was three feet three inches, the cross ties about a foot long, the beams six feet six inches, and twelve inches square.

The soil where the fabric was found was gravelly at the surface; lower down of a sandy loam.

The beams and planks were probably all hewn by the axe, yet were as neatly fitted and as well proportioned as if done by a skilful artisan in the present day, each mortised plank exactly corresponding with the alternate one above it.

We have been thus minute in detail, as we know of no other example of carpentry ever having been found so perfect, of the undoubted antiquity of the fabric we have described.

As it was cleared away from the soil, it loomed out against the dark earthen bed from which it had been excavated, like a mysterious record of a past and unknown age, exhibiting in some respects features new and strange.

The top of the shaft, when found, was covered with oaken planks, the structure being entirely filled with large flints. The workmen speedily broke down one side, and threw out the stones. As they approached the base, they came upon a single urn, about ten inches in height, and formed of bluish-black clay. It was protected by large flints, in some manner arched over it; beneath it was a layer of flints; then five urns, one central, and one in each corner of the shaft. Among the latter was an urn with a large piece of baked clay placed over its mouth.

The author of this paper was on the spot shortly after the contents were removed from the shaft, and found fragments in the soil taken out of it, and from the pieces he obtained, concludes there had been seven or eight urns included in the entombment.

The workmen having acted with the precipitancy usual upon such occasions, as soon as the urns were discovered, in their eagerness to obtain what they deemed the valuable contents of the jars, partially or wholly destroyed all of them but three.

Nothing but a soft white clayey matter was found within them. This might be burnt bones in a deliquescent state, for the shaft was very wet, having either acted as a drain to the soil in which it was placed, or having a small spring percolating through it. To this cause doubtless we may assign the perfect preservation of the oaken structure.

Some substance of a fibrous texture was found. This might have been yarn which went round the necks of the urns, or matting or woollen cloth laid over their mouths. Upon exposure to the air it speedily dissolved, as did for the most part some walnut or filbert shells.

Beneath the last deposit of urns was a flat piece of stone, over a concavity in the earth at the bottom of the shaft. It was kept in its place by six pegs, apparently of chestnut-wood, pinned round it.

On the stone imbedded in the soil was arranged a circle of horses' teeth.

Although every effort was made by the writer to preserve the shaft, it was soon partially destroyed by the workmen; while the continued rains, and the excavations going on in the cutting, undermined it and completed its destruction. Some of the timber however has been preserved.

In contemplating this strange resurrection from the past, we are reminded by its form and design of the Roman Columbarium; yet, composed of oak and buried at such a depth in the earth, where shall we find another example?

The urns are mostly of a fine dark material, very hard, some with a slight polish. Their height varies from nine to eleven inches; diameters eight inches; most of them with narrow necks and small mouths, some with marks of wickerwork pattern. One or two are of a coarser fabric. They have the character of Roman.

The 'Archæologia,' vol. xxvii. p. 148, contains an account of a planked pit or well, found in Lothbury, London, communicated in a paper by C. R. Smith, Esq. In this well were found earthen Roman vessels in considerable numbers. "Vases placed longitudinally on their sides, as if packed, and imbedded in the mud or sand. A coin of Allectus, and a small Samian patera of the ivy-leaf pattern border," were also found.

The character of the above discovery admitted of no doubt but that its contents were Roman. The place of deposit formed a pit "about three feet square, boarded on each side with narrow planks about two feet long," and exhibited all the character of being a well or pit, into which the relics had either been thrown or hastily deposited for security; the presence among them of two iron implements, one representing a boat-hook and the other a bucket-handle, the latter of no very ancient construction, seems to indicate the uses to which the place of deposit had been applied.

Pits and upright shafts have from time to time been found on our chalk hills and in other localities, but, devoid of woodwork as far as we know, they do not seem to offer any resemblance to the shaft at Bekesbourn.

What then is the nature of this singular relic, and by what people or tribe was it constructed?

We may answer the first query by assuming it to be sepulchral, and that the urns, one or more of them at least, from the contents found therein, contained the remains of burnt bones; the confined area of the shaft rendering untenable any idea that it was devoted to funeral rites by inhumation.

Was the fabric the funeral vault of a chief or leader and his family, or devoted to the burial of one individual? The urns being deposited in two or more layers, seem almost to favour the first hypothesis; yet we can hardly judge from circumstances so inconclusive, the Roman modes of sepulture being various.

The presence of the horses' teeth seems to refer to the rites or superstitions of a northern nation; but the flat stone at the foot of the shaft, which has been pronounced by some authorities to be a portion of a Roman millstone, seems to favour a different conclusion. Some of the urns doubtless were stored with such articles of food as the affection of survivors contributed for the use of the departed on his long and unrecorded journey.

The depth at which the shaft was buried in the earth, its entrance being about thirteen feet from the surface, is one remarkable character in the discovery; the elaborate nature of its construction is another.

We have not, that we are aware of, elsewhere, any similar example of a Roman interment. The Danes, who were sometimes in possession for months of this part of Kent, used much timber in their graves, and Worsaae's description of the barrow of Thyre Danebod at Jellinge, in Jutland, has some remarkable features in common with the shaft at Bekesbourn. The former is described as "being a burial-chamber, formed of wood, twenty-four feet long, four and a half feet high, and covered with beams of oak. The walls, which had been covered with woollen cloth, were formed of oak planks, behind which was a bed of clay, trodden down, in which the beams of the ceiling rested."

This oaken structure, unlike our example however, was horizontal, and, besides containing costly relics, was devoted to the practice of burial by inhumation. The carpentry was inferior; in fact, the planks, so far from being mortised and uniformly shaped and fitted, were merely placed together, resting on each other.

The ships of the Danes, however, their elaborately carved heads and sterns, and their dimensions, such as those of the ship recorded to have been built by Haco at Bergen, do not render the construction of the shaft by the artisans of this people a matter of impossibility.

The preponderating evidence favours the supposition that the structure was a Roman sepulchre; yet a strange and isolated example, exhibiting, after the lapse of ages, another phase of the rites and customs of a people: the silent exhumation of a single relic, or the resurrection of a buried city, alike attesting the dominating genius and the mighty energies which at one time subjugated half the world.

Note.—Since the above was written, additional remains have been discovered near the same spot. A shaft, but without timber, filled with flint stones; and, at the distance of about fifteen feet below the surface, two or three urns, and a vessel (for the writer has not seen it) answering in description to a large Roman amphora.

A HELP TOWARD A KENTISH MONASTICON.

BY W. E. FLAHERTY, ESQ.

REV. AND DEAR SIR,

I esteem myself pretty sure of your concurrence when I say, that a Society which has so rich and various a field as the Archæology of Kent before it, cannot fail to achieve permanent success, if but a fair proportion of its members will render such help as they may to the furtherance of its objects. The field indeed is so wide that there is ample room for all, however diverse may be their tastes and pursuits. While some discover, and describe from actual observation, the edifices or the sepulchres, the arms and the ornaments of our ancestors, others may, by the production of family papers, illustrate genealogy and history; and others, again, may draw from public records precise information on subjects that have been but lightly treated by authors, whose works are yet deserving of all the collateral help that can be bestowed on them.

Among such subjects I venture to class the monastic history of Kent. It is true that Dugdale and Tanner have touched on it (with that of other counties) in their valuable works, but much additional information is to be gained from a record now in the custody of the Master of the Rolls, and which, as far as I know, has not yet been printed, except a few fragments by Hasted,[1]

[1] And those not always correctly. *E.g.* Hasted says (vol. i. p. 220) from

Warner, and others; and wishing to do something toward the end that we all have in view, I beg to offer to the Society a transcript of the portion relating to Kent of Cardinal Pole's Book of Pensions (1556). If in future years some of our members will take up the subject, and give it such illustration as documents or local knowledge, or both, may enable them to bestow, I venture to say that their papers will not be inferior in interest or value to any in our Transactions.

I remain, Rev. and dear Sir,

Yours faithfully,

W. E. FLAHERTY.

The Rev. Lambert B. Larking,
Hon. Sec. K.A.S.

Cardinal Pole's Book—Kent.

In order to the understanding of this very curious and valuable record, it will be necessary to go back some twenty years prior to its date, to the first Statutes for the suppression of the Monasteries and the division of the spoil.

In the year 1536 two Acts were passed, which in the Record Commission edition of the Statutes are numbered chapters 28 and 27 of the 27th of Henry VIII. By the first of these Statutes, all the monasteries that had less than £200 of yearly revenue were suppressed, and their possessions of every kind granted to the Crown; by the second Statute, a court was established, which was "commonly to be called the Court of the Augmentations of the Revenues of the King's crown," for the purpose of managing the property thus acquired, and also of dis-

Browne Willis, there "the prioress and eighteen nuns of Dartford remained pensioned in 1553." Our document, dated three years later, contains twenty names.

pensing "some convenient charity" to such of the displaced religious as might choose to return to the world,[1] instead of entering the "honourable great monasteries" which were still allowed to stand.

Three years later, the Act for the Dissolution of Abbeys (31 Henry VIII. c. 13) was passed, when the conventual life was broken up, and, according to the received view of the case, a few subservient superiors were pensioned off, but the great majority of the monastic body was turned out literally to starve. Documents, however, exist, which show this to be untrue. There are four books of the Court of Augmentation (now in the Public Record Office, numbered 244, 245, 246, and 248) detailing the grant or the payment of monastic pensions, the last of which belongs to the year 1543 (34 Henry VIII.). There is also proof in another set of documents that these payments were kept up, at least until the year 1552. At that time commissioners were appointed in each county, who were to summon the recipients before them, and to learn whether any of them had assigned away their pensions, and what deaths had occurred among them. The returns that have been preserved are unfortunately very few, but in them we have the parties uniformly acknowledging that they have been "fully and duly paid unto this day."

We may fairly presume that matters remained the same when Mary came to the throne. As is well known, she gave up such Church lands as had not been already sold or granted away, but it was thought necessary to procure the formal sanction of Parliament for a new disposition of the first-fruits and tenths, which had been given to the Crown in 1534, by the 26th of Henry VIII. c. 3. Accordingly, in the end of the year 1555, the

[1] We have the good fortune to be in possession of an original of one of these dispensations under Cardinal Pole's seal, with his autograph,—of which we purpose to give a facsimile in our next volume.—ED.

Statute 2 & 3 Philip and Mary, c. 4, was passed "for the extinguishment of the first-fruits, and touching order and disposition of the tenths of spiritual and ecclesiastical promotions, and of rectories and parsonages impropriate remaining in the Queen's Majesty's hands." The first-fruits were to "cease and be clearly extinct and determined for ever," from the preceding August, but the tenths were to be received by a body of clerical commissioners, who were to pay thereout the pensions to the monastics, as long as any remained alive, after which time the tenths were to cease also. The carrying out of this measure was committed to "my Lord Legate's Grace" (Cardinal Pole), and he had power, according to his "godly wisdom and discretion," also to employ a portion of the tenths in the augmentation of poor livings, in finding preachers, and in exhibitions for poor scholars. After the death of the Legate the two Archbishops and the eldest Bishop by consecration were to execute the Act.

The Pension Book with which we are now concerned is in the form of an Indenture between the King and Queen on the one hand and Cardinal Pole on the other to give effect to the Statute. It bears date the 24th of February, 1556, and contains, in seventy-seven schedules, full particulars of the "rents, pensions, annuities, corrodies, fees, and other yearly payments," for which the Crown was liable in respect of the dissolved monasteries. These particulars are by the Act directed to be set forth "in a certain book indented," one copy of which was to be signed by the Queen, and the other by the Cardinal; it is the latter that has been preserved, and hence the name.

The book commences with Kent, the pensions payable in which, as will be seen, amount to £1263. 16*s.* 5*d.*; London comes next, at £1605. 16*s.* 8*d.*, and Middlesex, at £1075. 6*s.* 11*d.* The highest amount is Lincoln, at

£2008. 16*s.* 10*d.*, but Yorkshire is returned at only £875. 7*s.* 3*d.*, a small sum when we consider the extent of the county. We have no wish to intrude on the province of other Archæological Societies, and therefore will only further remark, that the sum total of payments is:

	£	*s.*	*d.*
To Monastics and those connected with them .	36,081	16	10
To Officers of the Court of Augmentations . .	660	0	0
To Shaxton, quondam Bishop of Salisbury . .	66	13	4
	£36,808	10	2

The volume, which is of large size, and handsomely written, commences with "𝔗𝔥𝔦𝔰 𝔍𝔫𝔡𝔢𝔫𝔱𝔲𝔯𝔢," etc., a document that recites the substance of the Statute; this is the only part that is in English. Next comes a formal specification of its object, as follows, verified by the signature of the Cardinal.—

"Specificantur et continent' in Septuaginta septem Cedulis Indentat' sequeñ tam nomina et cognomina diversaꝝ personaꝝ qm̃ eoꝝ separalia feoda añtes corrodia et penciones eisdem pro termino vitæ vel annoꝝ concessa nuper in Curiis Sc'cij et Ducatus Lancastrie de Thesauro Regio solut' ac imposteꝝ per Clerum vigore cujusdam Actus Parliamenti exonerand' et solvend' Videlt a festo sancti Michis Archi annis regnoꝝ Philippi et Mariæ dei gratia Regis et Reginæ Angliæ Franciæ Neapolis Jerlm et Hibniæ fidei Defensoꝝ Principum Hispaniaꝝ et Ciciliæ Archiducum Austriæ Ducum Mediolaniæ Burgundiæ ⁊ Brabantiæ Comitum Haspurgiæ Flandriæ et Tirolis Secundo et Tercio prout in separalibꝫ Comitatibꝫ subsequentibꝫ perticlariter apparet.

"Reg. Carlis Polus leg'.

Videlt."

The document has been put into English for the convenience of the general reader, but probably the antiquary may like to see a brief specimen of the original.

COMITAT⁹ KANCIE.

Scĩ Radigunđ nup̱ Monasteř	Annuit̃ Joħnis Russeƚƚ p̱ annū.	iiij.ƚi. xiij.s̃. iiij.đ.
	Pencio Thome Dale p̱ annū.	xiij.ƚi. vj.s̃. viij.đ.
Dover nup̱ Priorat.	Pencio Joħnis Lambert p̱ annū. . .	xx.ƚi.
Combewell nup̱ Moñ	Pencio Thome Vyncent p̱ annū	x.ƚi.

Tanner enumerates thirty-six religious houses in Kent, beside one alien priory and six colleges, but the names of only seventeen appear in our record, which, allowing for the hand of death among the pensioners in the course of near twenty years, is not surprising; it will be found, however, to mention some minor foundations, as chantries, of which probably no other memorial exists. The Order to which each house belonged, and its value, have been added, from Tanner, Dugdale, Speed, or Leland, as mere starting-points for the illustration that we trust the record may receive at the hands of those who have knowledge and time to devote to a subject that will repay any amount of labour bestowed thereon.

We will only further remark that the payments in the record are distinguished as "Pensions," "Fees," or "Annuities." The first of course represent the "convenient charity" of the Crown; by the second we understand (subject to correction) compensations for loss of office, as in the case of the clerk and the auditor of Dartford; and by the third, money payments for which the religious houses were liable at the time of their suppression. Those who wish to see the very various causes which led to such grants may advantageously consult the exceedingly curious Camden volume, "The Hospitallers in England," or, as that may not be so readily accessible, they will find a summary of it in the "Gentleman's Magazine" for June, 1857.

COUNTY OF KENT.

The late Monastery of St. Radigund.[1]

Annuity.

John Russell, per annum . . . . iiij.li. xiij.s. iiij.d.

Pension.

Thomas Dale, per annum . . . . xiij.li. vj.s. viij.d.

The late Priory of Dover.[2]

Pension.

John Lambert,[3] per annum . . . . xx.li.

The late Monastery of Combewell.[4]

Pension.

Thomas Vyncent,[5] per annum . . . . x.li.

The late Monastery of Bilsington.[6]

Pensions.

John Moyse, per annum . . . . x.li.
Thomas Cheltham, Bishop of Sidon, per annum . . . . x.li.

The late Monastery of Folkeston.[7]

Pension.

Thomas Barrett, per annum . . . . x.li.

The late Monastery of Dartford.[8]

Fees.

John Richardson, Clerk of the said late Monastery, per annum, lx.s.

[1] Premonstratensian Abbey, at Bradsole, near Dover. Value at suppression, £142. 8*s*. 9*d*., according to Speed.
[2] Benedictine. Value £232. 1*s*. 5½*d*., Speed.
[3] The prior.
[4] Augustinian Priory. Value £128. 1*s*. 9½*d*.
[5] The Prior.
[6] Augustinian Priory. Value £81. 1*s*. 6*d*., Speed.
[7] Benedictine Priory. Value £63. 0*s*. 7*d*., Speed.
[8] "Dertford." Augustinian Nunnery. Value £380. 9*s*. 0½*d*.

William Sydley, Auditor there, per annum . . . . . . lx.s.

Annuities.

Elizabeth, late wife of Sir Ralph Fane, Knt., per annum xx.li.
John Wyseman, per annum . . . . xl.s.
Thomas Golde, per annum . . . . liij.s. iiij.d.
Thomas Makyn, per annum . . . . xxxiij.s. iiij.d.
Richard Fyssher, per annum . . . . xl.s.
Robert Whalepole, per annum . . . . xl.s.
William Lycoras, per annum . . . . xx.s.
John Hollingeworth, per annum . . . . . . xxvj.s. viij.d.
John Ketle, per annum . . . . xl.s.
John Fryer, per annum . . . . iiij.li.

Pensions.

Joan Fane, per annum . . . . lxvj.li. xiij.s. iiij.d.
Elinor Wood, per annum . . . . xl.s.
Elizabeth Cresnore, per annum . . . . cvj.s. viij.d.
Mary Blower, per annum . . . . iiij.li.
Elizabeth White, per annum . . . . c.s.
Mary Bentham, per annum . . . . c.s.
Katherine Eflyn, per annum . . . . c.s.
Dorothy Sydley, per annum . . . . c.s.
Alice Grenesmyth, per annum . . . . xl.s.
Elizabeth Exmewe, per annum . . . . c.s.
Elizabeth Seygood, per annum . . . . xl.s.
Matilda Fryer, per annum . . . . c.s.
Katherine Garret, per annum . . . . xl.s.
Agnes Roper, per annum . . . . vj.li.
Anne Bosome, per annum . . . . c.s.
Alice Davye, per annum . . . . c.s.
Alice Bostocke, per annum . . . . xl.s.
Margaret Warner, per annum . . . . c.s.
Agnes Lego, per annum . . . . c.s.
Katherine Clovell, per annum . . . . c.s.

THE LATE FRIARY OF DARTFORD.[1]

Annuities.

Robert Strodle, per annum . . . . c.s.

[1] "Dertford nup. Domus Frm̃."

William Hastinge during the life of Elizabeth Cressenore, per annum . . . . lxvj.s. viij.d.

THE LATE MONASTERY OF HORTON.[1]

Annuity.

Richard Brysseley, per annum . . . . xv.li.

THE LATE MONASTERY OF MALLING.[2]

Annuities.

Rowland Ryce, per annum . . . . c.s.
Henry Fletcher, per annum . . . . c.s.

Pensions.

Agnes Weste, per annum . . . . liij.s. iiij.d.
Elizabeth Pympe, per annum . . . . liij.s. iiij.d.
Joan Hall, per annum . . . . liij.s. iiij.d.
Joan Randolphe, per annum . . . . lxvj.s. viij.d.
Juliana Whetenall, per annum . . . . liij.s. iiij.d.
Leticia Bucke, per annum . . . . liij.s. iiij.d.

THE LATE PRIORY OF LEEDS.[3]

Annuities.

Thomas Spilmane, per annum . . . . xl.s.
Arthur Seintcleger, per annum . . . . xvj.li.
Thomas Hendeley, per annum . . . . xx.s.
Sir Thomas Moyle, Knt., per annum . . . . . liiij.s. iiij.d.
Thomas Chapman, per annum . . . . vj.li.
Stephen Caldewell, per annum . . . . xl.s.
John Eshylowe and Richard Wheler, per annum . . . . c.s.
Thomas Dorrell and Anthony Hussey, per annum . . . xx.li.

Pensions.

William Heringe, per annum . . . . iiij.li.
William Dauncey, per annum . . . . cvj.s. viij.d.
John Drurye, per annum . . . . vj.li.
Richard Rogers, per annum . . . . vj.li.

[1] Benedictine Priory. Value £111. 16*s*. 11½*d*., Speed.
[2] "Mallinge." Benedictine Nunnery. Value £245. 10*s*. 2½*d*., Speed.
[3] "Leedes." Augustinian. Value £362. 7*s*. 7*d*., see p. 15.

Thomas Kayley, per annum . . . . cvj.s. viij.d.
Charles Walley, per annum . . . . . . vj.li. xiij.s. iiij.d.
Launcellett Gylbanke, per annum . . . . vj.li.
William Sheperde, per annum . . . . cvj.s. viij.d.
William Barker, per annum . . . . vij.li.
Thomas Daye, per annum . . . . iiij^{xx}.li.

The late Monastery of Rochester.[1]

Annuity.

Edward White, per annum . . . . lx.s.

Pensions.

William Chaunterburye, per annum . . . . c.s.
Robert Bacon, per annum . . . . c.s.
Robert Smythe, per annum . . . . x.li.
William Albon, per annum . . . . x.li.
Nicholas Spellehurste, *alias* Arnolde, per annum . . xl.s.

The late Monastery of St. Augustine.[2]

Annuity.

William Coppyn, per annum . . . . liij.s. iiij.d.

Pensions.

Thomas Edmonde, per annum . . . . . vj.li. xiij.s. iiij.d.
John Snothe, per annum . . . . c.s.
Edward Sawyer, per annum . . . . c.s.
George Amys, per annum . . . . c.s.
Robert White, per annum . . . . vj.li. xiij.s. iiij.d.
William Okenfeilde, per annum . . . . viij.li.
William Milles, per annum . . . . c.s.
Edward Mynge, per annum . . . . . vj.li. xiij.s. iiij.d.
John Hall, per annum . . . . vj.li. xiij.s. iiij.d.
John Hitchecoke, per annum . . . . vj.li.
Robert Davyson, per annum . . . . vj.li.
John Binge, per annum . . . . c.s.
William Mynge, per annum . . . . c.s.
William Jorden, per annum . . . . vj.li.
John Baynes, per annum . . . . vj.li. xiij.s. iiij.d.

[1] Benedictine Priory. Value £486. 11*s.* 5*d.*

[2] Benedictine Mitred Abbey. Value £1412. 4*s.* 7¾*d.*

John Wilborne, per annum . . . . . . xiij.li. vi.s. viii.d.

The late Monastery of Faversham.[1]

Fee.

Joseph Beverley, Auditor there, per annum . . lxvj.s. viij.d.

Annuities.

Philip Chowte, per annum . . . . lxvj.s. viij.d.
Thomas Persey, per annum . . . . xxx.s.

Pensions.

Peter Myntoo, per annum . . . . lxvj.s. viij.d.
Ralph Poste, per annum . . . . iiij.li.
Dunstan Goodhewe, per annum . . . . iiij.li.
Thomas Dove, per annum . . . . c.s.

The late Monastery of Mottenden.[2]

Pensions.

John Hendyman, per annum . . . . iiij.li.
William Barker, per annum . . . . liij.s. iiij.d.
Richard Brokehurste, per annum . . . . . . liij.s. iiij.d.
Andrew Pyttenden, per annum . . . . liij.s. iiij.d.

The late Priory of Christ Church, Canterbury.[3]

Annuities.

Thomas Herdes, Mariscall there, per annum . . . . viij.li.
John Leigh, for the term of lxxiiij years, per annum, liij.s. iiij.d.
John Johnson, per annum . . . . c.s.
Sir Anthony Aucher, Knt., Auditor and Supervisor there,
per annum . . . . vj.li. xiij.s. iiij.d.
Richard Engham, Steward of the Hall[4] there, per annum, viij.li.
Thomas Percey, per annum . . . . xl.s.

Pensions.

Thomas Nicholle, per annum . . . . x.li.

[1] "Fevershame." Benedictine Abbey. Value £286. 12*s*. $6\frac{3}{4}$*d*., Speed.

[2] "Modynden." Trinitarian Priory. Value £60. 13*s*., Speed; £30. 13*s*., Dugdale.

[3] Benedictine Mitred Priory. Value £2387. 13*s*. $3\frac{1}{2}$*d*., Speed.

[4] "Sen[li] Aule."

John Raspys, per annum . . . . xiij.li. vj.s. viij.d.
Thomas Payne, per annum . . . . . . xiij.li. vj.s. viij.d.
Richard Thornedon, per annum . . . . x.li.
William Goldwell, per annum . . . . vj.li.
John Throughley, per annum . . . . viij.li.
William London, per annum . . . . . . vj.li. xiij.s. iiij.d.
Robert Anthony, per annum . . . . vj.li.
William Caunterburye, per annum . . . . vj.li.
John Stone, per annum . . . . vj.li.
William Lychefeld, per annum . . . . x.li.
Nicholas Herste, per annum . . . . . . vj.li. xiij.s. iiij.d.
Richard Bonnyngton, per annum . . . . viij.li.
John Lambeherste, per annum . . . . . vj.li. xiij.s. iiij.d.
William Gregorye, per annum . . . . vj.li.
William Gillingham, per annum . . . . . xiij.li. vj.s. viiij.d.
Quintin Denys, per annum . . . . . . vj.li. xiij.s. iiij.d.

The late Monastery of La Maison Dieu,[1] Dover.

Pensions.

John Burnell, per annum . . . . vj.li. xiij.s. iiij.d.
Henry Wood, per annum . . . . vj.li. xiij.s. iiij.d.
John Thompson, per annum . . . . . . liij.li. vj.s. viij.d.

The late Monastery of Boxley.[2]

Annuity.

William Lorkyn, per annum . . . . xl.s.

Pensions.

Alexander Wimbhurste, per annum . . . . iiij.li.
George Downeham, per annum . . . . iiij.li.
George Squier, per annum . . . . iiij.li.
John Rede, per annum . . . . liij.s. iiij.d.
William Lorkyn, per annum . . . . iiij.li.

Chantries, Colleges, Fraternities, Free Chapels, and others of that nature, etc.

Pensions.

Thomas Johnson, late Incumbent of the Chapel of Crawthorne, per annum . . . . c.s.

[1] "Le Masendewe." Value £231. 16*s*. 7*d*.
[2] Cistercian Abbey. Value £218. 19*s*. 10*d*., Speed.

Mathew Goodricke, late Prebendary at Wingham,[1] per annum . . . . vi.li.
John Thorpe, another late Prebendary there, per annum, vj.li. xiii.s. iiij.d.
Richard Broke, [2] there, per annum . . xl.s.
Richard Turnore, [2] there, per annum . . xl.s.
Roger Lynsey, late Incumbent there, per annum . . iiij.li. v.s.
Augustin Quested, another late Incumbent there, per annum . . . . iiij.li. v.s.
Robert Collyns, another late Prebendary there, per annum . . . . vj.li. xiij.s. iiij.d.
John Blande, [2] there, per annum vj.li. xiij.s. iiij.d.
Henry Hollande, late Incumbent there, per annum, vj.li. xiij.s. iiij.d.
John Stone, [2] there, per annum . . . . c.s.
Edmund Cranemer, late Master of the said College of Wingham,[3] per annum . . . . xx.li.
Edward Cowdry, [2] there, per annum . xl.s.
Henry Sturgion, late Incumbent there, per annum . xl.s.

John Cleyton, late Incumbent in [2], per annum, vj.li. xiij.s. iiij.d.

John Porter, late Incumbent of the College at Maidstone,[4] per annum . . . . c.s.
Thomas Huggarde, another late Incumbent there, per annum . . . . xlvj.s. viij.d.
James Killingrewe, another late Incumbent there, per annum . . . . xl.s.
John Ware, *alias* Warde, another late Incumbent there, per annum . . . . xlvj.s. viij.d.
William Clere, another late Incumbent there, per annum, liij.s. iiij.d.
Arthur Butler, another late Incumbent there, per annum, iiij.li.
John Godfrey, another late Incumbent there, per annum, vj.li. xiij.s. iiij.d.
George Denham, another late Incumbent there, per annum, vj.li.

[1] Provost and secular canons. Value £84, Speed.
[2] Left blank in original. [3] "Wyngham."
[4] "Maydeston." Master and secular priests. Value £212. 5*s*. 3½*d*., Leland.

Arthur Burton, another late Incumbent there, per annum, liij.s. iiij.d.
George Prior, another late Incumbent there, per annum, iiij.li.
John Leyffe, late Master of the College of Maidstone aforesaid, per annum . . . . xlviij.li. xvj.s. viij.d.
Thomas Wade, another late Incumbent there, per annum, c.s.
William Rise, another late Incumbent there, per annum, xxvj.s. viij.d.
Thomas Pyne, late Incumbent at Maidstone aforesaid, per annum . . . . iiij.li.
John Pyersbye, another late Incumbent there, per annum, xxvj.s. viij.d.
John Weston, another late Incumbent there, per annum, liij.s. iiij.d.

Robert Bacon, late Incumbent at Dartford,[1] per annum . vj.li.
Edward Parker, another late Incumbent there, per annum, vj.li.

Roger Hewett, late Incumbent of the Chantry of Petham, lxxiij.s. iiij.d.

John Hall, late Incumbent of the Chantry called Burton Chauntrye, in Sandwich,[2] per annum . . . . vj.li.
John Stuarde, [4] there, per annum . . . vj.li.
William Lotte, another late Incumbent there, per annum, vj.li.
John Watson, late Incumbent of the Chantry called Grene Chauntrye, in Sandwich,[3] per annum . . . . . . vj.li.
Roger Powell, [4] per annum . . . . . . c.s.
John Motram, late Incumbent at Radfelde in Backechilde,[5] per annum . . . . xxxix.s. ix.d.
Philip Metcalfe, late Incumbent at Gillingham, per annum, vj.li.
John Castelyn, late Incumbent of the Chantry of Chilham, per annum . . . . vj.li.
William Hamon, late Incumbent of the Chantry in Ash,[6] called [4] per annum . . . . . vj.li. xiij.s. iiij.d.
Thomas Hewet, late Incumbent of the Chantry of Reculver, per annum . . . . vj.li.
Nicholas Thompson, *alias* Champyon, late Incumbent at Kingsbridge, in the city of Canterbury, per annum . vj.li.

[1] "Derteforde." [2] "Sandwiche." [3] "Sandwyche."
[4] Left blank in original. [5] *i.e.* Bapchild. [6] "Ayshe."

William Brigge, late Incumbent of the Chantry of Godmersham per annum . . . . c.s.
George Higge, late Incumbent at Harbledown,[1] per annum, vj.li.
William Hopkyns, late Incumbent at Sevenoaks,[2] per annum, vj.li.
Richard Hill, late Incumbent of the Chantry of Pepingbury, per annum . . . . vj.li. xiij.s. iiij.d.
Launcelot Peycocke, late Incumbent at Milkehowse, per annum . . . . vj.li.
William Deacon, late Incumbent of the Chantry of Hoath,[3] per annum . . . . vj.li.
Thomas Daye, late Incumbent of the Chantry of Newsted, per annum . . . . c.s.
Thomas Barret, late Incumbent of the Fraternity in Folkeston, per annum . . . . lx.s.
Henry Appevan, late Incumbent at Penshurst,[4] per annum, c.s.

Annuities.

Sir Richard Rede, Knt., issuing out of the late College of Maidstone,[5] per annum . . . . iiij.li.
John Weston, issuing out of the said late College of Maidstone,[5] per annum . . . . xl.s.

Sum of all payments in the aforesaid County of Kent, per annum . . . . Mcclxiij.li. xvj.s. v.d.

It will be an appropriate addition to our correspondents' communication if we here insert a list of the members constituting the Priory of Leeds in the early part of the sixteenth century. It was given to us many years since by the lamented Rev. Thomas Streatfeild, and extracted by him "from an original Roll in the hands of Mr. Thomas Rodd, the bookseller, in the year 1831, and brought from Leeds Castle."—Ed.

Dominus Prior.
Dominus Thomas Langley, *Supprior.*
Dominus Johannes Brenchisley.
Dominus Johannes London.

[1] "Herbaldowne." [2] "Sevenocke." [3] "Hothe." [4] "Pensehurste." [5] "Maydestone."

Dominus Willelmus Huntyngdon.
Dominus Johannes Goldston.
Dominus Robertus Bedirsden.
Dominus Johannes Leycest.
Dominus Willelmus Hollyngborne.
Dominus Thomas Harietsham.
Dominus Ricardus Goodherst.
Dominus Thomas Egerton.
Dominus Robertus Reynham.
Dominus Bartholomeus Lynsted.
Dominus Thomas Vyncent.
Dominus Thomas Lynden.
Dominus Johannes Wodrove, *Diaconus.*
Frater Johannes Tentirden, *Subdiaconus.*

Ricardus Roger.
Ricardus Ramsey.
Johannes Bawth.
Johannes Edynden.
Nicholas Ryder.
Robertus Roger.
Willelmus Coper.
Johannes Clayton, *Clericus ecclesie.*
Cristoforus Barbitonsor.
Johannes Bery, *Pincerna.*
Thomas Harritson, *Custos Equorum.*
Arnoldus Cokk.
Willelmus Benet, *Carpentarius.*
Thomas Joy, *Cocus.*
Antonius Breten.
Johannes Smyth, *Lixa.*
Jacobus Jenyn, *Pistor.*

Johannes Fox.
Johannes Archer.
Petrus Johnson.
Johannes Pettyt.
Edwardus Peverell.
Thomas Harlsey.
Johannes Lymden.
Thomas Byrche.
Willelmus Edward.
Thomas Chambir.
Willelmus Hardweyne, *Ballivus.*
Thomas Roger.
Robertus Cayme.
Robertus Yonge.
Thomas Rayman.
Johannes Hardgood.
Edwardus Filman.
Jacobus Arnold.
Johannes Clerk.

ANCIENT ROCHESTER, OR DUROBRIVÆ, VIEWED AS THE SITE OF A ROMAN CAMP AND STATION.

BY BEALE POSTE.

THE nature of this subject is such, that in order to supply due illustration to it, it is necessary to refer to the conquest of Britain by the Romans in the years 43 and 44 of the Christian era, and to ascertain what legions and troops were employed in that conquest; and to indicate what numbers those legions bore, as among them we may perhaps find one legion which was connected with forming the original military works at this place.

The first army, commanded by Aulus Plautius, a distinguished Roman senator and general, was, what was termed "double Consular," by which it is known to have consisted of four legions. To these are to be added, according to the customary arrangement of those times, an equal amount of auxiliary troops; and, as each legion was at that date 6,500 strong for its usual establishment, we shall thus find that the whole army must have amounted to about 52,000 men. The numbers of the said Roman legions are well known, and were the SECOND, the NINTH, the FOURTEENTH, and the TWENTIETH, and seem to have been specially appointed as the army which should occupy Britain, since none of them left the kingdom for about a quarter of a century afterwards.

At the end of the first year the issue of the war still remained doubtful; and in the beginning of the second year the Emperor Claudius, leaving his imperial metropolis, came over in person to endeavour to bring the contest to a conclusion: which indeed he effected. About the same time with him arrived also the Eighth legion, which—as we know the dangerous foes the Romans had to contend with in the Germanic nations, they having had three legions cut off in former years, under Varus, in the reign of Augustus—was no doubt extracted from the Continent with difficulty, and after its services in the field, might, for its winter quarters that year, have been stationed from prudential motives in some locality whence it might have advanced further into Britain, or have returned quickly to the Continent, as in either case its destination might have required. This legion, we may understand, formed the reinforcement which Zonaras, the Roman historian, informs us the Emperor Claudius brought over with him.

It may be asked: How do we know that the Eighth legion came over to Britain, since, strictly speaking, it is not mentioned by the Roman historians Dion Cassius, Tacitus, and Suetonius, nor even by the said Zonaras? This may be so; but an ancient Roman inscription, discovered formerly at Turin, and mentioned by Du Choul (p. 157), notices the circumstance, and leaves no doubt of it as a fact. I give it as under:—

C. GAVIO L. F.
STEL. SILVANO.
PRIMIPILARI LEG. VIII. AUG.
TRIBUNO COHOR. II. VIGILUM.
TRIBUNO COH. XIII. URBAN.
TRIBUNO COH. XII. PRÆTOR.
DONIS DONATO A DIVO CLAUD.
BELLO BRITANNICO
TORQUIBUS ARMILLIS PHALERIS
CORONA AUREA
PATRONO COLON.

There is no evidence that the Eighth legion remained

for more than a short time in England,—a few months perhaps. I have mentioned the EIGHTH legion as one which apparently wintered in Britain about this period, and possibly might have been connected with the ancient Roman *castrum hibernum*, or winter camp, at our *Durobrivæ*, or Rochester; but the discovery of inscriptions at this place like that at Turin, or of coins inscribed with the number of the legion, would be necessary to verify the fact, and such it must be admitted have not hitherto come to light.

However, whatever Roman legion may have formed the camp, it is now time to say a few words respecting it.

The city of Rochester then is very evidently laid out and disposed on the lines of an ancient Roman camp—one of that form which was called a *castrum tertiatum*; that is, a camp one-third longer than it was broad. The form is nearly quadrangular, and the four original gates, now long since removed, but the positions of which are still traceable, were placed opposite to each other. Faint traces of the *Via principalis*, anciently one of the most important features in a Roman camp, and invariably of the breadth of a hundred feet, are still to be seen, though of reduced dimensions, besides being built across in medieval times by the constructors of the Bishop's palace. This crossed the present High Street nearly at right-angles, leading from the former South-gate, pulled down in the year 1770, and passed through the site of the episcopal building just spoken of, to the former North-gate, which was called also Cheldegate. The *Via principalis* passed close by the doors of the present cathedral; and on the opposite or western side of this said *Via principalis*, the *Prætorium*, or *Basilica*, of the commander of the garrison, or, in other words, his quarters, would be to be looked for; contiguous to which would have been likewise the *Augurale*, or place of worship for the troops, where also their standards were deposited.

The space occupied by the former Roman circumvallation is twenty-nine acres, which, according to the best writers, ancient and modern, on Roman military affairs, would have been about the extent required for the encampment of a Roman legion, the strength of which was, as before said, in the first century 6,500 men. Numerous Roman coins of various emperors, early and late, have been found in the Castle enclosure, and in the garden plots and other pieces of ground which occupy the ditches which surround it.

The said Castle enclosure is considered to have formed the *Itinerary* station of the place mentioned in the *Itineraries* of Antoninus, under its name *Durobrivæ*, and placed as coming between *Vagniacæ* and *Durolevum* in the course of the road from London to Richborough, Dover, and Lymne. The present lofty castle keep or tower was built by Bishop Gundulph, at the end of the eleventh century; but the walls of the castle enclosure, or double ballium,—for there was anciently a middle wall,—were not constructed till after a considerable interval. In other words, Mr. King, in his 'Observations on Ancient Castles,' considers all balliums to Norman keeps to be of about the date of Edward I.

The Roman ramparts of the ancient town, city, or camp, including those of the station just spoken of, were without doubt earthen, and are rather to be supposed to have continued so through Saxon, Danish, and early Norman times, till, according to the historical accounts of the place, Henry III., in the year 1225, surrounded the city with a wall. There are no remains of Roman walls of masonry round the whole circuit of the place. Indeed I may here observe, that the entire absence of Roman foundations of every kind, both in the Castle enclosure and in every other part of the city, is very remarkable.

Henry III.'s walls of Rochester have one very remarkable peculiarity, that of being built on arches, as may be seen in the portion of them in the gardens near the end of Crow Lane, and in every other place where the earth has been removed to a sufficient depth. The walls of Lynn and Norwich are built in the same way, as also those of the Castle of Northampton. No cause can be assigned for this style of building,—certainly no good architectural reason. The walls of the Castle enclosure are no exceptions to those of the rest of the city, save only on the side towards the river, and are built on these arches; as can be seen opposite the cathedral. They were all then built at the same time, city walls and Castle-enclosure walls, as seems a very fair conclusion to form.

It is recorded, that the monks of St. Andrew's Priory obtained permission to alter a part of the line of the city walls in the year 1290, in the reign of Edward I. Which they did, and enclosed a piece of ground, of irregular shape, on the south side of the city, opposite the cathedral. But the original course of Henry III.'s wall and ditch is still plain enough to be seen in the garden of the Deanery. This wall, now removed, was built no doubt on the precise line of the Roman rampart, extending in a straight line to the Prior's Gate, and to the spot a little beyond, where the former South-gate stood, whence there is every reason to believe it went direct towards the river; though the ground has been so altered in that part that now no traces of it remain. The Roman rampart, in fact, with its ditch in front, may be considered, in this part of its transit, to have passed in a line parallel with the south wall of Gundulph's tower, or otherwise keep, and at a distance of about forty or forty-five yards from it.

The Prior's Gate seems to have been altered into a more ecclesiastical form than an Anglo-Norman city gate about the year 1330, or at some period between the Barons' Wars and the Wars of the Roses, which promised peace and security.

There may be a good reason assigned why Henry III.'s walls followed so closely the line of the Roman ramparts. In the first place the space they enclosed, twenty-nine acres, would apparently have contained all that was required for the site of an Anglo-Norman city of the thirteenth century; and secondly, the ramparts afforded firm ground to build the wall upon; and as the ditches with which the Roman ramparts were flanked were twenty-four feet wide and twelve deep, this might supply sufficient reason for not deviating from them unless some special cause required. The Anglo-Norman fortifiers enlarged these ditches, thus made ready to their hands, exceedingly. The eastern ditch in the gardens at the side of Crow Lane cannot be less than about eighty-five feet wide; and originally about twenty feet deep. Much of the earth, I may add, was probably carted down to the marshes, to make firm ground at the spot called the Common, and at other places.

There are appearances that the eastern wall had formerly been strengthened by a large square tower, from the cavities for fixing the floor-beams being still remaining in the wall. If so, nothing is now left of it. It adjoins the spot where the extension of the eastern wall by the monks began. These ecclesiastics, in prolonging their wall, threw a somewhat wide arch of construction over the former Romano-medieval ditch, crossing at right-angles at this place; the span of which was filled up with masonry. The foundations of the former wall in the Dean's garden before alluded to, according to information from a person accustomed to work there, are often struck against by the pickaxe and the spade in the usual cultivation of the soil.

Some foundations of walls were met with many years since, running diagonally across the Vines for some distance towards the south-west; but as there is nothing to induce a supposition that they were of the solid nature of city walls, and as they were not skirted by a ditch, so, they can only be regarded as remnants of strongly constructed enclosures for gardens, or for other purposes.

However, though the medieval architects of Henry III.'s wall showed their attachment to the Roman ramparts and were unwilling to leave them, yet they were obliged to make a decided *détour* in the south-west part of their circumvallations by an incidental circumstance, which was this. The Danes, arriving in great force, made a most vigorous though unsuccessful attack, in the year 884, on the ramparts and fortifications existing at that time in this quarter. Their proceedings are recorded in a somewhat brief form in the Saxon and other ancient chronicles, including also Asser's Life of Alfred. The chief feature in their attempts appears to have been, that they threw up immense mounds of earth to endeavour to overtop the works of the besieged, and by their superior advantages of position thus acquired, to drive them away from their defences by their missiles. When the siege was over, the mounds remained, and indeed even now remain. They seem in Gundulph's time to have supplied a reason for the position of his lofty tower, placed at the angle of the ballium, and intended to command them in its turn. These earthworks, then, of the Danes, now known as Boley Hill, had altered the features of the city in this part for attack and defence, and Henry III.'s medieval fortifiers of the city, not thinking Gundulph's tower a sufficient counteraction, enclosed them with a strong wall joining on to their other newly constructed walls at the South-gate, and thus made them a species of outwork to the castle and to the city. They seem to have been much lowered in modern times, particularly towards the Castle. The ancient boundary wall of this addition appears to have been met with, some years since, in digging the foundations of the Rev. Mr. Conway's house. It is described as standing parallel to the present brick walls, and as two feet within them. It is not impossible that this outwork might have been strengthened, like the city wall, with towers, but this point has not been hitherto ascertained.

The extent, limits, and direction of the whole of the south wall have been topics somewhat disregarded, and till quite of late years fallen much into oblivion among the inhabitants of this ancient city. Indeed it had been removed in places with great assiduity, and the ditch very completely filled up. Add to which, only the most vague accounts of its former course existed. With respect to the side of the city next the river, the discovery of authentic traces of the west wall and its gateway, excepting one short length of the former, has not yet been made.

References to the Plan of Rochester Walls.

AA. Line of original wall.
BB. Part added by the Ecclesiastics.
CC. Line of part of Roman rampart.
DD. Probable line of west wall.
E. The Castle.
F. The Keep.
G. Interior wall, removed.
H. The Barbican, now removed.
I. Southgate.
J. Northgate.
K. Prior's Gate.
L. Eastgate.
M. Square tower, removed.
N. The Cathedral.
O. The Bishop's Palace.
P. The Deanery.
Q. St. Clement's Church.
R. Boley Hill.
S. Remains of the city ditch.
T. Tower, with a shaft to the river.
U. Fisherman's cottage.
V. Castle ditch.
W. Probable continuation of city ditch.

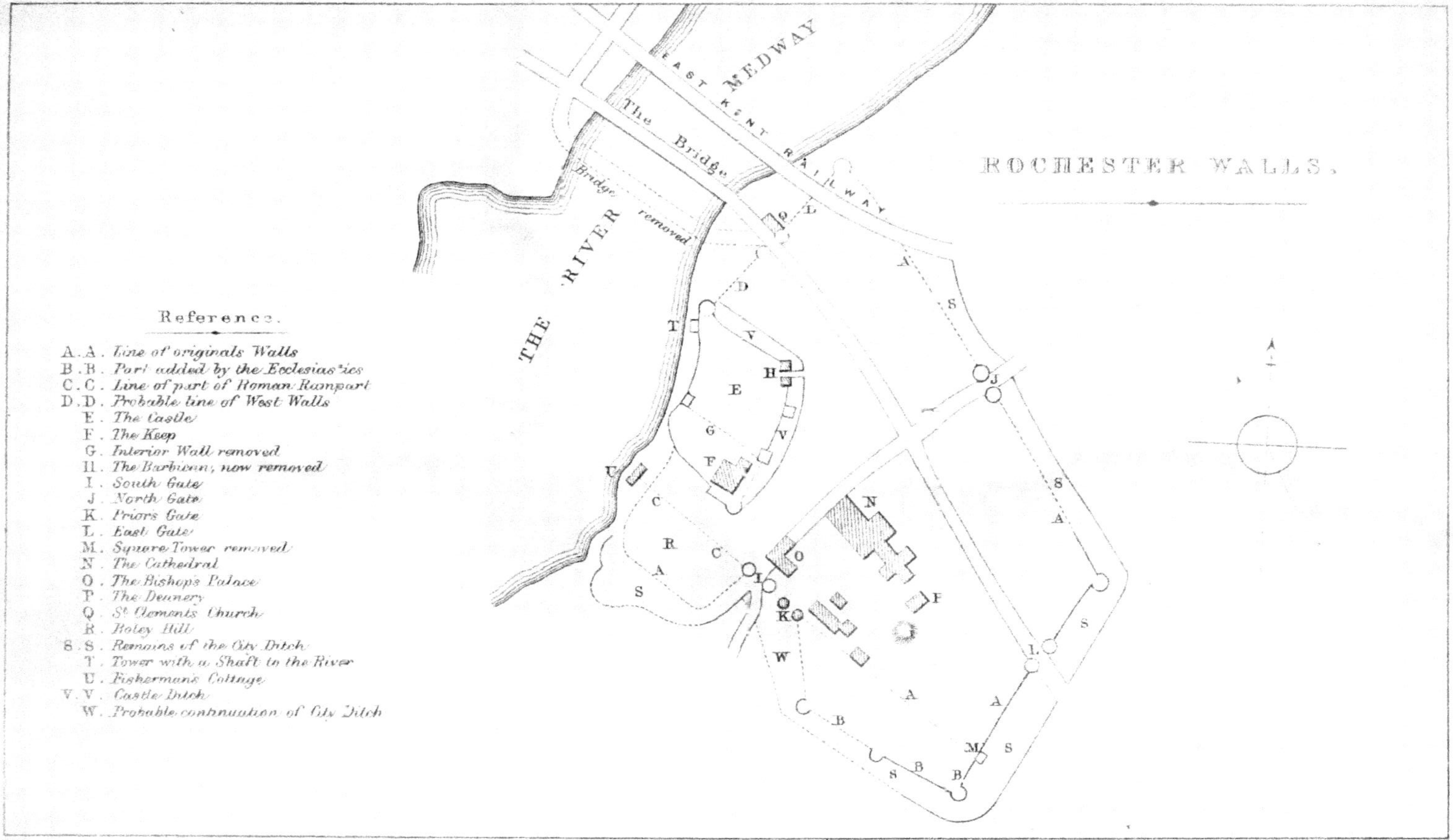

B. Poste del. J.R.Jobbins

ROCHESTER RECORDS.

BY ROBERT WILLIS BLENCOWE, ESQ.

By the kind courtesy of the Mayor and Corporation of Rochester,[1] in freely laying open their Records to our investigation, when we held our annual meeting in their ancient city, we are enabled to present our readers with transcripts of two very interesting and valuable documents, viz. the ancient Custumal of the city, temp. Edw. IV.,[2] and an account of the expenditure of the Corporation during two years' mayoralty of Richard Harlowe in 1578–9 and 1579–80, the earliest memorial of that nature among their Records.

Both these documents are full of indications of the position which Rochester occupied as the great thoroughfare between England and the continent, and the consequent necessity of stringent laws for facilitating and regulating the traffic.

In the latter of these records will be found many very curious entries, relating to the visits of grandees and high officials, when, in their passage through the city, they were received by the Corporation and treated

[1] We gladly take this opportunity of specially thanking J. Lewis, Esq., the late Town Clerk of Rochester, and R. Prall, Jun., Esq., the present Town Clerk, for the assiduous attention and great facilities which they have rendered us, in carrying out the permission of search so kindly accorded us by the Corporation.

[2] Since these lines were in type we find that the length of the Custumal precludes us from printing it in our present volume without great curtailment. We prefer therefore giving it in its entirety in our third volume, and limit ourselves at present to the accounts of the year 1578–9.

with civic hospitality. Thus we have items for wine and apples and lambs, etc., as given to my Lord of Huntingdon, and my Lord Cheney, and my Lord Deputy of Ireland, at a costly price, considering the value of money in those days.

When Duke Casimir, son of the Elector Palatine, came to England, to try his chance with many others for the great matrimonial prize, the hand of Queen Elizabeth, he seems to have caused some trouble and no small expense to the loyal citizens of Rochester, as the entries relating to his reception and entertainment in these accounts bear ample testimony.

It will be seen, too, by this document, that the assizes were occasionally held at Rochester, and that it was clearly high time that the Court House there should be put in sufficient repair to receive the Judges, and for the trial of the prisoners. And there is a curious charge of 3*s.* for the erection of the gallows, that great engine of punishment, which in those days, called by some "the good old days," groaned under the weight of its wretched victims.

Some of the items in this account are of peculiar interest, as evidencing the troubled and anxious condition of public affairs in England, and the plots that were formed against the life of the great Protestant Queen; such as the entries of sums paid to pursuivants for bringing down proclamations against the dispersing of seditious books,—against the flying of rebels out of the realm,—those relating to parties prosecuted for speaking words against the Queen's majesty, etc.

The entry respecting the probate of Mr. Watts's Will, will be read with considerable interest by our friends at Rochester. The tradition is still current, that Queen Elizabeth, in one of her progresses, spent four or five days at the Crown Inn, Rochester, from whence she removed to Mr. Watts's house on Boley Hill; upon leaving which she gave it the name of "Satis," to intimate her perfect satisfaction with the reception he had given her. Without pausing to inquire into the authenticity of this tradition, we may well pass on to remind our Rochester readers that this Will, whose probate is here recorded, was that containing the well-known munificent bequest of alms-houses by Richard Watts, which still render nightly service to the houseless poor wayfarer. He died 10th September, 1579. His will was dated September 10th, and proved September 25th, in the same year.

The entry relating to the "Banckite given by Mr. More at his decease" seems to require a passing notice. It was a common practice in those days for a testator to direct by Will what hospitalities should be exercised at his own funeral. They were often upon a very large scale, and there was much drunken revelry. Ralph Guy, a yeoman of Yorkshire,[1] in his Will dated 1550, directs that, for his funeral expenses, there shall be 7 sheep killed; xv^s was left for bread; vij^s for 4 gallons of ale; for 3 score gallons of beere, iv^s; for spice and honey, ii^s-$iiij^d$; for a quarter of wheat, $viij^s$-vj^d; a dozen of capons, vj^s; 4 pigs, x^s; and $viij^s$-$iiij^d$ was to be distributed at the church door. And another yeoman, Launcelot Gale, a few years later, directed that all his friends and neighbours who should offer within one day of his burial should have a dinner at his house, and that his body should remain unburied one day and one night, if God would permit it, to give time for them to be gathered together.

Another series of charges, viz. those relating to the expedition to London to answer Martin Coatis's suit before the Lord Chief Baron, suggest a lively picture for the imagination. We may well fancy the mayor and his brother aldermen mounted on their horses in the

[1] See Richmondshire Wills, published by the Surtees Society, p. 70.

early morn, making their way to Gravesend; "their coats, gowns, and cloaks," as Harrison describes the attire of that day, "of brown, blue, or purple, with some pretty furniture of velvet or fur, or a doublet of old tawney, or black velvet, or other comely silk." They reach Gravesend in somewhat sorry plight from the miriness of the road, but the "ostiler" soon scrapes the mud from their begrimed boots, and enables them to repair on board the tilt boat in trimmed attire, suited to their dignity. Arrived in London, we may picture to ourselves the inn to which they would resort. The archway, the large courtyard, the galleries, one above the other, on which the chambers opened, and the horses stabled underneath; each chamber containing many beds, and each bed probably more than one occupant; and the common room, where they supped, crowded perhaps with guests of all degrees. One item there is, the payment to the servants of the Lord Chief Baron, indicative of a private visit to the judge, and of evil omen to Mr. Martin Coatis, as to the result of the suit with the Corporation of Rochester, which brought them up to London.

But it is time that we admit our readers to the inspection of the accounts themselves, transcribed verbatim from the originals, as follows:[1]—

A note of all suche somes of money as have bine disbursed by me RICHARD HARLOWE, *maior of the Cittie of* ROCHESTER, *for the use of the saiede Cittie, anno domini* 1578, *as followeth :—*

Item, p^{d} to CHRISTOFER ANDROWES, for his paynes about the buttes[2] . . . . v^{li}

Imprimis, geven to my LORDE STRANGE his players . vj^{s}-viij^{d}

Item, to a Pursevaunt y^{t} broughte downe the proclamacions for ye prises of wine . . . . iij^{s}-iiij^{d}

[1] We confine ourselves to the disbursements. There is a single page of receipts; none of them, however, worth noting.

[2] ? "butter,"—the last letter is hopelessly blotted.

Item, spent upon the laste undershriffe, as touching matters for the Cittie . . . . ij^s

Item, for Timber and Ironwoorke for the bere belonging to St. Nicholas Churche, and for the makeinge of the said bere and Iron bowlts . . . . . . vj^s-viij^d

Item, for xxviij^{te} foote of Oken timber, for two Susters for the Stayers belonginge to the Towne Keaye and for a plancke for the foote . . . . vij^s-vj^d

Item, for iiij litter loads of Chaulke for the filling of the towne keaye, at iiij^s ye loade . . . . xvj^s

Item, for one litter loade of gravell for the paveinge of the same keaye . . . . v^s

Item, payed to John Nicolles, for makeinge and mendinge up of the Seller doore, where Mr. Sackeford's butter laye, and for a newe ride and naylles for the same . . . . ij^s

Item, for makeinge cleane of the Seller and for Sande vj^d

Item, payed to vj men for bringinge up of iiij score and ode barrells of Butter . . . . iij^s

Item, for a lincke ye same time . . . . iiij^d

Item, for wine and apples geven to my Lorde of Huntington, and my Lo: Cheney . . . . ij^s

Item, for wine and apples geven to my lorde deputie of Ierland . . . . iij^s

Item, for ij lambes geven to the saied Lorde deputie xiij^s

Item, for ij lambes geven to ducke Cassimere . . . . ix^s

Item, for one gallon of Sacke, and for v gallons of gascoyne wine geven to him . . . . x^s-iiij^d

Item, for appells geven to ye saied Ducke . . . . xij^d

Item, for a horsse hier for one of Bowles Searvants to ryde to Gravesende to bringe woorde when ducke Cassimerus shulde come . . . . xij^d

Item, for a horsshier for Wards mane to Gillinghame to geyte Oysters for ye ducke . . . . xij^d

Item, payed for halfe a Boushell and one gallon of oysters geven to the saied Ducke Cassimerus . . viij^d

Item, for ij Lambes geven to my Lorde of A Burgavenney . . . . ix^s

Item, for a horsse hier for Springfilde to carrye the saied Lambes my Lorde . . . . xij^d

Item, for ij Lambes geven to Mr. Justice Southcote . viij^s

Item, for fetching of the saied lambes at Di . . . s of Clife . . . . viij^d

Item, p^d for a hoshier for Edwarde Barker, to carrye those lambes to Gravesende . . . . viij^d

Item, p^d for apples and wine at the assembly of the Justices here at Rochester for the queenes majestes affayers . . . . vj^s

Item, for wine, breed, and bere geven unto my Lorde Cheffe baron . . . . ij^s

Item, for wine geven to Sr WILLIAM WINTER and Mr HOULDESTOCKE, at the same time y^t they graunted there goodwill for the Saylles for the assice howse xx^d

Item, for wine geven to Mr COPPINGER uppon a courte daye, when he dined at my howsse, viz. j pottell of Sacke, j gallon of gaskine wine, and halfe a pownde of sugar . . . . iij^s-vj^d

Charges bestowed uppon the ascehowse.

Imprimis, for lathes . . . . vj^d

Item, for Prigge and Trashe[1] . . . . ij^s-ij^d

Item, p^d to Thomas Sabine and his fellowe, for j dayes worke for to sawe rafters for the same howse . . ij^s

Item, for v Bushells of Lyme . . . . ij^s-j^d

Item, payd to George Ridsdale and his mane for mending ye same howse . . . . xvj^d

Item, for a boushell of heire . . . . iij^d

Item, for dim hundred of ij^s naylles . . . . xij^d

Item, for dim hundred of vj^d naylles . . . . iij^d

Item, for iij dayes worke to John Nicholles . . . iij^s

Item, p^d to Bartholmewe Roffe for iij dayes labour there . . . . xvj^d

Item, for a pece of ockeine timber to make the rafters xvj^d

Item, for slyttinge of a pece of timber for the saiede rafters . . . . iij^d

Item, to John Nicholles, for setting up of the gallowes xij^d

Item, for vj boundells of roushes . . . . xij^d

Item, for j C of iiij^d nayele . . . . iiij^d

Item, for xxvj^ti ij^s nayls . . . . vj^d

Item, for Shrimpes for ye Judges . . . . ij^s-vj^d

[1] Small nails and brads.

Item, for j dosser[1] of ffishe and for ye carringe of it to ye Judges . . . . x^s^

Item, for ij Bousshelles of oysters . . . . xx^d^

Item, for ij gallons of gaskine wine and one pottell of Sacke . . . . iiij^s^-iiij^d^

Item, payed for the fetchinge and caringe of the Sayles to the howse . . . . ij^s^-vj^d^

Item, payede to those y^t^ helped to cover ye howse wth the Sayles and to take theme downe for vitells at Stansales . . . . vj^s^-viij^d^

Item, p^d^ to William Rawlinge and Hughe Arudell for kepeing and layeinge of ye cousshings in the sice howse . . . . ij^s^

Item, payed to Nichollas White for ceartayne paynteing done by hime aboute the assice howse . . . xv^s^

Item, p^d^ for dim C of Elme boarde for to boarde up the hole in the assichowse . . . . ij^s^-iiij^d^

Item, p^d^ to Edward Barcker, for iiij C of Osterye ffaggotts at iiij^s^ the C, the wch weare geven to poore of the parishe . . . . xvj^s^

Item, p^d^ to Thomas Corke of Maydstone, pavior, for xiij Loods of Stones delivered at Mayedstone at the watterside there . . . . xvij^s^-iiij^d^

Item, p^d^ for the carraidge of ye same stones from Maydstone by watter to the Towne Keaye . . . viij^s^

Item, p^d^ for the certificate into the Chauncery, for eateing of fleshe in the Lente season . . . . . ij^s^

Item, p^d^ to Thomas Ffoule, masone, for ij dayes worke upon ye towne Keaye . . . . ij^s^-iiij^d^

Item, p^d^ to Thomas Waller, for iij ringells (? cingells) and iij Thimbles of iorne, wayeing xlviij^lb^, at ij^d^ of the pownde . . . . x^s^

Item, payed for a newe lande towe layeinge and for Timber . . . . ij^s^

Item, payed to Thomas Cooke ye Pavior for the Paveinge of 100 yards of paveing at the towne Keaye xx^s^-x^d^

Item, paied for one gooeinge up to London to put the certificate of the rate of Servant's wadges, and for his chardges ye same time . . . . v^s^

[1] dosser, 'a basket.'—*Halliwell.*

Item, payed to ye Poursivante for bringing the proclamacions for caringe of goñes and Longe Dudges[1] . ij^s^-vj^d^
Item, payed to Johne Pendellton for his chardges to to the Courte at Richemounte, w^t^ letters to the counsell there, for certayne woords, the which one Randalle Worsleye spake in Mr Edmunds howse againste the Queens Maigestie . . (ij^s^-vj^d^) . . x^s^
Item, paied for a newe markite bousshell and for the bindinge of the same . . . . v^s^
Item, paiede for the Queens Maigesties ffee farme, due unto her at the feaste of St Michaell tharchangell, anno domini , and in the xx yeare of her maigesties Raigne . . . . xiiij^li^
Item, paiede to the Poursivante for the bringeinge downe of ye proclamacions for the prisces of wines ij^s^-vj^d^
Item, payed to a Poursivante for the bringeinge downe of ye proclamacions for concealed lands . . . . ij^s^-vj^d^
Item, p^d^ to the Poursivante for the bringeinge downe of ye proclamaciones for the ffree libertie of wines for to be brought into this Realme . . . . . . ij^s^-vj^d^
Item, payed to a Poursivante for the bringeinge downe of the write and the Proclamacions for the gooeinge over of Woolles . . . . ij^s^-vj^d^

A note of suche Vittells as was expended at the Admirall Courte holden at Shiernas for the Cittie of Rochester, the xvj^th^ *daye of June, anno domini* 1579, *as hereafter followeth :—*

Item, payed for Beefe, boylled and rosted . . . . viij^s^-ix^d^
Item, payed for one lambe, backed and rosted . . . v^s^
Item, for Veale, backed and rostede . . . . iij^s^-vj^d^
Item, for Rabetts, backed . . . . xviij^d^
Item, payed for Courrants and Prevens . . . . . . vj^d^
Item, for Pepper to backe this meate . . . . ix^d^
Item, payed for ij^lb^ of Butter . . . . vj^d^
Item, payed for fflower . . . . xij^d^
Item, for a gammon of Backecon . . . . ij^s^
Item, for v doss of Breade . . . . v^s^
Item, for one killderkine of beere, being halfe stronge and halfe smale . . . . iij^s^

[1] Barrells.—*Halliwell.*

Item, p^d of one Pine of smalebeere . . . . vj^d
Item, payed for Wine . . . . ix^s
Item, payed for Vinier & Saulte . . . . ij^d
Item, payed for Svegar . . . . ij^s
Item, geven to the mariners for there paynes in roweinge of us downe to the Nasse and up agayne, and for ower drinckeinge at o^r comeinge to lande . . vj^s

Sm^a inde, xlix^s-ij^d

Item, payed for the dynner of the admirall courte holden by me, Richarde Harlowe, major of the Cittie of Rochester, for the saied Cittie, at HAWCKEWOODE. The xvj^th daye of October, anno 1578, as by the Recordes of the sayed courte dothe apper . vi^s
Item, p^d to the Pursivante for the bringinge downe of the proclamacions for appaerell, ssvardes, and longe rouffes . . . . ij^s-vj^d
Item, for a gallon of wine geven to Master Doctor Lewen at the probate of Mr WATTES his will of Bollyhill . . . . ij^s
Item, payed to Mr Fraunces Hille, for his paynes in goeinge up to London aboute the saied will of Mr Watts . . . . xiij^s-iiij^d
Item, payed the xxvj^th of November, a^o 1579, ffor the affirers dynner for affireing of the Lawedaye holden the Michaellmas before . . . . iiij^s
Item, payed for wine geven to my Lorde cheffe baron at his beinge at Rochester in the lente, comeinge frome his sircute . . . . iiij^s-viij^d
Item, payede to Richarde Claye for wine geven to my Lorde chefe barone at his going from Caunterburye to London . . . . ij^s-vj^d
Item, payede to the Exchetters bayelie, for bringeing of a parantarie daye for us to apper before the saied exchetor at Depforde . . . . ij^s-vj^d
Item, payed to Mr Wurdgers mane for writinge of ye coppie of Mr Watts will . . . . v^s
Item, payed for the Banckite geven by Mr More at his decease, expended at ye Signe of the White Harte at Rochester, being more then ye saiede Mr Moore allowed . . . . vij^s
Item, payed to a Poursivante for bringing downe of

proclamacions againste the disspersinge of sedicius boks . . . . ij^{s}-vj^{d}
Item, paiede to a Poursivante for the bringeinge downe of a proclamacion against the fflyinge of Reabells out of the Realme . . . . ij^{s}-vj^{d}

Monney layede owte by me, Richarde Harlowe, major of ye Cittie of Rochester, for the use of the saied Cittie, anno domini 1580.

Item, payed for the Certificate of the Eeating of ffleshe made by the saied Maior in to the Chancery for ye Lente . . . . ij^{s}
Item, payed to the Poursivante for the Bringeinge downe of the proclamacions for bredinge and increasse of horsses . . . . ij^{s}-vj^{d}
Item, geven to James Harrison for the caring of ij Salmons to my LORDE COBHAME'S . . . . xij^{d}
Item, paiede to Pendellton for his chardges to my LORDE OF ABURGAVENNEY'S in Sussex . . . . . ij^{s}
Item, paiede to those men, the wch caried the mariner to the assices, the wch mariner spake wordes agaynste the queen's ma^{ti} . . . . ij^{s}
Item, p^{d} for ye ffeefarme of ye Cittie this yere . . . . xiiij^{li}

Monney expended the iiijth *of Januairii, anno domini* 1579, *at the gooeing up of me,* RICHARDE HARLOWE, *maior, to London, and others of my Bretheren, to answer my Lord Chefebarone and others uppon a sute made to the saiede Lorde Chefe Baron by Martine Coatis.*

Item, ffor horshiers to Gravesende . . . . iiij^{s}-viij^{d}
Item, geven to the poore of White ditche . . . . . iiij^{d}
Item, geven to the ostiler at Gravesend for makeinge cleane of o^{r} bouttes . . . . vj^{d}
Item, for o^{r} Breakefaste there . . . . v^{s}
Item, for a tilte boote up to London . . . . iiij^{s}
Item, for a wherie thoroughe the bridge to the blacke-friers . . . . iiij^{d}
Item, paied for o^{r} Supper y^{t} nighte . . . . vij^{s}-x^{d}
Item, geven to my Lorde chefe barone his Butler and Portter . . . . iij^{s}
Item, for o^{r} Brekefaste uppon Tewsdaye . . . . . . ij^{s}

Item, for o^r^ dynner the same daye . . . . vij^s^-iij^d^
Item, for ower beddes and other necessaries, and to to the maiedes of the Inne . . . . ij^s^-viij^d^
Item, for our bote hier to Gravesende . . . . . iij^s^
Item, paied for Mr Maplesden his horse meate at Gravesend, and to the ostiler . . . . xij^d^
Item, for v horshiers for us to Rochester . . . . iij^s^-iiij^d^

Summa inde, xliiij^s^-xj^d^

A note of the expences of Vittels ye wch was expended at the Admirall Courte holden at Shiernas the of June, a^o^ domini 1580, by me, Richarde Harlowe, maior of the cittie of Rochester, for ye saied Cittie.

Imprimis, paiede for j lambe, bought of William Wilkinsonne . . . . v^s^
Item, p^d^ for dim Lambe, boughte in ye markit . . . xx^d^
Item, p^d^ to William Wilkinsonne for xij stone of Beefe at xij^d^ the stone, ye whiche was boylled and rosted . . . . xij^s^
Item, p^d^ Walter Powlter for one Loyne, one Shoulder, and a breste of Veale . . . . ij^s^-vj^d^
Item, for ij Pigges . . . . xx^d^
Item, for fflower and boutter to backe ye lambe . . xij^d^
Item, for courrants, pepper, and prevenes . . . . viij^d^
Item, for mousterde, viniger, and saulte . . . . . iiij^d^
Item, to Thom^a^s the baker for v doss of breed . . . v^s^
Item, paied for xiij quartts of gaskine wine . . . . vj^s^-vj^d^
Item, paied to Barker for a bottell of Sacke of v quartts ij^s^-vj^d^
Item, paied for a gallon of Sacke fechte at Queenborowe ij^s^
Item, paied to the mariners wch rowed in ij Pinsces downe to ye Nasse and up againe . . . . iiij^s^
Item, for a Samone, expended the same time at Shiernasse . . . . vj^s^
Item, paied to John Boutler for ij horse hiers to Canterburye ye same time that my Lorde Cheffe baron sente for ceartyne Presoners to come before hime, in the behalfe of the Queens Magestie to Canterburie v^s^
Item, p^d^ to Willcox the same time for the hier of ij horsses to Canterburie for those men . . . . . . v^s^
Item, payed for ij horse hiers to Birlinge for my selfe

and Springefild ye same time yt my LORDE OF ABURGAVENNEY sente for me and certayne other Alldermen to come to . at wch time he . alleged yt he hade wronge for yt he hade not the placeinge of the under stuarde of this Cyttie . . . . ijs
Item, pd to Thoms Watters ye same time yt he carried Becher and another younge mane to the conssell at the counselle's Comaundmẽte . . . . xs
Item, geven to Ussher and his men for takeinge up of a Samon upon the stadells, the wch Samon was geven to my LORDE COBHAME . . . . iijs-iiijd
Item, pd to my LORDE COBHAM his keper when he broughte us halfe a boucke at the same time to be merie wt . . . . iijs-iiijd
Item, payed for the affirers dinner at the affiringe of the lawedaye . . . . iiijs
Item, payed for a Courte dinner the 4 Julye, 1580 . vjs-viijd
Sma, lxli-iijs-vd

Then, in a different hand,—

Item, payed to Mr Wallis and others, aboute the probate of Mr. Watts's will of Bullyhill . . . . . . xxs-xd
Item, more Mr. Harlowe askethe allowance for his dyett for ij yeres . . . . xviijli
Sum Totall, iijxxjli-iiijs-iijd
Soe the hole expences and allowances is . . . iijxxxixli-iiijs-iijd
Whereof Mr HARLOWE hathe R . . . . lxvjli-iis-vd
Soe there is dewe unto Mr Harlowe by the citie . . xiijli-js-xd
More he askethe allowance for a dinner at the electinge of Mr HAULLE maior . . . . xijs-iijd
Soe his hole dewe to R is . . . . xiijli-xiiijs-jd
More Mr HARLOWE askethe allowance for xxxli of leade, at jd the pownde . . . . iijs-jd ob.
So that now the hole dewe to Mr HARLOWE owinge is . . . . xiijli-xvijs-ijd ob.

THE DUMB BORSHOLDER OF CHART, IN THE PARISH OF WATERINGBURY.

BY THE REV. HENRY STEVENS, VICAR OF WATERINGBURY.

MANY of the readers of the 'Archæologia Cantiana' may remember to have seen, among the curiosities and antiquities exhibited in the museum formed at the Deanery, Rochester, a somewhat cumbrous-looking club, with an iron spike at one end and an iron ring at the other, of which we furnish an engraving from a photograph drawing by our Honorary Photographer, Mr. Cruttenden. This is the Dumb Borsholder of Chart, whose history is here given, so far as it can be ascertained. The most authentic portion of that history is perhaps the "Extract from the Court Rolls of the Manor of Chart, in Wateringbury," for which thanks are due to our Secretary.

It would seem that a tything freeburgh, or decennary, originally consisted of ten freemen householders, who were answerable to the King for each other's good behaviour. Each tything formed a little state or commonwealth within itself, and chose its own dean or head, who was sometimes called the alderman of such a tything on account of his age and experience. Most commonly however he was called the borsholder, from the Saxon word *borh*, a 'surety,' and *alder*, a 'head' or 'chief.' The members of each tything, with their borsholder at their head, formed a court of justice, in which all the matters of dispute within the tything were heard

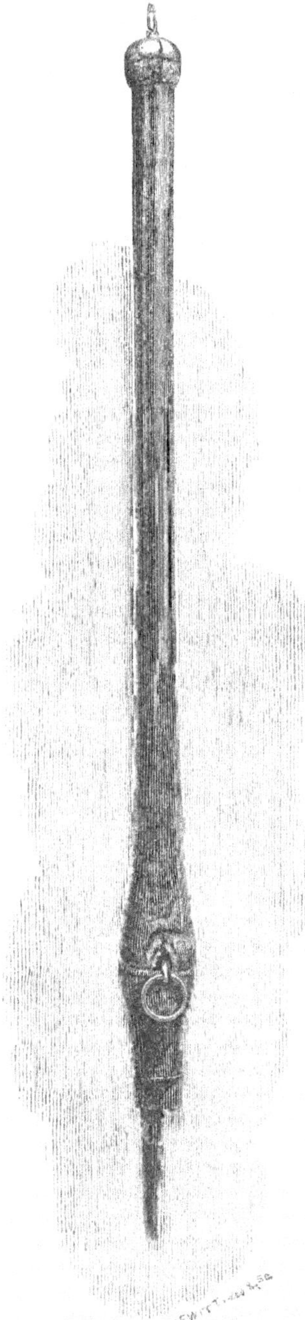

and determined. Thus much for the term borsholder.

In 4 Edw. II., A.D. 1310, Henry de Leybourne obtained a charter for a market in his manor of Wateringbury, to be held on every Tuesday; and a three days' fair on the vigil, feast, and morrow of St. John the Baptist (to whom the church is dedicated), *i.e.* on 23rd, 24th, and 25th of June; and free-warren in his demesne lands of his manors of Wateringbury and Chart (Rot. Cart. 4 Edw. II. No. 42). But it is probable that this market was never of any great account, in consequence of the vicinity of those more noted markets then in being, viz. Tunbridge, Malling, and Maidstone. Nor are we informed how long this market continued in force, or in what part of the parish it was held.

Come we now to our main subject of investigation. Pizein Well is a hamlet within the manor of Chart, in this parish. The "Dumb Borsholder of Chart," as he was called, formerly claimed a separate and exclusive jurisdiction over the inhabitants of that Liberty, which originally consisted of only twelve houses. This Dumb

Borsholder was always first called at the Court Leet holden for the hundred of Twyford; when his keeper (who was yearly appointed by this Court) held him up to his call, with a neckcloth or handkerchief put through the iron rings fixed in his top, and answered for him. This ancient custom has now been discontinued one hundred and four years, and the Borsholder put in by the Quarter Sessions for Wateringbury claims jurisdiction over the entire parish, including the liberty of Chart.

The Dumb Borsholder of Chart is a staff of wood, that by age has become perfectly black; it is three feet and half an inch long, and has an iron ring on the bottom. It once had four more by the sides near the top; three of these however are now wanting, though the marks remain where they were inserted. The circumference is greater at some places than at others, and it has a square iron spike fixed in the top, four and a half inches long, which perhaps was used to break a door open upon occasion, which was done without a warrant from a justice of the peace, when it was suspected that persons or things were unlawfully concealed in any of those twelve houses above mentioned.

As to the precise antiquity of this Dumb Borsholder of Chart it is not easy to determine, but we may with great probability take it as the type of the original staves borne by constables in early times.

The last person who acted as deputy for the Dumb Borsholder was Thomas Clampard, Blacksmith, who died in 1748. The following is the inscription on his tomb:—

> "My sledge and anvil I've declined;
> My bellows, too, have lost their wind;
> My fire 's extinct, my forge decayed,
> And in the dust my vice is laid;
> My coals are spent, my iron's gone,
> My nails are drove, my work is done."

We will close this short history with an extract from

the Court Rolls of the Manor of Chart, in Wateringbury. At—

"The Court Baron of Sir Roger Twysden, Knight and Barronett, holden there on Tuesdaie the twentieth daie of May, in the yeare of our Lord God 1657,"

among other returns from the Homage is the following:

"Item—they presente that within this mannor there is a custome, which is that the tennants belonging to this mannor have a staffe, which is the bosholder, and is called a dumbe bosholder, and that anie man liveing within this libertie, which are only twelve howses, may with the same staffe search within this precinct, and that this bosholder evrye yeare is carried to Yalding, to the Hundred Court, and there is called the ffirst of all the bosholders, and there does his service as a bosholder; and that whosoever of the Twelve carry him thether, eleaven howses paie a penny a piece to him that carried it, and that evrie one of the twelve take their turne for carrying of it.

"Affirors all the homage,

"*Examinatum per Senescallum ibidem,*

"THOM. TOMLYN."

NOTES FROM THE PAROCHIAL REGISTER OF ORLESTONE.

BY W. I. LIGHTFOOT, ESQ.

Index to the Register of Baptisms.

Abraham [Abram, 1574], 1641, 1643, [Abram, 1663, 1666, 1668.]
Allen, 1572, 1573 (2)*, 1575, [Allyn, 1577, 1580, 1582, 1585,] 1599, 1601, 1603.
Arnole, 1609 (2).
Ase, 1605, 1606.
Ashenden, 1668.
Avery, 1729, 1732, 1735, 1741.
Awstyn, 1578.
Baldwin, 1618, 1621, 1622, 1624.
Barber, 1613, 1614, 1617, 1620.
Barry, 1629.
Bayley, 1726.
Bene, 1764.
Birshel, 1643 (2).
Blasket, 1764.
Boulden, 1638, 1639, 1641.
Bowar, 1588.
Brett, 1623, 1668, 1670.
Brekenburye, 1575.
Bridger, 1626, 1627, 1629, 1630, 1631, 1632.
Brockenburye, 1596, 1598, [Brockenburye, 1599.]
Buckle, 1713.
Burtt, 1602, 1603.
Butcher, 1762.
Byshop, 1708.
Chaffinch, 1692, 1693 (2), 1697, [Caffinch, 1701.]
Chapman, 1736, 1739, 1741, 1742.
Chittenden, 1730.
Clark, 1747.
Cobb [Cobbe, 1735, 1737], 1740, [Cobbe, 1742,] [Cob, 1746,] 1747, 1749, 1758, [Cobbe, 1761, 1763.]
Colebrane, 1639.
Colebrone, 1614.
Coleburne, 1616.
Collins, [Collyns, 1570, 1576, 1599], 1717, 1720, 1722, 1724, 1731, 1734.
Comber, 1703.
Constick, 1746.

* (2) denotes that there are two baptisms of the name recorded in that year.

Cooper, 1578.
Coorlyng, 1573, 1579.
Crosson, 1597.
Cruchman, 1579 (2).
Cumber, 1719, [Comber, 1703.]
Culling, 1623.
Curling [Curlyng, 1568], 1571, 1665.
Dale, 1627, 1629.
Daniel, 1655, 1659, 1662, 1665, 1692.
Dastyn [Dasten, 1592], 1595, 1597, 1603, 1607.
Denton, 1579.
Derby, 1743.
Diprose, 1744.
Doo, 1580, 1583, [Dowe, 1586,] [Doe, 1590, 1593, 1595.]
Dorman, 1735, 1739, 1744, 1747, 1760, 1762, 1764.
Drawson, 1621, 1624, 1629.
Drure, 1555.
Edmunds, 1726.
Edwards, 1592.
Fagg, 1613 [Fag, 1623] [Fegg, 1700] [ffagge, 1703], 1707.
Figg, 1577, [Ffygge, 1575.]
Ffem, 1674.
Fenner, 1708.
Flye, 1584.
Fosier, 1659, 1663, 1664.
Foster, 1758, 1760.
Foord, 1677.
Ffranklin, 1635.
Freeman [ffreeman, 1699], 1700 [Ffreeman, 1703, 1704].
Ffuller, 1609, 1705.
Fumeth, 1614, 1617, 1619.
Furminger, 1639 (2), 1646, 1650, [Ferminger, 1641, 1652.]
Gill, 1641 (2).
Gimber, 1712, 1715, 1717, 1721, 1737, 1752, 1757.
Godfrye, 1554, 1559.
Goldwell, 1620, 1622.
Gorram, 1671 [Gorrham, 1674], 1681.
Green, 1717.
Grumbart, 1711.
Gullen.
Hadden, 1688, 1690, 1692, [Haddon, 1695,] 1696, [Haddon, 1700, 1701.]
Hadswell, 1614.
Hall, 1722.
Handy, 1603.
Harman, 1749.
Hart, 1577.
Harrisson, 1615.
Harselden, 1615, 1616.
Hatton, 1683.
Haul, 1562.
Haywood [Heywood, 1738, 1757], 1763.
Head, 1707, 1709, 1710, 1711, 1713.
Henman, 1676.
Hills, 1732.
Hodges, 1653 (2), 1647, 1662, 1671.
Holmes, 1725.
Homes, 1595.
Hull, 1588, 1589.
Hunt, 1727, 1730.
Johnson, 1637, 1638, 1639 (2), 1643, 1644, 1646, 1653, 1683, 1686, 1688.
Jorham, 1676.
Kedde, 1612.
Kesby, 1761, 1763.
Ketchley, 1745, 1749, 1754.

Kingsford, 1676, 1689, 1692, 1695.
Langly, 1617.
Lott, 1674.
Lynke, 1738.
Mapestone, 1635, 1639, 1641.
Marden, 1632, 1635, 1638, 1640, 1642.
Marten, 1643.
May, 1680.
Measit, 1675.
Merritt, 1676.
Millen, 1632, 1633, [Millin, 1654.]
Miller, 1594, 1596, 1599, 1653.
Milles, 1570.
Morley, 1686.
Morling, 1681, [Moorlyng, 1576.]
Mooerore, 1603.
Mooper, 1576.
Neals, 1663.
Netherfold, 1559, 1562, [Netherfolde, 1567.]
Nicolls, 1650, 1654, [Niclas, 1555.]
Nort, 1561.
Norton, 1563, 1566, 1567.
Nye, 1736, 1737, 1739, 1743, 1746, 1748, 1757.
Olillant, 1629.
Oultman, 1638.
Ourll, 1617.
Ouller, 1633.
Overington, 1555.
Padys, 1575.
Pain, 1720, [Paine, 1722,] [Payn, 1736,] [Payne, 1739, 1740, 1742 (2), 1743,] 1762, [Paine, 1764.]
Palmer, 1754, [Parmar, 1752.]
Parnell, 1595.
Paye, 1571.
Payner, 1563.
Pell, 1619.
Perry, 1696, 1699.
Phin, 1676.
Pierce, 1700, 1738, 1740, 1742.
Pollard, 1752, 1754.
Pointer, 1699, 1704.
Porter, 1724, 1726.
Portman, 1642, 1644, 1645, 1646, 1649, 1664.
Preston, 1605, 1607 (2), 1609.
Price, 1622.
Puket, 1564.
Rachel, 1717.
Raffell, 1598, 1606.
Raist (?), 1648.
Rayner, 1607, 1609.
Reader, 1695, 1697, 1699, 1701, 1705, 1727.
Reads, 1603.
Red, 1610.
Retchley, 1748.
Roberts, 1657.
Robson, 1610, 1613, 1618.
Robt, 1593.*
Rygden, 1668.
Sanderson [Saunderson, 1621, 1624 (2)], 1627, 1629.
Saunders, 1619.
Sawyer, 16—.
Saxby, 1689, 1692.
Sedwick, 1734.
Short, 1635.
Smith, 1617, 1619, 1622, 1629, 1681, 1688, 1751, 1752, 1755, 1756, 1757 (2), 1759, 1760, 1762.

* So written in the Register.—*W. J. L.*

Smyth, 1554, 1583, 1586, 1587, 1590, 1684.
Somfall, 1568.*
Somerfole, 1566.
Spicer, 1678, 1683, 1687.
Spratt, 1619, 1649, 1650, 1653, 1655.
Standen, 1594, 1606.
Stee, 1613.
Steed, 1752.
Stell, 1615.
Stevens, 1668.
Stocke, 1559, 1561, 1564, 1583, 1586, 1589, 1591.
Swaffer, 1575.
Swayne, 1616, 1619.
Swiome, 1623.
Symons, 1560, [Symon, 1561.]
Tarbton, 1610.
Tarrell, 1677.
Terrell, 1670 [Terrill, 1712 (2).]
Turrell, 1668, 1674, 1681.
Thurstan, 1745, 1747, 1749, 1752, 1754, 1757, 1762.
Tilden, 1722, 1725, 1727, 1728, 1731, 1732.
Tomlinson, 1681, 1682.
Towell, 1663.
Turner, 1747, 1749, 1753.
Tydale, 1723.
Upton, 1643.
Vale, 1621, 1639.
Vincet, 1706, 1708, 1709, 1713.
Vinset, 1717, 1718, 1729, 1731 (2), 1732, 1735 (2), 1737, 1739, 1740, 1742, 1746.
Virgoe, 1734.
Watome, 1581 (2).
Walker, 1711.
Webb, 1624.
Weeks, 1698, 1701, 1703, 1704, 1717, 1720, 1723, 1724.
Wells, 1604, 1624, 1628, 1630, 1633, 1634, 1637, 1644, 1661, 1665, 1668, 1670.
Wellward, 1694.
Weston, 1653, 1661.
What, 1706, 1715.
White, 1683, 1684, 1687, 1689, 1694, 1698, 1700, 1703.
Whithead, 1749.
Whookr, 1687.
Wicks, 1711, 1712, 1713, 1715, 1716.
Wickum, 1600.
Wiggs, 1708, 1710.
Wigmore, 1558, 1561, 1564, 1586, 1589.
Willes, 1555, 1589.
Willot, 1691.
Winder, 1710, 1712, 1714, 1716, 1717, 1723, 1724, 1736, 1738, 1741.
Winne, 1627, [Wine, 1633,] 1637.
Winterton, 1688.
Wioth, 1631, 1634, 1636.
Woodburn, 1686 (2), 1688, 1689, 1691, 1697, 1700.
Woolburn, 1685, [Wolburn, 1693.]
Wraight, 1629, 1650, 1656, 1671, 1760, 1761, 1763, 1765.
Wreight (same family as Wraight), 1666, 1668, 1669, 1670 (2), 1719, 1720, 1722 (2), 1724, 1725, 1726 (2).
Yeoman, 1628, 1630, 1634, 1637, 1660, 1663, 1667.

* So written in the Register.—*W. J. L.*

Names of the Rectors and Curates of Orlestone mentioned in the Register.

"Mr. Edward Preston, Parson of Orlestone, buried the 8th day of March, 1612."
Edward Harrison, Parson, 1613–1625.
Lancolet Harrison, Parson, 1629.
Johan Laury (?) Rector de Orlestone. From Reg. Baps. A.D. 1641.
Mark Sherman, Rector, 1656; buried Aug. 12, 1665.
Robert Richards, Rector, 1666.
Francis Cull, Curate, 1714.
John Lambe, Curate, 1716.
"Henry O'Neale, Curate of New Romney and Orlestone, 1734."
Blemell Pollard, Curate, 1736, and Rector in 1753.
Thomas Straker, Curate, 1744.
Thomas Hugill, Curate, 1747.
C. Wightwick, Curate, 1750.
Edward Thomas, Curate, 1751.

On the inside of the cover of the old Register is written, in the handwriting of Blemell Pollard, Rector, 1753,—

"Sir Philip Boteler,
Patron of Orlestone."

Names of Persons who signed the Register of Burials in Woollen-at-Orlestone.

Norton Knatchbull, 1681.
P. Honywood, 1682.
Nicho. Toke and Wm. Rondolph, 1683.
C. Digges and Wm. Brodaux, 1708.
W. H. Honeywood, 1710.
Wm. Hamilton and Thos. Wetherden, 1727.
J. Sawbridge, 1726.
Cha. Fagge and E. Dering, 1731.
Thos. May, 1732.
Granv. Wheler, 1736.
A. Filghman, 1742.
J. Brockman, 1748.

James Tunstall and Geo. Sayer, 1758.
Geo. Carter, 1762.

Some of the above names occur for several years in succession.

Names of Persons granting Affidavits mentioned in the Orlestone Register.

Thomas Fanny, Curate of Warehorne, 1681.
Robt. Richards, Rector of Snave, 1681.
Mr. Crofton, Curate of Bilsington, 1682.
Mr. Will. Burleston, Rector of Warehorne, 1684.
Henry Walker, Vicar of Wilsborough, 1684.
Mr. John Lodge, Curate of Warehorne, 1685.
Rd. Husband, Curate of Rucking, 1727.
Mr. Hugh Shaw, Curate of Warehorne, 1727.
Mr. Thos. Reader, of Kingsnorth, 1726.
Mr. John Bruce, Vicar of Brenzet, 1731.

COWLING CASTLE.

THE following transcripts of vouchers and receipts for moneys expended on the erection of Cowling Castle were exhibited when we visited that ancient dwelling in August last. Their appearance caused discussion at the time, and some doubt was raised as to their authenticity, because their dates did not exactly correspond with the period at which some of our members have conjectured that the Castle was built. To set the matter at rest, we give them as they were found among the muniments at Surrenden, leaving them to tell their own tale; and we complete their authenticity by furnishing a facsimile of one of them, in the unquestionable handwriting of the period. Still further to perfect our evidences of date, we give from the Patent Rolls a transcript of the original license to crenellate, thus furnishing a series of incontestable evidence as to the precise period when the castellation of Cowling was first made.

With these documents in hand, a very interesting survey might be made of the Castle, and much of the detail and measurements of its works verified and exactly dated.

I.

[Couling.—10 October, 48 Edw. III., 1374.]

Sachent touz gents moy WILLIAM ROBERTS, plomer de Loundres, avoir rescen de mons[r] JOHN seigneur de COBEHAM, qaraunte oept south[1] et dis deners en plein paiement des touz maners bargainz faitz peutre nous dil comensement de mounde taunke al jour de fesaunte du cestis.

Des qeux qaraunte oept south et dis deners, en plein paiement, come avaunt est dit, moy reconusse estre pleinement paie. Et le dit mons^r^ JOHN, ses heirs et executours estre quites par cestis presentz as touz jours.

En tesmoigne de quele chose, a ceste escript jay mis mon seal.

Done a Coulyng, le disme jour Doctobre, lan regne le roi Edward tierce puis le conquete quaraunte oeptisme.

[*Indorsed.*] Laquitaunce W. Plomer de Loundres, de xlviij^s^ x^d^ en plein paiement.

II.

[London.—11 May, 2 Ric. II., 1379.]

Sachient totez gentez, moy THOMAS WREK, mason, de Loundrez, avoir ressu de mons^r^ JOHAN DE COBEHAM, seigneur de Cobeham, cessaunte south en partie du paiement de quatorze livrez, siz souz, oept deners, que remeynt aderer[2] oultre certeyns paiementz faitz come piert par acquitaunce, en lez queux lavaundit mons^r^ JOHAN mest[3] tenuz pour une overayne[4] come piert par certeins endentures. Dez queux cessaunte souz en partie du paiement, come avaunt est dit, moy THOMAS reconusse estre paiez, et lavaundit mons^r^ JOHAN, ses heirez et executours quitz as touz jours par icestez presentz.

En tesmoigne de quel chose, moy THOMAS susdit ay mys mon seal.

Done a Loundrez, le unzime jour de May, lan du regne le roi Richard secounde, puis le conquete secounde.

[*Seal:* Red wax,—a Roman gem, genius holding a bunch of grapes and rod. Legend—Depar Deus.]

[*Indorsed.*] Aquitaunce de lx^s^ puis le payement feyt al dit

[1] South-souz—shillings.
[2] aderer, *i.e.* à derrier, 'in arrear.'
[3] mest, *i.e.* m'est.
[4] overayne, *i.q.* ouvre, 'work.'

Thomas que remeyneyt aderer xiiij^{li} vj^{s} viij^{d}. Et sy remeynt aderer onkor xj^{li} vj^{s} viij^{d}.

III.

Patent for Crenellating Cowling Castle,—Rot. Pat. 4 *Ric. II.* (1380–1) *pt.* 2, *m.* 24.

De Manso Kernellando—Cobeham.

Rex omnibus ad quos, etc.—Salutem. Sciatis, quod de gracia nostra speciali concessimus et licenciam dedimus, pro nobis et heredibus nostris, quantum in nobis est, dilecto et fideli nostro Johanni de Cobeham, quod ipse mansum Manerii sui de Coulyng, in Comitatu Kancie, muro de petra et calce fortificare, firmare, et kernellare, et mansum illud sic fortificatum, firmatum, et kernellatum, tenere possit, sibi et heredibus suis, in perpetuum, sine occasione vel impedimento nostri vel heredum nostrorum Justiciorum, Escætorum, Vicecomitum, aut aliorum ballivorum seu ministrorum nostrorum quorumcumque. In cujus, etc. Teste Rege apud Westmonasterium, x die Februarii.[1]

Per breve de privato sigillo.

IV.

[Coulyng.—29 September, 5 Ric. II., 1381.]

Sachount toutez genz, moy Henry de Ivelegh, masoun et citizein de Loundres, avoyr ressu de mons^{r} Johan de Cobeham, et par ses maynz payez de xx libres desterlyng, en le nom de Thomas Wrewk, masoun, des queux xx^{li}, come avaunt eśt dit, moy avaundit Henry reconuz estre perpayez[2] et lavaundit mons^{r} Johan, ses heyrs et executours quites atouz jours.

En tesmoynaunce de quele chose, a ceste lettre daquitaunce, moy avaundit Henry ay mys monn seal.

[1] This document is transcribed from the original Patent Roll in the General Record Office; all the rest are from the Surrenden Collection.

[2] perpayez, 'fully paid.'

Done a Coulyng, le jour seynt Michael larchaungele, lan du rengne le Roy Richard secounde puis le conqueste quintte.

[*Seal*: Red wax,—a dog seiant. "S . . . . . ."]

[*Indorsed.*] Aquitaunce, Henry Ivelegh de xx^{li} paye par Thomas Wrewk.

V.

[23 July, 6 Ric. II., 1382.]

Ceste endente fait parentre $mons^r$ JOHAN DE COBEHAM, seigneur de Cobeham, dune parte, et WILLIAM SHARNHALE, dautre part, tesmoyne que lavauntdit $mons^r$ JOHAN et lavauntdit WILLIAM, ount acompte et mesure les murs et tours deinz le mote de Coulyng, par mestre HENRY YEVELE, masonn.

Cestassavoir, del tour en le Southestcorner taunk al mur del graunt Chambre en le northcorner, oue les deux rondes tours del hautesse de deux perches oue crest et tout, qui amounte a cynkaunte et quartre perches, prenaunt pour le perche $viij^{li}$.

Et le hautement de les deux tours viij pees et j quart dun pee plus haute que les murs, qamonte treys perches, issuit que la somme des perches amounte, en tout, a Cynkaunt et sept perches, qui amounte en argent quatre Centz Cynkaunt et Sys libres. De quele somme lavauntdit $mons^r$ JOHAN ad paie al dit WILLIAM SHARNHALE, en partie de paiement de la somme suisdite, deux Centz Cessaunt et dys livres, dys south, et quatre deners; des queux $CClxx^{li}$ x^s $iiij^d$ lavauntdit WILLIAM SHARNHALE soy reconuz estre paiez, et lavauntdit $mons^r$ JOHAN, ses heires et executours, quites a touz jours par cestes presentes aquitaunces endentes, et entrechaungeablement enseales et baillez[1] entre les parties suisdites.

Done lendemayne de la maudeleyne, lan du regne le roi Richard secounde puis le conquete sisme.

[*Indorsed.*] Endentur come aquitaunce de Scharnhalle de payment de $cclxx^{li}$ x^s $iiij^d$.

[1] Enseales et baillez, 'sealed and delivered.'

---

ynhale deuers p(ar)t tesmoygne q(ue) lauantdit mons(ieur) John
r mestre Henry Yevele mason destassaud del tour en
tours del hautesse de deux perches ove crest e tout
t de les deux tours .viij. pees e .j. quart dun pee plus
ontinuant e sept perches q(ue) amountent en argent
William Shaynhale en p(ar)tie de paiement de la
ol xx. li. x. s. viij d. lauantdit William Shaynhale
testes p(re)sentes ajuntamentz endentez e entrechaungez
an du regne le Roi Richard secounde puis le conq(ueste).

(Endorsement.)

Endentur come aquitaunce
de Shaynhalle de payment
de cclx li x s iiij d

VI.

[25 November, 6 Ric. II., 1382.]

Sachount toutez genz, moy THOMAS CROMPE, masoun, avoyr ressu de mons^r JOHAN DE COBEHAM, syngn^r de Cobeham, oyt libres desterlyng, en perpayement de toute la graunde porte del outerwarde de Coulyng, le quel moy avaundit THOMAS et LAURENZ ATTE WODE avouns prys pour fayre, come apert par les dittez endenturs canselles, des queux oyt libres, en perpayement del dit overayne, come avaunt est expresse, moy avaundit THOMAS reconuz estre perpayes, et lavaundit mons^r JOHAN, seys heyrs et executours quietes a touz jours par cestes presentys aquitaunce, sur quel moy avaundit THOMAS ay mys mon sceal.

Done le jour seynte Katerine, lan de rengne le roy Richarde secounde, puis le conqueste sysme.

[*Indorsed.*] Aquitaunce Thomas Crompe dil graunde porte de Coulyng, de le perpayement pour iceles.

VII.

[Coulyng.—29 September, 8 Ric. II., 1384.]

Sachent touz gens, nous THOMAS CROMP et WILLIAM SCHARNALL, massonz, avoir resceu de mons^r JOHN DE COBEHAM, seigneur de Cobeham, cessauntes diz et oept south, en perpaiement pour larsure de siz centz et cinquaunte quarters de lym, de nous pris par WILLIAM BROWN, pour lez overaygnez le seigneur a Coulyng, dil feste seint Michael, lan du roi qui ore est septisme taunge le feste seint Michael proschein ensuit qest le jour de fesance du cestis. Dez queux cessaunte diz et oept south, en perpaiement, come avaunt est dit, nous nous reconons estre perpaiez. Et lavauntdit mons^r JOHN, sez heirs et executours, estre quites par ces presentz, as touz jours.

En tesmoigne de quelle chose, a yceste acquitaunce avons mys noz sealz.

Done a Coulyng, le jour saint Michael larchaungel, lan du regne le Roy Richard secounde puis le conquete oytisme.

[*Indorsed.*] Acquitaunce Cromp et Scharnal, en perpaiement pour arsur de lym, dez le jour Seint Michael a° vij° taunqz le feste Seint Simon et Jude [28th Oct.] a° viij° pour tout le seson entier.

VIII.

[London.—16 October, 8 Ric. II., 1384.]

Sachount toutez genz moy WILLIAM BESTCHERCHE, masoun, avoyr ressu de monsieur JOHAN DE COBEHAM, seigneur de Cobeham, cessaunte south desterlyng, en perpayement de toutes maneres dettez que lavaundit mons^r JOHAN estoit al avaundit WILLIAM BESTCHERCHE tenuz pour soun overayne fet de masonerye a chastel de Coulyng, des queux cessaunte south, en perpayement, come avaunt est dit, moy avaundit WILLIAM BESTCHERCHE me reconuz estre perpayes, et lavaundit mons^r JOHAN, ses heyrs et executours estre quitez a touz jours.

En tesmoynaunce de quele chose a yceste lettre de aquitaunce ay mys mon sceal.

Done a Loundres, le seszime jour Doctobre lan de rengne le Roy Richard secounde oytisme.

[*Indorsed.*] Laquitaunce William Bestcherche, masoun, de son overayne de Coulyng.

IX.

[29 September, 9 Ric. II., 1385.]

(The original is in Latin, of which the following is a literal translation.)

Know all men by these presents, that I, THOMAS CROMPE, mason, have received, on the day of the making these presents, of Sir JOHN DE COBEHAM, Lord of Cobeham, six pounds, thirteen shillings, and four pence sterling, in part payment of my work at the Castle of Coulyng, of which six pounds, thirteen shillings and four pence, in part payment, as is premised, paid to me, I acknowledge myself to be paid, and that the foresaid Lord of Cobeham, his heirs and executors, are acquitted thereof by these presents sealed with my seal.

Dated on the feast of St. Michael, in the ninth year of the reign of the King of England, Richard the second, after the conquest.

[*Indorsed.*] Acquittance of Thomas Cromp, mason, of ten marks paid to him, in part payment of his work of Coulyng, in the ninth year.

The sum total of this expenditure will be found to be as follows :—

		£	*s.*	*d.*
Plumber.	1374.—William Roberts	2	8	10
Masons.	1379.—Thomas Wreck, £3 on account of	14	6	8
	1381.—Ditto (by Henry Ivelegh) . .	20	0	0
	1382.—William Sharnhale, £270. 10*s.* 4*d.* on account of	456	0	0
	1382.—Thomas Cromp, for the great gate	8	0	0
	1384.—Thomas Cromp and William Sharnhale, limeburning . .	3	18	0
	1384.—William Bestcherche	3	0	0
	1385.—Thomas Cromp, on account of a larger sum	6	13	4
		£514	6	10

The Manor of Cowling was, from an early period, part of the possessions of the Cobhams, who only occasionally resided at the Castle. We have an old lease, dated 23rd May, 1429, by which Thomas Brook, Lord Cobham, lets to John Smith of Cowling, two houses, with a marsh called Leth . . . . for four years from Michaelmas next, at £5 per annum. One of the clauses in this lease is curiously indicative of the scantiness of furniture needed in those days. Among the conditions is one, that the tenant or his executors "straminabunt aulam et cameras de Castro de Coweling, cum cirpis de novo colligatis, contra quemlibet adventum predicti domini ad Castrum predictum."

To strew the floor with fresh rushes was nearly all the preparation needed to receive the lord on his arrival. The arras, the costers, dorsers, and bankers, and coverlets, etc., were shifted and brought with him; a few benches and stools, and steddles, and a few chairs formed the standing furniture of the house; and he could migrate from one mansion to another with his other furniture as readily as a soldier shifts his tent and its gear.

L. B. L.

Ashford

Betweene ye chancell and Fogges chappell now belonging to ye Ld. Tufton this monument thus circumscribed upon ye edge thereof.

" Edwardo quarti Regis specialis Amator
- -
" Semper Catholicus Populi vulgaris amicus
" Et sic decedens a mundo mente - - - - -

" Plenius hic sequitur qd fecerat iste Johannes
" Sumptibus ex proprijs eccliam renovavit
" Cum Campanili qd funditus ædificavit
" Pluribus atqz libris chorus hic q ēu veneratur
" Ac ornamentis altare Dei decoratur
" Vestibulum ditans as plume iocalia donans
" Vt patet intuitu pro posteribus memorandum
" Ad laudem domini cui laus sit nunc et in ævu.
Amen.

NOTES OF BRASSES, MEMORIAL WINDOWS, AND ESCUTCHEONS, FORMERLY EXISTING IN ASHFORD AND WILLESBOROUGH CHURCHES.

(FROM THE SURRENDEN COLLECTION.)

BY HERBERT L. SMITH, ESQ.

THE Englishman whose span of existence was allotted during the middle of the fifteenth century, or the thirty years' wars of the Roses, had but little settled peace. Whether he were prince, noble, or plebeian, the buckling on of his armour was not for the mere parade of chivalry or ornament of the gallant. The violence of partisanship cut asunder the dearest ties of family circle and friendly board.

It was through this period that he whose effigy lies before us lived.

Sir John Fogge, Knight, Privy Councillor, Treasurer,[1] Comptroller of the Household, personal friend, faithful adherent, and, by the Woodvilles, a family connection of Edward IV.,—for his first wife, Alice Haut, was first cousin to the Queen, her mother having been Elizabeth Woodville, a sister of Lord Rivers.—According to the evidence of the Patent Rolls, he received numerous grants from the Crown, and consequently may well be supposed to have played no trifling part in the stirring events of the agitated age in which he existed.

His devotional attitude in the brass, and that in which he appears in the memorial window of our third

[1] Anno 4 Edw. IV. *vide* p. 526 b, vol. v. Rolls of Parliament.

plate (although in most monumental representations a mere conventional form), and the many and still enduring acts of munificence which enshrine his name at Ashford, in his case seem almost the natural expressions of a mind alive with gratitude to that divine Providence which carried him through such vicissitudes, and ultimately gave him rest, and restoration of affluence, under the happy union of the long conflicting Roses.

We may reasonably suppose that when the romantic Edward raised the supplicating widow, and placed her at once on the throne of his affections and his realm, he drew around him all the adherents of her house, and among them Sir John Fogge; for, bearing in remembrance the fact that the first husband of Elizabeth de Woodville, Grey of Groby, perished as a Lancastrian in the second battle of St. Alban's, and that Sir John Fogge himself had been Keeper of the Wardrobe to the unfortunate Henry in the last year of his reign, we can scarcely fail to admit that his change of badge, from red to white, was due to this marriage.

It is by no means improbable that Sir John may have been with his kinsman Grey in the battles of St. Alban's on the side of Henry, and wearing the red rose on the snow-clad field of Towton, and at the subsequent sanguinary battle of Hexham. After which events occurred the marriage of Edward, and with it the family changes we have suggested.

At this period Sir John was a young man in the vigour of life, and henceforth must have played a conspicuous part in the stirring events of that distracted time, such as the banishment of Warwick and Clarence, and their return, the expulsion of Edward, and the restoration of the feeble Henry.

Much as the passions were excited by these events, we will hope that, though cognizant of the end of the unhappy master whom he once served, he in no way contributed to bring about the miserable death of that monarch, or the hard usage of the gallant Margaret. His counsels, if not his personal services, assisted doubtless in the subsequent invasion of France, and the many curious negotiations which ensued.

The trial and tragical end of the Duke of Clarence in the butt of Malmsey were events of his day, if not actually with his concurrence. Finally, it is very probable that he was about the King during his last hours, and, as a near kinsman and faithful servant, was among those who pledged their fidelity to the interests of the infant successor and his brother.

How, under the protectorship of the artful Gloucester, he escaped the fate of Hastings, Rivers, Grey, and others, seems surprising; for no time was lost by Richard in the attainder of Sir John, and in depriving him of all his possessions.[1] Perhaps he lay concealed, or escaped abroad. Possibly he might have been found amongst the two thousand followers of Richmond, when he landed in England, or was one of those who immediately repaired to his standard and played a part in the field of Bosworth; for the removal of the attainder, and the restoration of his honours and estates, are enrolled as occurring in the first year of Henry VII.[2]

The ensuing six years of his life seem to have been a period of peaceable possession of his restored fortunes, and to have been occupied in setting his house in order, and in preparing for the time of his departure, which occurred in 1499, the sixth year of Henry VII.

Some of the offices of Sir John Fogge have been already alluded to, but it may be well to observe some further particulars respecting him. The family of Fogge appear to have come originally from Lancaster, and to have been brought into the possession of Repton House,

[1] Anno 1 Ric. III. p. 245 f, vol. vi. Rolls of Parliament.
[2] Anno 1 Hen. VII. p. 273 a, vol. vi. Rolls of Parliament.

and large Kentish estates about Ashford, by marriage with an heiress of the house of Valoignes.

Sir John was more than once sheriff of the county. His benefactions to the town and church of Ashford were numerous and valuable, and, so far as we can ascertain, were commenced in the later and more peaceable years of the reign of Edward IV., in whose time he founded the choral college. He restored or rebuilt the church, built the bell-tower, enriched the church-porch, and greatly adorned the high-altar, and bestowed many jewels; "all which," as the inscription observes, "was manifest to the sight, and to be kept in remembrance by posterity to the praise of the Lord." In order more effectually to perpetuate the devotional deeds of his life, he bequeathed to the town of Ashford, in trust, lands and houses, for the maintenance of the repairs of the church and worship of God therein, which bequests at the present time produce about one hundred and twenty pounds a year.

On the decease of Sir John, he was buried beneath a handsome altar-tomb which still stands between the chancel and Fogge Chapel, and which appears to have retained until the days of Dering the greater portion of its original ornamentations: these consisted of brass effigies of himself and his two wives. He is attired in rich plate-armour, and decorated with the Yorkist collar of suns and roses, with the white lion of Marche attached.[1] His head reclines on his helmet, which is adorned with mantlings and crest. At his feet sits an Italian greyhound. On either hand lie his two wives, each the counterpart of the other in attitude, feature, and attire, as in name. Their mantles are fastened with roses; at the feet of each crouches a dog with knotted leading-strings. On one of the three sides of the tomb, which was enriched by panelling of Gothic arches, were

[1] As represented in the woodcut, Vol. I. 'Archæologia Cantiana,' p. 84.

three shields of arms, that to the right bearing Valoignes impaling Fogge, which arrangement can only be accounted for by some unknown marriage of a Valoignes with a lady of the family of Fogge, or by an error of the draughtsman in transcribing his notes,—dimidiating quarterly Fogge and Valoignes into Valoignes impaling Fogge. The centre shield had the arms of the first wife, Haut, and probably the third contained those of the second wife, Kiriel.

On the front of the tomb the centre ornament was an angel supporting an inscription-plate, within an endless circle formed of rose sapling sticks firmly bound together, perhaps to represent the stability of family unity, the vitality of which is also indicated by four small sprouts of rose-branches with leaves and blossoms. On the tablet are inscribed the Latin verses which are given in our plate: the whole of this is on one piece of brass, and was for a length of time removed from the monument to a place in the wall of the church, but is now restored to the tomb. Four large bosses of the united Roses proclaimed a Yorkist's acquiescence in the peaceable conclusion of intestine commotion. An inscription round the margin of the slab, of which only a part remained in the days of Dering, completed the memorial. It seems to have recorded "that Sir John was a special friend of Edward IV., ... and departed this world universally esteemed by the common people."

Dering has given us the notion that the figures were of a large size, whereas, judging by the chasings still left in the stone, they were smaller than life; they are now wholly gone, with the exception of the helmet and crest. It has been supposed that this destruction occurred at the same time the churchwardens, S. Worthy and another, defaced the high-altar, in 1644, or thirteen years after Dering's notes were taken.

Our next plate exhibits the outline of the complete

set of brasses which once existed in memory of Thomas Fogge, Esq., the son of the above Sir John. Of these only the labels, two children, and inscription-plate remain, thus inscribed :—

"Here under this stone lyeth the bodyes of Thoms Fogg, esquyer, lately Sergeant Porter unto the moste famous princes Kings Henry the VIJ. and the VIIJ., and Eliañr his wyf. The whiche Thomas deceased the XVI. day of August, ye yea^r^ of o^r^ Lord M^c^ V^c^ XII., and Eliano^r^ deceased the   day of the yea^r^ of o^r^ Lord M^c^ V^c^   on whose Soules I. H. U. have mcy."

Dering, though he gives this inscription, does not do so on the plate we have copied; it was therefore more convenient to introduce it into our text. Having compared the copy with the original brass, we find the spaces left for the date of the wife's decease were never filled up, which would lead to the conclusion that the wife survived her husband; but although every arrangement was thus made for burial with her late husband, whenever her death might occur, from some accidental circumstance her interment took place elsewhere, or if with her husband, the insertion of the dates was carelessly forgotten.

Dering has misplaced the inscriptions on the labels, giving to the man the wife's, and to the wife the man's; in other respects they are correctly rendered. The children should have been on the plinth between their parents, and the two lower shields of arms below the inscription.

Of the history of this Thomas Fogge we have but little to record. The thorough exhaustion produced by the past tumultuous reigns doubtless predisposed him to inaction and rest. Probably his time was divided between the routine of a quiet court, and the peaceable enjoyment of his country possessions. The office of Serjeant-Porter, however, implies an appointment of trust, and

Ashford

Thomas Fogge Esqr 1512.

Askford

In ẏ North window of ẏ crosse Ile This Figure Subscribed
Sr Joh.. Fogg------

In a North window in the gallery these armes.

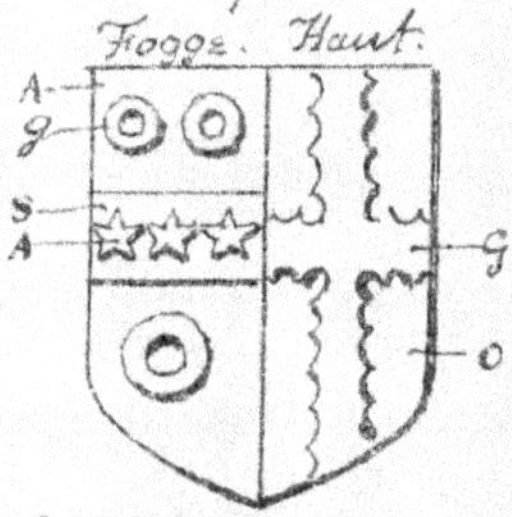

In ẏ ministers house

proves him to have been employed about the court in a confidential capacity.

In full armour, his feet rest upon his crest, a unicorn; his wife, without any accompaniment or distinction, is by his side. The first escutcheon bears the arms of Fogge; the second Fogge impaling Browne, the coat of the wife's family; the third Woodville and Fogge impaling Haut, which would seem to indicate that he was the son of Alice Haut, not of Alice Kiriel, as stated in the pedigrees, and that this Alice Haut had been the wife of a Woodville before she married Sir John Fogge, else the arrangement of the shield is a mere caprice; we are not, however, in a position to offer anything beyond this conjecture. The fourth shield is that of Browne quarterly.

By our third plate we are brought back to Sir John Fogge, who is represented in the coloured glass of a memorial window, northward in the cross aisle. He is kneeling at his devotions, in full armour, covered by a tabard of his arms, Fogge quarterly with Valoignes. Before him lies an open missal upon a table covered with a cloth diapered with roses, and the rose, probably of York, is repeated as the boss on a pendant over his head. The back was a coloured diapering indicated by the letters B and P. At the side is the representation of a church, the badge of a builder or founder. This window was probably executed in the later years of Edward IV.

In the north window of the gallery was a shield of the arms of Fogge impaling Haut, and another of an unknown coat, gules a fess between six martlets or, within a bordoure of —— argent and sable.

Amongst the coats of arms formerly in the windows of the minister's house is this,—Argent on a chevron between three boars' heads, gules a trefoil, or within a bordoure engrailed. Some correspondent may in our next Volume be able to appropriate these two coats and more completely emblazon them.

Our last plate is from the church of Willesborough, and presents us with the portraits of benefactors or builders. The inscriptions appear to have been very defective in Dering's time; the surname in one, and the Christian name in the other, being lost, also the date. Unfortunately one of these persons for whose souls we are invited to pray, has no cognizance by which we may be assisted in filling up the gap, "Rič̃i . . . Gen." Both name and tabard of the other indicate an individual of an ancient family flourishing in the period of Edward II., Brent of Charing: he was an ancestor of the Derings, and proprietor of the manor of Willesborough. Each of the above persons is praying before an open missal. The costume is that of the end of the fifteenth or beginning of the sixteenth century.

Below these, the two figures kneeling present us with the portraits of Richmond Bare and his wife Juliana, for the repose of whose souls there occurs the usual invitation to pray: they are both in the civil costume of the early part of the sixteenth century. The Bares were of an ancient family, whose ancestor, Sir John Bare, was a knight of great reputation in the reigns of Richard I. and Henry III. The Bare here represented was of the Mote House, Sevington, who died in 1463, or possibly his son.

Willesborough.

In ye windowe of ye north Ile, next unto ye Parson's chancell are these figures.

Orate p animab; Rici Gen quondam ------ Brent armigeri
Ex quorum bonis ista fenestra facta fuit Anno --- Ppitietur Deus.

" Orate pro animab; Rici Bare: & Juliane uxoris eius

FABRIC ROLL OF ROCHESTER CASTLE.

Among the documents deposited in the Public Record Office, there is a series of "Ministers' Accounts" relating to the repairs of Rochester Castle in the time of Edward III., one of which we here present to our readers. Although on the Pipe, and in other miscellaneous Rolls, we have general entries of repairs done to this fortress, yet they furnish us with very few particulars. The Roll before us is the earliest record with which we are at present acquainted, in which the details of repairs to this Castle are minutely given.[1] They are thus headed:—[2]

"Particule Compoti Johannis[3] Prioris Roffensis, Capitalis Magistri operacionum Regis apud Castrum Roffense. De receptis, misis, et expensis per ipsum factis in eisdem operacionibus, ab xi die Junii, anno regni Regis Edwardi tercii post conquestum xli° (1367–8) usque xi diem Januarii proxime sequentem, anno xlij° (1368–9), per visum et testificacionem Willelmi de Basyng magistri hospitalis de Strode, et Gilberti Geldewene supervisoris et Contrarotulatoris operacionum predictorum in Castro predicto."

Then follows the detail of Receipts for which the Master of the Works charges himself, to the amount of £1203. 15*s.* 4*d.*; and he next proceeds to those of Expenditure. They are written in abbreviated Latin, which we render into English as follows:—

[1] See Post Note, p. 131.

[2] For the annotations to this paper we are mainly indebted to Richard Hussey, Esq., F.S.A.

[3] John de Hertlip or Hertley.—*Anglia Sacra.*

Purchase of Stone.

Paid to Walter Byle, for 16 tons[1] of Beer freestone, bought of him for the works of our Lord the King in Rochester Castle, at 10*s*. per ton,—£8.

To Walter Coteler, for 18 tons of Beer freestone, bought of him for the said works, at 9*s*. 6*d*. per ton,—£8. 11*s*.

To Walter Byle, for 21 tons of Beer freestone, bought of him for the said works, at 9*s*. per ton,—£9. 9*s*.

To Thomas Ryder, for 62 tons of Caine[2] freestone, bought of him for the said works, at 9*s*. per ton,—£27. 18*s*.

To Henry de Yeflee, for 13 tons of Stapelton freestone, bought of him for the said works, at 8*s*. per ton,—118*s*.

To Thomas Fitz John, for 32 tons of Stapelton freestone, bought of him for the said works, at 8*s*. per ton,—£12. 16*s*.

To Philip Prophet, for 44 tons of Reygat[3] freestone, bought of him for the said works, at 6*s*. per ton,—£13. 4*s*.

To brother Robert Donyngton [Fr̃i Rob̃to Donyngton], for 195 tons of freestone from Farlegh,[4] bought of him for the said works, at 3*s*. 4*d*. per ton,—£32. 10*s*.

To Ralph Crompe, for 6 large pieces of Stone from Bocton,[5] bought of him for making lintels (*lintell*) for the said works, at 3*s*. 4*d*. the piece,—xx*s*.

To the said Ralph for one large piece of stone, called 'Nowel,'[6] bought of him for the said works,—2*s*. 6*d*.

[1] 'Pond Dol,' which we suppose to be the expression for Ton Weight, and so we render it throughout the Roll.

[2] *i. e.* Caen, in Normandy.

[3] *i. e.* Reigate, Surrey.

[4] Proved by other portions of these Fabric Rolls to be Fairlight, in Sussex, between Winchelsea and Hastings, still called by the common people, Farligh.

[5] Boughton Monchensea, or Monchelsea, about four miles south of Maidstone; quarries much worked to this day.

[6] 'Newel;' the central pillar round which the steps of a winding stairs turn: the end of each step is generally worked so as to form a portion of the Newel; the term is here applied to the entire steps. It will be observed throughout this Roll, that many of the stones were delivered from the quarry actually cut to their shapes ready for the builder, evidently the practice in those days. In the early part of the year 1859, on reopening some old quarries at Dean Street, in East Farleigh, several ancient fragments of finished stonework were found, such as parts of a Holy-water Stoup, arched mouldings and cusps of windows, etc. etc. The

To the said Ralph and his partners, for 60 pieces of stone, called 'Nowel,' bought of them for the said works, at 2*s.* per piece,—£6.

To the same, for 391¾ feet of stone, called 'Crest,'[1] bought of them for the said works, at 16*d.* per foot,—£26. 2*s.* 4*d.*

To the same, for 44¼ feet of stone, called 'Crest,' bought of them for the said works, at 12*d.* per foot,—44*s.* 4*d.*

To the same, for 47¾ feet of stone, called 'Crest,' bought of them for the said works, at 10*d.* per foot,—39*s.* 9½*d.*

To the same, for 40 feet of stone, called 'Lermer,'[2] bought of them for the said works, at 12*d.* per foot,—40*s.*

To the same, for 27 feet of stone, called 'Spaces,'[3] bought of them for the said works, at 10*d.* per foot,—22*s.* 6*d.*

To the same, for 408¾ feet of stone, called 'Spaces,' bought of them for the said works, at 8*d.* per foot,—£13. 12*s.* 6*d.*

locality would have induced us to speak of them as actual remnants of the stones prepared for these works at Rochester Castle, but that the Farleigh of our Roll is decidedly to be identified with Fairlight, near Hastings, for the reasons given in the foot-note; besides which, the entry at page 121 is actually accompanied by a specific charge for freight from Winchelsea.

In a communication with Mr. Hussey on this subject, he writes,—"The stones specified are Maidstone rag, Boughton, Beer, Reigate, Fairlight, Stapleton, Caen, and Caen-Grese; and the only kind of all these which seems to have been worked in the quarry is that from Boughton: this is a hard strong stone, which would bear the journey in a finished state, without much risk of injury, and is worked with least difficulty immediately after it is dug; so there were these two reasons why this should have been worked before it left the quarry: moreover, the overland carriage from Boughton to the river would have been lightened by reducing the stone to its finished condition. The Maidstone rag, of course, needed no working, as this was for the rough walling; but the other stones are charged by the ton, showing that they were delivered in blocks not ready worked. The accounts do not speak of a great deal of masonry which must have been wanted, and therefore was worked out of this block stone at the building: for instance, no masonry connected with either doors or windows is once mentioned; and the stonework for the vault ("*vausura*") within the gateway, for which a contract was made for the working and setting by piece-work, is not spoken of, though it was pretty sure to have been prepared on the spot from some of the stone delivered in block.

[1] Coping-stones, to cover the top of the walls and battlements.

[2] Stone worked with a projecting drip, to throw off the water and prevent it from running down the walls; the term is sometimes written Larmier and Lorimer.

[3] Coping-stones for the intervals, or *spaces*, between the battlements;

To the same, for 290¼ feet of stone, called 'Tablement,'[1] bought of them for the said works, at 6*d.* per foot,—£7. 5*s.* 1½*d.*

To the same, for 817¼ feet of stone, called 'Parpeincoins,'[2] bought of them for the said works, at 5½*d.* per foot,—£18. 14*s.* 6¾*d.*

To the same, for 1940 feet of stone, called 'Scuassheler,'[3] bought of them for the said works, at 20*s.* per hundred,—£19. 8*s.*

To the same, for 44¾ feet of stone, called 'Paas,'[4] bought of them for the said works, at 20*s.* per hundred,—8*s.* 11¼*d.*

To the same, for 2220 feet of stone, called 'Squarassheler,'[5] bought of them for the said works, at 16*s.* per hundred,—£17. 15*s.* 2¼*d.*

To the same, for 60 feet of stone, called 'Pament,'[6] bought of them for the said works, at 8*s.* per hundred,—4*s.* 9½*d.*

To the same, for 529 feet of stone, called 'Urnel,'[7] bought of them for the said works, at 6*s.* per hundred,—31*s.* 8¾*d.*

To the same, for 1850½ tons of stone, called 'Rag,'[8] from Maidstone, bought of them for the said works, at 40*s.* per hundred,—£37. 0*s.* 2¼*d.*

these openings were frequently called *spaces* in medieval times, and are still occasionally so called by workmen.

[1] This was formerly a general name for all horizontal mouldings, such as base-mouldings, strings, and cornices; the word is often united with a second term descriptive of the position of the moulding, as *base-table, crest-table.*

[2] 'Perpent-coins;' squared stones extending across the face of a buttress, or across the end of a wall where exposed to view, so as to form the coin at both angles.

[3] 'Skew-ashlar;' squared stones with one face worked sloping, or *askew*, such as are used at the set-off of a buttress, or over a projection formed by a reduction in the thickness of a wall, to prevent the lodgment of wet.

[4] 'Pace;' flat paving-stones; a term formerly applied to a landing on a stairs, a broad step, and a portion of a floor raised above the general level, here given to stones fit for such works.

[5] 'Square-ashlar;' *ashlar* is a general term for all kinds of worked stone. Ashlar-quoins, which will be found hereafter, are pieces of plain squared stone for forming the angles of the walls, buttresses, etc.

[6] 'Pavement,' or paving-stones. Pament of a strete; *pauiment, pauee.* —*Palsgrave.*

[7] We are unable to attempt any explanation of this term.

[8] Fragmentary stone of the district, used for the main substance of the walls.

To Thomas atte Pette, for 12 cart-loads of stone, called 'Rag,' bought of him for the same, in gross,—3*s*. 4*d*.

To the said Thomas, for 1 yard of squared chalk,[1] [j virḡ quar̃r̃ crete], bought of him for the said works, in gross,—10*s*.

To John Walsh, for 33½ tons of block chalk [peti crete], bought of him for the said works, at 3*d*. per ton,—8*s*. 4½*d*.

To John Cappe, for 5000 tiles, bought of him for the said works, at 3*s*. 8*d*. per thousand,—18*s*. 4*d*.

And all the above were applied and expended in the works of the said Castle, besides those which are noted on the dorse of this Roll.

Sum,—£276. 8*s*. 5*d*.

Burning Lime.

To John Walsh, for making and burning 2950 quarters of lime, burnt with the King's coal, at the kiln (*thorale*) of the said John, from his own quarry, at 10*s*. 6*d*. per hundred,—£15. 9*s*. 8*d*.

And all expended in the works of the said Castle.

Sum,—£15. 9*s*. 8*d*.

Smith's Work.

To Master Stephen, Smith of the Tower of London, for the ironwork of 14 windows of the said Castle, bought of him, weighing 5797 lbs., the 100 being computed at five score, at 2*d*. per lb.—£48. 6*s*. 2*d*.

To William Byce, for 2102 lbs. of iron, bought of him for the said works, at 6*s*. 4½*d*. per hundred, more in all, 3*d*.—£6. 14*s*. 3*d*.

To the said William, for 30 sheaves [garb̃][2] of steel, bought of him for the said works, at 8*d*. per sheaf,—20*s*.

To Mr. Stephen Smith, for an iron anvil, bought of him for the said works, weighing 221 lbs., the hundredweight being computed as above, at 2*d*. per lb.—36*s*. 10*d*.

To the same, for 12 'wrestlacches' of tinned iron, with their furniture, bought of him for the doors of the said Castle, at 5½*d*. a piece,—5*s*. 6*d*.

[1] Chalk was much used for internal vaulting in medieval buildings.

[2] "Garba aceris fit ex 30 peciis."—*Fleta*.

To the same, for 12 tinned iron rings,[1] with their furniture, bought of him for the same, at 4*d*. a piece,—4*s*.

To the same, for one lock bought of him for the same,—2*s*.

To the same, for 12 locks bought of him for the doors of the said Castle, at 17*d*. a piece,—17*s*.

To Nicholas Lethenard, for 1 lock, bought of him for the same,—20*d*.

To the same, for 2 locks, bought of him for the same,—15*d*.

And all the aforesaid were applied and expended in the works of the said Castle, besides those which are noted on the dorse of this Roll.

Sum,—£59. 8*s*. 9*d*.

Purchase of Nails.

To Nicholas Lethenard, for 100 great iron nails, called "Spykyng," bought of him for the said works,—18*d*.

To the same, for 350 iron nails, bought of him for the said works, at 12*d*. per hundred,—3*s*. 6*d*.

To the same, for 300 great iron nails, bought of him for the said works, at 11*d*. per hundred,—2*s*. 9*d*.

To the same, for 3350 iron nails, bought of him for the same, at 7*d*. per hundred,—19*s*. 6½*d*.

To the same, for 7100 iron nails, bought of him for the said works, at 5*d*. per hundred,—29*s*. 7*d*.

To Henry de War, for 1000 tinned iron nails,[2] bought of him for the doors of the said Castle,—8*s*.

To the same, for 2000 tinned iron nails, bought of him for the windows of the said Castle, at 4*s*. 9*d*. per 1000,—9*s*. 6*d*.

To Nicholas Lethenard, for 1000 iron nails, called 'Prig,'[3] bought of him for the said works,—18*d*.

To the same, for 3500 iron nails, called 'Prig,' bought of him for the said works, at 15*d*. per thousand,—4*s*. 4½*d*.

And all the aforesaid were applied and expended to various uses of the said Castle.

Sum,—£3. 3*s*.

[1] Probably the handles for the latches above mentioned; ornamental ironwork was formerly often tinned.

[2] This and the next item include the large headed nails intended for ornamenting the doors and window-shutters,

[3] This appears to be the original of the term 'sprig,' now given to headless nails, which are called also 'brads.'

Purchase of Timber.

To John Salot, for 41 pieces of oak timber, bought of him for the said works, at 2*s*. 4¾*d*. the piece, more in the whole 1¼*d*.,—£4. 18*s*. 4*d*.

To John Sandhell, for 18 pieces of oak timber, bought of him for the same, in gross,—53*s*. 4*d*.

To John Smyth, for 32 pieces of oak timber, bought of him for the same, at 19¼*d*. per piece,—51*s*. 4*d*.

To William Neweport, for 10 pieces of oak timber, bought of him for the same, in gross,—28*s*.

To William Sanskyn, for 10 pieces of oak timber, bought of him for the same, in gross,—24*s*.

To John Becheman, for 12 pieces of oak timber, bought of him for the same, in gross,—13*s*. 1*d*.

To John Heyton, for 6 pieces of oak timber, bought of him for the same, at 11*d*. per piece,—5*s*. 6*d*.

To John Clerk, for 5 sawn boards, called 'Rygol,'[1] bought of him for making the masons' moulds (*formis cementariorum*) for the said works, at 16*d*. a piece,—6*s*. 8*d*.

To John Pomfreyt, for 400 'estrichbords,'[2] called 'Wainscot,' bought of him for the doors, windows, and roofs for the said Castle, at 26*s*. per hundred,—104*s*.

To Richard de Euere, for 500 of the foresaid boards, bought of him for the same, at 22*s*. per hundred,—110*s*.

To Thomas Godet, for 40 oak boards, called 'Planchisbord,' bought of him for the foresaid works, at 6*d*. a piece,—20*s*.

To John Burgeys, for 28 poplar boards, bought of him for the same, in gross,—3*s*.

To Robert Couper, for 12 planks, called 'Shotbord,'[3] bought of him for the same, at a halfpenny a piece,—6*d*.

[1] 'Rygols' appear to be wooden patterns for the guidance of the masons in shaping stones; they are now usually formed of sheet-iron or zinc. When cut to represent the sections of mouldings, they are called *moulds*; but when made to represent the forms required to be given to stones which are to be fitted to each other, they are commonly called *templets*. The term is here applied to boards fit for making 'Rygols,' etc.; the moulds, or templets, are mentioned as the "*formæ cementariorum*." "Rewle: an instrument; *rigle*."—*Palsgrave*. "Reigle: a rule, canon, order, etc.; square, forme, patterne," etc.—*Cotgrave*.

[2] East country boards; the name 'wainscot' is still given to foreign oak.

[3] ? Gutter boards,—shootboards.

To Thomas Burre, for 300 laths, bought of him for the same, in gross,—16*d.*

To Thomas Warde and John Hamon, for 333 pieces of timber, called 'Scaffotlogg,' bought of them for the said works, at 1½*d.* a piece,—41*s.* 7½*d.*

To Nicholas Lente, for 112 hurdles[1] (*claiis*), bought of him for the 'scaffolds,' at 1½*d.* each,—13*s.*

To the same, for 3600 withes[2] (*virgulis*), bought of him for the same, at 1½*d.* per 100,—4*s.* 6*d.*

And all the aforesaid were applied and expended in the works of the said Castle, besides those which are noted on the dorse of this Roll.

Sum,—£28. 19*s.* 2½*d.*

Casting and Laying of Lead.

To John Plomer, for 9 cartloads and 8 weighs (*waug*) of lead, for melting, casting, and laying on the roof of the said Castle, at 5*s.* per cartload, 13 to each dozen in the work, for boot (*pro avantagio*),—42*s.* 1*d.*

Purchase of Sea-coal.

To Richard Hanekyn and John Walsh, for 165 quarters of sea-coal, bought of them, for burning lime for the said works, at 20*d.* per quarter,—£13. 15*s.*

And all was expended in burning lime for the works of the said Castle, and in the works of the fabric thereof.

Sum,—£13. 15*s.*

Purchase of Necessaries.

To Robert Graftone, for 2 large quires of royal[3] (*real*) paper, bought of him for inscribing the journal of the works of the said Castle,—2*s.*

[1] Hurdles were formerly used for the floors of scaffolding, instead of planks, which are now usually employed for that purpose.

[2] These may have been withes, used, instead of ropes, for tying the scaffolding; or thatching sticks; or twigs, to be twisted into a wooden partition, instead of laths, to carry plastering.

[3] "Paper riall, or royall paper. Charta Claudiana, Regia, Imperialis, Macrocolon. Plin. A staturæ cubitalis magnitudine. *Papier Royal, Imperial.*"—*Huloet's Dict. translated by Higgins*, 1572.

To the same, for 6 quires of paper, bought of him for registering the letters, precepts, and other necessaries concerning the said Castle, at 8*d.* per quire,—4*s.*

To the same, for red wax for the same, bought for sealing the said letters and precepts,—8*d.*

To Master William Herland, for 4 little brass wheels, bought of him to put in the hoisting engines (*vernis* or *verins*),[1] for drawing up the stone and timber on to the aforesaid works, at 3*s.* 4*d.* a piece,—13*s.* 4*d.*

To Nicholas Lethenard, for 32 hand-barrows (*siueris*[2]), bought of him for the said works, at 10*d.* a piece,—26*s.* 8*d.*

To Richard Stylle, for 128 'treyes,' bought of him, for carrying the mortar for the foresaid works, at 1½*d.* each,—16*s.*

To Nicholas Lethenard, for a wheel, bought of him for one barrow (*siuera*),—4*d.*

To John Heyton, for 100 'speldes,' bought of him for making the fire for melting the lead,—4*s.*

To the same, for 600 'bilets,' bought of him for the same, at 9*d.* per 100,—4*s.* 6*d.*

To Gilbert Geldewyne, for 2 casks, bought of him for carrying the lime from Frendesby[3] to the said Castle, at 22*d.* a piece,—3*s.* 8*d.*

To John Skynner, for 53 cartloads of loam (*lutei*), bought of him for the floors (*aras*) and walls of the said Castle, in gross, —3*s.* 4*d.*

To Nicholas Lethenard, for 54 wooden beetles [tribut], bought of him for the said works, at 1*d.* each,—4*s.* 6*d.*

To Thomas Hankyn, for 16½ pounds of tin, bought of the same for tinning different instruments, at 4¼*d.* per lb.,—20*s.*

To John Plomer, for 120 pounds of tin[4] for the leaden pipes, and making other joints in lead, bought of him at 3*d.* per lb., —30*s.*

[1] The precise character of this machine we are unable to describe. It was constructed of timber, and appears to have been provided with two pulleys, or blocks, with brass wheels. It will be seen hereafter that this term is sometimes written 'fernys' and 'fernes.' "Varin: a woodden engine, consisting of two vices and a skrue, and serving to lift up great pieces of timber, or of artillery."—*Cotgrave.*

[2] "Cenovectorium: *chivière.*"—*Gloss. de Lille.* "A hand-barrow: *civière, civière à bras.*"—*Cotgrave.*

[3] *i.e.* Frindsbury, near Rochester.

[4] For making solder.

To Hamo Chaundeler, for 1 large broom (*scopa*), bought of him for the said works,—4*d*.

To the same, for 12lb. of pitch, bought of him, for the said works, in gross,—9½*d*.

To Richard Hanekyn, for 2½lbs. of wax, bought of him, for making cement, at 7*d*. per lb.,—17½*d*.

To the same, for 9lbs. of rosin, bought of him for the same, at 1½*d*. per lb.,—13½*d*.

To John Marchant, for an ox-hide, bought of him, curried, for covering a pair of bellows therewith, in gross,—8*s*. 6*d*.

To William Marchal, for a whetstone [petra acutor̃], bought of him, for sharpening the axes and other tools of the masons and carpenters,—6*s*. 8*d*.

To Robert Couper, for repairing and binding the wooden vessels of the said Castle, with wooden hoops for the same, bought of him at various times,—5*s*. 4*d*.

To the same, for one wooden well bucket [situł] for drawing water and 1 wooden 'bokett' for carrying water, bought of him for the said works, at 7*d*. each,—14*d*.

To John Tornor, for 2 bowls [boll] and 6 'ladels,' bought of the same for the said works, in gross,—8*d*.

To Roger atte Fewe, for 1 pair of wheels, bought of him for the 'Poukweyn,'[1]—2*s*. 6*d*.

To the same, for repairing 3 pair of wheels, at Bokyngfold,[2] viz. for making and fixing on new fellies, for carrying timber to Newheth,[3] for each pair, 2*s*.,—6*s*.

To William Sharnhale, for 3 trusses [fassicłis] of hay,[4] bought of him, for plastering the walls of the said Castle,—3*d*.

To Nicholas Lethenard, for one sieve, bought of him for sifting lime and sand.

[1] This appears to have been some kind of wheeled truck, for moving timber and stone.

[2] Bokingfold was a royal manor, or park, of great extent, its demesnes being in the several parishes of Brenchley, Horsmonden, Marden, and Goudhurst. It had been formerly part of the possessions of the Crevecœurs.

[3] *i.e.* New Hythe, a small hamlet in the parish of East Malling, on the banks of the Medway. There is still a wharf there; but in the thirteenth and fourteenth centuries, and later, it was the great port for shipping goods from all the southern parts of Kent and a large part of the Weald.

[4] To be cut short, and mixed with the loam used for plastering the walls.

To John Lucas, for an iron anvil, hired from him for the said works,—3*s*. 4*d*.

To John Colyer, for 2 quarters of coals, bought of him for cementing[1] the stones, at 8*d*. the quarter,—16*d*.

To Adam Bocher, for grease, bought of him for greasing 'le Fernis'[2] and other necessaries of the said Castle, in gross,—8*d*.

To Walter Compton, for rushes, bought of him, to cover the new walls of the said Castle against the frost, in gross,—13*s*. 4*d*.

To John Roper, for 2 hempen cables, bought of him for drawing up stone, timber, and other necessaries on to the said Castle, 174lbs., at 1½*d*. per lb.,—21*s*. 9*d*.

To the same, for 7 hempen ropes, bought of him for the same, for drawing water, weighing 188 lbs., at 1½*d*. per lb.,—23*s*. 6*d*.

To Robert Graftone, for 7 skins of parchment, bought of him, for inscribing the roll of accounts, at 4*d*. a piece,—2*s*. 4*d*.

And all the aforesaid were applied and expended in the works of the said Castle, besides those which are noted on the dorse of this Roll.

Sum,—£12. 1*s*. 4½*d*.

Carriage and Carting.

To William Adekyn, for the freight of 13½ tons of Stapelton freestone from London to the said Castle, at 12*d*. per ton,—13*s*. 6*d*.

To the said William and his fellows, for freight for carrying 44 tons of Reygat freestone, from Batricheseye[3] to the said Castle, at 14*d*. per ton,—51*s*. 4*d*.

To Thomas Makerel and his fellows, for freight for carrying 195 tons of Farlegh stone from Wynchelsea to the said Castle, at 2*s*. per ton,—£19. 10*s*.

To Hugh Stace and his fellows, for freight for carrying 2289½ tons of Bocton and Maydestane stone from Maydestayne to the said Castle, at 5*d*. per ton,—£47. 13*s*. 11½*d*.

To John Walsh, for freight for carrying 33½ tons of block chalk [petr̃ crete] from Frendesby to the said Castle, at 2½*d*. per ton,—5*s*. 7*d*.

To the same John, for freight for carrying 360 quarters of

[1] Masons frequently use a cement for repairing their work, which requires the stones to be heated to make it adhere.

[2] See note to 'vernis,' or 'verins,' p. 119.

[3] Battersea.

lime from Frendesby to the said Castle, at ½*d.* per quarter,—15*s.*

To John Belherst and his fellows, for the carriage of 66 large waggonloads of timber from the park of Bokyngfold to Neweheth, at 2*s.* 6*d.* the waggonload,—£8. 5*s.*

To the same, for the carriage of 48 waggonloads of timber from the aforesaid park to Neweheth, at 18*d.* per waggonload,—72*s.*

To the same, for the carriage of 40 cartloads of timber from the said park to Neweheth, at 12*d.* per cartload,—40*s.*

To John Becheman, for the carriage of 6 cartloads of timber from Stapelherst to Maydestane, at 8*d.* per cartload,—4*s.*

To John Halle and his fellows, for the carriage of timber at Neweheth, in ships, for the whole year, in gross,—23*s.* 4*d.*

To John Watte and his fellows, for the freight of 292 tons of timber from Maydestane and Neweheth to the said Castle, at 5*d.* per ton,—£6. 1*s.* 8*d.*

To Roger Sengle, for the freight of ten cartloads of lead from Westminster to the said Castle, at 12*d.* per cartload,—10*s.*

For the carriage of ironwork, iron, locks, nails, boards, and other necessaries, as well from London as from other places, to the said Castle, in gross,—39*s.* 6*d.*

In the carriage of 44 tons of Reygate stone at Batriccheseye, by ship, in gross,—4*s.*

In the carriage and carting of ten cartloads of lead at Westminster, by ship, in gross,—5*s.*

To Richard atte Vyne, for freight of the stone of the doors, windows, and chimneys, at the Gore,[1] and for the carriage of 500 backstones[2] from the wall there pulled down, from Upecherch to the said Castle, and for the carriage and cartage of the same; by ship, in gross,—15*s.*

Total,—£96. 8*s.* 10½*d.*

Wages of Masons.

For the wages of Simon Hook, mason, being there and di-

[1] A manor in Upchurch, formerly called Le Gare, once the seat of a family of that name, and afterwards belonging to the De Leybournes, and conveyed by Juliana de Leybourne (see 'Archæol. Cant.,' vol. i. p. 347) to the King. Our text implies that the house was now demolished.

[2] A kind of tile, used for forming the backs of fireplaces. In a later Roll is an entry, "Tegula vocata Backston pro caminis."

recting the masons' work of the said Castle, and working there 288 days within the aforesaid time, at per day, 8*d*.,—£9. 12*s*.

For the wages of Richard Bal, Walter Gerard, Peter Payn, Thomas Conyngbrook, John Rook, Richard Rook, John Stone, and Bartholomew Wrek, 8 masons working on the said works, at 6*d*. per day each, for 252 working days within the time aforesaid,—£50. 8*s*.

For the wages of William Croydon, mason, working on the said works, at 6½*d*. per day, for 47 working days within the time aforesaid,—21*s*. 6½*d*.

For the wages of Gilbert atte Ford, Henry Payn, and John Rook, three masons working upon the said works, at per day 5*d*. each, for 183 working days within the aforesaid time,—£11. 8*s*. 9*d*.

Total,—£72. 10*s*. 3½*d*.

Setters'[1] *work, by the piece.*

To William Sharnhale, for a vault (*vausura*) within the inner gate of the said Castle, to be set complete, according to a certain agreement, by task-work,—106*s*. 8*d*.

Total,—106*s*. 8*d*.

Wages of Setters.

For the wages of William Sharnhale, William Loder, Richard Baker, William Lamb, William Crompe, Hamo Loder, Hamo Man, Richard Pathe, Ralph Loket, Henry Randulf, and William Hale, namely, 11 setters, setting the stones with mortar on the said works, at 6*d*. per day each, for 180 working days within the aforesaid time,—£49. 10*s*.

For the wages of Geoffrey Beneyt, John Beneyt, Robert Irland, Walter Vynet, and Walter Lexham, namely, 5 setters, working on the said works, at 5½*d*. per day each, for 172 working days within the aforesaid time,—£19. 14*s*. 2*d*.

For the wages of John Chipenham, William Walewer, Roger Curteys, and William Thornes, namely, 4 setters, working on

[1] "Opera positorum ad tascam."—These are the masons who fix the ashlar stonework in its place in the building. The name, however, does not appear, in medieval times, to have been confined to the workmen employed on the Ashlar, as "Rogh Setters" are mentioned in the contract for Fotheringhay Church, who were probably masons that built the ordinary walling.

the said works, at 5*d*. per day, for 175 working days within the aforesaid time,—£14. 11*s*. 8*d*.

For the wages of John Henill, a setter, working on the said work, at 4½*d*. per day, for 125 working days within the aforesaid time,—46*s*. 10½*d*.

For the wages of William Pathe, a setter, working on the said works, at 4*d*. per day, for 57 working days, within the aforesaid time,—19*s*.

For the wages of John Rykedon and Nicholas Pyk, 2 setters, working on the said works, at 3½*d*. per day each, for 172 working days, within the aforesaid time,—100*s*. 4*d*.

For the wages of William Lamb, a setter, working on the aforesaid works, at 3*d*. per day, for 97 working days, within the aforesaid time,—23*s*. 4*d*.

Total,—£93. 6*s*. 3½*d*.

Carpenters' work, by the piece.

To Henry atte Wode, for felling 36 oak trees at Bokyngfold, by a certain agreement, at task-work, at 2½*d*. each,—6*s*. 6*d*.

To the same, for felling, lopping [scindenđ], and squaring [scapulanđ] 22 oak trees, at task-work, at 14*d*. each,—25*s*. 8*d*.

To the same, for making one new building in the inner gateway (*pro j nova domo in interiori porta*) of the said Castle, in carpenters' work, with doors and windows pertaining to the same, according to a certain agreement at task-work,—£26. 13*s*. 4*d*.

Total,—£28. 6*s*. 6*d*.

Wages of Carpenters.

For the wages of Henry atte Wode, John Sharp, William Bereworth, Thomas Holbeme, and William Lymyndenne, namely, 5 carpenters, working at carpenters' work of the said Castle, as well in the wood as in the said Castle, at 6*d*. per day each, for 109 working days, within the aforesaid time,—£13. 12*s*. 6*d*.

For the wages of John Bryd and John Burgeys, 2 carpenters working on the said works, at 5½*d*. per day each, for 62 working days, within the aforesaid time,—56*s*. 10*d*.

For the wages of Henry Twysdenn and John Stace, 2 carpenters, working at the said works, at 5*d.* per day each, within the aforesaid time,—54*s.* 6*d.*

For the wages of Robert Courthope, a carpenter, working at the said works, at 4½*d.* per day, for 47 working days, within the aforesaid time,—17*s.* 7½*d.*

For the wages of John Lymyndenn, a carpenter, working at the said works, at 3*d.* per day, for 83 working days, within the aforesaid time,—20*s.* 9*d.*

Total,—£21. 2*s.* 3½*d.*

Wages of Smiths.

For the wages of Robert Pende, a smith, for making divers ironwork, as well for the doors and windows as for other works of the said Castle, namely, for rides [gumpħ[1]], bands [vertinelł], cramps, bands (*vinculis*), rings, bars, bolts, hooks, staples, large and small nails, irons for beetles [tribuł] and spades; in repairing, battering, and steeling axes [bat̃acōe et asceracōe secur̃] and other masons' tools, at 6*d.* per day, for 261 working days, within the aforesaid time,—£6. 10*s.* 6*d.*

Total,—£6. 10*s.* 6*d.*

Wages of Plumbers.

For the wages of John Plomer, a plumber, working on the works of the said Castle, in melting, casting, and laying lead, and for repairing various necessaries, at 6*d.* per day, for 36½ working days, within the aforesaid time,—18*s.* 3*d.*

For the wages of Richard Plomer, a plumber, working on the said works, at 5*d.* per day, for 15 working days, within the aforesaid time,—6*s.* 3*d.*

For the wages of Peter Plomer, a plumber, working on the aforesaid works, at 4*d.* per day, for 21 days within the aforesaid time,—7*s.*

Total,—31*s.* 6*d.*

[1] The *gumphæ* are the hooks, or rides (as they are called in Kent), of the hinges, which are fixed in the jambs of the opening; the *vertenellæ* are the straps, or bands, fastened on the door, which fit on the hooks. "Gomphose: a fastening of one bone within another, as of a naile, or wedge into a piece of wood; so are the teeth set into the jawbone."—*Cotgrave.* "Vertenelles; charnières pour tenir le gouvernail suspendu à l'étambor."

Wages of Carters.

For the wages of Stephen Fynel, Nicholas atte Melle, Reginald Palmer, and James Baker, four carters, with their own carts, carrying stone, lime, chalk, mortar, sand, timber, loam, and other necessaries, from the water and other places to the said Castle and to the works thereof, at 10*d.* per day each, for 176 working days, within the aforesaid time,—£29. 6*s.* 8*d.*

For the wages of Thomas atte Pette, William Panton, John Maykyn, and Thomas Thedom, four carters, carrying necessary things to the said works in their own carts, at 8*d.* per day each, for 125½ working days, within the aforesaid time,—£16. 14*s.* 8*d.*

Total,—£46. 1*s.* 4*d.*

Task-work of Labourers.

To John Emelyn and his fellows, for pulling down seven perches of the old wall of the said Castle, by task-work, at 3*s.* 4*d.* per perch,—30*s.* 4*d.*

Total,—30*s.* 4*d.*

Wages of Labourers.

For the wages of John Frensh, John Emelyn, John Sheredey, and Robert Bratyl, four labourers, labouring and working on the said works, at 4*d.* per day each, for 203½ working days, within the aforesaid time,—£13. 11*s.* 4*d.*

For the wages of John Wylmynsherst and Richard Lande, two labourers, labouring and working on the said works, at 3½*d.* per day each, for 142½ working days, within the aforesaid time,—£4. 3*s.* 1½*d.*

For the wages of Walter Smyth, Andrew Randulf, William Lambe, Richard Pende, Roger Brown, Richard Baker, Robert Cappedehust, John Rundel, John atte Mēr, John Clerk, Walter Proude, Richard Nase, Stephen Nichole, William atte Pette, William Spynner, Gregory Meller, Roger Stratford, Stephen Craye, John Kyng, William Trewelove, and Stephen atte Mōr, 21 labourers, labouring and working on the said works, at 3*d.* per day each, for 262 working days, within the aforesaid time, —£68. 15*s.* 6*d.*

For the wages of John Puttelady, Robert Westwode, Walter

atte Herst, Adam Sokelyng, William Tut, John Westwode, John Osebarn, David Meller, John Colchester, John Silvester, John Tanner, Richard Dynot, Richard Man, John Poltre, John Aleyn, William Pope, and Robert (*sic*), 17 labourers, labouring and working on the said works, at 3*d.* per day each, for 236 working days, within the aforesaid time,—£50. 3*s.*

For the wages of Simon Maykyn, William Bek, John Boydyn, John Large, Thomas Bocher, Hugh Baker, Robert Godard, Adam Rolf, Geoffrey Bradelee, Paul Betyl, and Thomas Wellys, eleven labourers, labouring and working on the said works, at 3*d.* per day each, for 132 working days within the aforesaid time,—£18. 3*s.*

For the wages of William Boleye, a labourer, labouring and working on the aforesaid works, at 2½*d.* per day, for 242 working days, within the aforesaid time,—50*s.* 5*d.*

For the wages of John Beneyt, a labourer, labouring and working on the said works, at 2*d.* per day, for 156½ working days, within the aforesaid time,—26*s.* 1*d.*

Total,—£158. 12*s.* 5½*d.*

Wages of Purveyor.

For the wages of Richard Porter, Purveyor of the said Castle, assigned by commission of our Lord the King, to make divers purveyances, from the first day of February in the 42nd year of the reign of the said King Edward to the 11th day of January next following in the said year, for 345 days, the first day being reckoned, at 6*d.* per day,—£8. 12*s.* 6*d.*

Total,—£8. 12*s.* 6*d.*

On the dorse of the Roll.

The same renders account of 193 pieces of stone of 'Caine Grese'[1] and of Beer, worked and prepared for doors, windows, and other things belonging to the within-written works; 68½ feet of stone called 'Crest,' 36 feet of stone called 'Spaces,' 52 feet of stone called 'Parpeincoins,' 63 feet of stone called 'Asshelercoin,' 40 pieces of stone called 'Corbell,'[2] 27 pieces of stone called 'Nowel,' 595 feet of stone called 'Assheler,'

[1] Coarse-grained stone from the neighbourhood of Caen, in Normandy: the common Caen stone is remarkably fine-grained.

[2] A corbel is a stone projecting from a wall to support something above.

324 feet of stone called 'Urnel,' 300 tons of stone called 'Rag,' one 'mouncelł'[1] of plaster of Paris;—and in the park of Bokyngfold, 105 large oak trees;—and at Neweheth, 3 large pieces of oak timber;—and in the within written Castle, 30 pieces of oak timber, 2 'fernys' nearly completed, 90 'standards' for scaffolds, 93 'pitsoules;'[2]—and at Neweheth, 16 'standards' for the same;—and in the said Castle, 100 cartloads of mortar, 100 cartloads of sand, 207 quarters 7 bushels of sea-coal, 40 large sheets (*pannis*) of lead, one large leaden cistern broken, 7 sheaves [garƀ] and 20 gadds[3] [gadđ] of steel, 18lb. of iron, four pairs of hengles [heng̃][4] and bands [vertinelł], 1400 iron nails called 'spikyng;' and smiths' tools[5] (*instrument fabri*), 3 sledges (*slegg*), 2 hammers (*martell*), 4 small hammers (*martell parv*), 2 'kervyngisnes,' 7 tongs, one 'nailtol,' one bickorn (*bicorne*), one 'spentonge,' 8 'punchons,' 5 files (*vyles*), one

[1] No indication can be given of the quantity described by this term. "*Congeries*,—monchell de pierres."—*Gloss. de Lille.*

[2] These appear to be connected with the scaffolding. In another Roll there is a entry of 'put sewels,' doubtless the same things. They may perhaps be the short pieces of timber laid across the scaffolding to carry the floor, now called 'put logs.'

These words, "93 pitsoules," are not in the counter-roll, and in this roll are in the margin.

[3] "Gadde of steele,—*quarreav dacier*."—*Palsgrave.* "A gad of steele,—*masse d'acier*."—*Cotgrave.* "Gad (from the Saxon, *Gaad*, i.e. the point of a spear) is a quantity of steel, of about two or three ounces."—*Blount's Gloss.*

[4] 'Hengles,' *i.e.* "hinges,"—hooks or rides for the bands.

[5] Most of these smiths' tools must remain unexplained. The 'slegg' are probably sledge-hammers; 'kervyngisnes' is sometimes written 'kervyngirnes:' they may be instruments for curving ironwork; 'nail tol' is doubtless an instrument for making some kind of nails; the name is still sometimes given to a tool used for making tire nails; 'bicorne' must be a small anvil with two pointed projections, or horns, such as is now called (perhaps by corruption of this older term) a beak-iron; 'punchons' may be punches, or pieces of iron with holes in them, on which thin iron is laid to be punched; a tool called a 'fuller' is now used by smiths for making mouldings in iron; the 'bolstres' were perhaps the pieces of iron on which the spindle of the grindstone rested, or they may have been pieces of iron to fix on to the spindle, to form square shoulders on the part passing through the stone; pieces of iron for making square shoulders to spindles are now called 'bolsters;' the 'gressor' appears to be a whetstone. "Grais: a hard and sparkling stone." "Grez: a greety, brown-gray, shining, hard, freestone."—*Cotgrave.*

'folo^r,' 1 washer (*wassh*), and one iron 'herth staf,' one stone called 'grindston' with an iron for the same, two iron 'bolstres,' one pair of bellows, one 'toyer,' and one grindstone (*gressor*) for sharpening the masons' tools, one bell with its furniture, weighing 60lb., 7 setters' hammers, two iron crows, 19 iron mattocks, 8 ironed beetles [tribuł], 17 beetles [tribuł] not ironed, 6 barrows (*siuer*), 4 wooden vessels for putting water in, 3 tubs (*cuvis*), one bowl [bołł], 8 trays (*treyes*), one bucket with an iron chain for the well, 2 hempen ropes of 42 fathoms, 2 sieves, one 'poukweyn,' 3 ells of woollen cloth for the accountant [compotor̃], one office seal, 80 hurdles (*claiis*), one hatchet [securuł],[1] received from Bernard Cok, clerk of the works of the aforesaid Castle, in the year last past, by indenture.

And of 55 tons of freestone from Beer, 62 tons of freestone from Caine, 45 tons of freestone from Stapelton, 195 tons of freestone from Farlegh, 483¾ feet of stone from Bocton called 'Crest,' 40 feet called 'Lermer,' 435¾ feet of stone called 'Spaces,' 290¼ feet of stone called 'Tablement,' 817¼ feet of stone called 'Parpeincoins,' 1940 feet of stone called 'Scuassheler' scappled[2] [scapulat̃], 60 feet of stone called 'Pament,' 5000 plain tiles, one iron anvil, 12 tinned iron 'wrestlacches' with their furniture, 12 tinned iron rings with their furniture, 15 locks, 129 pieces of timber, 900 'ertrichbord' (*sic*) called 'Weynscot,' the 100 computed at six score, four little brass wheels for the 'Fernes,' 32 barrows (*siuer*), 128 trays (*treyes*), 2 casks, one pail, 2 hempen cables, 7 hempen ropes,—purchased as within.

And of one iron sledge, 1 iron tongs, 2 'nailtols,' 2 files (*ryles*), one iron pound-weight for weighing divers necessaries, 4 iron bolts for the wheels in the 'fernes,' 2 iron crows, 12 irons for beetles (*tribul*), one iron chain for a bucket, made by the smith; and of 10 cartloads of lead, received from William Sleford, clerk of the king's works at Westminster, by indenture.

Of which the same renders in account, as expended and used up in the said works, 193 pieces of *Petr de Caine Grese et de Beer*, worked and prepared as above; 32 tons of Beer stone, 44 tons of Caine stone, 22 tons of Stapelton stone, 90 tons of

[1] 'Securula,' a little axe, a hatchet; possibly a knife.

[2] The modern term 'scappling' signifies rough hewing, usually done with a pick; but the name seems formerly to have been applied to finer work.

Farlegh stone, 1031¼ feet of stone called 'Crest,' 328¾ feet of stone called 'Spaces,' 258¼ feet of stone called 'Tablement,' 807¼ feet of stone called 'Parpeincoins,' 63 feet of stone called 'Assheler coin,' 33 pieces of stone called 'Corbell,' 18 pieces of stone called 'Nowel,' 1904 feet of stone called 'Scuassheler,' 345 feet of stone called 'Squarassheler,' 304 feet of stone called 'Urnel,' 290 tons of ragstone, 4000 plain tiles, 5 tinned iron 'wrestlacches' with their furniture, 5 tinned iron rings with their furniture, 9 locks, 53 large pieces of timber, 79 'scaffoldloggs,' 100 cartloads of mortar, 100 cartloads of sand, 207 quarters 7 bushels of sea-coal, 40 large sheets (*pannos*) of lead, 7 sheaves (*garb*) and 20 'gadds' of steel, 18lbs. of iron, 4 pair of bolts, rides and bands (*gumph* and *vertivell*), 1350 iron nails, 5 beetles not ironed (*tribul non ferr*), 26 barrows (*siuer*), 96 trays, 1 hempen cable, 6 hempen ropes, 26 hurdles (*claias*), 830 boards called 'Weynscot;' and in covering the dwelling of the said Castle [dom̄ dc̄i Castri], and making the gutters, 9 cartloads 5 weighs (*v waug*) of lead.

And there remain 23 tons of Beer freestone, of which there are in stone worked and prepared for the works of the Castle next year, 6 tons; 18 tons of Caine freestone, of which there are in stone worked and prepared as above, 7 tons; 23 tons of Stapelton freestone, of which there are in stone worked and prepared as above, 6 tons; 105 tons of Farlegh stone, of which there are in stone worked and prepared as above, 40 tons; 18 pieces of Bocton stone called 'Nowel,' 121 feet of stone called 'Crest,' 40 feet of stone called 'Lermer,' 43 feet of stone called 'Spaces,' 32 feet of stone called 'Tablement,' 62 feet of stone called 'Parpeincoins,' 6 pieces of stone called 'Corbell,' 36 pieces of stone called 'Scuassheler,' 150 feet of stone called 'Squarassheler,' 60 feet of stone called 'Pament.' Item, 20 feet of stone called 'Urnel,' and 10 tons of stone called 'Rag,' a 'mouncell' of plaster of Paris, 1000 plain tiles; and in smiths' tools,—1 iron anvil, 4 sledges (*slegg*), 2 great hammers (*gross martell*), 4 small hammers, 2 'kervyngisnes,' 8 'tonges,' 3 'nailtols,' 1 bickorn (*bicorne*), 1 'spentonge,' 8 punch irons (*ponchons*), 7 files (*vyles*), 1 'folor,' j wassher (*wassh*), 1 iron herthstaf, 1 grindstone with the iron thereto, 2 bolsters of iron, j pair of bellows, j 'toier,' 7 tinned iron 'wrestlacches,' 7 tinned iron rings, 6 locks, j iron pound weight for weighing different necessaries, 55 large pieces of oak timber, 39 other pieces of oak timber, 90 boards called 'Weynscot,' 2 'fernes' with 4 little brass wheels and 4 iron bolts for the same, 120 'scaffold-loggs,' 50 hurdles (*claie*), 4 weighs of lead, 1 large broken leaden cistern, 1 whetstone (*gressor*) for sharpening the tools of the masons, 1 bell with its furniture, 7 iron hammers for the setters, 4 iron crows, 19 iron spades, 2 ironed beetles (*tribul*), 12 barrows (*siuer*), 40 trays, 2 casks for carrying lime, 4 wooden vessels for holding water (*imponend*, i.e. 'putting water in'), 3 tubs (*cuve*), j bowl, 2 buckets bound with iron, with 2 iron chains for them for drawing water, 1 hempen cable, 2 hempen ropes, 2 sieves (*cribris*), 1 'Poukweyn,' 3 ells of woollen cloth for the accountant (*compotor*), 1 seal of office, and 1 hatchet[1] (*securul*).

POST NOTE.

Since the above paper was completed, we have found, among the Sheriff's accounts for the county of Kent, from Michaelmas, 2 Edward I. (A.D. 1272), to Michaelmas, 3 Edward I. (A.D. 1273), when William de Valoynes was Sheriff, the following statement of expenditure on Rochester Castle:—

Custus Castri Roffensis per tempus supradictum.

ss. In grosso mæremio empto	v^s-j^d
In xx cheveronibus[2] emptis	v^s-vj^d ob.
In plaunches[3] et aliis xij bordis	iij^s
In xxiij carectatis terræ[4] ad fodendum et cariandum .	xx^d
In daubura ad parietes cum stipendio facientis per x dies	iiij^s-iiij^d
In sabulone	iiij^s-vj^d
In calce	xij^s
In cariagio ejusdem in Castrum	xij^d
In tegulatore	x^s
In bordis ad hostia et fenestras et aliis emptis . . .	vj^s-j^d
In xxj legges[5]	vij^d
In mille lattorum de quercu	viij^s
In iiij^or carpentariis per x dies	xj^s-viij^d
Item in uno carpentario per tres septimanas, ad facienda et reparanda plura alia in eodem castro . .	iiij^s

[1] See note, p. 129. [2] Rafters. [3] Planks. [4] Loam.

[5] Ledges.—The cross-pieces at the back of a door, formed of upright boarding, are called *ledges*; these are, perhaps, what this item refers to. They may have been used in the construction of the doors and window-shutters (*fenestras*) mentioned in the preceding item.

In viij^{to} mille tegule[1]	xvj^{s}-iij^{d}
In tribus millibus skynill[2] ad easdem tegulas emptis	iiij^{d} ob.
In Gomfis et vertenellis[3] et iiij^{or} serruris	xxxij^{d}
In grossis clavis et parvis	xxxj^{d} ob.
In purgettura[4] parietum aule deintus et deforis et in dealbatura[5]	xxj^{d}
In reparacione garderobe forinsece	xj^{d} ob.
In quodam colerio ad pendendam portam posterne	iij^{d}
Item in Gumfis et vertenellis, clavis, et aliis ad hostia et fenestras, ad domum ultra portam	ij^{s}
In blumbo ad eandem domum emendendam	ij^{s}-iiij^{d}
In j plumbario per iij dies	xij^{d}
In stabulo emendendo et mangero de novo reficiendo, tam in mæremio quam aliis ad idem emptis	iiij^{s}-vj^{d}
In serruris et aliis ferrininis emptis ad aulam et cameram	xij^{d}
In prisona mondanda et emendenda	ij^{s} ob.

Summa,—cxv^{s} ob.

Summa summarum,—x^{li}-xiij-v^{d} ob.

[*In dorso.*] "Custus Castri Roffensis."

L. B. L.

[1] *Sic.*

[2] Probably a kind of nail, or perhaps tile-pegs. From the entry of "mille latt." above, they may have been for nailing the laths, but as here entered they seem to belong to the tiles. But 3000 pegs would only do for 1500 tiles, except that (nowadays) half the tiles get but one peg. If they are lath-nails, there would be three to a lath, a reasonable allowance.

[3] See p. 125. [4] "Pargetting," *i.e.* plastering. [5] Whitewashing.

[6] ? emptis,—it is written 'epm.'

MONUMENT IN FOLKESTONE CHURCH.

E Blore Esq FSA del — O. JEWITT SC

MONUMENT IN FOLKESTONE CHURCH.

MONUMENT IN FOLKESTONE CHURCH.

The engraving which we have here the gratification of presenting to our readers, is copied from an exquisitely beautiful drawing of an ancient monument in Folkestone Church, by Edward Blore, Esq., the distinguished artist and antiquary, who, with a rare liberality, has taken it from his own unrivalled collection, and most kindly placed it at our disposal to illustrate our present Volume. The monument stands against the north wall of the chancel, and is in a very dilapidated state, without arms or inscription to identify it with any individual or family. We are left therefore entirely to conjecture, who it is to whose memory this sumptuous tomb has been raised.

Mr. Blore unhesitatingly rejects Hasted's supposition, that it is "for one of the Fiennes family, a Constable of Dover Castle and Warden of the Cinque Ports;" the monument evidently belonging to a period much later than that to which Hasted's conjecture could be applicable; and we agree with Mr. Blore, that the ownership of the monument must rather be sought among the Lords of Folkestone, or of some of its dependent manors.

The first step in our inquiry, then, must be an endeavour to obtain a correct account of the descent of the manor and barony of Folkestone, and an authentic record of its successive lords down to the time when the monument was probably erected;[1] which, in Mr. Blore's

[1] The pedigree given at the end of this article will be found of great use in facilitating the study of the evidences which we here adduce.

opinion, was the latter part of the reign of Edward II., or very early in Edward III.

In the Inquisition, on the death of HAMO DE CREVECŒUR, taken at Folkestone, on 16th April, 47 Hen. III., A.D. 1263, the Jury return—

That HAMO DE CREVECŒUR died seized of eight hundred and twenty-five acres in his domain, pertaining to the manor of FOLKESTONE, as of the inheritance of his wife, MATILDA DE AVERENCHES (who was heir to her brother, WILLIAM DE AVERENCHES, in the barony of AVERENCHES); that her eldest daughter, AGNES, was married to JOHN DE SANDWYCO; that her second daughter, ISOLDA, had married NICHOLAS DE LENHAM, and, by him, had a son, JOHN, now aged twelve; that her third daughter, ELENA (or ELENOR), was married to BERTRAM DE CRIOL;[1] and that her fourth daughter was married to HENRY DE GAUNT; that the said three daughters and the said son of NICHOLAS DE LENHAM were her next heirs, " et debent tenere totum predictum MANERIUM de FOLKESTONE, cum pertinentiis suis, de domino Rege, in capite, per Baroniam."

The next evidence which we shall quote in tracing the descent is a document preserved among the " Inquisitiones post mortem," being an " Extent " or survey of the manor of FOLKESTONE, taken 55 Hen. III., *i.e.* A D. 1270–1271 (see Esc. 55 Hen. III., No. 34), eight years later than the Inquisition just cited, to the following effect, viz.—

That on the Monday " post dominicam qua cantatur mĩas domino" (? Monday after the second Sunday after Easter, *i.e.* 20th April), 55 Hen. III. (A.D. 1271), on a division of the inheritance of MATILDA DAVERENCHES, the MANOR OF FOLKSTONE, with its purtenances and the advowsons of the churches, fell to the purparts of JOHN DE SANDWICO and BERTRAM DE CRIOL, in the name of AGNES and ALIANOR, the eldest (*annatarum*)

[1] By the partition of the inheritance, as cited in the " Extent," 55 Hen. III., p. 4, and also by the " Quo Waranto," 6 Edw. II., p. 8, it would seem that the Jury were in error in this return, and that Eleanor was the second daughter and Isolda the third.

daughters and heirs of the said Matilda Daverenches in the barony of FOLKSTONE.

Four years later, in the Hundred Rolls, 3 Edw. I.,—

The Jury return that SIR JOHN DE SANDWICO and SIR BERTRAM DE CRIOLL hold the barony of FOLKSTONE of the King, *in capite*, whereof the said Sir John de Sandwico has seven fees, and Sir Bertram de Crioll seven fees, and that they hold in common[1] (*communiter*) the hundred of FOLKSTONE, by 20*s*. per annum, to be paid to the King, by the hands of the Sheriff.

Thus far, it seems that the two coheirs, on the partition of the inheritance, took the barony in divided moieties of seven fees each, and the hundred in undivided moieties. In the same way, in a Plea of Liberties, on the Quo Waranto Roll, 7 Edw. I., they claim to hold together the hundred of FOLKESTONE of the King *in capite*.

Sixteen years later, on the "Originalia" Roll, 19 Edw. I., rot. 6, we have this entry (12th Feb., A.D. 1290–1, *i.e.* twenty-eight years after the Inquisition on the death of Matilda Daverenches):—

"Rex commisit Ricardo Filiol et Johanni de Mose, custodiam MANERII DE FOLKESTAN, cum pertinentiis, quod est in manu Regis, ratione minoris etatis JULIANE filie et heredis JOHANNIS DE SANDWICO defuncti, qui de Rege tenuit in capite, usque legitimam etatem predicte JULIANE. Reddendo inde Regi, per annum, ad Scaccarium Regis, quinquaginta libras et unam, videlicet, medietatem ad scaccarium Pasche, et aliam medietatem ad scaccarium Sancti Michaelis. Teste Rege, apud Wanetinge, xij die Februarii.

Here, then, it is clear that, however the lands may have been apportioned among the four coheirs of MATILDA D'AVERENCHES, the eldest, AGNES, had taken the "caput manerii," according to the doctrine laid down, p. 31, *supra*; for her son and successor, JOHN DE SANDWICO,

[1] "Tenants in common" know not which is their particular part, but take the profits in common. By Common Law they are not compellable to divide their parts; but afterwards, by Statute Hen. VIII., they were.

is here recorded as having died lord of the manor of Folkestone, which, having been held by knight-service *in capite*, is taken into the King's hands during the minority of his daughter and heir JULIANA, and let to two parties at the very high rent of £51 per annum, evidencing thereby its great value and extent.

In the "Inquisitio post mortem" on BERTRAM DE CRIOL, held at Newington, near Hythe, 29th April, 23 Edw. I., A.D. 1295,—

The Jury return that he held the manor of TERLINGHAM, of the inheritance of ELIANORE, his wife (who still survives), of the King, *in capite*, by service of one-sixth of a knight's-fee, and that it is part of the barony of FOLKSTONE; and that he held half the hundred of FOLKSTONE, of the inheritance of the said ELEANOR his wife (who still survives), of the King, by fee-farm of 10*s*. per annum. That he held the manor of NEWINGTON, near HYTHE, of the same inheritance; and that JOHN, son of the said BERTRAM, is his next heir, and aged thirty-four years.

In a Plea on the Quo Waranto Rolls, 6 Edw. II. (A.D. 1313), rot. 1-d,—

JOHN DE SEGRAVE and JULIANA his wife, and RICHARD DE ROKESLE and JOAN his wife, are summoned to answer by what warrant they claim to have the hundred of Folkstone, "emendas assise panis et cerevisie," etc., "visum franci plegii, sok et toll, infangenthef, furcas," etc. etc. etc., "in omnibus dominicis terris suis de FOLKSTONE, TERLINGHAM," etc. They answer, that this said manor of FOLKSTONE, of which TERLINGHAM is a limb, was once in the seisin of MATILDA DE AVERENCHES, who died thereof seised; that after her death they descended to AGNES, ALIANORE, ISOLDA, and ISABELLA, as her daughters and heirs; that ISABELLA was dead without issue, her purpart falling to the other three sisters; that in the division between the coheirs, the said manor with its said limb were assigned to the purparts of the said AGNES and ALIANORE. From AGNES, the right of her purpart descended to her son JOHN, as son and heir, and from the said John to the claimant JULIANA. That from the foresaid ALIANORE, the right of her purpart descended to the claimant JOAN.

14 Edw. II. In the Inquisition on the death of RICHARD, son of JOHN DE ROKESLEE, held at Rochester, Saturday after the Feast of St. Dunstan the Archbishop, 14 Edw. II., A.D. 1320,—

The Jury return that he died seised of the manor of TERLINGHAM, which he, with JOAN his wife, had of ALIANORE DE CRYEL, to them and to their heirs for ever, by license of King Edward I.;[1] and that it is held of the King *in capite*, by one-eighth of a knight's-fee, and it is worth £40 per annum; and that JOAN, wife of WALTER DE PATESHULL, aged twenty-five, and AGNES, wife of THOMAS DE POYNINGS, aged twenty-two, are the next heirs.

16 Edw. II. In the Inquisition on the death of JOAN, widow of RICHARD DE ROKESLE, held 4th January, 16 Edw. II., 1322–3,—

The Jury return, that she held the manor of TERLINGHAM of the King *in capite*, by service of one-eighth and one-sixteenth part of a knight's-fee. That in the said manor is a capital messuage, worth 2*s*. per annum; and 200 acres of arable land, worth £6. 13*s*. 4*d*. per annum; and 200 acres of pasture, worth 66*s*. 8*d*. per annum; and 60 acres of wood, worth 20*s*. per annum; and a rent of 42 seams of oats, worth 70*s*. per annum; and £32. 3*s*. 5*d*. rents of assize; 9 hens, worth 13½*d*. per annum; 305 eggs, worth 12¼*d*. per annum; a watermill, worth 13*s*. 4*d*. per annum; a windmill, worth 20*s*. per annum; pleas and perquisites of court, worth 10*s*. per annum. That the said JOAN, together with JOHN DE SEGRAVE and JULIANA his wife, in right of said JULIANA, held the hundred of FOLKSTONE of the King, as pertaining to the said manor; and that JOAN, the wife of WALTER DE PATESHULL, aged twenty-six, and AGNES, the wife of THOMAS DE POYNINGES, aged twenty-three, are her next heirs.

On the Fine Roll, 17 Edw. II., No. 29, there is a partition, under the King's writ, of the inheritance of RICHARD DE ROKESLEE and JOAN his wife, by agreement of WALTER DE PATESHULL and JOAN his wife, the eldest

[1] This looks as if a division of the manor had been made, *temp*. Edw. I., by the King's license. The eldest, AGNES, taking the "caput manerii," FOLKESTONE; ALIANORE taking TERLINGHAM, a limb of FOLKESTONE.

daughter and heir, and THOMAS DE PAYNINGES and AGNES his wife, the other and younger daughter and coheir.

After dividing the lands, it is settled that the Ward to Dover Castle, and the Romscot of the church of Folkestone, shall be paid equally in even portions, by the two coheirs; and in the same way, the profits of half the hundred of FOLKESTONE, and wreck of sea, shall be divided evenly between the parties.

Even to this period, then, no actual division had yet been made of the hundred of Folkestone and its franchises; but, as stated above, it seems that the "caput manerii" was in AGNES, the eldest coheir of MATILDA DE AVERENCHES and her heirs.

Esc. 17 Edw. III., (1st No.) No. 52. Inquisition taken at Pynyndenne, on Monday after the feast of All Saints, 17 Edw. III. (3rd Nov., 1343).

The Jury say, that JOHN DE SEGRAVE LE UNCLE held, by the law of England, of the inheritance of JULIANA his wife, long since deceased, in the ville of FOLKSTONE, the MANOR OF FOLKSTONE; whose scite within the ditches, with the aisiaments within the same site, is worth 4*s*. They say also that he held there 300 and a half acres, pertaining to the said manor, which are worth 100*s*. and 2*d*., at 4*d*. per acre. Also he held there 12½ acres of meadow, which are worth 12*s*. 6*d*. per annum, at 1*s*. per acre. He also held there 30 acres of wood, which are worth 12*s*. 6*d*. per acre, at 5*d*. per annum. He also held there of rent of assise per annum, xiij^{li}-ix^{s}-ij^{d}; and the pleas and perquisites of court there are worth vj^{s}-viij^{d} per annum. They say also that all the foresaid lands and tenements are held of our Lord the King *in capite*, by service of half a knight's-fee, and the service of v^{s} per annum, for ward to Dover Castle, and one suit to the county of Kent every fourth weeek. They also say that the said JOHN DE SEGRAVE died on Thursday next . . . . the feast of the translation of King St. Edward in the foresaid year.[1] They say also

[1] It is impossible to decide with certainty which of the feasts of the Translation of King Edward this is, probably that held on October 13th; but then the scribe, in the Inquisition, has omitted to record whether it be the Thursday next *before* or the Thursday next *after* that feast.

that John de Segrave, son of the said John de Segrave, is the next heir of the said Juliana, and is twenty-nine years old. They also say that the said John de Segrave le Uncle held nothing by the law of England, of the inheritance of the said Juliana, of other lords in the said county.[1]

Esc. 23 Edw. III., pt. 2, (1st No.) No. 44. Inquisition taken at Canterbury, on Saturday after the feast of the Assumption of the blessed Virgin, 23 Edw. III. (22nd Aug., 1349).

The Jury say, that John de Segrave, of Folkestone,[2] held of our Lord the King *in capite*, on the day of his death, the manor of Folkstone, with its pertinencies, by the service of one quarter and a half of a knight's-fee, and it is worth per annum, in all, according to the true value of the same, 100 marks. They also say that the said John, on the foresaid day, held nothing of any others in the said county. They also say that the said John died on Wednesday after the feast of the Translation of St. Thomas the Martyr, in the foresaid year (*i.e.* 8th July, 1349), and that Maria, daughter of the said John, is his next heir, and is fifteen days old.

Esc. 23 Edw. III., pt. 2, No. 44. Inquisition held at Lymyng, 16th Sept., 23 Edw. III., 1349, on Maria,

1 John de Segrave le Uncle = Juliana.
Ob. Oct.?, 17 Ed. III., 1343. — Dead 1343.
Lord of Folkstone "jure uxoris." — Lady of the manor of Folkstone.

John de Segrave,
son and heir.
Aged 29, 1343.

2 "Of Folkestone." He must therefore have died at Folkestone.

John de Segrave, of Folkstone =
Lord of Folkstone.
Ob. 8th July, 23 Ed. III., 1349.

Maria, daughter and heir.
Aged 15 days, 1349.

[N.B.—It will be seen that his daughter died 25th August, 1349, surviving her father just seven weeks, and only three days after the Inquisition held on her father's death.]

daughter and heir of Sir John de Segrave, deceased, who "diem clausit extremum infra ætatem."

The Jury say, that MARIA, daughter and heir of the SIR JOHN DE SEGRAVE, Kt., on the day of her death, held of our Lord the King *in capite*, the MANOR OF FOLKSTONE, by service of one-fourth and one-half of a knight's-fee, and it is worth 100 marks per annum; that she died on Tuesday after the feast of St. Bartholomew in the foresaid year.

The rest of this Inquisition is given in full, p. 38.

In an Inquisition at Loden, Norfolk, 10th February, 25 Edw. III., A.D. 1350–1, Segrave is described as "JOHANNES DE SEGRAVE, DE FOLKSTONE," who held the manor of Loden in Norfolk, etc. etc., and died 23rd Sept., 23 Edw. III.; and that John de Segrave, "dominus de Segrave, consanguineus predicti Johannis, est heres ejus," is his next heir therein, and is thirty years old and more.

The conclusions to be gathered from these different records, seem to be these:—That the Barony of FOLKESTONE, with the manor and hundred, fell to the four daughters and coheiresses of MATILDA DE AVERENCHES, on the death of her husband, HAMO DE CREVECŒUR (the tenant by courtesy for life), 47 Hen. III., A. D. 1263. That in 55 Hen. III., A.D. 1271, a division of the inheritance was made, by which the Barony of FOLKESTONE, and its manors and purtinancies, were assigned as the purparts of the two eldest daughters, viz. AGNES, wife of JOHN DE SANDWICO, and ALIANORE, wife of BERTRAM DE CRIOL. In this division, the eldest, AGNES, seems to have taken, as of right, the "caput manerii,"—the manor of FOLKESTONE,—while its limb, TERLINGHAM, was assigned to her sister ALIANORE. The other demesnes and purtinancies were probably then regularly apportioned between them. The hundred of FOLKESTONE, with its franchises, seems not to have been divided, but to have been held "in common" between the heirs and their respective representatives; and in this state of undivided moieties it evidently remained in 17 Edw. II., at which period an apportionment of ALIANORE DE CRIOL's half of the inheritance had become necessary by its descent to her grandchildren, the two daughters and coheiresses of RICHARD DE ROKESLE.

From the above authentic history of the descent of the manor, and from the fact that these SEGRAVES were actually styled LORDS OF FOLKESTONE, and that the last of them, if not both, were resident in the palace of the manor[1] very early in Edward III.'s reign; we can hardly doubt that the monument is that of SIR JOHN DE SEGRAVE, Lord of Folkestone, the last of that line of Lords of Folkestone, who died 23 Edw. III., and who is most specifically recorded as "OF FOLKSTONE."

Since the completion of the above remarks, I have been favoured with the following communication from Mr. Blore, whose authority on such subjects is too great to justify the omission of his letter. He says:—

"I should have no doubt of your being right in assigning the Folkstone effigy to one of the SEGRAVES, as the documents to which you refer locate that family there so distinctly. The only difficulty I have is, the style of the armour, which, as far as my experience goes, belongs to the period of late Edw. II. or very early Edw. III.; I should rather think the former. It has occurred to me, that there is a remarkable resemblance between this effigy and the mutilated one in ST. CLEMENT'S, SAND-

[1] There was a large park and mansion at Folkstone, for in the extents set out in the different Inquisitions above cited, the services of the tenants in keeping up its fences are specified.

In the Northwood Genealogical Roll, p. 16, *supra*, the marriage settlement of Sir Roger de Northwode with Elizabeth, daughter of Sir John de Segrave, 25th June, 5 Edw. III., A.D. 1331, is cited as signed at FOLKESTONE, which is a strong indication that SIR JOHN DE SEGRAVE was then actually resident there.

On the Close Rolls (Rot. Claus., 22 Edw. III., No. 29), 22 Edw. III., A.D. 1348, there is a grant to John de Segrave, of two markets in Folkestone, and he is styled therein JOHN DE SEGRAVE, OF FOLKESTONE, as he is also styled in the Inquisition taken at Canterbury, 23 Edw. III., and none of the others are said to be "of Folkstone."

WICH, and the LAVEROCK in ASH Church—though there is great variety in the detail. There is a DE SANDWICH one also, in the Hospital at Sandwich, which I have not seen, not knowing of its existence when I was there; this may, possibly, further illustrate the subject. What occurs to me is, that, if the dates of the three first effigies agree, they may assist in identifying each other, provided the date of any one can certainly be ascertained. Besides which, if they can all be embraced in the same article,[1] it will add much to its value, though it will increase your labour, for which, perhaps, you will not thank me. It strikes me, with regard to these effigies, as well as those at Winchelsea, that they all, more or less, belong to official personages, Admirals of the Cinque Ports, Constables of Dover Castle, and such-like; and the evidence in favour of RICHARD DE ROKESLE (who died A.D. 1320, 14 Edw. II., see Inquisition, p. 137 *supra*) being an official character, has induced me very much to select him as the person represented at FOLKESTONE, added to his family connection with the place, and the style of the armour being suitable to the period."

In another communication, Mr. Blore observes:—

"In its perfect state, this must have been a very handsome monument. The mourners on the side of the tomb, though very much defaced, are designed in the varied attitudes and costumes of those on the tombs of Aylmer de Valence, Lady Montacute, and other monuments of the same period. The details of the effigy are nearly obliterated; but, as far as they can be made out, they correspond with numerous examples of the same period."

[1] Unfortunately, our Volume has been already too long delayed to allow of the adoption of this suggestion. We must leave the investigation to a future Volume, and invite the co-operation of our local antiquaries therein.

L. B. L.

ITED

3*

enham = Isolda, third daughter, and coheir to her mother. Dead 1263.

4

Henry le Gaunt = Isabella, fourth dau., and coheir to her mother.

Lenham.
1263.

le Crevecœur, the Jury
as third.

(To face p. 142.)

DISCOVERY OF A ROMANO-BRITISH CEMETERY AT WESTBOROUGH, MAIDSTONE.

BY BEALE POSTE.

THIS cemetery appears to have been rich in its contents, and would, no doubt, have proved very illustrative, had not by far the greater portion of the objects found been, through absolute neglect, broken in pieces, dispersed, and lost. The following are nearly all the particulars which can be collected in reference to it.

The cemetery appears to have occupied a long and rather narrow slip of ground, about one hundred and fifty feet by thirty, lying across the river, in the part of Maidstone parish called Westborough, and according to the map of Maidstone, four hundred and ninety-five yards west by north of All Saints church. It lay on the top of the bank of the former Tunbridge and Maidstone road, which is now removed to another direction, more to the north, and the site is part of the new nursery-ground of Mr. Epps, lying nearly parallel to his forcing-house for exotics, which indeed stands on a part of it. The eastern half of the cemetery only has been taken up. The remainder is crossed by a road, and being laid out and partially planted for nursery purposes, has not been disturbed. Strictly speaking, only one interment was found out of the limits assigned to the cemetery, which appeared to be by the side of a pathway lined with stones, extending in nearly a north-east and south-west direction, and approaching the cemetery from the river. This pathway was discovered on the ground being deeply trenched. These diggings and moving of the ground continued from about November, 1859, to February or March, 1860.

The quantity of ground to be trenched or otherwise moved being considerable, namely some five or six acres, the chief object of the workmen was evidently to get on as fast as possible with their task; nor did their foremen or directors, though otherwise men of intelligence, appear to have been in anywise sensible that the objects found were of the least consequence, or worthy of any particular notice. Thus no pains whatever were taken in extracting the various objects from the earth, or preserving them from being dashed to pieces by the workmen's tools; and so little was thought of the discovery, that it was almost entirely unmentioned in the adjoining town for some considerable time. The ruthless destruction which took place, leaves me but a short task.

As a general summary, and on a somewhat rough calculation, about twenty-five or thirty skeletons were dug up; as a cart-load of bones was mentioned as removed; and about one hundred and fifty urns, or sepulchral vessels, including some of glass, were met with, as also coins, as it was said, in gold, silver, and copper, were obtained: though I could not verify this last particular myself, not having succeeded in purchasing or meeting with a single one of them. The purpose of the workmen, as the reader will easily imagine from the previous observations, was by no means to dig down beyond their required depth, in search of urns or antiquities; we have therefore no means of knowing how much of this nature they may have passed over, undiscovered in the progress of their work. I will presently enter into a short detail of what the objects which were found principally consisted.

A very noticeable circumstance connected with this Maidstone, or rather Westborough cemetery, is, that it is exclusively Romano-British. These, from some cause not easily assignable, are far more rarely met with than those of the Anglo-Saxons. We find that Faussett, in East Kent, examined seven extensive cemeteries, of which six were Anglo-Saxon, and only the seventh Romano-British, though partially Anglo-Saxon likewise. A reason may be, that the Saxons did not always respect the sites of the burial-places of the former inhabitants when they wanted them for other purposes, but used up their sarcophagi, and other stonework of these repositories, if they required them (see Bede's 'Ecclesiastical History,' book iv. 19, and Mr. C. R. Smith's 'Collectanea Antiqua,' vol. i. p. 188). At other times, again, they used these places of sepulture for themselves, which had the effect of obliterating former interments.

Another thing to be observed in this cemetery is, that the interments are partly pagan and partly Christian. The burning the dead, and urn-burial, denote the former, and the skeletons the latter, as is now universally agreed since the late Mr. Kemble's admissions on the subject, published in the Journal of the Archæological Institute for 1855, No. 48. However, as to the distinction of pagan and Christian, I have met with nothing among the things found at the cemetery which could be construed as being a symbol of Christianity. The population which supplied the interments was apparently a limited number of families, who resided near the bridge or in the environs, of whom a relic, a small statuette or figure of Sylvanus, is engraved in our Vol. I. p. 166, which was found some three hundred yards to the north-east of the cemetery, in the garden of the former hospital of Newark.

Such details as could be procured have been collected respecting Roman Maidstone in our first Volume, pp.

154–175, from which the relative situation of the present cemetery, with respect to the supposed former site of the Roman military station, Vagniacæ, at the north-west extremity of the present town, and distant nearly a mile, can be sufficiently understood. There were, of course, numerous outlying hamlets, villas, and agricultural dwellings in communication with every Roman town or station; and the former existence of these is generally ascertained by the discovery of foundations, or of coins, or of objects of pottery, or of an ornamental nature. Accordingly, traces of Roman occupation have been found in various localities within a mile or two of the town, as in Hayle Place grounds, Postley Fields, Allington Fields, Grove Green, and Vinter's Park. Our present cemetery takes its place among these as one of the number connected with the former station.

No traces of Roman foundations have ever been recorded as having come to light at Westborough; but we see from the experience of the present discoveries how easily they may have been overlooked. Two hills, or declivities of the ground, on either side of the Medway, approached each other where the original Romano-British hamlet, near the present bridge, may be considered to have been situated, which made a favourable place for the passage of the river; since below, on the site of the Fair Meadow, was a small lake or sheet of water, as was shown by a deep longitudinal cutting made through it in the year 1852, for the purposes of the Public Baths and Washhouses; whilst immediately above, opposite the Palace, Church and College, there was another lake of some fifteen acres in extent, formed by the spreading of the channel of the river. These lagoons, or sheets of water, now mostly verdant meadows, were shown to be rather numerous along the ancient course of the Medway, by the borings for the projected atmospheric railway in 1848. The hamlet, then, or dwellings, to which the

Roman Cemetery at Westborough belonged, would appear to have been connected with the ferry or other passage across the river in those times, in this its narrowest part; it being sufficiently known that the present bridge was not built till long after the Conquest.

I need not say much on the subject of the date of this cemetery, concluding that it extended through the greater part of the period of Roman occupation: that is, beginning with the Emperor Antoninus, or about the year 150, down to the Saxon invasion, when, by the year 473, the Britons in Kent were either driven away, or thoroughly subdued, and the Anglo-Saxons occupied their places.

The objects found, as far as they have come to notice, may be now described.—

I. A large earthenware urn, of the species called "Olla," (by estimation) about one foot eleven inches in diameter, and rather more in height. It contained a globe of green glass, about ten and a half inches in diameter, which was filled with fragments of human bones. These glass globes are not uncommon without handles; the present specimen however had two very broad ones, set opposite to each other, and fluted. I conclude the pattern of this is rare, as I cannot find that any have been before found of the same form. The Olla was destroyed by a stroke of a mattock, and the same fate awaited the glass globe; some fragments of this last however were preserved by Mr. Barling, of Maidstone, to whom the Society is indebted for the first intimation of the existence of these interments.

II. Other glass vessels were found, but, as it should seem, not preserved. Among which was a cantharus, or libation vessel or jug, with a long narrow neck, about nine inches high, and in good preservation, except the handle. This specimen of ancient art, becoming the property of one of the labourers, was a few days afterwards, on the family moving, consigned, with two urns, to the parish dustman.

III. Samian ware. There is a patera of this species of pottery, of the unornamented kind, in Mr. Barling's possession. The maker's name is stamped upon it, very plain to be read,—

IV. Urns, sepulchral vessels, bottles of a rounded shape, pateras, drinking-cups of the ancient form, ampullæ, cruets, etc. etc., all in a very common sort of earthenware. Of these, Mr. Barling has seven or eight specimens, more or less perfect; two, also, are in my possession. I may refer to plates ix. and x., vol. i., of Mr. C. Roach Smith's 'Collectanea Antiqua,' for some good representations of these kinds of objects, as also for a great variety of them.

V. A ring, three inches and a quarter in diameter, of a species of bituminous shale, otherwise brown jet. This ring, which is in my possession, is of a thick form, the hoop or round of it measuring half an inch, notwithstanding its interior surface has been worked away, and made quite flat. The other dimension of the round or hoop, which likewise has been flattened on one of its sides to the extent of an eighth of an inch, measures three-quarters of an inch. One of these rings, but larger and more ornamented, is engraved in Douglas's 'Nænia Britannica,' plate xiv. fig. 1. Antiquaries are not decided as to their use. They have been suggested as being *armillæ*, that is, ornaments worn on the arms; and, again, as rings through which the hair was passed in female head-dress. Jet (in Latin *gagates*) was used as a charm, as we find by ancient authorities, which would not have interfered with either of the above uses. These rings are rather rare. In the present case a skeleton was found, towards the middle of which lay the bones of a dog, with this ring between; at least, so the account was given, which also added that nothing else was found.

ARCHBISHOP WARHAM'S LETTERS.

(*Continued from Vol.* I. *p.* 41.)

We have been compelled to diverge somewhat from our original intention, to make room for the Will of John Roper, of Eltham, father of William Roper, who married Margaret, the favourite daughter of Sir Thomas More. Besides its importance in relation to the controversy, perhaps the most serious, between Warham and Wolsey, this Will, as the testator seems to have anticipated, gave rise to much discussion, and was at last the subject of an Act of Parliament, passed in the year 1529. The succession to Roper's house in Kent, held by the custom of Gavelkind, appears to have produced disputes in the family, which could not be settled without so grave an interposition.

> "Nec Deus intersit nisi dignus vindice nodus
> Inciderit."

No private cause in England, whether considering the eminence of the parties concerned, or the issues involved in it, had, up to that time preferred so strong a claim on the majesty of Parliament.

This Will, and the Letters, are from originals in the Record Office, where further correspondence is preserved in connection with the Ropers, to which we may possibly have occasion to refer hereafter.

24. Archbishop Warham to Cardinal Wolsey.

Pleace it your grace to understand that now lately I receyved letters from thAbbat and Convent of Boxley, in whiche they offerred to bynd thaire house by thaire writings obligatorie, to be sealed with thaire convent seale, for the payment of all suche sommes of money as thAbbat oweth the Kinges highnes, bireason of his collect. Wherein, he and his said convent desireth respite, and favor, touching dayes of payment to bee graunted, for a tyme in that behalf.

In whiche matier, seing the said Abbey is an exempte place of your graces jurisdiction, I wold bee very lothe to medle, unles I were in maner forced thereto, by thact of convocation, auctorising me, and my lord of London, to make processe against suche collectors as pay not thair collect, accordingly as it is specified in the xviith and the xxith chapitur of the said convocation. And forasmuche as the said place is power, and much seking is thither to the rode of grace, from all partes of this realme, I wold be lothe, if I myght chose, to interdicte the place, or, to put the fruictes of the same, under sequestration, tyll the kinges highnes bee payed for diverse causes, whiche I doubt not, but your grace wol son coniect.

Whereupon, considering that it is an exempt place of your graces jurisdiction, whiche I wold bee lothe to interdict, or sequester the fruictes thereof, and considering this matier concerneth paymentes to be made to the kinges grace, wherein, I am not mynded to gyve dayes, without your graces pleasure knowen in that behalf. I entierly beseche your grace to advertise me by your moost honorable letters, what is your graces mynde and pleasure best to bee doon in this caas, outher to interdict the said monastery, and sequester the fruictes; orels graunt thaim som respite and dayes of payment, upon thair writinge obligatory under thair convent seale. Thabbat, as far as I can perceyve and lerne, is utterly disposed to lyve hardly and precisely, to bryng the place out of debt, and affore hand after this greate warnyng, and if I thought he wold not, I wold in no caas wrote or speke any letter or word in his favor. Diverse men bifore this, have fallen sore, whiche have arrisen and recovered; and have doon as well and better, than they whiche never fell, and so I trust this Abbat woll, orels it were piety that he shuld lyve muche longer to the hurt of so holy a place, where so many miracles be shewed. At my manor of Otford, the third day of May.

At your graces commandement,
WILL'M CANTAR.

To the moost Reverend Father in God, and my very singular good lord, my Lord Cardinall of York and legate de latere good grace.

·j·

---

25. FROM THE SAME TO THE SAME.

Pleace it your good grace to understand that I have receyved your moost honorable and loving letters, dated at your graces place beside Westminster, the secunde day of this moneth of Marche, by whiche I perceyve how graciosly ye take in good part my fre and playne writing to the same, whereof in my moost hertie wise I thank your grace, assuering you that unles I had had in your gracis undoubted favors and benignite towardis me verey singulier trust and confidence to write without displeasure, not only the playnes of my mynde, but also suche reportes as were brought unto me, I wold in no wise have attempted to disclose my said mynd and reportes so openly.

And where your grace adviseth me from hensfurth to give lesse credence to all thoes that have made suche untrue reaportes as bee conteyned in my said letters, studieng more to make division than to norisshe good amite and accorde bitwixt your grace and me. Suerly albeit I rehersed in my said letters suche reaportes as were writen and spoken unto me, and none otherwise, as I shall annswere affore god, yet I trust it cannot bee gatherd of my said letters that I gave any firme credence to thoes report. For unfaynedly whatsoever surmises sinister reportes or insinuations have been made or shalbe made unto me, by whatsoever menys they com, they have not, and shall not rayse, kendyll, or ingender in me any part of grudge of mynde towardes your grace, orels any mystrust in your singulier goodnes, favors, and benivolence towardes me, which evidently towardes me and myne by substanciall experiment appereth dayly more and more, which your graces manifold good dedes bee more depely fastened in myne hert and remembrance, than can bee removed by any wordes or reaportes whiche your graces goodnes I am not able to recompense with any other thing than with my feithful hert, true love, and dayly prayer for your grace, whereof your grace, being thus so good lord unto me, shalbee so well assuered as far as my litell power shalbe able to extende as of any thing in this worle, orels I were far unkynd and unthankfull.

And I beseche your grace to think none otherwise in me but that I esteme and set by the favor of your grace a hunderth tymes and incomparably more than by the privat cause of Jane Roper or any suche.

And forasmuche as your grace writeth that your grace is contented at my desire to forbere further proceding in the principal matier of John Ropers testament tyl I may awaite on your grace after Ester, I hertly thank your grace, and entend therefor to bee shorter in writing at this tyme, and to differ my ful annswer tyl I may have present conference and communication with your grace, trusting that none of your graces counsail whiche is groundly lerned hath or wol persuade unto your grace, that by vertue of your legacy, notwithstanding the composition that I made with your grace as legate de latere, ye may procede severally in knowlege of testamentarie causes, whiche heretofor have only apperteyned to the jurisdiction of my prerogative, and that without any breche of the said composition. If any lerned wol affirme and prove the same, suerly he hath seen other lawes, or other understanding of lawes than I could ever know or perceyve, and yet I have taken some payne to loke for suche matiers.

Finally, I trust when I shal com to your graces presence so to declare my mynde to the same in every thing that your grace of your goodnes shalbe right wel contented and pleaced there withall by the grace of God, who preserve your grace in highe honor and dignite, long life and good helth, as good as I can desir to have myself. At my churche of Cantrebury, the vi[th] day of Marche, [152$\frac{4}{5}$?]

At your grace commandement,

WILL^AM CANTUAR.

To the moost Reverend father in god and my verey singulier good lord my lord Cardinal of York and legate de latere good grace.

(Sealed.)

THE WILL OF JOHN ROOPER, ESQ.

In the name of God Amen. I John Rooper, of the paroche of Eltham, in the countie of Kent, the xxvii day of Januarye, in the xv yere of our sovereign lorde King Henry VIII., and in the yere of our Lorde God m^{l} v^{c} xxiij, being of hole mynde and good remembraunce, thankes be to God, make this my present testament in fourme folowing:—Furst, I bequethe my soule to Almightie God, our blessed lady sayncte Mary the Vyrgyn, and to all the company of heven, my bodye to be buryed in the churche of saincte Dunston without Westgate of Canterburye, in the chapell of Saincte Nycholas, in the same church where I have made my buryeng place. And I bequethe to the Vycar of the same churche, for my tythes necligently forgotten xiii^{s}-iiij^{d}. Item, to the reparacyons of the churche of holy crosse within the Westgate of Canterburye, xx^{s}. Item, to the Vycar of saincte Brydes in London, for my tythes forgotten, x^{s}. Item, to the Vycar of Eltham, for lyke cause, x^{s}. And to the reparacyons of the same churche, xx^{s}. Item, to the reparacyons of the paroche churche of Swalclyf, xx^{s}. Item, to the churche of Cosme and Damyane in the Bleen, for like cause, x^{s}. Item, for lyke cause to Whitstaple churche, xx^{s}. Item, to the reparacyons of the churche of Henn, xx^{s}. Item, to the reparacyons of the churche of Stowrmothe, xx^{s}. Item, to the reparacyons of the churche of Preston, beside Wyngham, x^{s}. Item, to the reparacyons of the churche of Ryver, beside Dover, vi^{s}-viij^{d}. Item, to the reparacyons of the churche of Ewell, vi^{s}-viii^{d}. Item, to the reparacyons of the churche of Saincte Stephin, besyde Caunterbury, xx^{s}. Item, I bequeth to the pryor of Christe Churche of Caunterbury forsaide, and to the convent of the same place, for a dyrige and a masse of requiem to be sayed and song there, by the same pryor and convent in convenyent tyme after my decesse, v^{li}, whereof the saide pryor to have xx^{s} for his labor, and the residue to be devyded amongst the convent of the same place, rateablye by the pryor of the same church for the tyme being by his discression. Item, I bequethe to the Abbot of saincte Austen's, without the walles of Caunterbury forsaide, and to the convent of the same place, iij^{li}-vj^{s}-viij^{d}, for lyke cause, whereof the saide Abbot to have for his labour xiij^{s}-iiij^{d} and the residue to be devyded, by the discression of the Abbot there for the tyme being, rateably amongst his convent. Item, I bequethe to the

Abbot of Batayllе in Sussex, and to the convent of the same place, for lyke cause, iij^{li}-vi^{s}-viij^{d}, whereof the Abbot to have xiij^{s}-iiij^{d} for his labour, and the residue to be devyded amongst his convent in lyke manner as, as aforsaide. Item, I bequethe to the Abbot of Feversham, and to his convent of the same place, for lyke cause, iij^{li}-vj^{s}-viij^{d}, whereof the same Abbotte then being to have for his labour x^{s}, and the residue to be devyded amongst his convent rateablye. Item, I bequethe to the pryour of saincte Gregorye, without the Northgate of Caunterbury forsaide, and to the convent of the same place, for lyke cause, xl^{s}, whereof the pryour of the same place to have for his labour x^{s}, and the residue to be devyded amongst his convent rateablye.

Item, I bequethe to the making of an horse way, for the fisshe wyves, and other, in the highway from Whitstaple, to the entring of the strete of saincte Dunston, without the Westgate of Caunterbury, in suche place, and places, as the Abbot of Feversham that now is, and other myn executours, shall thinke most necessary and convenyent, one hundredth markes, And the saide Abbot to have for his labour about the same xl^{s}. And I requyre myn executours to have at my buryeng dirige, and on the morow, xxx masses to be song and sayed, or mo by the discression of myn executours, without making of any gaye herse, other than iiij grete tapers of wex to be set about the herse, to be light at the servyce, and to be holden with iiij poure men with iiij blacke gownes, and iiij children with iiij blacke gownes, with iiij lesse tapers. And in lyke manner at my monethes mynde, And the prieste and clerke to have for theyr labours as myn executours can with them reasonably agree. And ferthermore, to order my buryall in such maner as my saide executours shall thinke necessary and convenyent. Not passing perfourming of my saide buryall, and monethes mynde, the expence of 100^{li} which I will be theruppon disposed by the advyse of my saide executors. And after yerely suche masses and dirige to be sayed ones in the yere, as in my last will shalbe declared, for the helth of my soule, and my frendes' soules, and all xtien soules.

And of this my testament I make and ordeyn the Reverende father in God the pryor of Christe churche of Canterbury forsaid, for the tyme being, Sir John Fyneux, knight, chief Justice of the King's benche, Richard Broke, Judge, to whom I bequethe iij^{li}-vi^{s}-viii^{d}, John Hales, one of the barons of the King his Exchequer, and Jane my wif, myn executours, for the assistence of the saide Jane in that behalf. And for the forther helpe of such labour and paynes as shall happen to be aboutte the accomplisshement of the premisses and perfourmyng of my testament and last will, I make also Christopher Hales, John Sethe, Robert Maycote, John Chilton, and John a Berry, myn olde servaunte, myn executours. And I bequethe to my wif Jane C.C.^{li}, and to every of the same pryor, and Lorde Fyneux, for theyr labor, x marks, and to the saide John Hales, iij^{li}-vi^{s}-viii^{d}, and to the saide Christopher, xl^{s}. And to every of the saide John Sethe, Robert Maycote, John Chilton, and John a Bery, xl^{s}. And these bequests beforesaied of one 100^{li} for my buryall, or more as my saide executours shall think necessary and conventyent, and the saide C.C.^{li} to my saide wif, to be levyed of my moveable goods and cattalles if it will thereof arryse, orells to be levyed of the yssues and proffytes of my manors, landes, and tenementes, as is conteyned in my last will. And all the residue of all my saide bequestes aforesaide to be levyed of thissues and proffytes yerely of my manors, landes, and tenementes in my last will specefied and conteyned: landes and tenementes lymyted to my wiffe, Joynctors and londs and tenementes lymyted to my soonnes Edwarde and Christofer, and londs and tenementes for our yerely obyt to be kept in my last will of my manors, londs, and tenementes conteyned and specefied onely excepted; and all the residue of my saide moveable goodes and catalles to be disposed by my saide executours in maner and fourme also as in my saide last will of my manours, landes, and tenementes is specefied and conteyned, desiring all my saide executours specyally of theyr charytees to cause this my present testament and last will to be fulfilled asmoche as they may. And if complaynte happen to be made uppon me after my decesse of any Injury or Wrong don by me in my lif to any person or persons, and theruppon lawfull profe therof had and made by any suche person or persons, then I will my saide executours make recompence and amendes to the same person or persons so complayning, or otherwise agree with them, which recompence and amendes I will shalbe levyed of thissues and proffyttes of suche manours, landes, and tenementes as in my last will be lymyted and appoynted for payment of my debttes and dyvers bequestes in the same last will also specefied and conteyned.

This is the last will of me the saide John Roper, made the

xxvii[th] day of January, in the xv[th] yere of the reigne of King Henry the VIII., as to the disposicyon of all my manours, landes, and tenementes, Rentes, Revercyons, Servyces, Advowsons, and other heredytamentes, with theyr appurtenances, Whereof I the saide John Roper ioynetlye with other be seased, or whereof any other person or persons ben seased to myn use, within the Counties of Kente, Surrey, the Cytee of London, or ellswhere, within the Realme of Englonde.

Fyrst, forasmoche as I have provyded and caused myn eldest soonne Willyam to be prefferred, and to be Joynt offycer with me in the office, of the chief clerke of our Sovereigne lorde the King, for plees before the same King to be holden, and perceyve the proffyttes thereof after my decesse, the Atteyning of which office was to me no litle charge, And also where the grete parte of my saide manours, landes, and tenementes, to the yerelye value of one hundreth poundes and above, ben of the tenure and nature of Gavylkynde, and that londes and tenementes of the same tenure and nature of Gavilkynde, within the saide Countie of Kent ben, and the tyme that no manne's mynde ys to the contrary, hathe ben parted and parteable emonge heyres males, and to thintente my soonnes after my decesse, shall have no cause to varye amongst them selffes, or to stryve for the partycyon and devyding of the same, I therefore openly declare this my saide last will concerning my saide manours, landes, and tenementes, by these presentes in fourme folowing, that ys to saye:

Fyrst, I will that all the saide persons, theyr heyres, and assignes, seased of and in all my saide manours, landes, and tenementes, Rentes, Revercyons, Servyces, Advowsons, and other heredytamentes, with theyr appurtenances aforesaide, shall after my decesse ymedyatly stonde and be seased of and in my manor place of Welhawe, Courtelage, Barnes, Stables, Gardeyns, Orchards, the motes and waters there, in the paroche of Eltham, with theyr appurtenances, in the saide Countie of Kent; And also of and in my pryncypall place, with the barnes, stables, courtlages, and gardeyns, with theyr appurtenances, in the paroche of Saincte Dunstons without the walles of Caunterburye, in the saide Countie of Kent; and also of and in my pryncypall place called Chestfelde, with the barnes, stables, gardeyns, and Orchards, with theyr appurtenances, in the paroche of Swalclyf, in the saide Countie of Kent: and of and in every of them, to the use of Jane my wif, aslong and all the tyme that the saide Jane do lyve sole unmaryed, without impechement of waste, wilfull waste as of plucking downe of houses onely excepted; And also of the pryncypall mansion place called the lodge, with the quadrante, the kitchen, the houses next adioyning to the same, called the milkehouse, the dof house, Gardeyn, and orchard, in the paroche of Linsted, during her lif, notwithstanding that she marye. Which pryncypall mansion place and houses in Lynsted aforsaid, amongst other landes and tenementes, Sir John Fyneux, knight, chief Justice of our sovereigne Lorde the King, at plees before the same King to be holden, by his writing gave and graunted to me, and to the saide Jane my wife for ever, to dispose it to any of the soonnes of me the saide John Roper and Jane, which it shoulde lyke us to lymyte yt unto. And over that I will that the saide Jane shall take and perceyve to her owne use, of thissues and proffyttes of all the saide manours, landes, and tenementes aforesaide, in such place and places as hereafter in this my last will shalbe appoynted, one hundreth markes, and fewell for her household yerely during her lyf. And also I will that the issues and proffyttes lymyted for the joyntour of the saide Jane shalbe at the lymytacyon and poyntement of the same Jane during the space of x yeres after her decesse, to be disposed at her Will if she lyve sole.

And Ferthermore I will my saide wif, lyvyng sole unmaryed, shall yerely after my decesse receyve and take xiij^{li}-vj^{s}-viij^{d} of thissues and proffyttes of the saide manor called the logge, and of all other landes and tenementes in Lynsted aforsaid, Dodington, Kingsdowne, and Norton, within the saide Countie of Kent, and of my londes and tenementes in Estgrenewich, and Candelwike Strete in London, till my Soon Edwarde cummeth to the age of xxiiij yeres, towardes the exhibycyon and fynding of my saide soon Edwarde to lerning, and to kepe my saide sonne Edwarde therewith honestly during the saide terme. And when my saide soon Edwarde cummeth to the age of xxiiij yeres, then I will that my saide wif shall trewly content and paye to my saide soone Edwarde, that ys to say, of the issues and proffytes of the saide manor called the Logge, and of the londes and tenementes in Lynsted, Kingsdowne, Norton, and Dodington; of the saide londes and tenementes in Estgrenewich, and also of the saide londes and tenementes in Candelwike Strete in London, xx^{li} at the feastes of Saincte Michaell the Archaungell and thannuncyation of our lady the Vyrgyn, by even porcyons yerely, as long as the saide Jane doth lyve sole unmaryed.

And if the saide Jane be maryed or decesse before thage of xxiiij yeres of the saide Edwarde my soone, then I will that my saide feoffes, theyr heyres and assignes, shall stonde and be seased of all the saide londes and tenementes in Lynsted, Kingsdowne, Dodington, and Norton, with theyr appurtenances, and of the saide londes and tenementes in Estegrenewiche and Candelwike strete in London, with theyr appurtenances, to the use and intente that the saide Edwarde shall have and perceyve of thissues and proffyttes thereof to his exhibicyon and fynding xiij^{li}-vi^{s}-viij^{d}, till he cum to the saide age of xxiiij yeres; and after when he cummeth to the age of xxiiij yeres, then the saide Edwarde to have and perceyve of thissues and proffytes thereof yerely xx^{li}, unto suche tyme as my dettes, bequestes, and legacies ben levyed and payed, or convenyently might be payed; and ymedyatlye after my dettes, bequestes, and legacies levyed and payed or might be levyed or payed, my saide feoffes, their heyres and assignes, shall stonde and be seased of the revercyon of the saide manor place in Lynsted, and of all other londes and tenementes in Lynsted, Dodington, Kingsdowne, and Norton, and of the londes and tenementes in Estgrenewiche, and Candlewyke Strete in London, with theyr appurtenances, to the use of the saide Edwarde during his lif, without impechement of waste; and after his decesse to thuse of his eldest issue male of his bodye, lawfullye begotten; and so from one the eldest yssue male to one other the eldest heyre and yssue male of his bodie begotten, for ever, Undevyded and not to be parted ne parteable emonges heires males.

And for lacke of suche issue male, then I will that of the same manours, landes, and tenementes, to the saide Edwarde before lymyted, my saide feoffes and theyr heyres and assignes shall stonde and be seased of them, to thuse that the doughter of the same Edwarde, if he happen to have yssue female, shall have, take, and perceyve of thissues and proffytes of the same manours, landes, and tenementes, one C^{li} [£100] to her preferrement. And if there be mo then one, the saide C^{li} to be egally devyded bitwen them. And after the saide C^{li} levyed and had, or convenyently might be levied and had to the use aforesaide, and my dettes and legacies levyed and payed, or might be levied and payed, then my saide feoffes, theyr heyrs and assignes, shall stonde and be seased of the reverceyon of the saide manours, landes, and tenementes before lymyted to the saide Edwarde, for lacke of such issue male of the saide Edwarde, to thuse of Christofer my youngest soon, for terme of his lyf, without impechement of waste; and after his dicesse to thuse of his eldest yssue male of his bodye lawfully begotten, for terme of his lyf, without impechement of waste; and after his decesse to one other the eldest next yssue and heyre male of his bodye cummyng, and so from one the eldest yssue male of his bodye begotten, to one other the eldest heyre and yssue male of his bodye begotten, for ever, undevyded, and not to be parted ne partable amongst heyres males as long as there ys or shalbe any yssue male of his bodye begotten.

And for lacke of suche yssue male, I will that my saide feoffes, theyr heyres and assignes, shall stonde and be seased of the same manours of Logge, landes and tenementes in Lynsted, Dodington, Kingsdowne, Norton, Estgrenewich, and London, to thuse of the doughters of my soon Christofer and theyr heyres for ever; and lyke wise I will that my wif Jane, lyvyng sole and unmaryed, shall take and perceyve yerely xiij^{li}-vj^{s}-viij^{d} of thissues and proffyttes of my manors of Welhaw and Esthorne, in Eltham, in the saide Countie of Kent, and of all my other londes and tenementes in Eltham forsaide, Modingham, Lee, Cheselherst, Kydbroke, Charleton, Woolwich, and Bexley, with theyr appurtenances, in the saide countie, tyll my saide soon Christofer cummeth to the age of xxiiij yeres, towardes the exhibyceyon and fynding of my saide soon Christofer to lerning, and to kepe him therewith honestly during the saide terme; and when that my saide soon Christofer cummeth to the age of xxiiij yeres, then I will that my saide feoffes, theyr heyres, and assignes, shall stonde and be seased of my saide manours of Welhawe and Esthorne, and of all my other manours, landes, and tenementes in Eltham, Modingham, Cheselherst, Lee, Kydbroke, Charleton, Wolwiche, and Bexley, with theyr appurtenances, to thintent that my saide wif, lyving sole unmaryed, shall yelde and paye yerely to the saide Christofer my soon of thissues and proffytes of them at the feastes of Saincte Michaell tharchaungell and thanaunceyacion of our Ladye, by even porcyons, xx^{li} yerely; and yf the saide Jane decesse, or be maryed before the saide age of xxiiij yeres of my saide soonne Christofer, then I will that my saide feoffes, theyr heres and assignes, from thensfourth shall stonde and be seased thereof, to the use and intente that the saide Christofer my Soonne shall have and perceyve of thissues and proffytes of the saide manours, landes, and tenementes, in Eltham, Modingham, Cheselherst, Lee, Kydbroke, Charleton, Wolwiche, and Bexley, $xiij^{li}$-vj^{s}-$viij^{d}$ towardes his exhibycyon and fyndyng; and when the saide Christofer cummeth to the age of xxiiij yeres, then I will my saide feoffes, theyr heires and assignes, shall from thensfourth stonde and be seased of the saide manours, landes, and tenementes in Eltham, Modingham, Cheselherst, Lee, Kydbroke, Charleton, Wolwich, and Bexley, to thintente that the saide Christofer shall have and perceyve of thissues and proffytes thereof to the yerely value of xx^{li} till my dettes, bequestes, and legacyes be levyed and payed or convenyently might be levyed and payed; and after my dettes, bequestes, and legacies levyed and payed, or might be levyed and payed, then and from thensfourth my saide feoffes, theyr heyres and assignes, shall stonde and be seased of the saide manours, landes, and tenementes in Eltham, Modingham, Lee, Cheselherst, Kydbroke, Charleton, Wolwich, and Bexley, to thuse of the saide Christofer during his lif, without impechement of waste, and after his decesse to thuse of the eldest issue male of the bodie of the saide Christofer lawfully begotten, and so from one the eldest heyre and yssue male to one other the next eldest yssue male of the bodye of the saide Christofer lawfully begotten, for ever, to be undevyded and not partable amongst heires males.

And for lacke of such issue male, then I will my saide feoffes, their heires and assignes, shall stonde and be seased of the same londes and tenementes to the saide Christofer before lymyted, to thuse that the daughters of saide Christofer, if he have issue female, shall have, perceyve, and take, of the issues and proffyttes of the same londes and tenementes lymyted to the saide Christofer, one C^{li} for her preferrement, and if there be mo then one, the C^{li} to be egally devyded bitwen them; and after the saide C^{li} levyed and had, or convenyently might be levyed and had, to thuse aforesaid, and my dettes and legacies levyed and payed, or might be levyed and payed, then my saide feoffes, theyr heyres and assignes, shall stonde and be seased of the same manours, landes, and tenementes assigned to the saide Christofer, to thuse of the eldest heyre male at the commune law, of my body begotten, during his lyf, without impechement of waste, and after his decesse to thuse of one the eldest next issue and heyre male of his bodye cummyng, and so from one the eldest issue male unto one other the eldest yssue male of his body begotten, aslong as there is or shalbe any issue male of his body begotten; and for lacke of suche yssue male I will my saide feoffes, theyr heyres and assignes, shall stonde and be seased of the saide londes and tenementes before lymyted to the saide Christofer, to thuse of the next heires of Willyam myn eldest soon, and of theyr heyres for ever.

Provyded alwaye that every of my soonnes Edward and Christofer, or theyr eldest yssue male, that shall happen to have and enjoye the saide londes and tenementes, to the saide Edwarde and Christofer severally in manner and fourme afore lymyted, shall and may make a joynctour to theyr wif or wiffes of the same, or of parcell thereof, to them appoynted for terme of theyr Wiffes' lyves, and that my feoffes, theyr heires and assignes, thereof shall during that tyme stond and be seased of the same, to thuse of the same wif or wiffes, as the saide Edward and Christofer, or the saide issue male, therunto shall appoynte and lymyte, during the lif or lyves of the same wif or wyves; and also may make exchaunge thereof for other londes and tenementes of like value or better Levyng, the same londes and tenementes taking in exchaunge in lyke wise and to like intent, and being of as just tytle as the saide londes and tenementes to the saide Edwarde and Christofer before lymyted ben.

Also I will that my feoffes of and in the londes and tenementes in Hakynton and Saincte Stephen, that I late purchased of John Lytilcote and his wif, and if it so may be, and which wern sumtyme Nycolas Sheldewiches, and of the landes and tenementes in the paroche of Saincte Dunstons next Canterburye, late Rycharde Filpottes, and the londes and tenementes late Elyzabeth Loveryke, widowe, decessed, in the paroche of Saincte Dunstons without the westgate of Canterbury, or any of them, and of and in a pece of lande called Brambiltighe, conteyning by estymacyon ix acres, lyeng in Hakynton, Whereof vij acres were sumtyme Selokkes, theyr heires and assignes shall from the tyme of my decesse suffer my saide wif and her assignes to take and perceyve yerely thissues and proffytes of them during her lif, she lyvyng sole unmaried, to this intent that the same Jane my wif shall yerely kepe the

Reparacyons of the houses of the same londes and tenementes, and also to pay yerely the quyterentes of the same londes and tenementes to the chif lordes of the fee, with parcell of the proffyttes of the same londes and tenements; and with the residue of the same yssues and proffytes that shall remayne yerely over and above the necessary reparacions of the same houses and paymentes of the saide quitrentes, I will that there shalbe by her one yerely obyte of one dirige and xxx masses kept in the churche of Saincte Dunstons aforesaide, the dirige to be song uppon the evẽ of that day that shall happen me to pass out of this present world; and upon the morow folowing the saide xxx masses, yerely for ever to pray for the helth of the sowle of the excellent prynce King Henry VIII., when he shall passe from this transitory lif, the soules of his progenytours and successours, and for my soule, my wiffes soule, when she shall happen to passe out of this worlde, my fathers soule, my mothers soule, the soule of John Rooper, Founder of the Chauntrye of Saincte Nycholas, in the saide churche of Saincte Dunstons, the sowle of Sir John Fineux, chief Justice of England, Father to my saide wif, when he ys departed from this worlde, and for the soule of dame Elizabeth, late his wif, Priour Sellinges soule, priour Goldestones soule, Sir John Wyllyamsons soule, Myldred Appultrefelde soule, the soule of Dame Elizabeth Borchier, Thomas Barrettes soule, John Herstes soule, his fathers soule, and his mothers soule, Wymarkes soule, Sir John Kysley soule, Willyam Maryners soule, Richard Bollinges soule, Jane Frognalles soule, Rycharde Gyttons soule, Agnes Letters soule, John Roo soule, clerke, all my childrens soules, my kynnys soules, my frendes soules, my servauntes soules, and all Christian soules, Whereof iij of the saide masses to be song by note, the furst of the trynytee, the seconde of our blessed lady, and the thyrde of requiem eternam; and that every pryest being at the dirige and masse, on the morrow; every of them iiij^{d}, and those iij that synge the saide iij masses by note, and being at dirige, every of them to have vj^{d}; and that there be spente uppon poure people in almes, in brede and chese, xx^{d}, and ij[^{s}] in ale; and to vj poure men, torcheholders, every of them ij^{d}; and for waste of wax at the dirige and the saide iij masses iij^{s}; amongst clerkes and children helping the pryestes at the masses, xx^{d}; and also vi^{s}-viii^{d} yerely to fynde brede and wyne and wax to the ij chauntrye preestes at the masses to be songen at the Aulter in the chappell of Saincte Nycholas in the saide churche of Sainct Dunstons. And also to a poure man that can helpe a pryest to sing, and being of honest disposicyon, yerely, towardes his fynding, xxxiij^{s}-iiij^{d}, to the intent that he shall daylie by the yere helpe the saide Chauntry preestes at masse when they be disposed to say masses; and also the same poure man to say ones a day wekely our Ladye's salter yerely, in the honor of our blessed lady, to pray for my soule, my wiffes soule, the soules of my father and mother, the sowle of John Rooper, Founder of the saide Chauntrye, and for the soules of all the other before named and specifyed. And that the saide poure man for the tyme being shall have the lytle house that goeth for v^{s} by the yere, and a gardeyn to the same, next adjoyning to the great tenement that I purchased of the saide Elizabeth Loveryk, to inhabyte and dwelle in during his lif, to this intente, that the same poure man for the tyme being shall have the keping of the grete place and gardeyns at sainct Dunstons forsaide, after my decesse, in the absence of my wif while she lyveth, and after in the absence of him that shalbe owner of the same place after the decesse of my saide wife, if my saide wif in her tyme, or the owner of the saide place, patron of the saide Chauntrye, will therwith be contente and pleased, and if not, then to helpe the preeste to theyr masses, and to say the psalter of our ladye daylie, and to pray for the soules before specefied. And also with thissues and proffyts of the same londes and tenementes I will there be a lampe brennyng yerely, by night and day, before the sacrement, in the quyer of the same churche of saincte Dunstons, in the honour of the holy sacrament.

And if it happen my saide Wif to Decesse or be maryed, then I Will my saide feoffes of and in my saide londes and tenementes to my saide wif in fourme beforesaide willed and assigned, to the saide obyt and other premisses to be pfourmed and kept, shall from and after the decesse of my saide wif, or after or fro her saide maryage, take and receyve yerely for ever the yssues and proffytes of the saide landes and tenementes to thintent to delyver and pay the saide yssues and proffytes yerely to the eldest chauntrye pryest of contynuaunce of the saide Chauntrye of saincte Nycolas for the tyme being, to thuse and intent that the same eldest chauntry pryest shall dispose and distribute the same of thissues and proffytes of the same londes in lyke manner and fourme as I have before willed and declared my saide wif to do, perfourme, and dispose, with thissues and proffytes of the same londes and tenementes, and to the same intente, for ever; and the same Chauntery priest to receyve for his diligence and labour yerely for the doing of the same vj^{s}-viij.

And if it happen the saide eldest Chauntry priest of contynuaunce in the saide Chauntrye for the tyme being, to make defaulte and to sease the perfourming of the premisses in manner and fourme aforesaide to be doon, then I will that Wyllyam my soon, the eldest heyre male of my body, owner in use of my saide grete place at sayncte Dunstons, and patron of the saide Chauntry, shall have the rule and disposicyon of the saide yssues and proffyttes, therwith to do and perfourme this my last will in manner and fourme aforesaide During his lyf; and after his decesse, one suche issue male as there shalbe or ought to be my next heyre male of my bodye begotten, owner in use to the saide place, Patron of the saide Chauntrye, shall have the rule and disposicyon of the saide yssues and proffyttes, therewith to do and perfourme this my last will in fourme aforsaide During his lyf. And after his decesse, one suche yssue male as there shalbe or ought to be my next heyre male of my bodye begotten, owner in use of the saide place, patron of the saide Chauntrye, shall have the disposicyon and rule of the saide yssues and proffyttes of the same londes and tenementes to perfourme my saide last will in fourme aforsaide During his lif. And so one other myn eldest and next heyre male of my body after one other my next eldest heyre male of my body shall have the Rule and disposycyon of thissues of the same landes and tenementes to perfourme this my last will in manner and fourme aforsaide for ever.

And as to all thissues and proffyttes of all the residue of manours, landes, and tenementes, Rentes, Revercyons, servyces, Advousons, and other heredytamentes, within the saide Shire of Kent or elles where, except the saide manours, landes, and tenementes before limyted to the saide Edwarde and Christofer, and except the saide pryncypall place, Courtelage, barnes, stables, gardeyns, or orchardes, that is to say, sainct Dunstons, Chestfelde, Welhawe, and Logge, in manner and fourme aforsaide, to my saide Wif before lymyted, and thissues and proffyttes of my saide other manours, landes, and tenementes, to the value of the saide C markes yerely hereafter lymyted to my saide wif, and the saide londs and tenementes assigned to the saide obyte and Almes, I will that the same yssues and proffyttes shall from the tyme of my decesse be receyved and taken by myn executours, and by them fully and hollye to be imployed and bestowed to and for the paymentes of my bequestes, dettes, and legacyes, and perfourmaunce of this my will. And after my dettes, bequestes, and legacyes in this my last will specefied ben of thissues and proffyttes thereof levyed, fulfilled, and trewly perfourmed, or convenyently might be perfourmed, then I will that all my saide feoffes, theyr heyres and assignes, being seased of and in all the same manours, landes, and tenementes, Rentes, Revercyons, servyces, Advousons, and other heredytaments, with theyr appurtenaunces, except before lymyted to the saide Edwarde and Christofer, obyt and almes, shall stonde and abyde seased thereof to the use of my saide wif as long as she lyveth sole unmaryed. And if my saide Wif happen to mary or to Decesse before my saide dettes, bequestes, and legacies be levyed and payed, or might convenyently be levyed and payed, then I will that thissues and revenues of all my londs and tenementes abovesaide, except the landes and the tenementes lymyted to my soonnes Edward and Christofer, obyt and Almes, and the saide mansion place, and landes, houses and orchards, called the logge, and the saide C marks yerely to be to the saide Jane, shalbe taken, receyved, and imployed by myn executours to the perfourmance and payment of my dettes, bequestes, and legacyes, unto the same my Dettes, legacies, be or shalbe fully levyed and payed, or might be fully levyed and payed. And after the same my dettes and legacies shall or might be of the issues and proffyttes in fourme abovesaide, of the residue of the saide manours, landes, and tenementes, except before in this my last will to my said soonnes Edwarde and Christofer, obyt and almes, and C marks to my saide Wif Jane, in manner and fourme before lymyted, my saide feoffes, theyr heyres and assignes, from thensfourth shall stonde and be seased of the same residue to thuse of the saide Willyam myn eldest sonne during his lif, without ympechement of waste. And after his decesse to the next eldest yssue and heyre male of the bodye of the saide Willyam, lawfully begotten. And so from one the next and eldest heyre and issue male of the bodye of the saide Willyam begotten, to one other the next and eldest yssue male of his bodye begotten for ever, to be undevyded and not ptable amongst heyres males.

And for lacke of suche issue male, I will that my saide feoffes, theyr heyres and assignes, of all my saide manours, landes, tenementes, Rentes, Revercyons, servyces, advousons, and other heredytamentes, with theyr appurtennces, shall stonde and abyde seased thereof to the use that the doughters of the saide Willyam, if he happen to have yssue female, shall have, take, and perceyve of thissue and proffyts of the same manours, landes, and tenementes lymyted to the saide Willyam C.C.li to her pferrement. And if there be mo then one, the same C.C.li to be equally devyded bytween them. And after the saide C.C.li be levyed, had, and payed, or convenyently may be had, levyed, and paied, then I will my saide feoffes, theyr heires, and assignes, shall abyde and stond seased of all the saide residue of the saide manours, lands, and tenementes, Rents, Revercyons, servyces, advousons, and other heredytamentes within the Countie of Kent aforsaide, except before excepted, as well of landes and tenementes, advousons, and other heredytaments thereof of the saide teanure and nature of Gavilkynde, as of the other lands, advousons, and other heredytaments thereof, being at the comune law to thuse of suche one yssue male as then shalbe or ought to be my next heyre male of my bodye begotten, at the saide comune law of this Realme, And to the londes and tenements being holden by knightes servyce, for terme of his lif, without impechement of waste, So that alwaye I will that one person being my next and eldest heyre male of my body begotten, shall have in severaltee all my saide manours, landes, and tenementes, Rentes, Revercyons, servyces, advousons, and other heredytamentes, with theyr appurtenances, except before excepted, and lymyted to my soonnes Edwarde and Christofer during his lif, without impechement of waste. And so from one myn eldest and next heyre male of my bodie to one other eldest and next heyre male of my bodie for ever, to contynue without dyvision or partycyon thereof, to be made bitween or emonges the heires males of my bodye after the custome of landes of the teanure and nature of Gavilkynd.

And for lacke of such issue male, then my said feoffes, theyr heyres and assignes, shall stonde and be seased from thensfourth of the saide residue of the saide manours, lands, and tenementes, advousons, and other heredytamentes before lymyted to the said Wyllyam, to thuse of the Doughters and heyres of the saide Edwarde, and of theyr heyres for ever, provyded alwaye that after the Decesse of my saide soonne Willyam, when my next heyre male or any of his eldest yssue male shalbe maryed, my saide feoffes, theyr heyres and assignes, shalbe seased of and in landes and tenementes for a joynctour to her that at such tyme is or shalbe wif to the eldest yssue male of the saide Willyam, to her use onely for terme of her lif, as the saide eldest and next heyre male of the saide Willyam or his eldest yssue male of his body for the tyme being shall lymyte and thinke to be behofull and necessary, so that the Joynctour passe not above xl[li] by yere.

And I will that my feoffes, theyr heyres and assignes shall not delyver ne execute any estate to any of my soonnes for terme of lif, ne otherwise onely to any other person or persons; But that the same feoffes, theyr heyres and assignes, shall stonde and abyde seased thereof, thuse and intent abovesaide. And also I will that when all my saide manours, landes, and tenementes, with theyr appurtenances shall happen to cum to ij[o] or iij of my feoffes, that then the over lyver of them shall make or cause to be made a new feoffement thereof by thadvyse of my saide soones Willyam, Edwarde, and Christofer, and other my or theyr eldest heyre male for the tyme being, and such other then lyvyng as apparantly may or might be heyrs male to me the saide John Rooper, or the more parte of them. And if all my saide feoffes dye without making of any suche feoffement of my saide manours, landes, and tenementes, to thuse and intent afore specefyed, then I will that the heyre or heyres of him that survyveth and that longest lyveth of my saide feoffes shall make or cause to be made a feoffement of the same by the saide advyse of myn eldest heyre male, and of my other heires males for the tyme being as ys before expressed in lyke manner as ys beforesaide to other persons, and theyr heyres and assignes, in lyke uses and to lyke intentes as ys afore specefyed; And so for ever from tyme to tyme lyke feoffementes to be made thereof, when nede shall requyre, to the saide uses and intentes aforsaide for ever, without making any estate or estates of the saide manours, landes, and tenementes, or of any of them, to any such yssue or eldest heyre male, but alway to contynew in use in my saide feoffes, and Survyver or Survyvours of them and theyr heyres, unto to such tyme as the saide feoffementes be made to other persons and theyr heyres to the same uses afore specefied, according to the trew mynde and fulfilling of this my last will.

And over that I will that my saide Soonnes Edwarde and Christofer, till they cum to the Age of xxiiij yeres, And my Doughters Elizabeth and Agnes till they be maryed or otherwise advanced, shalbe in the governance and Rule of my saide wif if she so long lyve, and she to receyve and take yerely the yssues and proffytes and somes of money to suche of them and every of them bequethed and lymyted in this my last will and testament for theyr fynding, and also to take and levye of thissues and proffytts of the saide manours, landes, and tenementes, except before excepted and lymyted to the saide Edwarde and Christofer, and the saide C marks to my saide Wif hereafter lymyted, towardes the perfourmaunce of my saide dettes and bequestes as long as my saide wif lyveth sole unmaryed. And if my saide wif mary or dye before my bequestes and dettes be payed and fulfilled, then and from thensfourth I will that thissues and proffytts of all my saide londes and tenementes and other heredytamentes shalbe yerely taken up and receyved by the pryour of Christes churche of Caunterburye for the tyme being, towardes and to thintent that the pryour of the same churche of christ in Caunterbury for the tyme being shall suffer my saide wif, during her lyf, to have out of my manours of Chestfelde, and other my londes and tenementes in Whitstaple, Swalclyf, Hern, Cosme, and Dannyane Le Bleen, and Recolver, within the saide Countye of Kent, And out of my manour of Hakynton, landes and tenementes in the saide paroche of saincte Stephins, in the Countie aforsaid, the saide C marks of good and laufull money of Englond.

If my saide Wif Do not let the perfourmaunce of this my last will, then the same my wif to have onely xl marks out of the same manours, landes, and tenementes, of lauful money, yerely payable at the feastes of the Natyvyte of our lorde god, and the Natyvytee of sainct John Baptist, by even porcyons. And my saide wif to have non further occupacyon and possession of my saide manours, landes, and tenementes, but onely the saide mansion place of the logge aforesaide During her lyf. And ferther I will that the saide C marks yerely lymyted to my saide Wif, to be made as sure unto her During her lif upon condycyon to be perceyved out of the saide manours, landes, and tenementes aforesaide, payable at the saide feastes, as by the same Jane my Wif and her counsaill shalbe devysed, in full recompence and satisfaction for her Dower and ioynctour. And then I will that the residue of thissues of my saide manours, landes, and tenementes be levyed yerely towarde the fulfilling, perfourming, and payeng of my saide Dettes and legacies before specefied, the unperformed and not payed. And over that to the fynding of every of my saide Doughters Elizabeth and Agnes iij^{li}-vj^{s}-viij^{d} till my saide Doughters be maryed or otherwise advaunced. And also to every of my saide Doughters maryages C.C. marks, if they shall not be maryed in my lif, or otherwise by some other covvenantes of their maryages by me in my lif provyded, and if any of them Dye before maryage or covvenantes and bondes made by me for the same, then her parte to sease. And if they or any of them entre into religion, then they or she so entering into Religion to have xl marks, and no more. And the saide Edwarde and Christofer to have to theyr fynding till they cum to the age of xxiiij yeres, of thissues and proffytts of the same manours, landes, and tenementes to them before lymyted, every of them the saide xiij^{li}-vi^{s}-viij^{d} as is before saide, till they cum to the saide age of xxiiij yeres. And at the age of xxiiij yeres every of them to have xx^{li}, till my dettes, bequestes, and legacyes ben levyed and payed, or might convenyently be levyed and payed, as ys above specefied, and also to be levyed of thissues and proffyttes of the same manours, landes, and tenements. I will and bequethe to my wif Jane above, her owne apparell C.C.^{li}, and to my Doughter Agnes, the Nunne of Dartford, to pray for my soule, xiij^{li}-vj^{s}-viij^{d}, and to the pryoresse and convent of the same place, for lyke cause, iij^{li}-vj^{s}-viij^{d}. And to my Lady Fyneux, Suppryoresse of Dartford, xl^{s}. And to every of my Doughters Elyn and Margaret x^{li}.

And I will that of thissues and proffyttes of the same manours, landes, and tenementes, except before excepted, there be levyed for every of my Systers, being alyve at my Decesse, iij^{li}-vj^{s}-viij^{d}, and for every of my Clerkes, being with me in my houseolde at my Decesse, xx^{s}. And to every other houseolde servante x^{s}. And I will that John a Bery, my servante, have the issues and proffytts of my tenement in Candelwyk strete, in London, which Willyam Harryson holdeth, during the lif of the same John a Bery, Any thing in this my will to the contrary Notwithstonding. And also I will there be levyed of thissues and proffytts of the saide manors, landes, and tenementes, except before excepted, to thuse of every of my saide soones Edwarde and Christofer, if they lyve to the age of xxiiij yeres, towards their preferment, in maryage or otherwise, or for landes to be purchased for them or every of them, C.C.^{li}. And also I will that every place of freers in Caunterbury have xx^{s}, and every place of harbaldowne and saincte Johns in Caunterbury xx^{s}. And to Maynards spyttell, being to the Castelwarde of Caunterbury x^s. And to every of the pryson houses Westgate and the Castell x^s. And I will that my Dettes, bequestes, and other Somes of money by me in this my last will willed, be fully levyed onely of thissues and proffytes of my saide manours, landes, and tenementes, except before excepted, as it will arryse, before my saide sonne Willyam take and have my saide manours, landes, and tenementes, or any of them, to him in manner and fourme before lymyted. And that myn executours dispose my goods and cattalles after suche meanes as I have before declared. And the residue by me not declared ne bequethed, to be distributed and disposed by my saide executours, by theyr discressions, towards the ferther Reliffe of my saide wif, and for the welth of soule, my frends soules, and all Christen soules, as by the said Jane my wif and myn executours shalbe thought convenyent, if she so longe abyde and be sole unmaryed. And if it happen my saide executours by any accyon or otherwise by the law be compelled to pay any of my det or dettes of my moveable goods before they have levyed the saide Dettes and bequestes aforesaide of thissues and proffyts of the saide manours, landes, and tenementes, thereunto before lymyted, then I will that my saide wif and other myn executours shall kepe the saide manours, lands, and tenementes, and thereof take thissues and proffyts of the same manours, landes, and tenementes, till they have receyved and levyed the same Dettes so payed of my moveables, and all my other Dettes and bequestes aforesaide of the same issues and proffyttes in lyke manner to be levyed or convenyently might be levyed, as is afore rehersed.

Also I will that the saide pryour for the tyme being to have for the trew executing of this my last will, if my wif dye or be maryed before the performance of this my saide will, xx marks yerely of thissues and proffyttes of my saide manours, landes, and tenementes, Whereof x^{li} to thuse of the same pryour, and iij^{li}-vj^s-$viij^d$ to suche one person as the saide pryour shall appoynt to receyve the issues and proffyttes of the same manours, landes, and tenementes, And that as long and unto the tyme this my last will be fully perfourmed, or reasonably might be perfourmed. And Furthermore, I will that if my saide soonne Willyam, his heyres and assignes, do lette, interrupte, or distourbe the perfourmaunce of this my testament and last will in parcell thereof, that then my saide feoffes, theyr heyres and assignes, shall ymedyatly from thensfourth stonde and be seased of all my manours, landes, and tenementes, before lymyted to my saide sonne Willyam within the same Countie of Kent, to the use of the saide Edwarde my sonne, During his lif, without impechement of waste. And after his decesse to thuse of his eldest yssue male of his bodye begotten. And so from one the eldest yssue male to the eldest yssue male of his bodye begotten, Undevyded, and not to be parted ne partable emonges heires males.

And for lacke of suche yssue male of his bodye begotten, then I will my saide feoffes, theyr heyres, and assignes, shall stonde and be seased of the same manours, landes, and tenementes, before lymyted to my saide Soone Willyam, to thuse of the saide Christofer my sonne, During his lif, without impechement of wast. And after his decesse, to thuse of his eldest yssue male to one other the eldest yssue male of his bodye begotten. And so from one his eldest yssue male to one other the eldest yssue male of his bodye begotten for ever, Undevyded, and not to be parted ne partable emonges heyres males. And for lack of such issue male, then I will my said feoffes, theyr heyres and assignes, shall stond and be seased of the said manours, landes, and tenementes, before lymyted to my saide Sonne Willyam, to thuse of theldest heyre male, at the comen law, of my bodye begotten, During his lif, without impechement of Waste. And after his Decesse to one theldest and next yssue male of his body cumyng. And so from one theldest yssue male to one other theldest yssue male of his bodye begotten, as long as there ys or shalbe any yssue male of his bodye begotten. And for default of such issue male, to thuse of the Doughters of the saide Edward, and of theyr heyres for ever. And if my sonne Edward, his heires, or assignes, do let, interrupte, or Distourbe the perfourmaunce of this my last will in any thing, or in any parcell thereof, then I will my saide feoffes, theyr heyres and assignes, of and in the saide manours, landes, and tenementes before lymyted to my saide Soonne Edwarde, shall ymedyatly from thensfourth stond and be seased of the same manours, landes, and tenementes to thuse of my saide sonne Christofer for terme of his lif, without impechement of waste, And after his Decesse to thuse of theldest issue male of his bodie begotten, And so from one the eldest issue male to one other the eldest yssue male of the bodie of the same Christofer laufully begotten for ever, to be undevyded, and not to be parted ne partable emonges heires males.

And for lacke of suche yssue male, then I will that my feoffes, theyr heires and assignes, of the same manours, landes, and tenementes, before appoynted to the saide Edward my sonne, shall stonde and be seased thereof to thuse of the eldest heyre male at the comen law, of my bodie begotten, During his lif, without impechement of waste, And after his decesse to thuse of one the eldest next yssue male of his bodie cumyng, And so from one theldest yssue male unto one other theldest next yssue male of his body begotten, as long as there ys or shalbe ony yssue of his body begoten. And for lacke of suche yssue male of his bodye begotten, then I will my saide feoffes, theyr heires and assignes, shall stonde and be seased of the same manours, landes, and tenementes, before lymyted to the saide Edwarde, to thuse of the Doughters of my saide sonne Christofer, and of theyr heyres for ever. And in like wise, if my saide sonne Christofer, his heyres or assignes, do let, interupte, or distourbe the perfourmance of this my last will above specefied, in every thing or in any pcell thereof, then I will that my saide feoffes, theyr heyres and assignes, of and in my saide manours, landes, and tenementes, before lymyted to the saide Christofer, shall ymmedyatly from thensfourth stonde and be seased thereof to thuse of the saide Edwarde, During his lif, without impechement of waste, And after his decesse, to the use of the eldest yssue male of his body begotten, And so from one the eldest yssue male to one other theldest yssue male of the body of the saide Edwarde laufully begotten for ever, to be undevyded and not to be parted ne partable emonges heyres males. And for lacke of such issue male, then I will my saide feoffes, theyr heyres and assignes, of and in the saide londes and tenementes lymyted to the saide Christofer, shall stond and be seased thereof to thuse of theldest heyre male at the comen law, of my body begotten, for terme of his lif, without impechement of waste, And after his Decesse, to thuse of one theldest next yssue male of his body begotten, And so from one the next eldest yssue male unto one other theldest yssue male of his body begotten, to be undevyded and not to be parted ne partable emonges heyres males. And for lacke of suche yssue male of his body begotten, then I will my said feoffes, theyr heyres and assignes, of and in the same londes and tenementes before lymyted to the saide Christofer, shall stonde and be seased thereof, to thuse of the saide Willyam myn eldest sonne, and of his heyres for ever.

Also where John Morton Esquier, late one of the gentilmen Sewers of the quenes chamber, by his indenture, bering date the fyrst day of December, the xth yere of the reigne of king Henry the viij[th], made a lese to me and to John Morton, his brother, decessed, of his manours of Cosyes and of all his landes and tenementes in Romford and Havering at the Bowre, in the countie of Essex, for terme of xl yeres, yelding and payeng therefore yerely to the same John Morton, Esquier, During the same terme, xv[li] of laufull money of Englond, at the feastes of thanuncyacon of our lady and saincte Michaell the Archangell, by even porcyons, as by the same indenture more playnely may appere, And over that where I have Receyved yerely sythen the tyme and day of this saide lease xv[li]-xiij[s]-iiij[d], by even porcyons, at the saide feastes of thanuncyacon of our ladye and saynete Michaell the Archangell, of his manour of Allerston, in the Countie of Warwyk, I will that thereof, for his fynding and his servantes mete, Drynke, fyer, candell, bed, and bourde, by the yere; for fynding of one horse for his servaunte to Ryde upon his maisters bysynes, by the yere, xx[li] yerely to be allowed to me and to myn executours, and also allowed for the charges spent uppon the same John Morton, Esquier, for his clothing, hose, and shoes, and other necessaryes for his bodye, and for his servauntes wages, and for the reparacons of his saide manours necessary to be Don yerely; that then the residue above the saide fynding, clothing, and wages of his servante, and other charges aforesaide, fyrst payed and allowed, I Will it be disposed to William Morton the elder, and Willyam Morton the yonger Brethern, to the saide John Morton, esquier, and to Anne and Elyn his Systers, which have nothing toward theyr preferrement, equally to be dyvyded bitween them as long as it shall happen the same John Morton, esquier, to remayne in the custody of my wif, myn executours, and assignes.

Pme Johem Roop.

The bequestes specefied in the testament of John Rop *Esquier.*

Imprimis, to the vycar of sainct Dunstons . . xiij[s]-iiij.

Item, to the reparacyon of the churche of holy crosse within the westgate of Canterbury . . xx^s
Item, to the parson of saincte Bryds, in London x^s
Item, to the

The above Will furnishes us with the following bit of pedigree :—

John Roper, Will 1523. = Jane. 1523. Daughter of Sir John Fyneux, Chief Justice of the King's Bench, 1523.

William Roper, eldest son and heir, 1523, a Clerk of the Pleas.	Edward. 1523. inf. æt.	Christopher. Youngest son inf. æt. 1523. N.B. The grandson of this Christopher was created Baron Teynham in 1616, direct ancestor of the present Lord Teynham.	Agnes. A nun of Dartford, 1523.	Elizabeth. 1523.	Agnes. 1523.

SIR ROGER TWYSDEN'S JOURNAL.

(*Continued from Vol. I. p. 214.*)

41. To wch purpos it may heere deserve a place what a friend of myne writ unto me soone after the bill for continewing their sitting, and ye Act of Poll mony, in wch I was a Commissioner, had past, and finding sundry doubts troubling me how to proceede in it, I imparted them to my cosen Richard Browne,[1] a Parliament man (whose memory is ever deere unto me), for hys advise, who returned me answer the 24th of July, 1641, That he feared it might bee unseasonable to produce those my doubts, though just; for he had seene of like nature moeved lately w^th^out successe; That hee did hope the very good lawes allready made, and endeavors for more, would cause ye kingdome to bear wth the inequalities, considering what was rendered them again, wherein both howses had beene bold wth themselves, having payd allready, and the City and Westminster goe on freely; and then proceeds thus:—

"Onely some popish and some episcopall men do cunningly indeavour to infuse, especially in both the Universities, ill opinions, as if all learning were falling, and the Universities fayling, if Lords, Bishops, and Deans, etc., should bee altered, wherein what is indeavoured were too long to write; but, in generall, ye ayme is, to commit the episcopall jurisdiction to Laymen in every county,[2] and to give Orders by learned Ministers, upon examination of parties that are to enter into Orders,

[1] Of Great Chart. He was Member for New Romney.

[2] This formed a part of a scheme drawn up by Sir Edward Dering.—Ed.

intending to provide for every parish a resident painfull preacher, and for that preacher a competent maintenance, where it shall bee least an 100^{l} per An^{m}, and to some double, treble, quadruble, or more; and when this is setteled for a tyme, I beeleeve there will bee many learned men called together, to confer of one discipline through all the reformed churches, as neere Christ's owne Ordinances as may bee. But, Sir, these last are but some private opinions and desires; and when our bill of Episcopacy comes to the Lords, wee doubt it will bee buryed in a Lawne wynding sheete. Sir, you see how willing I am to emparle wth you, whose presence heere might have affourded much counsell, both in these and other things, as now for setteling the Armes of ye Kingdome, in some legall posture, for the defense of the Kingdome, by taking away, or by regulating, Deputy Lieutenants; but I must leave writing, etc.

"Your truly affected friend, and kinsman,

"RICHARD BROWNE.

"*24th July*, 1641."

42. To wch letter I find this answer amongst my papers:—

"Sir,—I am much bound unto you for your kind letter, as for y^{t} you write, of inequalyty in ye law of Pole mony, I hope and doe not think it will make any dispute in this country. And certaynly the good Acts past this session deserve as much as wee have payd. I confesse, if it bee lawfull for me to speak my owne thoughts, the thing I most mislike in our payments is, that the two howses are as well expenditors as grauntors of them, wch I apprehend is a poynt may prove dangerous; for certaynly your nwe officers must eat up much of what wee pay, beesides what else.

"But as for that you write is endeavoured about Episcopacy, I professe I see a great tempest hanging over ye Kingdome; for beesides y^{t} remoeving ordination from ye Bishop is questionlesse that will give our adversaries advantage, who could never fixe it as not Apostolicall in this Church, and what I am persuaded, ye King and Lords will never be induced to passe, I doe take many things annexed to their calling not absolutely spirituall, yet not so proper for lay men to meddle wth. But to let that passe,—where you say it is desired 'every

Ecclesiastique cure may have a paynfull resident preacher, none of w[ch] to have lesse than an hundred pound a year, treble, quadruble, or more, etc.' This is, suer, a thing to bee hoped rather then expected. Truly no honest conscientious man but doth wish, when the great inundation happened on y[e] Ecclesiastiques in Henry y[e] 8[ths] tyme, many appropriations, wth the religious howses to w[ch] they perteyned, coming to y[e] Crowne, but y[t] the Parlyament would have given them to y[e] Parishes to w[ch] they first beelonged; but they beeing now in Lay hands, I see no possibilyty of doeing it, unlesse by applying that little remayns from Bishops and Cathedrall churches to y[e] parochiall incumbent, w[ch] is y[t] I can not desire ever to see done; first, in respect of y[e] revenue of y[e] crowne; for I hold it an undoubted Maxime, the Kingdome must maynteyn y[e] King; and there is no question but any Prince may wth lesse envy rayse somes of mony from them then the Lay, they beeing, for y[e] most, as a body that gives rather then perticular persons, and w[ch], beeing ritch, is not subject to so great expences as the temporalyty, and therefore better able to spare it, as their payments are greater; but it is a dangerous president to take from them what by Law and long continuance is setteled upon them. When y[e] yce is once broken for eyther Prince or any else, by these extraordinary ways of assuming the estates of others (of what condition soever), it is hard to say where it will stoppe. The 27th Hen. 8th, cap. 14, was so far from taking away y[e] universities, as it made hon[ble] mention of the greater religious howses, w[ch] yet in y[e] printed is omitted. (And this I take to bee y[e] first that ever any Parlyament by meere power divested eyther socyety or corporation of their estates.) The 31st Hen. 8th, cap. 13, tooke them away; yet heere it stopt not; for the 37th of Henry y[e] 8th, cap. 4, put chantries, Colledges, both the universities, into y[e] King's hands; so that there was not, to my understanding, much of publique to bee had now from them: certaynly it was more then hys Ma[ty] did think fit to make use of, and was onely in part renewed to hys Sonne (1st Ed. 6th, cap. 14), who finding nothing left to bee taken from that body, the Commons were forced (2[d] et 3[d] Ed. 6th, cap. 36) to ayd hym with a nwe invention of Reliefe out of sheepe, cloaths, goods, debts, etc., for three years, so heavy as y[e] Parlyament next ensuing (the 3[d] and 4th Ed. 6, cap. 23), they were constreyned to desire hys Ma[ties] mitigation, the clothier beeing in a manner discouraged from making cloath; yet I can not find all this made ye Crowne ritch. Henry ye 8th (the first of any English Prince), 1544, made abundance of base money. Camden observes he left England *opibus exhaustis*,[1] that Queene Elizabeth received it *afflictissima, ære alieno quod Hen.* 8 *et Edw*^d^ 6 *contraxerat oppressa*;[2] Heyward[3] that Edward ye 6^ths^ debts were sayd to be 251,000 pounds; and this, after so large contributions, as, for my part, I can not reckon the treasure spent in fiefteene years, what in subsidies, fiefteenths, and other graunts, lesse (rather more) then ye value of half ye kingdome to bee sold. I shall conclude this long letter wth one observation: that whilst the Church was ritch (in taking away or altering whose estates, I doe not onely looke at them, but myself; for who doth from one may from ye other), there was no compulsory Act for relieving ye Poore, growne now so numerous, as you well know how burthensome they are. I have heard, ye 39 Eliz., there was not lesse than eleven bylls propounded for their reliefe. My earnest desire of ye good of this kingdome hath made mee thus far enlarge myself. You will pardon it in

"Your poore kinsman that truly loves you,

"ROGER TWYSDEN.

"*Aug.* 2, 1641, *East Peckham.*"

The reader will, I hope, pardon this digression.

43. Whilst wee lay thus imprizoned, dayly attending what would bee done wth us, Mr. Benyon, a worthy citizen, now Sir George Benion, empeached by the Commons, for somewhat concerning a petition they misliked, came to a censure beefore the Lords,—in what kind he was culpable I can not now say,—but, beeing fined, and by them committed to the Tower, I heard a Member aske the Black Rod, whither his fine were to ye King or to bee employed towards ye Irish wars now broken out. It was answered, all fines were to hys Mat^y^; to wch he replyed, he would have had hym lost

[1] In Apparat. Annal. Eliz.—T. [2] Ib. anno 1558.—T.
[3] In Vitâ Edw. VI. p. 155.—T.

hys hand for it. This was spoken by Mr. George Peard, a Lawyer who, notwithstanding his beeing one of ye severest men you could meete w^{th}, told me the Howse of Commons could distinguish beetweene faults, that he saw very little against me.

44. Yet, for that onely (however, not impeached), I was, wth others, committed, lay at a place in Covent Garden, such as ye Sergeant assigned us, all in one howse, tyl, ye 8th April, I procured a petition, beeing not very well, and in a streight howse, to bee delivered to ye howse of Commons, shewing—

That, having beene committed to their Sergeant, and remeyned in hys custody many days, to ye prejudice of my helth, examyned on severall articles, to wch I had declared my knowledge, I did desire that, beeing infirme of body, they would bee pleased to accept of Bayl for my appearance, at such tyme as they should think fit, I beeing very sorry to have had hand in any thing hath offended y^{t} hon^{ble} howse, etc.

45. Upon it, ye 9 April I was bayled, and so was Mr Spencer (Sr George Stroode lying longer), but were not to goe at all into Kent, nor more than 8 or ten miles out of London. As for bayling men by Order of ye howse of Commons, it was never before this Parlyament; neither is it any formall way, by entring into Recognizance, as in Courts of Record (an undoubted signe they have not an absolute illimited power in committing), but by giving bond to their Sergeant, who requyred of me, (by their directions I suppose,) no lesse then xx^{ty} thousand Pounds for my appearance w^{th}in four and twenty houres after I should bee called for by the howse. Truly the summe was so immence, I at first resolved to lye by it; for who could I procure to enter into so vast an Obligation? But beeing told it was onely forme, not really good in Law if it could be examyned by it, would never be looked after, and find-

ing my very noble friends, my unkle, Francis Finch, and Sr Robert Filmor,[1] ready to joyn, each in a bond of 5,000^l^, and myself of 10,000^l^, I did, in ye end, submit unto it, though tyed not to make a steppe into Kent.

46. Where now much endeavour was had, to make the Country disclaym the former petition; and, for y^t^ end, to ye next Quarter Sessions (wch beegan on Tuesday, April ye 19, at Maydstone) there came y^t^ had not of some tyme[2] usually appeered on ye Bench; but they met wth so great contradiction, and so earnest an affirming by many, that it did conteyn ye desires of ye County, there was nothing considerable could bee effected by them to stop the subscrybing of it,[3] wch went on cheerefully, and on ye day appoynted, it was brought up by many. When they came to ye Bridge, they found ye Gate of it shut against them by ye Sheriff of London, and there they were forced to quit their swords, beefore they might bee admitted to enter ye Cyty; so much mislyked it was to see men not willing to combyne wth ye howse of Commons in ruining the present government in Church or State; or rather, that it did appeere, there were had so much wit, as to foresee the commanding by Votes, Orders, Ordynances, and not by Lawes, must terminat in an enslaving them and their posteryty; and so much courage as to let them know they would not willingly contribute to their owne misery.

47. After this petition, wch they entended thus to have styfled, was delivered, and they saw ye worst was intended, I beegan to be a suitor for liberty to goe into Kent, (where I had left my wife ille and great wth chyld,)

[1] Of East Sutton, Knt., a steady loyalist, and author of many loyal tracts, chiefly in defence of the rights of the Crown. He was a great sufferer in the cause.—Ed.

[2] Sr Walter Roberts, as hymself told me.—T.

[3] The Grand Jury, however, sent a disclaimer to the House, as appears by the Journals.—Ed.

wch after some tyme I obteyned, and ye 17 May returned to my howse, there resolving to live quyately and meddle as little as possible wth any buisinesse whatsoever; Yet, beeing a Justice of Peace, and having a tryall, I went to ye Assizes then next following, in July 1642, of wch, beeing the last publique meeting I was ever an actor in, it will bee necessary to make particular mention.

48. Beeing thus drawne to Maydstone, there came to th' Assizes a very large Committee of ye Howse of Commons; all I think had any reference to ye County of Kent and were members of it (unlesse old Sr Henry Vane): I asked one, to whome I was well known, what the intent was of so many gentlemen's coming from ye Parlyament? He told me, about somewhat had reference to ye peace of ye County. This increased my wonder; it beeing in a firme peace, wthout any probabylyty of other; except some of ye Parlyament's faction made it otherwise. After dinner, the Justices of Peace received this Order, and these instructions from ye sayd Committee, as coming from the Howse of Commons.

"Die Veneris, 22o Julii 1642.

"Whereas this howse hath beene credibly informed, that some ille affected persons, with in the County of Kent, are now endeavouring to disperse rumors to the scandall of the Parlyament, and to censure their proceedings against the promoters of ye late dangerous Petition, and that they have plotted for this purpos to meete at th' Assizes, the farther to extend their malitious designes; It is therefore thought fit, and ordered, by the sayd Howse, that Sr Edward Hales,[1] Sr Henry Heyman,[2] Sr Edward Partridge,[3] Sr Thomas Peyton,[4] Sr Thomas Walsingham,[5] Sr Henry Vane,[6] Senr et Junr,[7] Sr Francis Barnham,[8] Sr Peter Wroth,[9] Sr Norton Knatchbull,[10] Sr Humfry Tufton,[11] Sr

[1] Member for Queenborough.
[2] Member for Hythe.
[3, 4] Members for Sandwich.
[5] Member for Rochester.
[6] Member for Wilton.
[7] Member for Hull.
[8] Member for Maidstone.
[9] Member for Bridgewater.
[10] Member for New Romney.
[11] Member for Maidstone.

Edward Boys,[1] Mr Browne,[2] Mr Skinner,[3] Mr Lee,[4] Sr Edward Masters,[5] and Mr John Nutt,[6] shall forthwith goe downe unto ye sayd Assizes, and use all diligence to prevent all such inconvenience, or any other attempt that shall bee offered to ye prejudice of ye Parlyament, and by all lawfull wayes and means to preserve ye sayd County, not onely in peace amongst themselves, but in a right understanding of the proceedings of Parlyament.

"H. Elsing, Cl. P. D. Com."

The Instructions wch they acquainted us wth, were these,—

"49. You shall acquaynt the Justices of Peace at the Bench wth the contents of this Order, and let them know, that, out of ye howse's tender care and affection to ye peace of that County, and the Kingdome, they have sent you downe wth Order and Instructions, to use all lawfull wayes and means to preserve the sayd County, not onely in peace amongst themselves, but in a right understanding of the proceedings of Parlyament; and doe not doubt of their readynesse to comply wth the desire of this howse therein."[7]

Then from themselves was added,—

"It is desired, according to the Instructions of ye Howse of Commons, that you will give your best ayde and assistance to this Committee, in their performance of the commands of the Howse, expressed in their Order herewith delivered:

"That, to this End, this Committee may bee seated at the Bench, sutable to ye auctoryty and trust they represent, to bee ready to performe the commands of the howse, as occasion shall requyre."

50. The Committee, coming from Westminster, thus

[1] Member for Dover.
[2] Member for New Romney.
[3] Member for the County.
[4] Member for Rochester.
[5, 6] Members for Canterbury.
[7] By a reference to the Journals of the House, it will be seen that this Committee came down charged with instructions more extensive, and involving a more unwarrantable usurpation of power, even than that contained in the above.—Ed.

armed, first made their publique appearance on ye Bench on Saturday, July ye 23, in ye afternoone; when they desired, by Sr Henry Heyman, their Speaker, a printed order, touchinge the illegalyty of hys Maties Commission of Array, might bee openly read; wch Mr Justice Mallet (though he spake not one word as approving of it) did not think fit to give way unto, conceiving hys power beeing deryved unto hym by ye Great Seal, he could not admit of ought came not that way.

51. On Munday ye 25 July, Sr Edward Hales, and some others, made a shewe of coming to ye Bench; but the Court beeing just risen, they applyed themselves to ye Judge, who wished what they would impart to hym might bee publick beefore all ye Justices of ye Peace: and, to y^t end, sent to them to meete at his lodging after dinner, whither the Committee soon after came, Sr Henry Vane, Jun., beeing their mouth, who told hym he was "to impart somewhat unto hym from the Howse of Commons." To wch in effect he answered, "That he came thither to administer Justice agreable to ye Law, that any thing concurring wth that, and coming from y^t body he should willingly embrace, and desired to know whither that they had to say to hym might not bee publick." It was replyed, "it should bee afterwards; but they first thought fit to acquaynt hymself wth it." On wch he asked "whither it did not concerne the King?" The answer was, "Not more then all things perteyning to ye government of ye Kingdome." Upon this Sr Henry Vane and hymself went into a private roome together, (whether any others were wth them I can not now call to mynde) stayd there pryvately about half an houre; when they came out, what had past beetweene them was read to us, beeing in effect denyalls to what had beene propounded unto hym; and then these former Orders and Instructions were made knowne to ye Justices of Peace,

52. Who the same afternoone fell into a sadde and serious consideration what answer was fit for them to returne. One was drawne; but, as that wch issues from heads of differing tempers doth not ever pleas all, (but is eyther too long, too short, something or other will want, or abound,) so that thus framed was cast on the table, where it lay as y^t^ was not approved, yet none taking it in hand to reforme; upon this I tooke it up, thinking onely to abbreviate it for my owne satisfaction, as indeed I held it somewhat too long; when I had done, I read it to them, and I know not by what fate, it was generally so well liked as, very few words altered or added, it was delivered to ye Committee.

"The Answer of ye Justices of Peace the sayd 25 July, 1642.

"1. That the first demand beeing grownded (as wee conceive) upon misinformation, and in it a great aspersion layd on this County, wee not knowing of any such endeavors as are expressed, it beeing, as wee hope, likely to continue in a secure peace; his Maties Justices of ye Peace, having their auctoryty committed unto them under the Great Seal of England, dare not, in ye execution of it, joyn wth any not so authorized.

"2. That beeing demanded this Committee may sit upon ye Bench for ye performing ye commands of ye Howse of Commons, (unknowne to us,) wee doe not know what place may bee sutable to the authoryty and trust they represent; nor that wee have power to place any on ye Bench not sent thither by ye like auctoryty wee sit there."

53. But these giving no satisfaction, the 26 of July, 1642, the Committee replyed thus, and sent it us by Sr Norton Knatchbull, a very honest gentleman.

"Die Martis, July ye 26, 1642.

"Whereas this Committee have received an answer yesterday in ye name of hys Maties Justices of Peace of the County of Kent, wth wch they are alltogether unsatisfyed, and wch tends very much to the disservice of ye Howse of Commons; They, therefore, according to the Instructions they have received from that howse, (whereof a copy is hereunto annexed,) doe require the sayd Justices, in the name of that howse, to be assistant to this Committee in the execution and performance of the Orders and Commands of that Howse, as they will answer the contrary to the sayd howse. And for this purpos this Committee doth declare that they doe resolve to make their repayr to the Bench, from tyme to tyme, (as they shall see cause,) during these Assizes, there to put in execution the Orders and commands of that Howse as occasion shall require."

"The instructions of the Howse of Commons to the Committee.

"And for your better performing of the Orders, Instructions, and commands you heerewith received from this howse, the Sherifs, Justices of Peace, Mayors, and all other his Maties Officers are hereby requyred to bee assistant to you in execution and performance of the sayd Orders and Instructions."

54. In the after noone, according to theyr Reply, they all came to the Bench, but there they found Mr Justice Mallet, (who onely attended these Assizes,) not at all readyer to comply wth their desires. Sr Henry Vane (who as Chayr man of ye Committee, managed the conference, and spake exelently well, temperately, and soberly,) shewde a desire of propounding somewhat tended to ye good of ye King, peace of ye County, mayntenance of ye lawes, and Religion. The Judge, on the other side, seemed to doubt whither those he intended to deliver were so, and therefore excused hys giving way to their propositions unlesse first made knowne unto hym; sayd he was most willing to obey the howse of Commons in any thing consisted wth hys charge, and the preservation of ye Law; but whilst this was in agitation, so loude acclamations were heard, and such fear of styrrs beegan to bee apprehended, the Judge told hym if it went on so he should bee forced to adjourne ye court. And a whyle after, Sr Henry Vane, by command of the Committee, retyred himself, and that night went home to

Fayr Lane. At their going of, some few followed them crying for the "Parlyament," but beeing persons neyther for number or qualyty greatly considerable, were not as it seemed to me greatly regarded.

55. After this I retyred to my lodging, intending to make myself ready to goe to my howse; but hearing a very lowde shute, I went down to ye Bench, and found divers young Gentlemen, vizt Sr John Mayny,[1] Sr John Tufton,[2] Sr Edward Filmor,[3] Mr Wm Clark (slayn afterward in ye King's army),[4] had brought wth others certayn Instructions to ye Knights of ye shire to acquaynt the Parlyament w^th^, w^ch^, wth a Petition by them likewise presented, were to bee sent hys Ma^ty^ at Yorke. When I came, these had not beene read nor received by any. The Clark or hys agent refused ye doing of it, they beeing offerd to me, I excused the accepting, in reguard persons before me were on ye Bench. Sr John Baker, Mr Spencer, etc. At last a young youth (I think ye Undersherif's clark) was got to read them; some Parlyament men sitting amongst others on ye Bench (having shewed no mislike whilst it was in reading,) at ye conclusion of all, desired to know whither they were conceived to sit there as Justices of Peace; for if so, they must protest against whatsoever had thus past: it was answered they were not understoode to have approved any thing they heard. These Instructions were sent to the Knight of the Shire[5] by Mr George Chute and some

[1] Of Linton Place, near Maidstone. He commanded the Royalists in the gallant defence of Maidstone against Fairfax in 1648.—Ed.

[2] Eldest son of Sir Humphrey Tufton, of the Mote, mentioned p. 181, *supra*.—Ed.

[3] Eldest son of Sir Robert Filmer, mentioned above, p. 180, and brother to the first Baronet of the name.—Ed.

[4] At Cropredy Bridge. He had raised a regiment at his own expense, at the head of which he was slain in the above battle, at the early age of thirty-six. He was of Ford in Wrotham.—Ed.

[5] Augustine Skinner, of Tutsham Hall, in West Farleigh, near Maidstone. He was substituted for Sir Edward Dering on his expulsion.—Ed.

other; but he would not take them. I heard they were after throwne unto him.

56. And, beeing indeede full of resentment, did require Mr Augustine Skinner, as their Servant, to certify the howse of Commons there was no grownd for such an information as had beene made of ye County, desiring the Informer, of what qualyty soever, might receive condigne punishment. Then, as Loyall subjects and good patriots, they require hym to offer their humble advise for ye setteling the distractions of ye tymes, wch might bee in giving hys Maty satisfaction in four particulars.

1. In leaving ye Towne of Hull in the same state it was before Sr John Hotham's entrance.

2. In laying aside the Militia till a good law may be framed.

3. That ye Parlyament bee adjourned to an indifferent place, where hys sacred Maty, all ye Lordes, and ye Members of the howse of Commons may meete wth honor, freedome, and safety.

4. That hys Maties Navy may bee immediately restored unto hym.

To these Advises were joyned certayn reasons, and ye Petition beefore mentioned, wch beeing after printed at York and London, I shall forbear farther to mention, then that on Thursday the 28th July, Sr John Mayny, hys brother in law Mr Richaut, Sr Edward Filmor, Sr Thomas Boswell, Mr Clark (after Sr William Clark, slayn at Cropready brydge, June ye 29, 1644), carryed to Hys Maty at York what had beene thus concluded; from whense it was by ye presse divulged; but at London, where the Parlyament bare rule, it was stopt, divers copies taken from ye Printer, and few suffered to bee vented, none exhibited unto them.[1]

[1] We are enabled to lay before our readers a perfect copy of these requisitions, which seem to have been so eagerly suppressed by the Parliament.

"*Instructions from the County of Kent, to Mr Augustine Skynner.*

"WHEREAS,

"A Committe from the House of Commons is now sent down to the

57. And heere I think I may note, y[t] beefore this, there was never any men who so represented others in Councell, as wth out their election they had no right of sitting in it, that ever refused to hear what was presented unto them by so considerable a party. If what was propounded were not fit to bee graunted, certaynly it did not ill beecome to say so, wth out using farther extreamities. How this would have beene interpreted in the Netherlands, where the elected are so strictly tyed to the Elector's instructions, as fayling in performing of them, they are subject to their censure; I shall leave others to conclude from ye Decree of Holland and West Friseland, 1587, lately printed in ye Reepublica Hollandiæ.

Assizes upon a credible Information (as they say) that something should be done at this Assize to the disturbance of the peace of this County; We the Commons of *Kent* require you Master *Augustine Skynner*, as our servant, to certifie to that honorable House, that you found the country in full peace, and that there was no ground for any such Information; and that you desire in our names to know the particular of that Information (which it seems you are ignorant of) and the Informer, that this County may have full reparations in honour against so scandalous an aspersion cast upon them; and that the Informer, of what quality soever, may receive condigne punishment.

"And that the House of Commons may understand our desires, not onely to preserve the peace of this County (which by God's blessing, and the help of the good and known Laws of this Kingdom, we are confident we shall maintain) but also of the whole Kingdom, being now in so great a distraction, that every man stands at a maze to see what the event is like to be, and well weighing what a great fire a small spark may kindle, abhorring and detesting the thought of a Civil War: we forthwith require you to offer our humble advice, as faithfull and loyall Subjects to His Majestie, and good Patriots, and lovers of our Country, for setling the distractions of these times, one principall means to effect it, we conceive will be to give His Majestie full satisfaction in His just desires in these four particulars, *viz.*) In presently leaving the Town of *Hull* in the same state it was before Sir *John Hotham's* entrance into it, and delivering His Majestie His own Magazine. Secondly, in laying aside the *Militia*: untill a good Law may be framed, wherein care may be taken, as well for the Liberty of the Subject, as the defence of the Kingdom. That the Parliament may be adjourn'd to an indifferent place, where His sacred Person, and all the Lords and Members of the House of Commons may meet, and treat with honour, safety and freedom. Fourthly, that His Majestie's Navie may be immediately restored to him."

58. What had thus past at Maydstone very much offended the Howse of Commons, who, enraged to think they might meete with any opposition, the 2 of August, 1642, ordered their Sergeant at Arms, hys Deputy or Deputies, to repayr to ye bayle or Suerties of Sr George Stroode, Sr Roger Twysden, and Mr Spencer, to cause them, according to the condition of their bonds, personally to attend the howse. Upon wch Mr George Brag his servant gave notice to my Unkle, Francis Fynch, at Kensington, (though ye condition of my obligation requyred it should have beene at my howse in Redcros-streete,[1]) who, somewhat timorous, sent hys man to me all night to make me hast up. So I went immediately, leaving my deere wife nwely brought a bed and very weak.

59. When I came and had rendered myself to ye Parlyament, the 5th of August, w^th^out ever any examination I was committed to the Sergeant, who sent me to ye three Tobaccopipes, nigh Charing Crosse, as a prisoner, where having remayned about 15 dayes, never sent unto, charged, or questioned, in ye least measure whatsoever; they finding nothing could possibly bee objected against me, one came and told me ye howse was willing I should goe to my Brother Cholmley's[2] at Isleworth, wch I absolutely refused, seeing that must bee but to make another sute I might bee released thence; onely I desired I might bee charged wth ye breach of any Law; to wch the answer was, "In these tymes the Howse could not looke at ye nice observance of Law;" I replyed, "that might bee wth those *qui belli sunt participes*, where the Armies lay; but for those did not at all engage, *contra hos nullum*

[1] It was the corner house of Red Cross Street and Barbican.

[2] Sir Hugh Cholmley, of Whitby, in Yorkshire, who, at this time, was a strong Parliamentarian. He afterwards deserted their cause, when in command of Scarborough, which he delivered up to the Queen at a very critical conjuncture. His history is too well known to need further remark here.—ED.

est jus bellicum," and alledged Grotius for my opinion.[1] Whilst I continewed there, I grewe acquainted wth two noble gentlemen, Sr Basill Brook, and Sr Kenelme Digby, persons of great worth and honor, who, whilst they remayned wth me, made the Prison a place of delight, such was their conversation and so great their knowledge; but Sr Kenelm Digby was soone released, his innocentie appearing to ye close Committee; and ye other, having compounded wth ye Sergeant and payd hys fees, was remoeved to ye King's bench; where, though he were received by a very honest gentleman, ye Speaker's brother,[2] yet hys charge was far greater then wth me, paying at first 3^l^ per weeke for hymself and man in his howse, wch after was reduced to fifty shillings, wch beeing constantly payd, I have heard hym sometymes say he was as well as at hys owne home. But this summe, however it might perhaps not bee great for the one to receive, yet was excessive for hym, whom the Parlyament had stript of all, to pay; and might bee one cause wth other vexations, of concluding hys days in that Prison.

60. During this my restreynt, an horrid outrage was committed by Coll. Edwin Sandis,[3] and others, sent by the Close Committee, at ye Howse of Sr Wm Butler,[4] in Teston; his servant tortured by fyer, hymself, then at ye wells nigh Tunbridge, on the nwes, flying to ye King. This beeing the next day divulged, dispersed all my famyly in Kent; it beeing beelieved and given out, they intended to bee at my howse the night following. My

[1] Grotius De Jure Belli et Pacis, lib. iii. cap. 17, n. 1.—T.

[2] Sr John Lentall.—T.

[3] Second son of Sir Edwin Sandys, the author of 'Europæ Speculum,' who was, as Wood says, "an excellent patriot, faithful to his country, without any falseness to his Prince." Sir Edwin was second son of the memorable reformer, Edwyn Sandys, Archbishop of York. The Parliamentary Colonel ended his days and his outrages at his seat at Northborne, near Deal, of a wound received in the battle of Worcester in 1642.—Ed.

[4] He was afterwards killed in the battle of Cropredy Bridge, at the head of his regiment which he had himself raised.—Ed.

poore wife, never strong, but then exceeding weake, not recovered of her lying in, having placed her children wth my sister Twysden,[1] full of fright and fear came up to London on horsback. The rest shifted to one place or other where they might shroude themselves; onely a few servants were left to prove the extreamyty, who, under God's protection staying in it were safe.

61. Of this Inhumane Action (for who can think or call it otherwise, that knwe how it past, or hath read the first Mercurius Rusticus) I shall say no more; but onely it was so disguised aboue, that I myself speaking of it to a Parlyament Man, he told me there was much more made of it then it deserved. The truth beeing, y^{t} Col. Sandis, lead in scorn by one of S^{r} W^{ms} servants into a privy howse, he, to make hym sencible of ye affront, caused some pouder to bee put in ye palme of hys hand, and so, after a military Punishment, had it set on fyer, wch though more then he wisht, was nothing in comparison of what was spoke; and this I neede not doubt to bee all ye truth, he having received it from one of ye Committee[2] employed in ye scrutyny of that fact.

62. But as the servant told me, they did know better then so how he had beene used; for he, soone after the inquiry, making complaynt to my Lord of Essex of hys Usage, hys Lord^{sp} spake honorably unto hym, as if hys information were trwe, he should bee so far from protecting Sandis, as he should have reparations: after wch he could never get accesse to ye Earl, wch made hym

[1] Wife of his brother Thomas, who was afterwards created a Baronet, and was one of the Justices of the Court of King's Bench temp. Car. II. She was sister of Matthew Tomlinson, who commanded the guard that had charge of Charles from St. James's to Whitehall; and on the scaffold, Charles gave him his gold toothpick in remembrance of his kind demeanour to him, which, with the Ribbon of the Garter worn by Charles at his execution, and handed to T.'s charge, we have often seen at Bradbourne, the family seat of the Judge.—Ed.

[2] Sir Philip Stapleton.—T.

convert hymself to M[r] Pym, whose zeal to Justice was so great as he held

> "his dearest blood
> Too small a prise to worke his countrie's good:"[1]

but he spake otherwise; told hym perhaps he would petition the Parlyament; if he did, he assured hym y[e] Collonell should find those in y[e] howse would answer for hym and justyfy what he had done.

63. Certaynly, if he did countenance so abomynable an action, (for I have no other then y[e] partie's owne relation, whome yet otherwise I never found false,) hee must maynteyn the liberty of y[e] subject (so much talked of and so little practist) some other way, in y[e] propryety of their goods and freedome of their persons, then by the known lawes of y[e] Kingdome.

64. My Wife upon this, weak and sick as she was, retyred to her howse in London,—my famyly dispersed, myself in prison, out of mynd,—S[r] Basill Brooke, an honest, worthy gentleman, (whom I found in y[e] Sergeant's custody,) remoeved in to y[e] King's bench, and I now solytary alone in a pryvate howse,—I beegan to think of delivering a Petition, and the 8th of August, 1642, procured a Petition to bee delivered, w[ch] in effect spake thus:

"To the hon[ble] howse of Commons, etc.

"That beeing brought in by my bayl, I had attended their pleasure more then a month, to y[e] prejudice of my health, beeing streightly lodged, not permitted to styr to Church, that I had nothing hytherto objected against me. That I never enterteyned other thoughts then what might tend to the good of y[e] Kingdome, and therefore desired I might not lie under the heavy burthen of their displeasure, but retyre to my owne Lodgings, etc."

[1] Writ under hys pycture en taylle douce, and otherwise.—T.

65. Upon this petition I was again bayled ye 12th of September, 1642, but advysed not to goe into Kent, wch I had no mind to doe, things standing in the posture they then did; yet, at ye giving securyty to ye Sergeant of the Mace, I made knowne unto hym I had a resolution to travell, as I had a passe for y^t^ purpos lying by me. And I well remember, Sr John Finch told me, if I gave hym warning, he would goe wth me; but y^t^ noble gentleman, beeing soone after, by an unfortunate fall from an horse, taken away, left me to prosecute the designe alone.

66. Beeing got now to my howse in Redcros Streete, the Kingdome in a flame, I endeavoured to settle some particular businesses I had as well as I could; and trusting my chyldren to an old faythfull servant,[1] of whom I therefore asked no rent for my howse and land I had used to it in East Peckham and thereabouts, intended ye making myself fit for a journey into France; and having sent my poore weake wife to take order about some things in Kent, having beene myself hardly ten days out of prison, certeyn officers of ye Parish there, Zelots for ye Parlyament, came to me to know what I would give upon the propositions of Publick faith.[2] I told them how much I had suffered by beeing long imprisoned, for nothing that I knewe, now enforced to stay from my famyly in ye country; That mony I had none, That little plate I had, must of necessyty serve to feede me and myne; yet I could give them no certeyn answer,

[1] George Stone.—T.

[2] By the active influence of Pennington, Lord Mayor of London, an overture was made by "divers (in the City) under the style of affected persons, that they would advance a considerable number of soldiers, for the supply and recruit of the Parliament Forces, and would arm, maintain, and pay them for several months, or during the times of danger and distractions; provided that they might have the public faith of the Kingdom, for repayment of all such sums of money, which they should so advance by way of Loan." An Ordinance was immediately framed and passed both Houses, "That all such as should furnish men, money, horse, or arms for

my wife beeing away, who knwe better then myself what I could doe, to whose returne I must remit them.

67. They seemed wth this reasonably well satisfyed, saying they would stay tyl they heard she was come; yet afterwards they never came to my howse to enquire of me; onely casually meeting one of them in Barbycan, he asked me what I intended to doe; to whom I answered I was not yet resolved; and so I heard no more tyll upon ye Ordinance of y 29 November, somebody left at my howse a Tycket of 400 pounds, for my twentyeth part. But y^{t} ordinance extending onely to th' Inhabytants of London and parts adjacent, I did not take myself at all included in it, my abode beeing there rather by constreynt then choice. Yet when their Offycers came to gather it, I shewde them my howse, asked them whither they conceived all I had in it to bee worth 400 pounds, much lesse was that ye xx^{th} part of what I had; That I was no Inhabitant of London, but remayned in towne onely to bee ready if the howse of Commons called for me; That I desired they would make this knowne to such as employed them, wch they promysed to doe, but sayd it would bee better done by myself; to wch I replyed, ye summe was so immence, wth out all proportion, as I thought it would bee better from them who saw what I had, and therefore would bee credited. They told me I might bee heard if I would pay them ye first 200 pounds, wch I had not to lay downe; after this I heard no more of them tyll some came w^{th}

that Service, should have the same fully repaid again, with interest for the forbearance thereof, from the times disbursed. And for the true payment thereof, they did thereby engage to all and every such person and persons, the public Faith of the Kingdom."—Clarendon, vol. ii. p. 60. This Act or Ordinance was published about this time, and "the active Mayor and Sheriffs appointed a Committee of such Persons whose inclinations they well knew, to press all kind of People, especially those who were not forward, to new subscriptions; and by degrees, from this unconsidered Passage, grew the monthly Tax of six thousand pounds to be set upon the City for the payment of the army."—Ed.

carts and carryed away what I had, and so I think had ye 20th part, for they lef nothing worth ought beehynd.

68. By this I easyly saw how hardly men would be prest could not concur in making themselves slaves: for what was it other, to have our goods taken from us at ye will of others,[1] wth out any dwe processe of Law? and resolved agayn to goe beeyond sea; onely I desired to see the issue of a Treaty about this tyme beegun at Oxford, beetweene the King and Parlyament, the carryage and conclusion of wch I leave you to see in ye second tome of ye Collection of Orders,[2] and shall onely say heere, that this was ye onely tyme in wch there was any probabylyty of an accommodation; yet was clogd by the two howses wth five such[3] bylls, as if hys Ma^ty^ had past them, they would, to my understanding, have brought such innovations in ye Church, as must have given no small scandall to many honest persons; and in fine have beene found advantagious to none but ye Roman party.

69. During this winter that I abode in Redcrosstreete, I had often recours to ye tower, had ye sight of sundry the auntyent Records of Parlyament there reserved, some of wch I procured to bee transcribed, of wch hereafter.[4]

70. When I was nwely freede, Sr Francis Barnham,[5] a right honest Gentleman, and a very noble friend of myne, desired to speak wth me, wch he did at the Temple. The effect of what he sayd was, to perswade me to give

[1] See Justice Crook's argument against Shypmony, p. 17.—T.

[2] Collect. of Orders, tom. ii. p. 49 et seq., and p. 118.—T.

[3] The Bill for "taking away superstitious innovations;" that "for the utterly abolishing and taking away all Archbishops, etc. etc. etc.;" that "against scandalous ministers;" the Bill "against pluralities;" and that "for consultation to be had with godly, religious, and learned divines."—Ed.

[4] Perhaps this was the foundation of that taste for the antiquities of British History, which so distinguished Sir Roger Twysden, and which led to such valuable results in the 'Decem Scriptores,' and other works of our learned author.—Ed.

[5] Formerly of Hollingbourne Hill, but now of Boughton Monchensey. He was the member for Maidstone.—Ed.

somewhat on ye Propositions, that ye Howse of Commons would goe very high against such as did not joyn with them, would maynteyn any man did ought against the disaffected party; That Sr John Sedly [1] and Sr Anthony Weldon [2] now ruled all Kent; and many other such weighty reasons as might come from a person of great wisdome and judgment; to all wch I could onely answer that the thing alone restreyned me from giving was ye poynt of conscience. That ye Howse, of wch hymself was a member, had urged me to promis I would defend the liberties of the subject; That I held nothing more against them then to have men forced from their estates for fear; That I had out of that respect, when I was not tyed wth a Protestation, refused Shypmony; That to give now would shew I did it not then out of other then a refractory spirit, or some sinister end; That I saw, if this war continewed, it would prove ye ruine of ye Protestant religion and ye lawes of ye Land. Beside I did not love to have a King armed wth booke law against me for my life and estate. He told me to ye last it would not bee possible, should hys Ma^ty^ come in a Conqueror, (wch I wisht not,) he could, in so generall a defection, take away all men's estates; but there would bee some means found to gayn a generall pardon for ye lives and estates of ye most, as had beene in former Civil wars; That hymself had given, and shewde me the manner of it. That it was wth out ye least thought of doing ought against ye King, his person or power, but for conserving no other then ye lawful and just rights of ye subject, and added in effect that of Sr Edward Cooke, *Salus populi suprema lex.* [3] To wch I answered that of ye same auctor, [4] *Optima*

[1] Of the Fryars, in Aylesford, near Maidstone. He was father to Sir Charles Sedley, the celebrated wit and profligate in the time of Charles II.—ED.

[2] Of Swanscombe.—ED.

[3] Cooke, lib. 10, fol. 139 b.—T.

[4] Cooke, lib. 2, fol. 3 b.—T.

regula, qua nulla est verior aut firmior in jure, neminem oportet esse sapientiorem legibus. That those wch had somewhat must bee onely the loosers by these wars. I have made the more particular mention of the discourse I had wth this worthy Gentleman, not onely to shew what reteyned me from joyning wth the Parlyament; but y^t the reader may see how men of wisdom, honesty, and judgment, wch none y^t knwe hym can deny to have beene dwe un to hym, wer at first led away by ye Protestations, promises, and pretenses, of those who ment nothing lesse then that they held out to ye world.

71. About ye beegining of 1643, Sr Christofor Nevil, a noble gentleman, and my very worthy friend, came to me, told me there would bee no abode for us in ye Parlyament's quarters; and not long after going to see hym, he shewde me a Proclamation,[1] sent hym wth advise from Oxford, of not at all complying wth ye Parlyament; that hys sister Goring had received ye like; that he was resolved to get a passe and goe out of their quarters; that If I would, he could procure my name and my wive's to bee inserted in it. I profess I was at first sight amazed to see a King not able to give protection to hys people, yet declare it high treason to pay any assessment or contribution unto them, as y^t wch was ayding or assisting of them, prohybyted by ye Act of ye 25 Ed. 3. And where the Parlyament[2] (for so men now called ye two howses) had publisht a Sequestration of ye Estates of those had voluntaryly contributed to hys Ma^{ty}, not lying under ye power of any part of hys Army; The King in this adds no qualyfication whatsoever; and yet I have beene taught since,[3] the giving ayd in such a case not to have beene treason.

1 Collect. of Orders, tom. ii. p. 27, 28, at Oxford, 7 of April.—T.

2 1 April, 1643. Collect. of Orders, tom. ii. p. 13.—T.

3 Cooke, Instit. iii. p. 10, § "It was."—T. See 6 Ric. II. cap. 3, stat. 2.—T.

72. By this all Men saw if hys Ma^{ty} prevayled, they must looke for nothing but ye extreamyty of Law, wch in so generall revolts, Princes have seldome put in execution, and never fortunate in professing beeforehand; as indeede what effect did it produce? but by making ye adverse party more firmely combyne against hym from whom they expected no favor, in ye end was a cause of hys utter ruine.

73. Some tyme after this, I asked Mr. Adrian Scroope what course he tooke (beeing ye Duke of Richmond's steward) to preserve hys Lord^{ps} goods at Cobham; he protested unto me, he durst take none; having received an expresse charge from my Lord y^{t} he should not; and yet, says he, I know there is a pycture of hys mother's he values above any thing; by all this I saw the King was in good earnest had he prospered; and y^{t} Men wth in ye Parlyament's power must deal waryly not to forfeit all.

74. But to Sr Christofor Nevel, first giving hym many humble thanks for hys kind offer, as it well deserved, I answered, "that I had no estate in ye world but what lay wthin ye Parlyament's quarters; that I had a wife and five small children, beesides old servants, to provide for, left me by my friends, wch I could not shake of; that staying heere I might hope to get somewhat, but going to the King I did certaynly expose myself to their fury that resolved (for ought I saw) ye ruine of all men's estates could not joyn wth them. That I was not (for certaynly so I tooke myselfe) wth in any ye words of ye Ordinance for Sequestrations. That I should not contribute to them willingly; that what was forced from me the King, in justice, could not take amisse. That my body was not able to endure ye toyle of war, and should bee ashamed to live in Oxford and not bee in ye Army; that of this I had good experience in my youth, when I was both more able and had fewer to care for then now.

That for these reasons I durst not accept hys kind offer. But if he went one way, I would an other;" beeing resolved to goe into France, against wch I thought there could be no exceptions, the law of Ric. ye 2^d^ beeing repealed.[1]

75. Upon this I intended to hastene my journy to those parts; and the 15 of May, 1643, some friends of myne going thither, I sent my eldest sonne, then not much above seven years old, wth them, and Hamnet Ward, now Doctor Ward, as Tutor wth hym; meaning myself speedyly to follow them. And heere, that ye reader may ye better judge how I was brought to conclude upon this journy in my declyning age, I think it not amisse to take a short vieue of ye state or posture of the kingdome, how ye Justice of it was managed by severall Committees, both in this and some other years.

76.[2] The disputes beetweene the King (now in ye North) and the Howse of Commons growing, upon every message, higher and higher; his Ma^ty^, by Sr John Hotham, denyed entrance into Hull; and resolute to hynder ye howses from enforcing their ordinances on ye subject as bynding; many of eyther side beegan to fear the differences would not bee decyded onely by words: but mony, ye sineues of war, beeing in plenty to neyther party, it was hoped each would encounter so great difficulties in endeavoring to rays an army, as might persuade the most averse to fit termes of peace.

77. But to shew how they should bee supplyed, the two howses first brake ye yce, many of themselves subscribing to a contribution of Arms the 10th of June, 1642,[3] and inviting all others to doe ye like; suggesting, such as were about ye King, wth out eyther fear of God or the

[1] 5 Ric. II. cap. 2.—Ed.

[2] I return to my oun story, not tyll No. 113.—T.

[3] Collect. of Orders, tom. i. p. 340.—T.

Lawes, were ready to commit all manner of outrage and violence tending to ye dissolution of this government, the destroying of our Laws, liberties, and propriety, etc.; that they did, therefore, for prevention of such evills, excite all persons well affected, to afford their best assistance, according to a Protestation by them lately framed for ye mayntenance of the Priviledges and beeing of Parl^nts^; promising not onely 8^l^ per cent. for all mony so brought to Guildhall, (for of late the Exchequer was kept there by certayn officers of ye Cyty,) but consideration for ye fashion of all plate, etc.

78. What a vast proportion of treasure was carryed in upon these propositions (the repayment of wch beeing never executed, if at ye first intended, turned in ye end ye name of Publick Ffaith to Publick fraud, in Latin, "*Publica fides, Punica fides*") I shall not heere enquyre; it shall suffice me to say, it was so immence, it enabled them to rayse an Army, and, by the power of it, maynteyning a maxime (on what grownds I know not) xl^y^ made an howse of Commons, and three an howse of Peeres, did frame Orders and Ordinances commanding ye subjects' estates, freedom, lives, after ye most absolute, if not Tyranicall, way hath beene ever seene amongst Christians; for whereas th' Hollander [1] hath reference to carry hymself after their instructions and advise who depute them; the Venetian [2] makes no newe law, nor doth any thing extraordinary, but in an assembly of 600; the Florentine hath a councell of xlviii; [3] the French a Parlyament to counsell or revise what passeth the Prince; these forty and their Committees, responsable to none but themselves, not supervised by any whomsoever, did

[1] *Vide* "Edictum de antiquo jure Reipub. Batavicæ, dat. 16 Octobris, 1587," nuper impress. Latine, scilic. 1630, in libro dicto "Respublica Hollandiæ," pag. 165; vid. et pag. 180 ad finem.—T.

[2] Botero della Repub. Venet. lib. 1, cap. "Governo," fol. 30 a.—T.

[3] Adriani, lib. 1, pp. 7 et 8.—T.

exercise the most absolute, arbitrary, illimited power, Europe ever saw; having no colourable defence to uphold the injustice of sundry their doings, but "*that necessyty compeld them*," "*the preservation of the kingdome lead them to it*," "*that it was carryed by a few votes in eyther howse*;" to whom, as it seemed, all men were to submit, as well their Judgment as obedience. Lord, of his goodness, grant England never see ye like!

79. And though their wanted not men of integrity and wisdome that showed the absurdyty of such like positions, and that men were not to submit their opinions to any Votes whatsoever, but their obedience to Laws made by King, Lords, and Commons; yet, having a sword to bear them out, there was nothing of the contrary to bee harkened unto, how reasonable soever, but that they voted was to bee credited, as what the whole nation was obliged to beelieve ye best and most just.

80. And thus, under pretence of mayntеyning the religion of the Church of England, they defaced (as superstitious or superfluous) all ye antique monuments of pyety and devotion; ruined the Cathedrals; found means on easy terms (as not beeing payd what was dwe for service in ye wars or otherwise) to divide amongst themselves those lands the Church had beene so many years possest of; denyed all former rights of Monarchy, yet wth a Protestation of defending hys royall person, honor, and estate; Seated in themselves an absolute power of taking from the subject all he could call hys owne, yet professing an upholding them in their lawfull rights, propryety of their goods, and liberties. W^th^ ye first and second of these, as proper for the generall history of the tymes, I will not take on mee heere to meddle.

81. Of ye third I shall remember, that, having got an Army, and finding Committees ready to forward their commands in all parts, they did, by little and little, force from the subject the greatest masse or treasure so short

a tyme had ever expended; yet first trying how it would rellish. So, upon a pretence diverse in and about London and Westminster had not payd equally to others for ye beginning this war, the 29 November, 1642,[1] they made an order for assessing such as had not contributed at all, or not proportionably to their estates at the xx^th^ part; allthough, in their declaration of 10 June, 1642, they had exprest no man's affection should bee measured by the proportion of ye offer, so that he exprest his good will to the service in any proportion whatsoever, yet that expression now must not bee lesse than a xx^th^ part of his Estate.

82. This carryed on by so high an hand, as it found no great opposition, the 7th May, 1643, produced another Ordenance[2] for "persons in all parts to pay the fifth part of their yearly revenue, and ye xx^th^ of goods and chattels;" but heere was a mischiefe to bee remoeved. By these Ordinances Parlyament men themselves might come to bee taxed by others, as in former tymes had beene ever done; to avoyd w^ch^, care was taken ye 16 December, 1642,[3] That no Member or Assistant to eyther Howse should bee rated but by that howse where they attended. By w^ch^, all Parlyament men (except such as absented themselves, not able to comply wth their horrid injustice) escaped for ye most these taxes, as did the active Committee men in some Counties.

83. How contrary this was to former presidents, every man knows y^t^ remembered ye Acts of Subsidies; out of wch none was excepted from beeing assesst by hys neighbours *eo nomine* 'that he was lately or at present of ye Parlyament.' I have seene many Petitions[4] on ye Parl^nt^ Rolls, y^t^ no Member should have any thing to doe w^th^

[1] Collect. of Orders, tom. i. p. 764.—T.

[2] Collect. of Orders, tom. ii. p. 169.—T.

[3] Collect. tom. i. p. 777.—T.

[4] Rot. Parl. 22 Edw. III. n. 24; 45 Edw. III. 43; 51 Edw. III. n. 48; 6 Hen. IV. n. 9; and he that hath not ye leisure of searching all, may

assessing, collecting, or being Controuler in ye guift given; but never any that themselves should not bee assesst as others were; of w^{ch}, no question, one and an especiall reason was, y^{t} the country might see their integryty, and they who gave bee rated to ye guift by those that had no hand in it; when now, ye same that gave, were not onely Commissioners, but forced others to pay what them listed; levyed it, and expended it so as did onely conduce to their owne ends.

84. Now if any Ordenance did at first speak wth some moderation, in ye execution they and their Committees (who[1] were to bee borne out by both howses) were most barbarous. And therefore they made them so ambiguous as they might bee interpreted variously, according to successe; wch increasing, was allwaies ye more severe and tyranous to such as, standing for ye auntient laws and trwe liberty of the subject, did seeme to mislike or oppose their arbytrary government; or, if he lived quiatly, had a good estate, and did not comply wth them farther then necessity (for ye saving of it) inforced hym, something or other must bee found to bring hym wth in ye list of men to bee sequestred: and this went much according to ye qualyty and revenue of the person; of wch take this one of many may bee produced.

85. A gentleman,[1] riding abroad in ye country, meetes a stranger unknowne to hym coming from London; asks hym, what nwes there? The party tells (that wch was indeede false) of a defeat geven to ye Parlyament's forces. He, upon this, told it others, so as in ye end it came to ye Committee's ears, who sent for hym, told hym he must reveal to them how he came by ye report.

Rot. Parl. at West. 2 Rich. II. n. 51; 13 Hen. IV. n. 10, in fine. Of which ye last is, "they should not bee Collectors, Assessors, Controulers, nor Commissioners for raysing ye subsidy then given."—T.

[1] Collect. of Orders, tom. i. p. 776, *et alibi, passim*.—T.

[2] Sergeant Hatton, of Surry.—T.

The man did; but nothing would serve, he must produce hys Auctor, or if not, Sequestration. What should he doe? The person was unknowne to hym; how to find hym impossible. But see ye chance. They gave hym some tyme to seeke hym, during w^{ch}, riding abroad, he lighted on ye same body, whom he carryed beefore ye Committee, y^{t} did not deny to have told it hym, and y^{t} he had it from such an one in London. When they saw there was no way by this stratagem to bring in the Gentleman y^{t} had somewhat, ye others not so considerable, they let ye inquisition fall.

86. But to cast an eye upon y^{t} is more generall, and is by themselves printed, the 2 of October, 1643.[1] Upon a pretense of saving Tymber Trees, wch ye poore, necessitated for want of fewell, (hys Ma^{ty} having Newcastle,) did in many parts destroy, they allowed certayn to enter in to and cut onely the fellable woods of Bishops, etc., and such as were described in an Act of Sequestration (of wch hereafter). But finding the King's army eyther not able or not willing to help the oppressed, and men ready to execute their commands (for *prima dominandi spes in arduo; ubi sis ingressus, adesse studia et ministros*,[2] etc.), the 16 April, 1644, they fell upon ye Tymber of sundry persons; and amongst others, of Sr George Sonds,[3] of Kent, who was so far from beeing at Oxford, or in Arms against them, as he hath publisht[3] in print (to wch I have not heard any thing in opposition), that beeing forced to compound for hys estate, they could not charge

[1] Collect. of Orders, tom. ii. p. 351.—T.

[2] Tacit. Annal. iv. p. 152.—T.

[3] Of Lees Court, near Faversham. He was imprisoned several years, his house plundered more than once, and his estate sequestered; but this was the smallest of his misfortunes. He was the father of George and Freeman Sondes, whose unhappy story is too well known to need repetition here. At the Restoration he was created Earl of Faversham and Viscount Sondes.—Ed.

[4] Sonds hys Narrative, p. 2.—T.

hym wth any delinquency, but about a taxe, wch, beeing unequall, he refused, yet, upon abatement, payd; notwithstanding was sequestred, seven years imprisoned, and forced to 3,500l composition.

87. What the Ordinances of Sequestration were I shall shew elsewhere. It shall suffice heere to remember, that having them for a cullor, they and their Committees (for what one did, the other would make good) did exercise a tyranny no tyme or hystory can paralell; depriving men of their estates, who never had part in ye war; forcing them to a sute beefore a Committee of Lords and Commons (wch, under ye two howses, or rather ye howse of Commons, was ye supreame Court of Judicature in those cases) for recovery of that was illegally, by power of ye sword, taken from them (for they ever put ye accused to play ye after game); seizing at ye first upon all he had;[1] beeginning with execution, wch ye party, beeing stript, must at hys unspeakable charge seeke to get of. Now, if there were no colourable shew of contynewing ye Sequestration made, to defer judgment so as they might, eyther by delays weary hym out, or by hys necessities enforce hym to give over the sute; but, if that would not bee, but that they must come to a Resolution, and ye Committee, from whom hee appealed, would have hym sequestered that they might pray longer on hys estate, then, though the Ordenance[2] described onely certayn notorious Delinquents, yt had beene causers or instruments of ye publique calamyties, as subject to that punishment, they would (to bring him under it) enforce a construction contrary to all rules of former tymes for interpreting statutes yt ever yet was seene. Neither was there hope what they thus by violence tooke from him might in fine satisfy for his

[1] See Bracton, lib. iii. de Corona, cap. 8, n. 5, p. 123, a, stat. 1 Ric. III. cap. 3.—T.

[2] 1 April, 1643.—T.

error, as was ye use of our princes, when a subject had hys land extended[1] for a Fine on a Misdemeanor in ye Star Chamber; but what ever they made, eyther by sale of wood, receipt of revenue, or otherwise, must bee reputed as nothing when he came to repurchase his estate. But if any were so fortunate as to get out of y^e *Premunyre*, which was rare (had he a considerable Estate), it was allmost an impossybilyty to get satisfaction for y^t he had beene by force depryved of. Why? Beecaus ye Souldyary were possest of it; and they, ye Committee, could not tell how to pay it but out of their own purses. Of all or most of which I had the sad experyence as the reader will see.

88. Certaynly their severyty was so notorious, and their extortions so full of scandall, as ye Officers of ye Army (who ever seemed to me more full of Honor and mercy then ye howse of Commons) did desire,[2] ye first of August, 1647, Compositions on Sequestrations might bee lessened; and Cromwell, in hys speech of ye 12th of September, 1654,[3] told the Parlyament then assembled, "Poore Men under their arbitrary power were driven like flocks of sheepe, by forty in a morning, to ye confiscation of Goods and Estates, without any man beeing able to give a reason that two of them had deserved to forfeit a shilling." But to look a little farther into their Ordenances.

89. The first Order[4] for sequestrations was, that those by them employed should bee subject to such dyrections for alowance to Delinquents as both howses did require.

[1] *i. e.* surveyed and valued.—Ed. [2] Proposals, p. 117.—T.

[3] To ye Parlyament, page 8.—T.——Sir Roger had originally written, "My Lord Protector, in his speech," etc.; but he subsequently seems to have been influenced by the issue of public events in his designation of Cromwell, for the MS. was apparently revised by him after the Restoration, in consequence of which, he has drawn his pen through "My Lord Protector," and substituted "Cromwell."—Ed.

[4] Collect. of Orders, tom. ii. p. 15, 1 April.—T.

By wch, whilst it resided in the Parlyament, some (as my Lady Finch of Forditch) hyred their husband's estates by friends made in one or other howse; so as they lived and supported themselves. But ye King, after the taking of Bristoll, sitting downe beefore Glocester, and not likely to carry it, they, out of fear of hys approach to London,[1] ye 19 August, 1643, issued a second, leaving the conferring this to their Committees, or any two or more of them; and where ye former words were for alowlance to bee given Delinquents in generall, these were restrictive for their wives and children onely; so as one unmarryed could not get a farthing; and yt they did give was so pared by their officers, as little or nothing came to the distressed man's purs. If I forget not, Sr George Sonds told me the Committee of Glocester, of whom he hyred hys estate, (it beeing by ye two howses assigned to mayntein their Guarrison,) did alow him, for ye taxes and payments by hym made on their Ordenances, xiiijs and vid in ye pound. An other gentlewoman[2] spake of a greater proportion out of land she had.

90. But their Armies prospering, this (though not so beneficiall as ye first) was in a great measure taken of,[3] it beeing made voyd[4] to all whose fathers or husbands abode in the King's quarters, by a subsequent one of ye 8 of September, 1645. And afterward, ye 17 March, 1648–9, assigning a very short tyme for men to come in and perfecting their Compositions, they resolved all persons not rendering themselves and submitting according to ye tymes and rates by them prefixed (wch were greater then formerly) to have their estates confiscate, no further alowance to wife or children.

91. Now a certayn consequent of Sequestration, especyally of an estate lay nigh London, was felling ye

[1] Collect. of Orders, tom. ii. pp. 296, 299.—T. [2] Mrs. Legat.—T.
[3] *i.e.* "taken off." [4] Collect. of Orders, tom. ii. p. 726.—T.

woods upon it, in w^ch^, if any did complayn their Agents went further than ye Ordenance warranted, the first difficulty was to get any witnesse alowed; but if that could not bee absolutely, at least some exception must bee layed to enervate his testimony, as beeing malignant, ill affected to the proceedings of Parlyament, or such like; then to delay the tryall from day to day, to ye starving a suitor (so far as ye expectation was as insupportable as ye injury); to question whither it were Tymber they had felled, though oke of thirty years' grouth, wherein, all that grewe out of old stocks were, by their interpretation, to bee cast out, of what growth so ever, contrary to ye Kentish Proverb,—

> "The tree that growes on ye father's head,
> Is as good Tymber as ever was bread."

92. But if the suitor would not desist, and, having overcome the tedious difficulties of sending to, and returns from, ye Country Committees (for they above were to credit nothing but as ye other their Agents, and ye parties against whom ye complaynt came, did certify), expected their resolution and some rights to bee done hym; there appeering nothing to justyfy the insupportable oppressions by hym susteyned, but ye will of y^em^ that did it; the Chayrman would give an Order, eyther for hys absolute Sequestration on their desires, or, at least, such as did rather embolden them in what they did, then any way discountenance them for ought they had done; beecaus they were not to discourage the wel-affected, nor incourage ye other party; and this, too, after that boord (if not ye very persons themselves, upon certifycat, of ye County) had by letter answered, "There did appeere to them no cause of sequestration," upon ye same evidence hath beene done.

93. And heere I must adde a word, though, in effect, but a repetition of what is allready, that these men,

following Rhadamanthus his example, *Castigatque auditque dolos subigitque fateri*, first seized on your Estate, wch was easyly done, had you any one enemy in ye Committee, bee ye fault what it would: then you were to sue to understand what your crime might bee (wch was enough, if you could not approve and run mad in complying wth their horrid ways), wch they would not bee willing to tell you, especially if there were any opinion you were not w^th^in ye Ordinance, but would put you of [1] y^t^, "perhaps it came from above to them," "they could say nothing, beeing not a full Committee," or ye like: if upon this, you applyed yourself to them at Westminster, the first question wth them would bee, "whyther you had not beene sequestred by the Howse," then a day must bee given for y^t^ inquiry: if, at the tyme prefixt, y^t^ were not found to have beene, then all you could hope for was, they would send to your Country to understand the causes of it; they and their Agents, in ye mean tyme, receiving ye rents, cutting downe ye woods, and possessing all as absolute masters of ye Estate; terryfying ye party, "it should bee worse wth hym, if he did not submit unto them, and acknowledge hymself a Delinquent."

94. But if he could not bee induced, neyther by ye threats were voyced abroad, nor by ye delays of each Committee, to quit hys owne innocentie; but y^t^ they must deliver the causes brought hym w^th^in Premunire; and hys Delinquentie were not notorious, but questionable; some while after, he should have the accusation delivered hym, but might not know hys accusers; and then perhaps he might obteyn an Order to stoppe the felling of wood, wch was not absolute tyl hys cause were determined; but tyll such a day, at wch time ye Committee were free, and their Ministers again beegan to make havock, then they, at their great charge, must get

[1] *i.e.* "off."

counsel to move again. Thus men were at continuall expence; all they had taken from them; in the end forced to confesse themselves offenders, though nothing contrary to law was objected against them, and were so far from having any part whatso ever in ye wars, as they lay imprisoned for ye most during ye continuance of them, as I myself can testyfy.

95. As these were their comportments to privat persons, so were they not lesse tyranous in theyr publick exactions. I shall not (rather I can not) remember all ye ways the people were by them peeled. It shall suffice to remember they first brought in y^t Monster *Excise*, unknowne to our Auncestors, wth so great exclamations detested in former Parlyaments, erected an office for regulating of it, declared, the 22 July,[1] 1643, what should bee payd for Tobacco, Wine, Beere, strong and small, Syder, Perry, Grocery, Silks imported, Furs, Linnens, Thread, Wyer imported.

96. This beeing publisht about ye 1 of August, no peny was demanded on it, tyll they did perceive how it would bee swallowed; and indeede the very name having beene heeretofore so odious, as nothing more, it was wisely done, many hoping it would not have beene diegested; themselves, I beeleeve, beeing of y^t persuasion; for having, ye 8th of October, 1642,[2] declared a rumor which was then spread, that the Howse intended to assesse men's peuter, and lay excise on that and other commodities,[3] to be false and scandalous, raysed by ill-affected persons, and that tended to ye disservice of ye Parlyament, it was fit first to make an essay how it would rellish.

97. The 11 of Sept., 1643,[4] this Ordinance was

[1] Collect. of Orders, to. ii., p. 267, 1643.—T.

[2] Collect. of Orders, tom. i., p. 638.—T.

[3] "Nemo repente fuit turpissimus."—Juv., Satyr 2, vers. 82.—T.

[4] Collect. of Orders, tom. ii., p. 313.—T.

annulled, and another Excise or new impost set upon Tobacco, Wynes, Strong Waters, Beere, Ale, Cyder, Perry, Grocery, Druggs, Mercery, Silks imported, Linnen, Drapery of Linnen, Haberdashery, Upholstery, Saltery, Soape, Drapery of Wollen, nwe and old Skins, and leather imported, Glasse men. But this, if ye rates were more moderate (wch I leave to ye search of ye curious), as pretended, yet ye number of things exciseable were increased, was immediately put in execution by a power, found more ready obedience then ship mony; and beeing for ye most upon imported commodities, it was hoped they would not have forced men to pay for that of necessity went into ye mouth. But ye 9 January, 1643–4,[1] assured ye contrary, they then imposing it upon flesh, victuall, salt.[2] And now, when wee had neither Silk, Linnen, nor wollen to cloth us with; flesh, beere, nor salt, to put in our bellies, untaxed; I could not imagine how they could goe farther, and I conceive all history would bee at a stand; yet, after all, they found a nwe invention to cheat their stomachs, who dwelt about ye City, compelling all, no members of eyther Howse, or Assistant of ye howse of Peers, to pay for a weekely meal, as it should bee taxed or assessed by certayn therein appoynted.

98. This Excise upon flesh (as what the poore beegan to feele made us of a free people slaves) was very grievous, and much resented by many, and caused a great insurrection of ye Butchers and others in London, ye 15 of February, 1646–7. Upon w^ch^, the two howses, ye 22 of February following, taking into consideration the many tumults it had raysed, declared that, As nothing could have draune them to the resolution of that imposition, but ye preservation of ye Kingdome, Religion, Lawes, and Liberty, from utter ruine, so they could not find any other means to draw in ye malig-

[1] Collect. of Orders, tom. 2, p. 410.—T. [2] Ibid., p. 467.—T.

nants and neutralls, who had endeavored all cunning ways to evade what y[e] well affected had so willingly bore; that, considering the great difficulties they had overcome by the receipte and credit of this Excize and some other helps, as maynteyning armies, relieving Ireland, satisfying, in some measure, y[e] Scots, they did hope no well affected person would look what they had contributed that way. That for y[e] continuance, if it shall bee considered to how many well affected they had allready engaged for monies borrowed the Excise; what expence they must bee at for setteling this Kingdome, and reducing Ireland; they were confident no understanding person can desire or expect this leavy (w[ch] they found the most equall and indifferent course to goe through so many great affayres) should ceas. Yet they declare, when they shall have overcome, in some good measure, these engagements, they shall make it appeere how much more ready they are to eas the people of this charge, then they were willing at first to impose y[e] same.

99. This declaration printed fild y[e] world with astonishment, and such as had beene wholy devoted to y[e] two howses beegan to fear they should not meete wth more liberty then they had enjoyed beefore these warrs: but indifferent men saw playnly they must never see that monster totally buryed, it beeing the most equall course to rayse mony. They laught to see them keepe their first principles of abusing y[e] people by promises of better tymes. And I doe well remember some did then say, there was nothing but y[e] Army could moderat the Tyranny the subject lay under; and for my part, I am confident that Howse of Commons had never redrest it in the least, had they beene sollicited by any of lesse power to persuade then the Officers of y[e] Army; upon whwse intreaty,[1] and their drawing nigh London,

[1] Proposalls. p. 118, § 1.—T.

th' Excise was taken of[1] from somthings most burthensome.

100. About wch tyme there happened to me a passage not unworthy the remembring, in effect as followeth:—Going up to the Parlyament wth one of ye Howse of Commons, a person who stoode in ye Lobby beefore ye entring in, wth severall petitions in hys hands to present them each member, gave me one (as supposing me one of ye number), couched in very high language (such as at other tymes would not have beene endured), concerning certayn prisoners had, by some power deryved from them, beene restreyned. Going downe the stayres, I cast myne eye upon it, when one of them following, told me he saw I looked on their petition. I replyed, "I did on one was given mee above, that mee thought spake very boldly." "Sir," says he, "it is tyme, for wee see these men that sit there have nether truth nor honesty; for they have had our persons and estates at their command; and now, instead of ye lyberty they promysed, and wee expected, they imprison us (who have gon along wth them) on every slight occasion. And of their truth wee have had a late experyment, for upon ye rising of the Butchers, they declared nothing but necessity had enforced them to ye raysing mony by way of excise. That they could not take it downe, it beeing securyty to other men for monies lent; yet now (says hee) the Army is coming up to London, they, apprehending the Butchers and common People may joyn wth it, pull them out and shake of[1] their auctoryty, they can lay it downe in some particulars, as flesh, etc.; if it bee for securyty of others, how can they meddle wth it? If not, why did they not doe it beefore? And onely now they may apprehend the army will enforce them."

101. I thought not fit to hold long discourse wth so discontented an humor; though, for my part, I could

[1] "off."

not tell how to answer hym; but I told it a Parlyament man,[1] who seemed to me to think he spake in a great measure truth, but that their intent was, to satisfy those creditors otherwise. Certaynly these ways by wch they made men hope for liberty were very rugged to get to it.

102. And indeede when I consider, how is it possible to bee otherwise? for who ever undertooke to deal in y^t^ is improper for them but it proved so? If the hand would walk, the feete write, how unapt were they! So, if the Howse of Commons, who were chosen to petition and expedite the affayres of others; to assent in making lawes by which themselves as well as ye poorest is to bee governed; to see how ye necessary charges of ye commonwealth may bee furnished; will apply that care should bee for ye generall, to conduce onely to their owne private ends; if, in lieu of making lawes to bee governed by, they will themselves bee governors; if, instead of beeing givers to ye King, they will bee the expenditors themselves, as well as ye graunters of ye taxe, wee have of late had experyence how beneficiall it is.

103. But beecause the pretence ever was, *Necessyty enforced them to lay those immence burthens on ye people*, wch no age will, I fear, ever see taken off; it will not bee amisse to cast an eye a little upon it, and what they were, so pressing, that forced them to such nwe unheard of paths to draw mony from ye subject. And, for my part, I professe I can not imagine other then their owne ambitious appetites, wch ye whole Kingdome could not suffice for. It is not conceivable, that, in effect, the King and Princes revenues, the inhaunced customs, the ordinary payments of Subsidies, Pole-mony, etc., would not have defrayed th' expence of any home war whatsoever, wth out such nwe unheard of ways, as excise,

[1] M. Richard Browne.

sequestration, and ye like, for drayning their purses and ruining their estates, wch they ought by good lawes make more suer, not, by arbitrary ordinances, destroy and ruine.

104. This Island hath had in former tymes both domestick and forrayn wars, yet the subject never prayd upon as by these Men. When Edward ye 3 enterd upon those great expeditions against France, hee easyly saw he was to receive great support from hys people in assisting Flanders, and carrying his armies into France. The 13 Ed. 3,[1] it fell in consideration, and propounded to give hys Ma^ty the tenth Lambe, Fleace, etc., for two years, wch ye Lords easyly assented to; but ye Commons excused themselves tyll they could confer wth their Counties. The issue was, a Parliament was concluded to meete ye 21 January following; when ye Commons thought fit[2] to present the King wth xxx thousand sacks of wool, the Lords styll continewing in their former persuasion of ye x^th fleece, etc. About the middle of Lent following, an other Parl. met, in wch hys Ma^ty had that imposition first layd[3] upon merchandize, is since knowne by ye name of "Tunnage and Poundage,"[4] and likewise the ix^th Lambe, fleece, sheafe, etc.

105. These, I think, were ye greatest guifts were ever given or taken from ye subject beefore these tymes; and the collection of this latter was so full of trouble, so much to ye vexation of ye Commons, as the second[5] payment seemes to have beene bought out for xxx thousand sacks of wool.[6]

[1] Rot. Parl., quinze St Michell, 13 Edw. III. n. 4, 5, 8, etc.—T.

[2] Rot. Parl., Octav. St Hillaire, 13 Edw. III. n. 7, 8.—T.

[3] Statut. 14 Ed. III. cap. 21.—T.

[4] Rot. Parl., en my quaresne, 14 Edw. III. n. 6, et stat. impess. cap. 20.—T.

[5] Confer Rot. Parl., en my quaresne, 14 Edw. III. n. 6, wth 15 Edw. III. n. 48, et 17 Edw. III. 27.—T.

[6] "The King, in return for the concessions he made, obtained from the barons and knights an unusual grant, for two years, of the ninth sheaf,

106. But the King's needes were pressing, and ye Lambe for hys Ma^{ty} was not yeaned, nor ye fleece shore, or Sheafe cut, and God had blessed hym wth a great Victory at Sea, by wch this kingdome was secured; but hys necessities encreased for want of treasure to keepe hys allies together and firme unto hym. Upon w^{ch}, he sent the Earls of Arundell, Glocester, and Sr Wm Trussell, wth Letters to ye Prelats,[1] Earls, etc., expressing the same: who found no other way of relief, but to assiste hym wth xx thousand sacks of Wool, by ye way of Lone, to bee sold ye Merchant a marke cheaper then ye ordynary rate, to pay for ye custome of every sack 40^{sh}, the prise of ye sayd Wooll to bee repayd out of ye second year's fleece, etc. And this proceeding from the Lords the Knights of Counties were to make knowne at home.

107. After which I doe not meete wth any great nwe extraordinary charge (more then ye subsidy of Tunnage and Poundage continued) given to y^{t} Prince, tyll ye 51

lamb, and fleece on their estates; and from the burgesses a ninth of their movables at their true value. The whole Parliament, also, granted a duty of 40*s.* on each sack of wool exported, on each three hundred wood fells, and on each last of leather, for the same term of years. But, dreading the arbitrary spirit of the Crown, they expressly declared that this grant was to continue no longer, and was not to be drawn into precedent. Being soon after sensible that this supply, though considerable and very unusual in that age, would come in slowly, or would not answer the King's urgent necessities, both from his past debts and his preparations for war, they agreed that 20,000 sacks of wool should be immediately granted him, and their value be deducted from the ninths which were afterwards to be levied."—*Hume.*—Ed.

"N.B.—The knights often, at this time, acted as a separate body from the burgesses, and now made some scruple of taxing their constituents without their consent. They desired the guardian whom Edward had left in England to summon a new Parliament, which might be properly empowered for that purpose. Both this and the old one were rather unsparing in the conditions required by them before they would make the grant; but Edward himself came over, called a new Parliament, and contrived to get what he wanted granted, as above, on more moderate terms, and with the sacrifice of fewer concessions."—*Ditto.*—Ed.

[1] Rot. Parl. post transl. S^{ti} Thomæ, 14 Edw. III. n. 10, 11.—T.

Ed. 3,[1] when was graunted, considering "*Les grandes charges et insupportables despenses*" hys Ma^{ty} was at every day, more and more, of every person above 14 years old (beggars onely excepted), iiij^d per teste, wch certaynly amounted to no great summe.

108. For 1 Ric. 2, a Parlyament, meeting the 13 of October, taking notice of the kingdome beeing in greater peril to bee lost then it had ever beene,[2] gave his Ma^{ty} out of all Cities, Burgs, and other lay persons whatsoever, two 15^{ths} and Two 10^{ths}, to bee payd by Candlemas ensuing; wch ye year following, in ye Parlyament held at Glocester,[3] is sayd to have beene ye greatest guift had beene ever given any prince to bee payd in so short a tyme. And the same year, at Westminster,[4] they renwe teste mony, setting an higher rate then in Edward ye 3^{ds} days, and where the Parlyament, beefore[5] they had increased ye subsidy of Tunnage and Poundage to a marke more on every sack of wool, and so on others, beesides 6^d ye pound on marchandize, on this gift hys Ma^{ty}, coming into Parlyament, was pleased to take them downe. It were tyme lost to run through all ye Kings of this Island; no one of them will ever be found to have demanded so much as these men did actually leavy from ye people. When King Hen. ye 8,[6] 1523, joyning wth Charles ye 5th, intended such a war in France as had not beene seene, he demanded onely a fifth, vizt. 4^{sh} ye pound, in four years to bee payd, wch could not bee gayned.

109. When Hen. ye 5th was engaged in y^t great war

[1] Rot. Parl. 51 Edw. III. n. 19.—T.

[2] Rot. Parl. 1 Ric. II. n. 27.—T.

[3] Rot. Parl. at Glocest. 2 Ric. II. Rehersayl faict par la Cōē de lour charge done et lour response.—T.

[4] Rot. Parl. at West. 2 Ric. n. 14.—T.

[5] At Glocester, n. 29, 30.—T.

[6] Herbert's Hist. Hen. VIII. p. 144, 146.—T. (Lord Herbert of Cherbury's Life of Hen. VIII.—Ed.)

against ye French, he managed wth no extraordinary levies yt I find, but onely

2 Hen. 5th,[1] Tunnage and Poundage 3 years; wch, 3 Hen. 5 (Sr Edward Cooke says),[2] was first given for life; yet see 21 Ric. 2, cap. 15.

2 Hen. 5,[3] two xvths and 2 xths.[4]

3 Hen. 5,[5] Tunnage and Poundage, given yt Prince for life; one xvth, one xth, formerly given, ye Payment accelerated; Item, one xvth and one xth *de novo*, of wch, at a Parlyament held ye same year,[6] ye payment was a little quickened.

4 Hen. 5,[7] two xvths and two xths.

5 Hen. 5,[8] two xvths and two xths.

7 Hen. 5,[9] one xvth and one xth, the third part of a xvth, and a xth.

9 Hen. 5,[10] n. 10, one xth, one xvth.

110. With these helps from his subjects, yt victorious Prince made all his conquests in France. And, to speak of latter tymes, queene Eliz.,[11] who found her Crowne "*afflictissima*," engaged in a war wth Scotland and Ffrance, a potent enemy of ye Pope, had ye Protestant party to assist all her tyme. Beeing left by her Friends after the ye treaty of Vervins, had, in effect, the strength of all ye Popish party in Europe turned upon her, and ye Netherlands (whom she assisted hourly);—Had ye Spanyard, fayling in hys attempt against England (1588), fallen wth a potent army (1601) into Ireland, and thence

[1] Rot. Parl. at Leycester, n. 11.—T.
[2] Instit. iv. p. 32.—T.
[3] Parl. at West. n. 11.—T.
[4] On the subject of fifteenths and tenths, vide note to pp. 215, 216.
[5] Parl. omnium Sanctorum, n. 4, 5.—T.
[6] Parl. 10 March, 3 Hen. V. n. 10.—T.
[7] Parl. 19 Octobr. n. 9.—T.
[8] Parl. 16 Novembr. n. 9.—T.
[9] Parl. 16 Octob. n 8.—T.
[10] 1 December, 9 Hen. V. n. 10.—T.
[11] Camden, ano. MDLVIII.—T.

by ye valor of ye English expeled, payd styll her armies both there and heere;—Had never at one tyme two subsidies graunted, beefore 31st of her raign, nor ever after to bee payd more then one and two fifteens in a year, or there abouts;—did make knowne to her Parl. (1601) that the French owed to her Ma^ty^ 13 hundred thousand pounds, ye low countries 900 thousand pounds, the charge of Ireland when my Lord of Essex made hys expedition 300 thousand pounds; yet dyed ritch, beeloved of her people, and dreaded of her enemies.

111. By all wch it is more than manyfest, the paying an army could not take from ye subject so great a masse of treasure as they forced from them: and who can doubt it, when the event prooves (what all good men feared) their chiefest end of raysing one was no other but to gayn a power, by wch they might beecome masters of ye wealth, and appropriate to themselves the goverment of ye Kingdome, wresting it out of their hands in wch it was legally seated, and everting all laws in opposition.

112. But, for governing a war, or counseling the King in y^t^ kind, certaynly former Parlyaments have rather sought to bee excused in, then to take that any way upon themselves. The 13 Ed. 3,[1] it was recommended to ye Commons (of whom I speak) to take in to consideration ye guarding of ye seas, and give hys Ma^ty^ counsell therein; to wch they make answer, "*endroit de guarde sur mere, prie la cōē q'ils ne soient chargez a conseil donner, es choses des queux is n'ont pas conisance,*" etc. And ye 21 Ed. 3,[2] their advice beeing asked touching the wars then in hand, their returne is onely thus, "*Tresredoute Seig^r^, quant a vostre guerre et L'arraye d'icelle, nous somes si misconisantz et simples, qe nous ne scavons ne poons ent conseiller; de quoy nous prions a*

[1] Rot. Parl. Quinye St Michel, 13 Edw. III. 3, 11.—T.

[2] Rot. Parl. 21 Edw. III. n. 5.—T.

vostre gracious Seig^{rie}, nous avoir de L'ordinance pour excusez." Thus the Commons did not heretofore think it their part to bee counselors in ye making a war, much lesse to be the sole managers of one, wch whither they have of late done, wth so great advantage to ye common good, I shall leave ye judgment to others, and turne to what happened to me, from whense I have somewhat strayed.

I left myself engaged in a resolution to follow my sonne into France,[1] wch I shall now goe on with.

[1] See before, No. 75.—T.

MISCELLANEA.

UNDER the above title we propose, in future, to reserve a small portion of our Volume as a depository for short contributions and annotations,—for the occasional Queries of correspondents, and such additional information or amendments of our published papers as they may be enabled to furnish.

Suggestions on any points of local antiquarian interest, archæological "waifes and estrayes" in any department of the science, will always be acceptable, and will be duly recorded in this department of our 'Archæologia,' which shall be, as it were, a "Spicilegium," a gathering up of fragments; at the same time it shall be a vehicle for proclaiming our "desiderata" to all who may be able and willing to supply them.

We commence by notices of the errors and pretermissions of our first Volume.

NOTE ON PP. 52–54, VOL. I. 'ARCHÆOLOGIA CANTIANA.'

Since the publication of our first Volume, we have ascertained beyond a doubt, that the document given by Dering to Cotton was not a copy of the "Articles," but the Great Charter itself.

We have in our possession Sir Roger Twysden's own interleaved copy of Cowel's Interpreter, copiously annotated with his autograph MS. "adversaria."

Among them, *sub titulo* "Magna Charta," he writes :—"Y^e^ "King finding himself allmost alone, forsaken by hys nobylyty, "condescended to a meeting at Runningmead, (wee call it "Renymed,) nigh Stanes, in Middlesex, ye 15 of June, 1215, "where he graunted to them Magna Charta, *one copy of which*

" I my self have seene, under hys Seale, in ye hands of Sr Edward " Deering, who gave it Sr Rob. Cotton."

This, at once, identifies the copy of the Great Charter, with the Great Seal attached, in the Cotton Collection, as that which was presented by Sir Edward Dering to Sir Robert Cotton. It is the copy, damaged by the fire, which is exhibited, framed and glazed, in the MSS. Room in the British Museum.

But how are we to account for Dr. Smith's assertion, by which we were led astray in the observations (now proved to be erroneous) pp. 52–54 of our first Volume? He either spoke from mistaken recollections, or he must have seen and handled some other copy, (abstracted from the collection before the fire) which he erroneously supposed to have been Dering's copy, or Dering must have given him a copy of the Articles as well as one of the Charter itself. Be this as it may, it is due to the cause of Truth, to acknowledge the error into which Dr. Smith beguiled us, and to announce the important discovery which we have made among the valuable remains of the learned Sir Roger Twysden.—L. B. L.

NOTE TO P. 45, VOL. I. 'ARCHÆOLOGIA CANTIANA.

After our first Volume had issued from the press, it was cursorily intimated to us that the beautiful Anglo-Saxon Relics collected by W. Gibbs, Esq., at Faversham, were excavated from a field called the "King's Field," in that parish.

This seemed to us too important a fact to be passed over unnoticed; because, if we could ascertain that they were so found, and that the field in question had borne the designation of the "King's Field" from early times, we might infer from the richness of the ornaments, and the burial of the war-horse, that Mr. Gibbs's relics are those of a royal sepulture. We therefore placed ourselves in communication with that gentleman, and were much gratified at receiving the following reply:—

"The field where they were dug up has been from time "immemorial, known by the name of the 'King's Field;' an "antiquarian friend of mine, who has been for some years "engaged on a history of Faversham, can trace the name for "upwards of eight hundred years past. I may add, that a por-"tion of the relics were found in making the railroad through "the field in question, and the others in digging out the "earth for brickmaking."

We feel that we are only carrying out faithfully the objects of our Volume in recording this important communication among its pages.—L. B. L.

NOTES FOR THE HISTORY OF COBHAM CHURCH AND COLLEGE.

I.

(License from the Prior and Convent of St. Saviour's, Bermondsey, to the Master and Brethren of Cobham College, to erect a range of buildings, the entire width of the churchyard, viz. thirty-seven feet, on the south part of the said churchyard, and extending the whole length of the church and chancel, on condition that they leave a sufficient width for processions on the south side of the church. Dated 24 June, 44 Ed. III., 1370.)

[From the Surrenden Collection.]

Universis presentes literas inspecturis. Nos Petrus Prior Sancti Salvatoris de Bermundeseye et ejusdem loci Conventus, Ordinis Clunacensis, Wyntonie dioceseos, ecclesiam parochialem de Cobeham, Roffensis dioceseos, obtinentes in proprios usus, salutem in Domino sempiternam.

Noverit universitas vestra, quod dilecti nobis in Christo, Magister et Confratres Collegii sive Cantarie de Cobeham, dicte Roffensis dioceseos, Vicariam ipsius ecclesie de Cobeham, sibi et Collegio suo predicto, de consensu nostro expresso, alias in ea parte prestito, rite et legitime obtinentes appropriatam, nuper nobis supplicarunt, quod, cum ipsi Magister et Confratres, quedam edificia sive domus cultui divino, utilia quamplurimum et necessaria, in solo cimiterii dicte ecclesie, ex parte australi ejusdem, per totam latitudinem dicti cimiterii, que triginta et septem pedes hominis, juxta mensuram per nos habitam, non excedit, et per totam longitudinem dicte ecclesie et cancelli ejusdem extendere se debencia, affectent, ut asserunt, suis propriis sumptibus construere et edificare, quatinus dictis constructioni et edificacioni nostram preberemus auctoritatem et consensum. Nos igitur, considerantes dictorum Magistri et

Confratrum propositum in ea parte pium et laudabile, opusque predictum ecclesie prefate utile existere et necessarium, nec in aliquo nobis aut parochianis dicte ecclesie hoc fore nocivum aut prejudiciale, ut prefati Magister et Confratres dicta domus et edificia in solo ipsius cimiterii, ex parte australi ecclesie, predicte latitudinis dictorum triginta et septem pedum, edificare et reedificare, presertim quatinus longitudo dictorum ecclesie et cancelli se extendit, et cum edificata vel reedificata fuerint, reparare tociens quociens opus fuerit in futurum, liberumque ingressum in eadem et egressum ab eisdem, et eorum usum continuum habere valeant inperpetuum, absque nostra aut successorum nostrorum molestacione, calumpnia, contradiccione, seu soli predicti vendicacione quibuscunque, de Fratrum nostrorum unanimi consensu et assensu habito, primitus inter nos super hoc tractatu diligenti ac informacione pleniori, ceterisque omnibus de jure requisitis in ea parte concurrentibus, dum tamen via processionalis, ex parte australi ecclesie predicte consueta, in perpetuo in futurum pateat, et salva sit parochianis ecclesie predicte et eorum successoribus, saltim matutinarum missarum et vesperarum temporibus, et per edificia predicta, dictis temporibus, non impediatur via antedicta, pro nobis et successoribus nostris, quatinus in nobis est, ipsis Magistro et Confratribus et eorum successoribus, licenciam concedimus et plenam potestatem.

In cujus rei testimonium, sigillum nostrum commune fecimus hiis apponi.

Datum apud Bermundeseye, in domo nostra capitulari, in festo Sancti Johannis Baptiste, anno Domini millesimo tricentesimo septuagesimo.

[*Seal gone.*]

[*In dorso.*] "De edificando in parte australi Cimiterii de Cobeham, per licenciam Capituli de Bermondesey."

L. B. L.

II.

(Extracts from the Will of Elena, widow of Thomas Jemes, of Cobham, relative to the disposal of sixteen marks. Probate 30 January, 14 Hen. VI., 1435-6.)

[From the original Will in the Surrenden Collection.]

Summo altari de Cobham, xv^{d}.

Lumini Sancte Marie Magdalene ecclesie predicte, viij^{d}.

Lumini Sancte Crucis, viij^{d}.

Luminibus in capella Beate Marie Virginis, xij^{d}.

Lumini Sancti Nicholai, vj^{d}.

Altari ejusdem Sancti, suum optimum lectistitium.

Facture stallorum ecclesie predicte, vj^{s}-viij^{d}.

Et vult predicta Elena ut ipsi predicti feoffatores et executores Michael et Robertus dent, seu dari faciant, pelvim et lavacrum nova fonti ecclesie predicte, ad usum levantum pueros de sacro fonte.

Et insuper vult predicta Elena ut ipsi predicti Michael et Robertus solvant, seu solvi faciant, viij^{s}-iiij^{d} pro centum missis celebraturis, pro anima sua et animabus omnium benefactorum suorum; vij^{s}-vj^{d} pro xxx^{ta} missis celebraturis de tricentinali beati Gregorii.

Et preterea vult ut ipsi predicti Michael et Robertus per annum idoneum habeant capellanum divina celebrantem in ecclesia predicta, pro anima sua, et animabus omnium benefactorum suorum.

Residuum vero pecunie predicte, debitis que debet prius solutis, expendatur in reparacione ecclesie predicte, et elemosinarum largacione, et viarum pupplicarum emendacione, prestita in omnibus supradictis caucione sufficienti.

WILLELMUS PEPIR,
Capellanus Ecclesie predicte.

Proved at Malling, before the official of Rochester, 30th January, 1435.

[*Indorsed.*] "Codicillum Elene de Cobham."

L. B. L.

NOTES OF VINEYARDS.

In the Surrenden Collection there is a Roll of Accounts of the Abbey of St. Augustine's, Canterbury, the date of which, judging by the handwriting, is early in Edw. III. There are the following entries with respect to Vineyards:—

EXPENSE IN VINEIS.

Iidem computant de stipendio vineatoris de NORHOME,[1] per annum	lij^{s}
Et solut̃ fodientibus in eisdem per totum annum .	xliij^{s}-j^{d}
Et in scalet̃[2] emptis pro eisdem, cum cariagio . .	xxxiij^{s}-xj^{d}
Et in vanges,[3] howes, et aliis utensilibus pro eisdem	v^{s}-ij^{d}
Et in stipendio et vadiis vineatoris de CHIST⁹, per annum	lij^{s}
Et solut̃ fodientibus in eisdem, cum xv carectatis de scalet̃ emptis pro eisdem	xix^{s}-vj^{d}

Summa, x^{li}-v^{s}-viij^{d}.

COLLECTANEA FOR A HISTORY OF THE FAMILY OF COBHAM; WITH MUCH OF THE CITY OF ROCHESTER.

I.

[No date: it appears to be about A.D. 1200–1220.]

(Bartholomew and Matthew, cutlers, sons of Wulfwin, smith, of Strode, confirm to Henry de Cobbeham, son of Serlo de Cobbeham, and his heirs, a rent of thirty-eight pence per annum, of which Amfrid Tincturarius used to pay fourteen pence per annum, out of three acres of the land of Itherdene; Adam Pelliparius twelve pence per annum, out of . . . . acres of the land of Itherdene; Sefader Sefare atter Strehende ten pence per annum, out of land at Sorere ?; and Godwin, son of Osbern de Culinge, two pence per annum, out of a messuage in Strode, near the shop. To be held of the said grantors, by said Henry de Cobbeham and his heirs, by two pence per annum. For this grant, the said Henry has paid twenty-four shillings for the purchase.)

[N.B. The property is in Strood, as shown by the indorsement "Strodes."]

Sciant presentes et futuri, quod ego BARTHOLOMEUS, et ego MATTHEUS, fabri, cultellarii, filii WLFWINI, fabri, de STRODE, de-

[1] 'Nordhome;' an estate belonging to the Abbey, in St. Martin's parish. Abbot Ralph Bourne (elected 1309, died 1334), according to Thorne, caused vines to be planted there; it had before been a hiding-place for thieves.

[2] 'Scalettis;' little ladders, or trellises: not mere stakes, as for non-climbing plants.

[3] 'Vanges;' spades.

dimus et concessimus, et presenti carta nostra confirmavimus, Henrico de Cobbeham, filio Serlonis de Cobbeham . . . .[1] et heredibus suis, triginta et octo denarios redditus nostri, cum omnibus utilitatibus inde surg . . . . bus . . . nnibus casibus; unde Amfridus Tincturarius nobis annuatim reddere solebat xiiij denarios. Scilicet, in die Incarnationis . . . . Pentecostes, apud Strode, de tribus acris terre Itherdene; et Adam Pellifarius xij denarios ad predict . . . . acris terre Itherdene; et Sefader Sefare atter Strehende x[d] ad predictum terminum . . . . . terre et dimidia apud Sorere ?; et Godwinus filius Osberni de Culinge ij[d], ad sepe [dictum] t[erminum] : . . . . quodam mesagio in Strode, quod jacet juxta fabricam.

Tenendos et habendos jure hereditario in perpetuum, de nobis et heredibus nostris, reddendo inde annuatim, nobis et heredibus nostris, scilicet ad predictum terminum, apud Strode duos denarios, pro omnibus servitiis et consuetudinibus et demandis temporalibus.

Et ego Bartholomeus, et ego Mattheus, et heredes nostri, guarantizabimus totum predictum redditum, cum omnibus utilitatibus inde surgentibus in omnibus casibus, predicto Henrico et heredibus suis, contra omnes homines et omnes feminas, per predictum servicium.

Pro hac autem confirmatione nostra, ad stabilitatem ejus perpetuam, appositis sigillis nostris fi . . . . munita, dedit nobis predictus Henricus vigintiquatuor solidos sterlingorum in gersumam.

Hiis testibus,—Johanne filio Roce, Willelmo . . . . , Radulpho Coiteman, Duket de Strode, Prekelinger, Waltero, Nauta, Johanne de Hacke, Jacobo de Porta, Hugone de Dudintone, Thoma de Dene, Malgerio clerico, Roberto clerico, Johanne de Chilingeham, et multis aliis.

Serlo de Cobbeham =

|

Henry de Cobbeham.

L. B. L.

[1] After 'Cobeham' three letters are gone; part of the last of them remains, it is apparently the top of the letter *l*, and the missing letters may have been "mil," for kt., but this must be taken only as conjecture. If the grantee be (as is most probable) Sir Henry de Cobham, we are supplied with his father's name, Serlo, which is not noted by Dugdale.

Ego, vero, Helte, et heredes mei, warantizabimus predicto Henrico et heredibus suis, totum jus et hereditatem predictam, contra omnes homines et feminas.

Pro hac dimissione et concessione, et quietaclamacione et presentis carte mee confirmacione, sepe dictus Henricus dedit . . . . . marcas.

Hiis testibus,—Roberto de Sancto Claro, Simone de Berherse, ... Waltero filio Ricardi de Cobeham, ... Roberto . . . . , Willelmo Potin . . . . Waltero Hod . . . . . Elya Mercatore.

Gudrid Creac = of Rochester

Helte. — Wimarea.

L. B. L.

III.

[No date: it appears to be about A.D. 1230–1240.]

(Alan Schipwerchte, for sixteen shillings, sells to Henry de Cobbeham, a rent-charge of two shillings and sixpence, without Chealdegate, in Rochester,[1] of which Alexander Midnicth is to pay twenty pence per annum, and Helyas Sutor ten pence per annum, to the said Henry de Cobbeham.)

[N.B.—This was tied up with No. II.]

Sciant presentes et futuri, quod ego Alanus Scipwerchte,[2] vendidi Henrico de Cobbeham duos solidatos et dimidium redditus, extra Chealdegate, pro sexdecim solidis sterlingorum, de quo redditu Alexander Midnicth reddet predicto Henrico de Cobbeham, vel heredibus suis, viginti denarios per annum, et Helyas Sutor decem denarios similiter per annum, et heredes eorum.

Habendos et tenendos, sibi et heredibus suis, de me et de heredibus meis, libere, jure, et in pace; ita quod nec ego predictus Alanus, nec aliquis heredum meorum, versus predictum Henricum de Cobbeham, vel heredes suos, de prefata venditione nichil juris calumpniare poterimus. Et ego predictus Alanus, et heredes mei, predicto Henrico, vel heredibus suis, prefatam venditionem warantizare debemus contra omnes homines et omnes feminas.

[1] It is in Rochester, as shown by the indorsement "Roffa."

[2] On the indorsement it is "Schipwerchte," *i.e.* Shipwright.

Hiis testibus,—Johanne filio Rocii, Willelmo Potin, Petro de Thalamo, Durante Wisdom, Humfrido Vinitore, Geldewino Maceccario, Alexandro Coco, Adam Mercatore, Yvone Portario, Magistro Euerardo, Henrico Portario, Helie Grangier, et multis aliis.—L. B. L.

NOTES OF WILLS.

The following is a summary of the Will of HENRY STIDOLF, of Tudely, ancestor, in the female line, of the FANES of MEREWORTH, Earls of Westmoreland, who inherited from him their large estates in TUDELY and BRENCHLEY, which are still possessed by his direct lineal representative the VISCOUNTESS FALMOUTH. The Will is registered in the official Registry of the Bishop, at Rochester, and is to the following purport:—

HENRY STIDOLF, of TUDELE, 24 September, 1474, leaves to the High Altars of CAPEL BRENCHLEY and TUDELY various small sums.

To RICHARD KNIGHT, two cows; to JOHN MICHELL, a heifer; to JOHN PENYALE, a heifer. MARION, my wife, and THOMAS A STONE, Junior, to be Executors; WALTER ROBART, Esq., of CRANBROOK, to be Supervisor; MARION, my wife, to be Residuary Legatee. Witnesses,—WILLIAM, Vicar of TUDELEY; WALTER ROBARD, Esq.; THOMAS A STONE, etc.

Then as to his real estate:

Sir JOHN CULPEPER, Knyght; RICHARD CULPEPER, of OXENOTH, Esq.; JOHN SAMPSON, Gent.; JOHN DOD, RICHARD LATTER, and THOMAS A STONE, my Feoffees, to deliver to MARION, my wife, a messuage, etc., called PEERS SMYTHES, late George Burrys's, in TUDELY and BRENCHLEY; also five pieces of land called POCOKS, and another called ROWPOLE, in BRENCHLEY, for life. Also, to sell a tenement in EADMANSTR, which I lately bought of WILLIAM ATTE CROCHE and JOHN COSYNES, to pay debts. To deliver all my lands and tenements, etc., to THOMAS, my son, in fee simple, when he is twenty-four years old. My wife MARION to receive the profits meanwhile, keeping my son THOMAS to school, etc. etc. My son THOMAS, when he is sixteen years old, to receive certain profits of the land, at the discretion of WALTER ROBERTS, Esq. and THOMAS A STONE. If my son THOMAS marry before he be twenty-four, to have such profits of the estate as the said WALTER

ROBERTS and THOMAS A STONE may, in their discretion, assign, provided he marry with their consent; otherwise, the said profits, till he be twenty-four, to be expended in masses.

If the said Thomas die under twenty-four, then to MARION, MARGERY, and AGNES, my daughters, with benefit of survivorship, to be under the same guidance and conditions, as to marrying, as THOMAS my son. If WILLIAM CARDWELL pay 40^{s} within two years of my death, he is to have a piece of land called KEYSERSCROFTE, in fee simple. If my daughters MARION, MARGERY, and AGNES, die without issue, then my manor of BADSELLE, its rents and appurtenancies, to be delivered to THOMAS STIDOLF, son of GEORGE STIDOLF, in fee simple: and all the lands and tenements purchased by THOMAS STIDOLF, my father, and HARRY STIDOLF, to be sold for masses, repairs of roads, etc.

Witnesses,—WALTER ROBARD, Esq.; Sir WILLIAM, Vicar of TUDELY; JOHN GODYNS; THOMAS A STONE; RICHARD A STONE; THOMAS HERMAR; RICHARD WRYNGE, etc. etc.

The following pedigree results from this Will:—

Harry Stidolf.

Thomas Stidolf ═ Dead 1474.

George Stidolf ═

Henry Stidolf of Tudely, 1474. ═ Marion. 1474.

Thomas Stidolf Devisee in remainder, 1474.

Thomas Stidolf. Under 16, 1474. | Marion. 1474. | Margery. 1474. | Agnes. 1474.

With the possibility that any of these may have been by a different mother.

L. B. L.

NOTICES OF KENT WORTHIES.—CAXTON.

In his Preface to the 'Historyes of Troye' Caxton says: "I was born and learned mine English in Kent in the Weald." How he would have pronounced his own name, we may gather from a comparison with the mode in which others were pronounced in that district, and this we learn from the form in which they present themselves in old manuscripts, at a time when the scribe wrote by ear, and had no settled law of spelling to guide him.

In manuscripts of the fourteenth and fifteenth centuries, we find Hadlow invariably written Haudloo or Haulo; Francklyn is written Frauncklyn; Alchin, Auchin; Malling, Mauling; Wanting, Waunting; Addington, Audinton. These names are all selected from the Weald, or the neighbourhood of Hadlow. Were it necessary, we could yet add a large number more. We have however cited sufficient to prove that in the Weald, and specially in that part in which Hadlow is situated, the *a* was pronounced broad. It is also well known that at the above period *x* was pronounced something very like *ss*. Thus Vaux is frequently written Vauss; Fyneux, Fyness; and we have Exhurst as often as Esshurst, for one and the same place, just as the English rendering of Bruxelles is to this day Brussels. Admitting therefore the pronunciation of *a* and *x* to be as we have stated (and there is hardly any doubt that it was so), CAXTON, in speaking of himself, would have called himself CAUSSTON. But we have a most decided exemplification of this in reference to Caxton in Cambridgeshire. In Rot. Origin. 41 Edw. III., rot. 42, there is the following entry:—"Cantebr. Johes Freville dat viginti marcas, etc." In English thus:—"Cambridgeshire, John Freville gives twenty marks for license to enfeoff John de Carleton and John de Selvte in the manor of CAUSTON." In the 'Inquisitiones post mortem,' 4 Ric. II., No. 23, in a record of the same estate, we find Elena, the widow of Sir John Frevill, having, as her dower, the third part of the manor of CAXTON in Cambridgeshire. It must therefore have been pronounced CAUSSTON, or it never could have appeared in that form in the 'Originalia.' In the fourteenth century, then, CAXTON and CAUSTON were one and the same name.

Fuller says that, "William Caxton was born in that town" (*i.e.* Caxton). Caxton, as we have seen, tells us himself that he was born in the Weald of Kent. We must look, therefore, for CAXTON, *alias* CAUSTON, in the Weald, for his birthplace. Now, in the parish of Hadlow (*alias* Haulo) in the Weald is the manor or ville of CAUSTON. Late in the fourteenth century it was possessed by a family of the same name, "DE CAUSTON," one of whom we conclude to have been our illustrious Typographer.

It may be well to add that the manor of CAUSTON was held of the honour of Clare, the lords of which, in the fifteenth century, were that ducal and royal house by whom William Caxton was warmly patronized. Their forest of South Frith, close to Causton, descended, through one of the coheiresses of Gilbert de Clare, Lord of Tunbridge, to Richard, Duke of York (father of the Duchess of Burgundy and Edward IV.), whose widow possessed it at her death.

We think, from the above premises, we can with safety assert that CAUSTON in Hadlow may take to itself the honour of having been the birthplace of William Caxton, and our Society may congratulate itself on having been the first to decide this interesting fact, which has been hitherto a subject of hopeless inquiry.—L. B. L.

ANCIENT LETTERS OF MEN OF KENT.

For the following letter, and the interpretation of many passages in it, we are indebted to the kind attention of W. B. Sanders, Esq., of the General Record Office. The writer of the letter seems to have been GREGORY DE ROKESLE, who in the thirteenth century was owner of large estates in the county of Kent. In 7 Edw. I. he was Mayor of London, and in the same year was appointed one of the keepers of the Mint.[1] [See Originalia, 7 Edw. I., rot. 1; Pasch. Commun., 7 Edw. I., rot. 6; Trin. Commun., 7 Edw. I., rot. 6.]

By the return of the Jurors in the Inquisition upon his death,

[1] According to Madox (History of the Exchequer, Edw., 1711, p. 198), there were several mints in England, viz. at Winchester, Canterbury, Lincoln, Lynn, Norwich, etc. etc. etc., which, with their officers, were under the supervisal and direction of the Chief Justiciar, or the Treasurer and Barons of the Exchequer.

Assays were made at the Exchequer of the money minted at the respective mints. King Edward I. (anno 9 or 10), by his writ, commanded the Barons to take with them GREGORY DE ROKESLE, and straightway, before they retired from the Exchequer, to open the boxes of the assay of London and Canterbury, and to make the assay in such manner as the King's Council were wont to do. [Trin. Commun., 9 & 10 Edw. I., rot. 5 a.]

it appears that he died 13th July, 19 Edw. I., A.D. 1291, and Roger de Rislepe, son of his sister Agnes, was his heir.[1]

It will be seen, that a tame stag having devoured despatches entrusted to Rokesle, he writes as follows to his friend Jakes :—

"A son cher ami especiel Jakes le seu Gregre de Rokesle. Saluz, e ceo qil peut de honeur e damiste.[2] Pur ceo qe jo ws[3] disei nad geres de tens qe jo ws chargereye de akunes bosoignes fere e ke ws deveryez pur moi travailer, jo ws pri especialment ke ws voilez resseivere les lettres ke jo envei a mon Seignur e le vostre, e bailez[4] les la ou il voud. E estreceo pursure les peticions ke sunt continuees en memes celes lettres, cest a dire dever mon Seignur le Eveske ij peires de lettres, cest a saver, une a Visconte de Nicole,[5] pur carier ces vins e son pesson de la Seint Botulf gekes a Cestre, e une autre lettre mon Seignur le Eveske a celuy qi ressevra ces vins e son pesson[6] a Cestre. E dautrepart, v paire des lettres le Rei, une a Visconte de Nicole, la secunde a Senescal e la Bailif de Seint Botulf, la terce au Meyre e a Bailif de Lenne, la qarte a Sire Hamon Hautein, e la qinte a Conestable de la Tour de Londres; Richard de Waldegrave, kil seit a socié par lettres patentes a Sire Hamon Hautein a deliverance de la Gayole de Newegate. Cest priere ws fay jo mout[7] especialment pour une meschance ke me est avenue, ke par le ov Jon de Maydestane avoit porte de la Court tens[8] lettres come jo vois[9] ore demandand[10] e mis sur un es-

[1] There is much confusion and error in Hasted's different accounts of the family of Rokesly. In his history of the manor of Foot's Cray he names Roger de Rokesle as the son of Gregory, while, in the descent of the manor of North Cray, he represents Sir Richard de Rokesle as the son of Gregory; whereas, according to the Inquisition, Gregory died without issue, his nephew Roger de Rislepe being his heir. This Roger, in all probability, was afterwards styled Roger de Rokesle, from the place of his residence and his heirship. In a Subsidy Roll for the hundred of Rokesly, 30 Edw. I., in the General Record Office, the chattels of ROGER DE ROKESLEE, in Foot's Cray, are valued at £25. 4*s*. This, doubtless, is the same individual, and mistaken by Hasted for the son of Gregory.

[2] amitié. [3] vous. [4] deliver them.

[5] Nicole,—the old name for Lincoln.

[6] poisson. [7] much, very. [8] for 'telles.'

[9] for 'vais.' Literally, "I go now asking."

[10] The interpretation of the entire paragraph will be: "John of Maidstone has brought from the Court such letters as [or letters similar to those] I am now asking for."

cheker[1] en ma chambre, vint le Cerf ke Jo tene en mon hostel, si les devora issi ke ren ne demorre de cyre ne de parchemyn.

"Pur amor de moi pursue ben ceste chose ke jo sei vostre a touz jours."

L. B. L.

CHURCH BELLS.

Any information or extracts from churchwardens' or parish accounts, relating to the inscriptions, arms, medallions, stops,

[1] 'Escheker.' "The Exchequer took its name from the chequered cloth which was wont to be laid upon the table there" (*Madox*, p. 110). In the Dialogue of the Exchequer, printed in Madox, we read as follows:—

"*Discipulus.*—Quid est Scaccarium?

"*Magister.*—Scaccarium tabula est quadrangula, quæ longitudinis quasi decem pedum, latitudinis quinque, ad modum mensæ circumsedentibus apposita, undique habet limbum altitudinis quasi quatuor digitorum, ne quid appositum excidat. Superponitur autem Scaccario Superiori pannus in Termino Paschæ emptus, non quilibet, sed niger virgis distinctus, distantibus a se virgis, vel pedis vel palmæ extentæ spacio. In spaciis autem Calculi sunt juxta ordines suos de quibus alias dicetur. Licet autem tabula talis Scaccarium dicatur, transmitatur tamen hoc nomen ut ipsa quoque Curia qua consedente Scaccario est Scaccarium dicatur; adeo ut si quandoque per sententiam aliquid de communi consilio fuerit constitutum, dicatur factum ad Scaccarium illius vel illius anni. Quod autem hodie dicitur ad Scaccarium, olim dicebatur ad Taleas.

"*D.*—Que est ratio hujus nominis?

"*M.*—Nulla mihi vereor ad presens occurrit, quam quod Scaccarii lusilis similem habet formam.

"*D.*—Nunquid antiquorum prudentia pro sola forma sic nominavit, cum et simili ratione Tabularium appellari?

"*M.*—Merito te scrupulosum dixi. Et est alia, sed occultior. Sicut enim in Scaccario lusili quidam ordines sunt pugnatorum, et certis legibus vel limitibus procedunt vel subsistunt, præsidentibus aliis et aliis præcedentibus. Sic in hoc quidam præsident, quidam assident ex officio. Et non est cuiquam liberum leges constitutas excedere; quod erit ex consequentibus manifestum. Item, sicut in lusili, pugna committitur inter Reges; sic in hoc inter duos principaliter conflictus est et pugna committitur, Thesaurarium scilicet, et Vicecomitem qui assidet ad compotum; residentibus aliis tanquam judicibus ut videant et judicent."

Whether the 'Escheker' of our text was an actual chessboard, or a "pannus niger virgis distinctus," a chequered cloth, such as that used in the Exchequer, we must leave our readers to determine. Madox conjectures the author of the Dialogue to have been Richard Fitz Nigell, Bishop of London *temp.* Ric. I.

weights or dimensions of Church Bells, or the original costs, or any faculty for recasting, with the expenses; or the frames, stocks, wheels, rules for ringers, or payments to them, or the expenses in any way relating to the bells of the county of Kent, will be most thankfully received by J. R. Daniel Tyssen, Esq., of Rock Gardens, Brighton, who is collecting materials for the History of Kentish Bells.

DESIDERATA.

We close this department of our Volume by submitting the following list of subjects, on which information is much desiderated:—

Early notice of the discovery or supposed existence of Primæval Relics;—Genealogies of Kent Families;—Ancient Heraldry of Kent Families;—Ancient Seals of Kent Families and Officials;—The Archbishops of Canterbury;—The Bishops of Rochester;—The Cathedrals of Canterbury and Rochester;—The Deans and Chapters of Canterbury and Rochester;—Ancient Charters relating to the County, whether from public records or private archives;—The Cinq Ports;—The Ancient Castles of the County;—The Ancient Mansions and Manor-Houses of the County;—The Churches of the County;—Architecture, Ecclesiastical and Civil;—Ancient Bridges, Roads, etc.;—Ancient Customs in the County;—Ancient Proverbs in the County;—Dialects and Provincialisms of the County;—The History of Gavelkind and its peculiarities;—Lists of Manors and Lands exempted from the custom of Gavelkind;—Monumental Inscriptions;—Indices to, and Notes from Parochial Registers;—Parochial Annals.

On these subjects, and any others calculated to illustrate the Topography and early History of the County, we ask the hearty co-operation of all our Members.

We also invite their assistance in supplying annotations and corrections of the papers which we may from time to time publish.—L. B. L.

PEDES FINIUM.

PEDES FINIUM.

(Continued from Vol. I. p. 280.)

XLIX.—(Jo. No. 11.)[1]

[21st June, 1199, 1 Jo.][2]

(Mageria de Sconinton acknowledges to Ailnod de Broc and Mabilia his wife one yoke and the eighth part of a yoke of land in Hokeling. For which they grant the said land to the said Mageria and her heirs, to be held of them and their heirs, by the free service of twelve pence per annum.)

Apud Westmonasterium,[3] die Lune proxima post octavas Sancte Trinitatis, anno regni Regis Johannis primo.

Coram G. filio Petri, magistro Thoma de Husseburn, Willelmo de Warenn, Ricardo de Herierd, Simone de Pateshill, Osberto filio Hervei, Johanne de Gesling, Justiciariis, etc.[3]

Inter Ailnodum de Broc et Mabiliam uxorem suam, petentes, et Mageriam[4] de Sconinton,[5] tenentem.

De j jugo, et de octava parte j jugi terre, cum pertinentiis, in Hokeling.[6]

[1] These numbers "(Jo. No. 11)" etc. in parenthesis, are the references to the original Record.—John No. 11. etc.

[2] Although Richard I. died on 6th April, John's reign is always dated as commencing at his coronation, viz. 27th May, Ascension Day, 1199; and in public documents his regnal years are computed from Ascension Day to Ascension Day. We have adopted this practice in fixing the dates of these Fines.

[3] To economize space, we shall in future omit expressions of mere form and of constant recurrence, such as the initiatory words of every Fine: "Hec est finalis concordia facta in curia domini Regis;" and the words which always follow the enumeration of the presiding judges: "et aliis fidelibus domini Regis tunc ibidem presentibus."

[4] *Sic.*

[5] ? Sconniton.

[6] There was land called Hokeling in the Isle of Sheppey, belonging to Domus Dei Ospringe, temp. Hen. III. ? if this be the same.

Unde placitum fuit inter eos in prefata Curia, scilicet quod predicta MAGERIA recognovit totam predictam terram, cum pertinentiis, esse jus et hereditatem predictorum AILNODI et MABILIE.

Et pro hoc fine et concordia et recognicione, predicti AILNODUS et MABILIA concesserunt predicte MAGERIE totam predictam terram, cum pertinentiis, tenendam de eis et heredibus eorum, sibi et heredibus suis, in perpetuum, per liberum servicium xij denariorum per annum, pro omni servicio, salvo forinseco servicio, unde prius non reddidit nisi vj[2] denarios, reddendorum ad festum Sancti Michaelis.

Ailnod de Broc = Mabilia.
1199. 1199.

L.—(Jo. No. 9.)

[1st July,[3] 1199, 1 Jo.]

(Stephen de Deninton acknowledges one virgate of land, called Gare, in Essedeford, to be the right and inheritance of William de Essedeford, to hold, to him and his heirs, of the said Stephen and his heirs, by the free service of three shillings per annum.)

Apud Westmonasterium, in octavis Sancti Johannis, anno regni Regis Johannis primo.

Coram G. filio Petri, etc. [ut in No. 49.]

Inter STEPHANUM DE DENINTON,[4] petentem, et WILLELMUM DE ESSEDEFORD, tenentem.

De j virgata terre, cum pertinentiis, in ESSEDEFORD,[5] que vocatur GARE.

Unde placitum fuit inter eos in prefata Curia, scilicet quod predictus STEPHANUS recognovit predictam terram, cum pertinentiis, esse jus et hereditatem predicti WILLELMI, tenendam

[2] ? "nisi vj." The words are nearly obliterated.

[3] *i.e.* if in octaves of St. John Baptist; but if "Sancti Johannis" here stands for St. John the Evangelist, then the date of the Fine will be 4th January, 1199-1200.

[4] ? Denniton.

[5] Probably Ashford.

de ipso STEPHANO et heredibus suis, sibi et heredibus suis, in perpetuum, per liberum servicium iij solidorum per annum, pro omni servicio, reddendorum ad festum Sancti Michaelis.

LI.—(Jo. No. 8.)

[8th July, 1199, 1 Jo.]

(Nicholas Fitz Richard quitclaims to William de Barnefeld, and his heirs, all right in half a virgate of land in Petham [? Peckham], for three and a half marks.)

Apud Westmonasterium, die Jovis proxima post octavas Apostolorum Petri et Pauli, anno regni Regis Johannis primo.

Coram G. filio Petri, etc. [ut in No. 49.]

Inter NICOLAUM FILIUM RICARDI, petentem, et WILLELMUM DE BARNEFELD,[1] tenentem.

De dimidia virgata terre, cum pertinentiis, in PETTHAM.[2]

Unde placitum fuit inter eos in prefata Curia, scilicet quod predictus NICOLAUS remisit et quietum clamavit predicto WILLELMO et heredibus suis, totum jus et clamium quod habuit in predicta terra, de se et heredibus suis, in perpetuum.

Et pro hoc fine et concordia et quieta clamancia predictus WILLELMUS dedit predicto NICOLAO iij marcas et dimidiam argenti.

LII.—(Jo. No. 10.)

[10th July, 1199, 1 Jo.]

(In a recognizance of Mortdauncestor, Thomas de Ospring quitclaims to Emma de Creuequer all right in three messuages in Lamberhurst, for two marks.)

Apud Westmonasterium, die Sabbati proxima post octavas Apostolorum Petri et Pauli, anno regni Regis Johannis primo.

Coram G. filio Petri, etc. [ut in No. 49.]

Inter THOMAM DE OSPRING, petentem, et EMMAM DE CREUEQUER, tenentem.

[1] It is "B̃nefeld" in the original.

[2] ? Peccham for Peckham, but Pettham is the most probable reading.

De tribus mesuagiis, cum pertinentiis, in LAMBURHERST.

Unde recognicio de morte antecessoris summonita fuit inter eos in prefata Curia, scilicet, quod predictus THOMAS remisit et quietum clamavit predicte EMME, et heredibus suis, totum jus et clamium quod habuit in predictis mesuagiis, de se et heredibus suis, in perpetuum.

Et pro hoc fine et concordia et quieta clamancia predicta EMMA dedit predicto THOME ij marcas argenti.

LIII.—(Jo. No. 5.)

[17th October, 1199, 1 Jo.]

(In a recognizance of Mortdauncestor, Thomas de Esse acknowledges half a yoke of land in Audinton, to be the right and inheritance of Richard and John de Lee, and quitclaims it to them and their heirs, for twenty shillings.)

Apud Westmonasterium, in vigilia Sancti Luce, anno regni Regis Johannis primo.

Coram G. filio Petri, magistro Thoma de Husseburn, Willelmo de Warenn, Ricardo de Herierd, Simone de Pateshill, Johanne de Gestling, Justiciariis, etc.

Inter RICARDUM et JOHANNEM DE LEE, petentes, et THOMAM DE ESSE, tenentem.

De dimidio jugo terre, cum pertinentiis, in AUDINTON.[1]

Unde recognicio de morte antecessoris summonita fuit inter eos in prefata Curia, scilicet quod predictus THOMAS recognovit totam predictam terram, cum pertinentiis, esse jus et hereditatem predictorum RICARDI et JOHANNIS, et reddidit et quietam clamavit, de se et heredibus suis, prefatis RICARDO et JOHANNI, et heredibus eorum, in perpetuum.

Et pro hac recognicione et quieta clamancia, prefati RICARDUS et JOHANNES dederunt ipsi THOME viginti solidos esterlingorum.

[1] There is nothing to indicate whether this be Aldington or Addington, we write it therefore exactly as it is in the original, "Audinton," without attempting to offer any conjecture on the subject.

LIV.—(Jo. No. 4.)

[31st October, 1199, 1 Jo.]

(In a recognizance of Mortdauncestor, Thomas Long acknowledges a messuage in Westgate to be the right and inheritance of Roger and Nicholas, for which they have granted, to him and his heirs, the said messuage, to hold of them and their heirs by sixpence per annum. For which grant the said Thomas has given them twenty shillings.)

Apud Westmonasterium, in vigilia Omnium Sanctorum, anno regni Regis Johannis primo.

Coram G. filio Petri, etc. [ut in No. 53.]

Inter ROGERUM et NICHOLAUM, petentes, et THOMAM LONGUM, tenentem.

De j mesuagio, cum pertinentiis, in WESTGATE.[1]

Unde recognicio de morte antecessoris summonita fuit inter eos in prefata Curia, scilicet quod predictus THOMAS recognovit predictum mesuagium, cum pertinentiis, esse jus et hereditatem predictorum ROGERI et NICHOLAI.

Et pro hac recognicione predicti ROGERUS et NICHOLAUS concesserunt predicto THOME totum predictum mesuagium, cum pertinentiis, tenendum de eis et heredibus eorum, sibi et heredibus suis, in perpetuum, per servicium sex denariorum per annum, reddendorum ad festum Sancti Michaelis, pro omni servicio, salvo forinseco servicio.

Et pro hac concessione predictus THOMAS dedit predictis ROGERO et NICHOLAO viginti solidos esterlingorum.

LV.—(Jo. No. 2.)

[7th November, 1199, 1 Jo.]

(John Patric acknowledges six acres in Plumsted to be the right of Hugh Fitz Norman and his heirs, to hold of him and his heirs by the free service of thirty-two pence per annum. For which the said Hugh has given the said John fifteen shillings.)

Apud Westmonasterium, dominica proxima post festum Omnium Sanctorum, anno regni Regis Johannis primo.

[1] Probably the ville of Westgate, Canterbury. There was however a manor called Westgate in Birchinton.

Coram G. filio Petri, etc. [ut in No. 53.]

Inter HUGONEM FILIUM NORMANNI, petentem, et JOHANNEM PATRICIUM, tenentem.

De quatuor acris terre, cum pertinentiis, in PLUMSTED.

Unde placitum fuit inter eos in prefata Curia, scilicet quod predictus JOHANNES recognovit totam predictam terram, cum pertinentiis, esse jus predicti HUGONIS, tenendam de se et heredibus suis, sibi et heredibus suis, in perpetuum, per liberum servicium xxxij denariorum per annum, pro omni servicio, salvo forinseco servicio, reddendorum ad quatuor terminos anni, scilicet, ad Natale, viij denarios,[1] et ad Pascham viij denarios, et ad festum Sancti Johannis viij denarios, et ad festum Sancti Michaelis viij denarios.

Et pro hoc fine et concordia et recognicione, predictus HUGO dedit predicto JOHANNI xv solidos esterlingorum.

LVI.—(Jo. No. 7.)

[25th November, 1199, 1 Jo.]

(Bernardus, son of Robert de Cobeham, quitclaims to Robert Fitz Nigell and his heirs, all right in one yoke of land in Cobeham. For which the said Robert Fitz Nigell has granted to the said Bernard one acre of the said land in Adgaresfeld to the north, to hold to him and his heirs, of the said Robert Fitz Nigell and his heirs, by one pound of pepper per annum. Besides this, the said Robert Fitz Nigell has given the said Bernard five marks.)

Apud Westmonasterium, in die Sancte Katerine, anno regni Regis Johannis primo.

Coram G. filio Petri, Willelmo de Warenn, Ricardo de Herierd, Simone de Pateshill, Osberto filio Hervei, Johanne de Gestlinges, Justiciariis, etc.

Inter BERNARDUM filium ROBERTI DE COBEHAM, petentem, et ROBERTUM FILIUM NIGELLI tenentem.

De j jugo terre, cum pertinentiis, in COBEHAM.

Unde placitum fuit inter eos in prefata Curia, scilicet quod

[1] "Denarios."—It is the mode of extending these clauses adopted by the scribe when written *in extenso*.

predictus Bernardus remisit et quietum clamavit predicto Roberto et heredibus suis, totum jus et clamium quod habuit in predicta terra, de se et heredibus suis, in perpetuum.

Et pro hoc fine et concordia et quieta clamancia predictus Robertus concessit predicto Bernardo j acram de eadem terra que jacet in Adgaresfeld versus aquilonem, tenendam de se et heredibus suis, sibi et heredibus suis, in perpetuum, per servicium j libre piperis per annum, pro omni servicio, salvo forinseco servicio, reddende ad Pascham.

Et preter hoc, idem Robertus dedit predicto Bernardo v marcas argenti.

Robert de Cobeham =

Bernard de Cobeham.

LVII.—(Jo. No. 6.)

[23rd April, 1200, 1 Jo.]

(In a recognizance of Mortdauncestor, William de Moriston acknowledges five acres and a half in Sittingbourne to be the right of Aldina Fitz Wulmar. For which she grants the said land to him and his heirs, to hold of her and her heirs by the free service of eighteen pence per annum. For which grant the said William gives the said Aldina one mark.)

Apud Westmonasterium, a die Pasche in xv dies, anno regni Regis Johannis primo.

Coram G. filio Petri, Willelmo de Warenn, Ricardo de Herierd, Osberto filio Hervei, Johanne de Gestliges, Hugone de Boby, Justiciariis, etc.

Inter Aldinam filiam Wlmari, petentem, et Willelmum de Moriston, tenentem.

De v acris terre et dimidia, cum pertinentiis, in Sidingeburn.

Unde recognicio de morte antecessoris summonita fuit inter eos in prefata Curia, scilicet quod predictus Willelmus recognovit totam predictam terram, cum pertinentiis, esse jus predicte Aldine.

Et pro hac recognicione et fine et concordia, predicta Aldina concessit predicto Willelmo, et heredibus suis, totam predictam terram, cum pertinentiis, tenendam de se et heredibus suis, in perpetuum, per liberum servicium xviij denariorum per annum, pro omni servicio, salvo forinseco servicio, reddendorum ad festum Sancti Michaelis.

Et pro hac concessione et fine et concordia predictus WILLELMUS dedit predicte ALDINE j marcam.

LVIII.—(Jo. No. 1.)

[26th April, 1200, 1 Jo.]

(In a recognizance of Mortdauncestor, Thomas de Fugeleston acknowledges one messuage and half an acre in Sittingbourne, and two acres in Egsted [? Hysted] to be the right of Aldina Fitz Wulmar. For which she grants them to the said Thomas and his heirs, to hold of her and her heirs by eight pence per annum. For this grant the said Thomas gives the said Aldina one mark.)

Apud Westmonasterium, in crastino Sancti Marci, Evangeliste, anno regni Regis Johannis primo.

Coram G. . . . . , Simone de Pateshill, Osberto filio Hervei, Johanne de Gestling, Justiciariis, etc.

Inter [ALDINAM FIL]IAM WULMARI petentem, et THOMAM DE FUGELESTON tenentem.

De j mesuagio in SIDINGEBURN, et dimidia acra in eadem . . . . et duabus acris terre in Egsted.

Unde recognicio de morte antecessoris summonita fuit inter eos in prefata Curia, scilicet quod predictus THOMAS recognovit predictum mesuagium et predictam terram esse jus predicte ALDINE.

Et pro hac recognicione et fine et concordia predicta ALDINA concessit predicto THOME predictum mesuagium et predictam terram, cum pertinentiis, tenendam sibi et heredibus suis, de se et heredibus suis, in perpetuum, per servicium viij denariorum per annum, pro omni servicio, salvo forinseco servicio, reddendorum ad festum Sancti Michaelis.

Et pro hac concessione et fine et concordia, predictus THOMAS dedit predicte ALDINE j marcam argenti.

LIX.—(Jo. No. 3.)

[14th May, 1200, 1 Jo.]

(Christiana, widow of William Fitz Odo, acknowledges thirty-nine acres in Natindon to be the right of Godfrey Sceredust and Matilda his wife. For which they grant, to her and her heirs, twenty-two acres of the same land lying near her capital messuage in Natindon, to hold of them and their heirs by twelve pence per annum.)

Apud Westmonasterium, a die Pasche in v septimanas, anno regni Regis Johannis primo.

Coram G. filio Petri, R. de Herierd, S. de Pateshill, O. filio Hervei, J. de Gestlinges, H. de Wicheton, Eustacio de Fauconberge, H. de Boby, Justiciariis, etc.

Inter Godefridum Sceredust et Matillidem uxorem suam, petentes, et Cristianam que fuit uxor Willelmi filii Odonis, tenentem.

De xxxix acris terre, cum pertinenciis, in Natindon.[1]

Unde placitum fuit inter eos in prefata Curia, scilicet quod predicta Christiana recognovit totam predictam terram, cum pertinentiis, esse jus predictorum Godefridi et Matillidis.

Et pro hac recognicione et fine et concordia predicti Godefridus et Matildis concesserunt predicte Christiane xxij acras terre, cum pertinentiis, de eadem terra que jacent juxta capitale mesuagium predicte Christiane, in villa de Natindon, tenendas sibi et heredibus suis, de se et heredibus eorum, in perpetuum, per servicium xij denariorum per annum, pro omni servicio, scilicet, ad Nativitatem Sancte Marie vj denarios, et ad medium Quadragesime, vj denarios, salvo forinseco servicio.

Godfrey Sceredust —	Matilda.	William Fitz Odo =	Christiana.
1200.	1200.	Dead 1200.	1200.

[1] Now called "Nackington."

LX.—(Jo. No. 17.)

[11th June, 1200, 2 Jo.]

(William Noel grants to Ralph de Deniton, and his heirs, the entire ville of Deniton [Denton], to hold of him and his heirs by the free service of six marks per annum.)

Apud Westmonasterium, in octabis Trinitatis, anno regni Regis Johannis secundo.

Coram G. filio Petri, Ricardo de Heriord, Simone de Pathill, Johanne de Gestling, Eustachio de Faucumbge, Justiciariis, etc.

Inter Willelmum Noel, petentem, et Radulphum de Deniton, tenentem.

De tota villa de Deneton,[1] cum pertinentiis.

Unde placitum fuit inter eos in prefata Curia, scilicet quod predictus Willelmus concessit predicto Ralulpho et heredibus suis, predictam villam de Deniton, cum pertinentiis, habendam et tenendam, de se et heredibus suis, in perpetuum, per liberum servicium vj marcarum argenti per annum, pro omni servicio, reddendarum ad duos terminos anni, scilicet, ad festum Sancti Michaelis xl solidos, et ad Pascha xl solidos.

Et pro hac concessione et fine et concordia predictus Radulphus dedit predicto Willelmo . . . . marcas argenti.

LXI.—(Jo. No. 18.)

[12th June, 1200, 2 Jo.]

(Emma de Pirifeld quitclaims to Thomas son of Geoffrey and Hamo son of Matthew, all right in half the ville of Pirefeld, which she claimed as dower from her late husband, Richard de Loses, except eleven acres of the same land, viz. seven called "Alard's land," and four other acres, and two acres of meadow in Perifeld Park, towards the west of Dudewisse.)

Apud Westmonasterium, in crastino Sancti Barnabe Apostoli, anno regni Regis Johannis secundo.

[1] The grantor in this Record being William Noel, and Richard Noel (see 'Inquisition post mortem,' No. II.) dying in 20 Hen. III., A.D. 1236, possessed of lands and rents in Milton and Faversham, leaving a son and heir William, we may conjecture that this ville was the manor of Denton, *alias* Plumford in Ospringe. There were, however, other parishes and manors called Denton in Kent.

. . . . filio Petri, Ricardo de Heriord, Simone de Pathill, Osberto filio Hervei, Johanne de Gestling, Henrico de Wichinton, Eustachio de Faucunberge, Justiciariis, etc.

Inter EMMAM DE PIRIFELD, petentem, per Magistrum BENEDICTUM, positum loco predicte EMME, ad lucrandum vel perdendum, et THOMAM FILIUM GAUFRIDI, et HAMONEM FILIUM MATHEI, tenentes.

De medietate ville de PIRIFELD, quam predicta EMMA clamabat pertinere ad rationabilem dotem suam, quam habet ex dono RICARDI DE LOSES, quondam viri sui.

Et unde placitum fuit inter eos in prefata Curia, scilicet quod predicta EMMA remisit et quietum clamavit predictis THOME et HAMONI et heredibus eorum, totum jus et clamium . . . . habuit in predicta medietate ville de PIREFELD, preter xi acras terre, et duas acras prati de eadem terra, et in eadem villa . . . . ipsi Emme, tota vita sua, nomine dotis; scilicet vij acre que vocantur terre ALARDI, et quatuor acre in cultura . . . . et due acre prati in parco de PERIFELD versus occidentem de DUDEWISSE.

Richard de Loses = Emma de Pirifeld.
Dead 1200. 1200.

LXII.—(Jo. No. 14.)

[18th June, 1200, 2 Jo.]

(In a recognizance, whether twelve acres in Easling be a lay fee, or belonging to the church of Easling in frank almoign, Philip, the Parson of Easling, acknowledges the three acres next the west to be the lay fee of Alexander de Eslinges, who thereupon quitclaims the remaining nine acres to the Church of Easling; Richard de Eslinges, the Patron of the said Church, being present.)

Apud Westmonasterium, a die Sancte Trinitatis in xv dies, anno regni Regis Johannis secundo.

Coram G. filio Petri, etc. [ut in No. 61.]

Inter ALEXANDRUM DE ESLINGES, petentem, et PHILIPPUM, Parsonam de ESLINGES, tenentem.

De duodecim acris terre, cum pertinentiis, in Eslinges.

Unde recognicio summonita fuit inter eos, utrum ille xij acre essent laicum feodum ipsius Alexandri, an libera elemosina ecclesie de Esling; scilicet quod idem Philippus recognovit tres acras propinquiores versus occidentem de prefatis xij acris esse jus ipsius Alexandri, et ejus laicum feodum.

Et pro hac recognicione et fine et concordia predictus Alexander quietas clamavit novem acras, de predictis xij residuas, predicte ecclesie, de se et heredibus suis, in perpetuum.

Et hoc factum fuit per assensum Ricardi de Eslinges, patroni illius ecclesie, et eo presente.

LXIII.—(Jo. No. 19.)

[13th October, 1200, 2 Jo.]

(Stephen Haket quitclaims to William Haket and his heirs all right in twenty-one acres in Hoo, Ringeton, and Hemwold, for forty shillings.)

Apud Westmonasterium, a die Sancti Michaelis in xv dies, anno regni Regis Johannis secundo.

Coram G. filio Petri, Ricardo de Herierd, Simone de Pateshill, Johanne de Gestling, Eustacio de Faucunberg, Henrico de Wichenton, Godefrido de Insula, Hugone de Boby, Waltero de Creping, Justiciariis, etc.

Inter Stephanum Haket, petentem, et Willelmum Haket, tenentem.

De xxj acris terre, cum pertinentiis, in Ho et in Ringeton, et in Hemwold.

Unde placitum fuit inter eos in prefata Curia, scilicet quod predictus Stephanus remisit et quietum clamavit predicto Willelmo, et heredibus suis, totum jus et clamium quod habuit in predicta terra, de se et heredibus suis, in perpetuum.

Et pro hac quieta clamancia et fine et concordia predictus Willelmus dedit predicto Stephano quadraginta solidos esterlingorum.

LXIV.—(Jo. No. 12.)

[20th November,[1] 1200, 2 Jo.?][2]

(The two brothers Lefward and Edwaker acknowledge eight acres in Halstow to Godwin de Wibbing. For which acknowledgment he grants to the said Lefward and Edwaker half the said land, viz. three acres lying near their house, and the superplusage of his own half towards the brook of Wibbing, to hold of him and his heirs by three pence per annum. The said Lefward and Edwaker on the one part, and the said Godwin on the other, to be answerable to the lord of Milton each for the respective moieties.)

Apud Westmonasterium, in die Sancti Edmundi, anno regni Regis Johannis .... Ricardo de Herierd, Johanne de Gestlinges, Godefrido de Insula, Waltero de Creping, Ricardo Fleming, Justiciariis, etc.

Inter GODIWINUM DE WIBBING, petentem, et LEFWARDUM filium .... et EDWAKER, fratrem ejus, tenentes.

De viij acris terre, cum pertinentiis, in HALEGESTOWE.

Unde placitum fuit, quod predicti LEFWARDUS et EDWAKER recognoverunt totam predictam terram, cum pertinentiis, esse jus ipsius GODWINI.

Et pro hac recognicione et fine et concordia predictus GODWINUS concessit predictis LEFWARDO et EDWAKER, totam medietatem predicte terre, cum pertinenciis, scilicet iij acras terre que jacent circa domum predictorum LEFWARDI et EDWAKER, et superplusagium medietatis sue versus orientem del Broc de WIBBING, tenendam de se et heredibus suis, in perpetuum, per servicium trium denariorum per annum pro omni servicio, reddendorum ad Pascha floridum.

Et sciendum, quod predicti LEFWARDUS et EDWAKER defendent medietatem suam versus capitalem dominum de Middelton et idem GODWINUS medietatem suam.

[1] If St. Edmund, King, Martyr,—but if St. Edmund, Archbishop of Canterbury, Nov. 16 or 17.

[2] The Regnal year is gone from the original. This however seems to be the proper place for this Fine. Walter de Crepping and Godfrey de Insula first appear as judges in the Fine immediately preceding this. It could hardly have belonged to 1199.

LXV.—(Jo. No. 13.)

[25th November, 1200, 2 Jo.]

(In a plea of "warantia carte,"[1] Amfridus de Dene acknowledges to John de Bilsinton[2] sixty acres of land in Oswardestone. For which acknowledgment the said John grants to the said Amfrid and his heirs all the said land, to hold of him and his heirs by the free service of fourteen shillings per annum. For which grant the said Amfrid gives the said John one mark.)

Apud Westmonasterium, in die Sancte Katrine, anno regni Regis Johannis secundo.

Coram G. filio Petri, Ricardo de Heriert, Johanne de Gestling, Godefrido de Insula, Waltero de Crepping, Ricardo Fleming, Justiciariis, etc.

Inter Amfridum de Dene et Johannem de Bilsinton.[2]

De lx acris terre, cum pertinentiis, in Oswardestan.

Unde placitum warantie carte summonitum fuit inter eos in prefata Curia, scilicet quod predictus Amfridus recognovit totam predictam terram, cum pertinentiis, esse jus ipsius Johannis.

Et pro hac recognicione et fine et concordia idem Johannes concessit predicto Amfrido totam predictam terram, cum pertinentiis, tenendam de se et heredibus suis, sibi et heredibus suis, in perpetuum, per liberum servicium xiiij solidorum per annum, pro omni servicio, salvo forinseco servicio; scilicet ad festum Sancti Johannis Baptiste, vij solidos, et ad festum Sancti Michaelis, vij solidos.

Et pro hac concessione, idem Amfridus dedit eidem Johanni j marcam argenti.

[1] A writ "warantia carte" lieth where a man is infeoffed of lands with warranty, which warranty has not been made when he is sued for the lands by a third party, then he has his action against the feoffor to compel him to warrant. (*Vide* Fitzherbert, Jacob, etc.)

[2] ? Billinton.

LXVI.—(Jo. No. 15.)

[20th January, 1200-1, 2 Jo.]

(Alexander Fitz Osbert acknowledges one knight's-fee in Plumsted to Roger Percesvil. For which acknowledgment the said Roger grants to the said Alexander and his heirs the whole of the said fee, except a rent of sixteen shillings which William, son of Isabella, holds, (the reversion thereof being in the said Roger,) to hold of him and his heirs by the services thereto belonging. The said Roger has received the homage of the said Alexander. And the said Roger has granted to William Percesvil, his brother and his heirs, for his homage and service, the said rent of sixteen shillings, to hold of him and his heirs by one pair of gilt spurs per annum. The said sixteen shillings rent are in the ville of Plumsted.)

Apud Westmonasterium, in octabis Sancti Yllarii, anno regni Regis Johannis secundo.

Coram G. filio Petri, Ricardo de Herierd, Johanne de Gestling, Henrico de Wichinton, Godefrido de Insula, Waltero de Crepping, Justiciariis, etc.

Inter ROGERUM PERCESVIL, petentem, et ALEXANDRUM filium OSBERTI, tenentem.

De feodo unius militis, cum pertinentiis, in PLUMSTED.

Unde placitum fuit inter eos in prefata Curia, scilicet quod predictus ALEXANDER recognovit totum predictum feodum, cum pertinentiis, esse jus ipsius ROGERI.

Et pro hac recognicione et fine et concordia idem ROGERUS concessit ipsi ALEXANDRO et heredibus suis, totum predictum feodum, cum pertinentiis, preter sexdecim solidatas redditus, cum pertinentiis, quas WILLELMUS filius YSABELLE tenet, que remanent ipsi ROGERO; tenendum de se et heredibus suis, per servicium quod ad predictum feodum pertinet. Et inde recepit predictus ROGERUS homagium predicti ALEXANDRI.

Et sciendum est, quod predictus ROGERUS concessit WILLELMO PERCESVIL, fratri suo, pro homagio et servicio suo, predictas sexdecim solidatas redditus, cum pertinentiis, tenendas de se et heredibus suis, sibi et heredibus suis, in perpetuum, reddendo inde annuatim j par calcarium deauratorum ad Pascha.

Sunt autem predicte sexdecim solidate redditus in villa de Plumsted.

Apparently the following may be deduced from this Fine:—

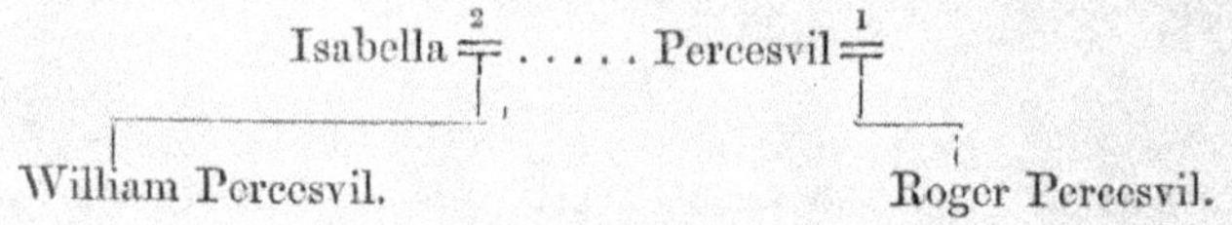

LXVII.—(Jo. No. 16.)

[27th January, 1200-1, 2 Jo.]

(Richard de Pirie acknowledges half a yoke of land in Pirie to Reginald de Faversham and Gloria his wife. For which acknowledgment, they grant it to Ranulph son of the said Richard, and his heirs, to hold of them and their heirs by the free service of sixpence per annum. For which grant the said Ranulph pays them two and a half marks.)

Apud Westmonasterium, a die Sancti Yllarii in xv dies, anno regni Regis Johannis secundo.

Coram . . . . Ricardo de Herierd, Johanne de Gestling, Henrico de Wichinton, Godefrido de Insula, Waltero de Crepping, Justiciariis, etc.

Inter Reginaldum de Faveresham et Gloriam uxorem suam, petentes, et Ricardum de Pirie, tenentem.

De dimidio jugo terre, cum pertinentiis, in Pirie.[1]

Unde placitum fuit inter eos in prefata Curia, scilicet quod predictus Ricardus recognovit totam predictam terram, cum pertinentiis, esse jus predictorum Reginaldi et Glorie uxoris sue.

Et pro hac recognicione et fine et concordia predicti Reginaldus et Gloria concesserunt Ranulpho filio ipsius Ricardi, totam predictam terram, cum pertinenciis, tenendam sibi et heredibus suis, de eis et heredibus eorum, in perpetuum, per liberum servicium vj denariorum, vel unius libre piperis, ad festum Sancti Michaelis, et faciendo forinsecum servicium capitali domino.

[1] Probably Perry Court, in Preston-next-Faversham.

Et pro hac concessione, predictus RANULFUS dedit predictis REGINALDO et GLORIE duas marcas argenti et dimidiam.

Reginald de Faversham = Gloria.
1200-1. 1200-1.

Richard de Pirie =
1200-1.
|
Ranulph de Pirie.
1200-1.

LXVIII.—(Jo. No. 27.)

[9th May, 1201, 3 Jo.]

(Walter Maleterre acknowledges two parts of half a carucate of land in Wickham to John de Lidesings and Robert his brother. For which acknowledgment they grant the said land to the said Walter and his heirs, to hold of them and their heirs by sixpence per annum, with covenant of warranty.)

Apud Porecestre, die Mercurii proxima ante Pentecostem, anno regni Regis Johannis tercio.

Coram G. filio Petri, Comite Essexie, et Simone de Pateshill, Eustachio de Fauconberge, magistro Radulpho de Stok, Justiciariis, etc.

Inter JOHANNEM DE LIDESINGS et ROBERTUM fratrem ejus, petentes, et WALTERUM MALE-TERRE, tenentem.

De duabus partibus dimidie carucate terre, cum pertinentiis, in WICHAM.[1]

Unde placitum fuit inter eos in eadem Curia, scilicet quod ipse WALTERUS recognovit predictam terram, cum pertinentiis, esse jus et hereditatem predictorum JOHANNIS et ROBERTI.

Et pro hoc recognicione, et fine, et concordia, predicti JOHANNES et ROBERTUS concesserunt predictam terram, cum pertinentiis, eidem WALTERO, tenendam sibi et heredibus suis, de ipsis et heredibus suis, per servicium sex denariorum per annum, reddendorum ad festum Sancti Michaelis, pro omni servicio, salvo forinseco servicio, et prefati JOHANNES et ROBERTUS, et heredes eorum, warantizabunt totam prefatam terram, cum

[1] There is nothing in the body of the Fine to indicate to which of the Wickhams it relates.

pertinentiis, prefato WALTERO, et heredibus suis, contra omnes homines.

. . . . de Lidesings ⚭

John de Lidesings. 1201. — Robert. 1201.

LXIX.—(21 Jo.)

[27th May, 1201, 3 Jo.]

(In a plea of "Warantia Carte," Ralph Chanu, for three and a half marks, warrants to Daniel, son of Alexander de Lodeneford, one carucate, which the said Alexander held of him in Lodingford; and further warrants the charter (reciting it) by which, for twenty shillings, he had granted the said land to the said Daniel, to hold freely of the said Ralph and his heirs by twelve shillings per annum, for all service except the King's, and when that is demanded, if it be a mark, the proportion to be paid by said Daniel shall be sixteen pence; if one pound . . . .)

Apud Westmonasterium, in octavis Sancte Trinitatis, anno regni Regis Johannis tercio.

Coram G. filio Petri, Ricardo . . . . Johanne de Gestling, Henrico de Wicketon, magistro Radulpho de Stok, Godefrido de Insula, Waltero de Crepping, Justiciariis, etc.

Inter DANIELEM DE LODENEFORD, petentem, et RADULPHUM CHANU, tenentem.

De j carucata terre, cum pertinentiis, quam ALEXANDER pater predicti DANIELIS tenuit in LODENEFORD.[1]

Unde placitum warantie Carte summonitum fuit inter eos in prefata Curia, scilicet quod predictus RADULPHUS warantizat predicto DANIELI, et heredibus suis, totam predictam terram, cum pertinentiis, et cartam quam ei fecit de predicta terra, in hec verba:—"RADULPHUS CHANU omnibus hominibus suis francis "et anglicis, clericis et laicis, tam presentibus quam futuris, "salutem. Sciatis me concessisse et hac mea carta presenti "confirmasse DANIELI filio ALEXANDRI DE LODENEFORD, terram "quam pater ejus tenuit, illi et heredibus suis, tenendam de me "et de heredibus meis, libere et quiete, reddendo annuatim xij

[1] Probably LODINGFORD, in YALDING.

"solidos, pro omni servicio; scilicet ad festum Sancti Michaelis "iiij solidos, et ad Natale iiij solidos, et ad Pascham iiij solidos, "salvo servicio . . . . si hoc contingat quod miles dat marcam "argenti, ipse dabit xvj denarios, et si miles dat xx solidos, "predictus Daniel . . . . . . pro hac concessione et confirma-"cione dedit mihi predictus Daniel xx solidos."

Et pro hac warantia et fine et concordia predictus . . . . Radulpho tres marcas argenti et dimidia.

Alexander de Lodeneford =

Daniel de Lodeneford.

1201.

LXX.—(32 J.)

[21 August, 1201, 3 Jo.]

(Ralph ate Berne grants to Juliana de Gren half of two and a half acres in Grain for life.)

Apud Bermundesciam, die Marcii proxima ante festum Sancti Bartholomei, anno regni Regis Johannis tercio.

Coram Ricardo Herierd, Reginaldo de Cornhell, Johanne de Gkestleng, Justiciariis, etc.

Inter Julianam de Gren, petentem, et Radulphum ate Berne, tenentem.

De ij acris terre et dimidia, cum pertinentiis, in Gren.[1]

Unde placitum fuit inter eos in prefata Curia, scilicet quod predictus Radulphus concessit medietatem terre predicte, cum pertinentiis, habendam et tenendam, tota vita ipsius Juliane, per servicium inde faciendum predicto Radulpho, vel heredibus suis, quod ad predictam medietatem pertinet. Et post obitum predicte Juliane predicta terra redibit predicto Radulpho, vel heredibus suis, soluta et quieta, de heredibus predicte Juliane.

[1] Probably the Isle of Grain.

LXXI.—(22 J.)

[6th October, 1201, 3 Jo.]

(In a recognizance of Mortdauncestor, Crispin Fitz Geoffrey quitclaims to William de Mares all right in forty acres in Mapelderesfeld. For which Reginald de Mapeledurefeld (who ought to warrant the said land to the said William de Mares) has granted to the said Crispin and his heirs fifteen shillings rent in Mapeldurefeld, which the said Crispin before held of him the said Reginald by four shillings, to hold of him by the free service of three shillings per annum for all service to the ward of Dover Castle.)

Apud Westmonasterium, in octabis Sancti Michaelis, anno regni Regis Johannis tercio.

Coram G. filio Petri, Ricardo de Herierd, ... de Patishill, Johanne de Gestling, Eustachio de Fauconberg, Godefrido de Insula, Henrico de Wichinton, Waltero de Crepinges, Justiciariis, etc.

Inter Crispinum filium Gaufridi, petentem, et Willelmum de Mares, tenentem.

De quadraginta acris terre, cum pertinentiis, in Mapelderesfeld.

Unde recognicio de morte antecessoris sumonita fuit inter eos in prefata Curia, scilicet quod predictus Crispinus remisit et quietum clamavit predicto Willelmo et heredibus suis, totum jus et clamium quod habuit in predicta terra, de se et heredibus suis, in perpetuum.

Et pro hac quieta clamancia, et fine, et concordia, Reginaldus de Mapeledurefeld, qui terram illam predicto Willelmo de Mares warantizare debuit, concessit predicto Crispino quindecim solidos redditus, cum pertinenciis, in Mapeldurefeld, quos idem Crispinus prius tenuit de predicto Reginaldo pro quatuor solidis, tenendum de se et heredibus suis, sibi et heredibus suis, in perpetuum, per liberum servicium trium solidorum per annum, pro omni servicio ad wardam de Doure.

LXXII.—(23 J.)

[20th October, 1201, 3 Jo.]

(Assignment of dower by Alan de Elmestede[1] to Roheisia de Caggeworth, in Caggeworth, viz. all the land which she before held there in dower, to hold it of him and his heirs for life, by twenty shillings per annum. The eight shillings per annum which the said Roheisia pays to Eugenia, mother of said Alan, she shall, on the death of said Eugenia, pay to said Alan (should he survive his mother), besides the said twenty shillings per annum. After death of said Roeisia the said land to revert to said . . . . . . and his heirs.)

Apud Westmonasterium, a die Sancti Michaelis in tres septimanas, anno regni Regis Johannis tercio.

Coram G. filio Petri, Ricardo de Herierd, Simone de Patshill, Johanne de Gestling, Eustacio de Faucunbrege, Godefrido de Insula, Waltero de Creping, Justiciariis, etc.

Inter Alanum de Elmestede, petentem, et Roeisiam de Caggewrth, tenentem.

De admensuratione dotis ipsius Roheisie in Caggewrth.

Unde placitum fuit inter eos in prefata Curia, scilicet quod predictus Alanus concessit predicte Roheisie totam predictam terram, cum pertinentiis, quam ipsa prius tenuit in dote, in eadem villa, tenendam de se et heredibus suis, tota vita ipsius Roeisie, per servicium xx solidorum, reddendorum per annum ad duos terminos; scilicet ad Purificacionem Sancte Marie decem solidos, et ad Nativitatem Sancti Marie, decem solidos, salvis tamen viij solidis quos predicta Roeisia annuatim solebat reddere Eugenie matri predicti Alani. Et post decessum predicte Eugenie reddet ipsa Roeisia predictos viij solidos, simul cum predictis xx solidis, predicto Alano vel heredibus suis, quolibet anno, ad predictos terminos, si idem Alanus matrem suam supervixerit. Et post decessum ipsius Roeisie, tota predicta terra, cum pertinentiis, redibit . . . . heredibus suis quieta.

. . . . . de Elmestede = Eugenia.
Dead 1201. 1201.

Alanus de Elmestede.
1201.

[1] Apparently this Alan inherited the estate from Roheisia's husband, charged with her dower; and by the charge to the mother, Eugenia, it would seem that Roheisia's husband had been an elder brother of Alan.

LXXIII.—(28 J.)

[12th November, 1201, 3 Jo.]

(John Fitz Jordan acknowledges to Margaret and Cristiana, daughters of William Cauuel,[1] a messuage in Canterbury, abutments given. For which acknowledgment they grant the said messuage to said John and his heirs, to hold of them and their heirs by the free service of two pence per annum. For this grant the said John gives them two shillings.)

Apud Westmonasterium, in crastinum (*sic*) Sancti Martini, anno regni Regis Johannis tercio.

Coram G. filio Petri, Simone de Pathill, Johanne de Gestling, Godefrido de Insula, Waltero de Crepping, Justiciariis, etc.

Inter MARGARETAM et CRISTIANAM filias WILLELMI CAUUEL, petentes, per ipsam Margaretam, positam loco ipsius Cristiane ad lucrandum vel perdendum, et JOHANNEM FILIUM JORDANI, tenentem.

De uno mesuagio, cum pertinentiis, in CANTUARIA, quod jacet inter domum Johannis Pistoris, et domum Cristine la Grandame.

Unde placitum fuit inter eos in prefata Curia, scilicet quod predictus JOHANNES recognovit predictam mesuagium, cum pertinentiis, esse jus predictarum MARGARETE et CRISTIANE.

Et pro hac recognicione et fine et concordia, predicte MARGARETA et CRISTIANA concesserunt predicto JOHANNI et heredibus suis, totum predictum mesuagium, cum pertinentiis, tenendum de se et heredibus suis, in perpetuum, per liberum servicium duorum denariorum per annum, pro omni servicio, reddendorum ad mediam quadragesimam.

Et pro hac concessione predictus JOHANNES dedit predictis MARGARETE et CRISTIANE duos solidos sterlingorum.

William Cauuel =

Margaret. | Cristiana.

[1] ? Canuel or Caunel.

LXXIV.—(20 J.)

[12th November, 1201, 3 Jo.]

(Aelfegus Lamb acknowledges to Margaret and Christiana, daughters of William Cauuel, twenty-one acres in Yoclete as their right and inheritance. For which acknowledgment they grant the said twenty-one acres to the said Aelfegus and his heirs, to hold five acres of the said land as they themselves did of the Abbot of St. Augustine and his successors (to which the said Aelfegus called the said Abbot to warrant), and the remaining sixteen acres of the said Margaret and Christiana and their heirs, by the service of half a mark yearly.)

Apud Westmonasterium, in crastinum (*sic*) Sancti Martini, anno regni Regis Johannis tercio.

Coram G. filio Petri, etc. [ut in No. 73.]

Inter MARGARETAM et CRISTIANAM, filias WILLELMI CAUUEL, petentes, per ipsam Margaretam, positam loco ipsius Christiane ad lucrandum vel perdendum, et AELFEGUM LAMB, tenentem.

De xxj acris, cum pertinenciis, in YOCLETE.[1]

Unde placitum fuit inter eos in prefata Curia, scilicet quod predictus AELFEGUS recognovit predictas xxj acras terre, cum pertinenciis, esse jus et hereditatem predictarum MARGARETE et CRISTANE.

Et pro hac recognicione, et fine et concordia, predicte MARGARETA et CRISTIANA concesserunt predicto AELFEGO, et heredibus suis, predictas xxj acras terre cum pertinenciis. Ita quod idem AELFEGUS et heredes sui teneant de ABBATE SANCTI AUGUSTINI, et successoribus suis, quinque acras terre de predicta terra, sicut eas prius de eo tenuerunt, de quibus ipse AELFEGUS vocavit ad warantiam ipsum ABBATEM. Et sexdecim acras terre residuas teneant de predictis MARGARETA et CRISTIANA, et heredibus suis, in perpetuum, per servicium dimidie marce per annum; scilicet quadraginta denariorum ad festum Sancti Michaelis, et xl denariorum ad mediam quadragesimam, pro omni servicio, salvo forinseco servicio.

Et pro hac concessione predictus AELFIGUS dedit predictis MARGARETE et CRISTIANE . . . . .

[1] Probably YOKLET borough in WALTHAM.—There was, however, land called YOKLET in SALTWOOD.

LXXV.—(30 J.)

[21st November,[1] 1201, 3 J.]

(Emma, widow of Osbert le Husier, and her son Alexander, for twenty shillings each, quitclaim to the Abbot of Boxley all their right in a yoke of land in Halsted, which the said Emma had in dower.)

Apud Westmonasterium, in crastino Sancti Edmundi, anno regni Regis Johannis tercio.

Coram G. filio Petri [ut in No. 73.]

Inter Emmam, que fuit uxor Osberti le Husier, et Alexandrum, filium et warantum suum, de dote sua, petentes, et Robertum Abbatem de Boxleḡ, tenentem.

De uno jugo terre, cum pertinentiis, in Halsted, quod ipsa Emma clamat in dotem, de dono Osberti le Husier, quondam viri sui.

Et unde placitum fuit inter eos in prefata Curia, scilicet quod predicta Emma remisit et quietum clamavit predicto Abbati et successoribus suis, totum jus et clamium quod habuit in predicta dote. Et predictus Alexander quietum clamavit, de se et heredibus suis, predicto Abbati et successoribus suis, totum jus et clamium quod habuit in predicta terra.

Et pro hac quieta clamancia, fine, et concordia, predictus Abbas dedit predicte Emme xx solidos esterlingorum, et Alexandro filio . . . viginti solidos.

Osbert le Husier = Emma.
dead 1201. 1201.

Alexander.
1201.

[1] *i.e.* If the feast of St. Edmund, King and Martyr; but if St. Edmund, Archbishop, then the date would be 17th or 18th November.

LXXVI.—(26 J.)

[20th January, 1201-2, 3 Jo.]

(Mauricius de Langdon and Brictina his wife acknowledge to Anselm, son of Roger de Nordburn, twenty acres of land in Langdon, as his right and inheritance. For which acknowledgment the said Anselm grants the said twenty acres to them and the heirs of the said Brictina, to hold of him and his heirs by two shillings per annum, with warranty against all men. The said Maurice and Brictina, and the heirs of the said Brictina, to do the "forinsecum servicium.")

Apud Westmonasterium, in octavis Sancti Yllarii, anno regni Regis Johannis tercio.

Coram G. filio Petri, Ricardo de Herierd, Simone de Pateshill, Johanne de Gestling, Eustacio de Faucunbge, Godefrido de Insula, Waltero de Creping, Justiciariis, etc.

Inter ANSELMUM filium Rogeri de Nordburn, petentem, et MAURICIUM DE LANGEDUN et BRICTINAM uxorem suam, tenentes, per ipsum MAURICIUM, positum loco ejus ad lucrandum vel perdendum.

De viginti acris terre, cum pertinenciis, in LANGEDONE.

Unde placitum fuit inter eos in prefata Curia, scilicet quod predictus MAURICIUS et BRICTINA uxor sua recognoverunt totam predictam terram, cum pertinenciis, esse jus et hereditatem predicti ANSELMI.

Et pro hac recognicione, et fine, et concordia, predictus ANSELMUS concessit predictis MAURICIO et BRICTINE, et heredibus ipsius BRICTINE, predictas xx acras terre, cum pertinenciis, tenendas de se et heredibus suis, in perpetuum, per servicium duorum solidorum per annum, pro omni servicio, reddendorum ad festum Sancti Michaelis, salvo forinseco servicio, quod idem MAURICIUS et BRICTINA uxor ejus, et heredes ipsius BRICTINE, facient. Et ANSELMUS et heredes sui warantizabunt predictis MAURICIO et BRICTINE, et heredibus ipsius BRICTINE, predictam terram contra omnes gentes.

Et pro hac concessione predictus MAURICIUS et BRICTINA dederunt . . . . . mo tres marcas argenti.

Roger de Nordburn ╤
Anselm. 1201-2.

Mauricius de Langedon = Brictina.
1201-2. 1201-2.

LXXVII.—(31 J.)

[20th January, 1201-2, 3 Jo.]

(Felix, Prior of Dover, quitclaims to Stephen de Kenerdinton and his heirs, two parts of some marsh land in Romney, whereof a view was taken by twelve jurors thereto appointed. The other third part remains to the said Prior and his successors.)

Apud Westmonasterium, in octavis Sancti Yllarii, anno regni Regis Johannis tercio.

Coram G. filio Petri, Simone de Patishill, Johanne de Gestling, Eustachio de Fauconberge, Godefrido de Insula, Waltero de Crepping, Justiciariis, etc.

Inter Stephanum de Kenerdinton, petentem, et Felicem Priorem de Douer, tenentem.

De terra de marisco in Rumenell.

Unde placitum fuit inter eos in prefata Curia, scilicet quod predictus Prior recognovit et quietas clamavit predicto Stephano et heredibus suis, duas partes predicte terre versus orientem, unde visus factus fuit per . . . ec . . . ratores inde electos. Et tercia pars predicte terre remanet predicto Priori, et successoribus suis, quieta de predicto Stephano et heredibus suis.

LXXVIII.—(24 J.)

[3rd February,[1] 1201-2, 3 Jo.]

(Edith Fitz Nigell, for two marks, grants to Richard . . . . . a messuage before the gate of St. Trinity, Canterbury, which she claims as her dower from her late husband, Richard, to hold of her for life by three pence per annum.)

Apud Cantuariam, in crastino Sancti Laurencii, anno . . . . Ricardo, de Herierd, Johanne de Gestling, Reginaldo de Cornhll, Justiciariis, etc.

Inter Editham filiam Nigelli, petentem [et Ricardum . . . . . tenentem].

[1] The regnal year is gone, but in the office arrangement it is entered among the Fines of the 3rd John: as such it takes its place here.

De j mesuagio, cum pertinenciis, in civitate Cantuarie, ante portam Sancte Trinitatis, quod ipsa EDITHA clamat versus ipsum RICARDUM, ut rationabilem dotem suam, que eam contingebat de dono RICARDI quondam viri sui.

Unde placitum fuit inter eos in prefata Curia, scilicet quod predicta EDITHA concessit predicto RICARDO et heredibus suis, illud mesuagium, cum pertinentiis, tenendum de ipsi (*sic*) tota vita sua, reddendo ipsi EDITHE, et heredibus suis, iij[d] per annum, pro omni servicio, ad festum Sancti Michaelis, salvo forinseco servicio.

Et pro hac concessione, fine, et concordia, predictus RICARDUS dedit predicte EDITHE duas marcas argenti.

LXXIX.—(25 J.)

[10th February,[1] 1201-2, 3 Jo.]

(In a trial by Wager of Battle,[3] Simon de Averenches and Baldwin, Earl of Guines, divide between them the manor of Newington near Hythe.)

Apud Westmonasterium, a die Sancti Yllarii in j mensem, anno regni Regis . . . .

Coram G. filio Petri, Ricardo de Herierd, Simone de Pateshill, Johanne de Gestling, Eustacio de Faucunbge, Godefrido de Insula, ... Creping, Justiciariis, etc.

Inter SIMONEM DE AVERENCHES, petentem, per . . . . . and (?) fratrem suum, positum loco suo ad lucrandum vel perdendum, et BALDEWINUM COMITEM DE GUINES, tenentem.

De toto manerio de NEWETON,[2] cum pertinentiis.

Unde duellum[3] vadiatum armatum et percussum fuit in pre-

[1] The regnal year is gone, but in the office arrangement it is entered among the Fines of the 3rd John: as such it takes its place here.

[2] NEWINGTON was a limb of FOLKSTONE, of which manor the AVERENCHES were lords.

[3] The Wager of Battle—"duellum vadiatum et armatum"—was a species of trial of great antiquity, and abolished only as recently as 59 Geo. III. "It seems," says Blackstone (bk. iii. c. 22), "to have owed its original to the military spirit of our ancestors, joined to a superstitious frame of mind: it being in the nature of an appeal to Providence, under

fata Curia; scilicet, quod predicti Comes BALDEWINUS DE GUINES et SIMON DE AVERENCHES dimidiaverunt totum predictum manerium, cum omnibus pertinenciis suis, scilicet in dominicis et serviciis, et in advocacionibus ecclesiarum. Ita quod WILLELMUS DE CERINTON, cum omnibus tenementis suis de feudo illo, remanet in parte que predictum COMITEM vel heredes suos contingit; et predictus SIMON .... sui, habuerunt ad electionem suam, tantum servicium quantum predictus WILLELMUS DE CERINTON facit predicto COMITI DE .... Et omnes qui fefati fuerunt de eodem feudo, die quo placitum monitum inter eos, tenebunt ipsi .... omnia tenementa sua per idem servicium quod fecerunt predicto Comiti, cuicunque parti illa tenementa occid ..... predicti, scilicet, COMES et SIMON, et heredes eorum, tenebunt partem suam de domino Rege, per servicium .... pertinet.

---

an apprehension and hope (however presumptuous and unwarrantable) that heaven would give the victory to him who had the right. This trial was introduced into England among other Norman customs by William the Conqueror; but was only used in three cases, one military, one criminal, and the third civil. The first in the court-martial, or court of chivalry and honour; the second in appeals of felony; and the third upon issue joined in a writ of right, the last and most solemn decision of real property. For in writs of right the *jus proprietatis* (right of ownership), which is frequently a matter of difficulty, is in question; but other real actions being merely questions of the *jus possessionis* (right of possession), which are usually more plain and obvious, our ancestors did not in them appeal to the decision of Providence. The last trial by battle that was waged in the Court of Common Pleas at Westminster, was in the thirteenth year of Queen Elizabeth, A.D. 1571, as reported by Sir James Dyer: and was held in Tothill Fields, Westminster, '*non sine magna jurisconsultorum perturbatione*,' saith Sir Henry Spelman, who was himself a witness of the ceremony. The form, as described by authors writing while this kind of trial existed, was as follows:—When the tenant in a writ of right pleads the general issue, viz. that he hath more right to hold, than the demandant hath to recover; and offers to prove it by the body of his champion, which tender is accepted by the demandant; the tenant in the first place must produce his champion, who, by throwing down his glove as a gage or pledge, thus *wages* or stipulates battle with the champion of the demandant; who, by taking up the gage or glove, stipulates on his part to accept the challenge. The reason why it is waged by champions, and not by the parties themselves, in civil actions, is because, if any party to the suit dies,

LXXX.—(29 J.)

[10th February, 1201-2, 3 Jo.]

(Robert, son of Richard *extra portam*, and Gunnora his wife, for twenty shillings, acknowledge and quitclaim to Reginald de Beseville fifteen acres of assart[1] in Farningham, as his right and inheritance.)

Apud Westmonasterium, a die Sancti Hillarii in unum mensem, anno regni Regis Johannis tercio.

Coram G. filio Petri, etc. [ut in No. 79.]

Inter REGINALDUM DE BESEVILLE, petentem, et ROBERTUM filium RICARDI extra portam, et GUNNORAM uxorem ejus, tenentes.

De quindecim acris terre, cum pertinenciis, in FERNINGEHAM, que vocantur assart.

Unde placitum fuit inter eos in prefata Curia, scilicet quod predicti ROBERTUS et GUNNORA uxor sua, recognoverunt totam

the suit must abate and be at an end for the present; and therefore no judgment could be given for the lands in question, if either of the parties were slain in battle: and also that no person might claim an exemption from this trial, as was allowed in criminal cases, where the battle was waged in person. A piece of ground is then in due time set out, of sixty feet square, enclosed with lists, and on one side a court erected for the judges of the Court of Common Pleas, who attend there in their scarlet robes; and also a bar is prepared for the learned serjeants at law. When the court sits, which ought to be by sunrising, proclamation is made for the parties, and their champions; who are introduced by two knights, and are dressed in a coat of armour, with red sandals, barelegged from the knee downwards, bareheaded, and with bare arms to the elbows. The weapons allowed them are only batons, or staves of an ell long, and a four-cornered leather target; so that death very seldom ensued from this civil combat; though in the court military they fought with sword and lance, according to Spelman and Rushworth. When the champions, thus armed with batons, arrive within the lists or place of combat, the champion of the tenant takes his adversary by the hand, and makes oath that the tenements in dispute are not the right of the demandant; and the champion of the demandant, then taking the other by the hand, swears in the same manner that they are; so that each champion is, or ought to be, thoroughly persuaded of the truth of the cause he fights for. Next an oath against sorcery and enchantment is to be taken by both the champions, in this or a similar form: 'Hear this, ye justices, that I have this day neither eat

[1] "Assart" is forest land grubbed and brought into cultivation.

predictam terram, cum pertinenciis, esse jus et hereditatem predicti REGINALDI, et eam remiserunt et quietam clamaverunt predicto REGINALDO et heredibus suis, de se et heredibus suis, in perpetuum.

Et pro hac quieta clamancia et recognicione et fine et concordia, predictus REGINALDUS dedit predictis ROBERTO et GUNNORE viginti solidos sterlingorum.

Richard *extra portam* =

Robert = Gunnora.

LXXXI.—(52 J.)

[2nd October, 1202, 4 Jo.]

(In a recognizance of Mortdauncestor, Ralph de Pencherst acknowledges all the land of Lagerham to Ela de Marti, as her right and inheritance. For which she grants it to said Ralph and his heirs, to hold of her and her heirs by the free service of seven shillings and four pence per annum; she and her heirs warrant it against the chief lord. For this grant he gives her one mark, and he and his heirs are to do the "forinsecum servicium." The said Ela takes the homage of the said Ralph.)

Apud Beremundescyam, die Mercurii proxima post festum Sancti Michaelis, anno regni Regis Johannis iiij[to].

drank, nor have upon me, neither bone, stone, ne grass; nor any enchantment, sorcery, or witchcraft, whereby the law of God may be abased, or the law of the devil exalted. So help me God and his saints.' The battle is thus begun, and the combatants are bound to fight till the stars appear in the evening: and, if the champion of the tenant can defend himself till the stars appear, the tenant shall prevail in his cause; for it is sufficient for him to maintain his ground, and make it a drawn battle, he being already in possession; but, if victory declares itself for either party, for him is judgment finally given. This victory may arise from the death of either of the champions: which indeed hath rarely happened; the whole ceremony, to say the truth, bearing a near resemblance to certain rural athletic diversions, which are probably derived from this original. Or victory is obtained if either champion proves *recreant*, that is, yields, and pronounces the horrible word of *craven;* a word of disgrace and obloquy, rather than of any determinate meaning. But a horrible word it indeed is to the vanquished champion: since as a punishment to him for forfeiting the land of his principal by pronouncing that shameful word, he is

Coram G. filio Petri, Ricardo de Heriord, Osberto filio Hervei, Jordano de Turri, Justiciariis, etc.

Inter Elam de Marti,[1] petentem, et Radulphum de Peneherst, tenentem.

De tota terra que vocatur Lagerham.

Unde recognicio de morte antecessoris summonita fuit inter eos in prefata Curia, scilicet quod predictus Radulphus recognovit totam predictam terram, cum pertinenciis, esse jus et hereditatem ipsius Ele.

Et pro hac recognicione et fine et concordia, predicta Ela concessit predicto Radulpho et heredibus suis, totam predictam terram, cum pertinenciis, tenendam de se et heredibus suis, in perpetuum, per liberum servicium septem solidorum, et iiij denariorum per annum, pro omni servicio, scilicet ad festum Sancti Michaelis xij denarios, et ad Natale xij denarios, et ad Annunciationem Beate Marie ij solidos, et ad Pascham xij denarios, et ad festum Sancti Johannis Baptiste xij denarios, et ad festum Sancte Marie Magdalene xvj denarios. Et predicta Ela et heredes sui warantizabunt et defendent totam predictam terram, cum pertinenciis, versus capitales dominos.

Et pro hac concessione predictus Radulphus dedit predicte Ele j marcam argenti. Et predictus Radulphus et heredes sui facient forinsecum servicium de predicta terra.

Et modo predicta Ela cepit homagium ipsius Radulphi.

condemned, as a recreant, *amittere liberam legem,* that is, to become infamous, and not be accounted *liber et legalis homo;* being supposed by the event to be proved forsworn, and therefore never to be put upon a jury or admitted as a witness in any cause. This is the form of a trial by battle; a trial which the tenant, or defendant in a writ of right, had it in his election to demand; and which was the only decision of such writ of right after the Conquest, till Henry II., by consent of Parliament, introduced the *grand assize,* a peculiar species of trial by jury, in concurrence therewith; giving the tenant his choice of either the one or the other."

---

[1] ? Marci.

LXXXII.—(36 J.)

[3rd October, 1202, 4 Jo.]

(In a recognizance of Mortdauncestor, William Fitz Alur[1] acknowledges sixteen acres in Eynesford to Henry, Reginald, and Alexander de Derentef[ord],[2] as their right and inheritance. For which they grant the said land to him and his heirs, to hold of the said Henry and his heirs by the free service of twelve pence per annum, the said William acquitting it from all service to the chief lord, and paying them for this grant ten shillings.)

Apud Beremundeseiam, die Jovis proxima post festum Sancti Michaelis, anno regni Regis Johannis iiij^{to}.

Coram G. filio Petri, etc. [ut in No. 81.]

Inter Henricum et Reginaldum et Alexandrum de Derentef',[2] petentes, et Willelmum filium Alur,[1] tenentem.

De xvj acris terre, cum pertinenciis, in Eineford.

Unde recognicione de morte antecessoris summonita fuit inter eos in prefata Curia, scilicet quod predictus Willelmus recognovit totam predictam terram, cum pertinenciis, esse jus et hereditatem predictorum Henrici et Reginaldi et Alexandri.

Et pro hac recognicione et fine et concordia, predicti Henricus et Reginaldus et Alexander concesserunt predicto Willelmo et heredibus suis, totam predictam terram, cum pertinenciis, tenendam de predicto Henrico et heredibus suis, in perpetuum, per liberum servicium xij denariorum per annum, pro omni servicio; scilicet ad Pascham vj denarios, et ad festum Sancti Michaelis vj denarios.

Et predictus Willelmus, et heredes sui, aquietabunt totam predictam terram, cum pertinenciis, versus capitales dominos, de omni servicio quod ad terram illam pertinet.

Et pro hac concessione predictus Willelmus dedit predictis Henrico et Reginaldo et Alexandro x solidos esterlingorum.

[1] Probably for "Aluredi."

[2] Doubtless for Derenteford.

LXXXIII.—(51 J.)

[3rd October, 1202, 4 Jo.]

(In a recognizance of Mortdauncestor, Thurgar de Erthe, for sixteen shillings, acknowledges five acres in Crayford as the right and inheritance of Alice, wife of Simon de Craiford, and quitclaims them to the said Simon and Alice, and the heirs of the said Alice for ever.)

Apud Beremundeseyam, die Jovis proxima post festum Sancti Michaelis, anno regni Regis Johannis iiij^{to}.

Coram G. filio Petri, etc. [ut in No. 81.]

Inter SIMONEM DE CRAIFORD et ALICIAM uxorem suam, petentes, et THURGARUM DE ERTHE, tenentem.

De v acris terre, cum pertinenciis, in CRAIFORD.

Unde recognicio de morte antecessoris summonita fuit inter eos in prefata Curia, scilicet quod predictus THURGARUS recognovit totam predictam terram, cum pertinenciis, esse jus et hereditatem ipsius ALICIE, et eam remisit et quietam clamavit predictis SIMONI et ALICIE, et heredibus ipsius ALICIE, de se et heredibus suis, in perpetuum.

Et pro hac recognicione et quieta clamancia, et fine et concordia, predicti SIMON et ALICIA dederunt predicto THURGAR xvj solidos esterlingorum.

Simon de Craiford = Alice.
1202. 1202.

LXXXIV.—(42 J.)

[4th October, 1202, 4 Jo.]

(In a recognizance of Mortdauncestor, Hugh and Briethina his mother acknowledge eight acres in Minster as the right and inheritance of Edilda and Hagenilda, daughters of Anketill. For which acknowledgment the said Edilda and Hagenilda quitclaim to the said Hugh and Briethina, and the heirs of said Hugh, three and a half acres of the said land lying next the land of Ailmar Cittepere, to the west, and half an acre thereof lying next the head of the said Ailmar's land, to the north.)

Apud Beremundseiam, die Veneris proxima post festum Sancti Michaelis, anno regni Regis Johannis iiij^{to}.

Coram G. filio Petri, etc. [ut in No. 81.]

Inter EDILDAM et HAGENILDAM filias ANKETILLE, petentes, et HUGONEM filium BRICTINE, et BRICTHINAM matrem suam, tenentes.

De octo acris terre, cum pertinenciis, in MINSTRE.

Unde recognicio de morte antecessoris summonita fuit inter eos in prefata Curia, scilicet quod predicti HUGO et BRICTHINA recognoverunt totam predictam terram esse jus et hereditatem predictarum EDILDE et HAGENILDE.

Et pro hac recognitione et fine et concordia, predicte EDILDA et HAGENILDA concesserunt et quietas clamaverunt, de se et heredibus earum, predictis HUGONI et BRICTHINE et heredibus ipsius HUGONIS, iiij acras terre de eadem terra, scilicet iij acras terre et dimidiam, juxta terram AILMARI CITTEPERE, versus occidentem, et dimidiam acram terre ad caput terre ipsius Ailmari, versus aquilonem, tenendas de capitali domino.

LXXXV.—(48 J.)

[4th October, 1202, 4 Jo.]

(In a recognizance of Mortdauncestor, Ralph, Prior of Rochester, for half a mark, acknowledges fifteen acres in Eleham to be the right and inheritance of Alan Fitz Henry and his heirs, to hold of the said Prior and his successors by the free service of five shillings per annum.)

Apud Beremundeseyam, die Veneris, etc. [ut in No. 84.]
Coram G. filio Petri, etc. [ut in No. 81.]

Inter ALANUM FILIUM HENRICI, petentem, et RADULPHUM PRIOREM ROUECESTRENSEM, tenentem.

De xv acris terre, cum pertinenciis, in ALEHAM.[1]

Unde recognicio de morte antecessoris summonita fuit inter eos in prefata Curia, scilicet quod predictus PRIOR recognovit totam predictam terram, cum pertinenciis, esse jus et hereditatem ipsius ALANI, tenendam de se et successoribus suis, ipsi ALANO et heredibus suis, in perpetuum, per liberum servicium v solidorum per annum, pro omni servicio; scilicet ad festum Sancti Michaelis xv denarios, et ad Nativitatem xv denarios,

[1] "Aleham," *i.e.* Eleham.

et ad Pascham xv denarios, et ad festum Sancti Johannis Baptiste xv denarios.

Et pro hac recognicione et fine et concordia, predictus ALANUS dedit predicto PRIORI dimidiam marcam argenti.

LXXXVI.—(49 J.)

[4th October, 1202, 4 Jo.]

(In a recognizance of Mortdauncestor, Amiot de Wodestok acknowledges four acres and one perch of land in Shelve, to be the right and inheritance of John Fitz Stephen, who, for this acknowledgment, grants the said land to the said Amiot for life, to revert at his death to the said John and his heirs. To be held of William Fitz Wido and his heirs by the service pertaining thereto. The said William being present and assenting to this grant.)

Apud Beremundeseyam, die Veneris, etc. [ut in No. 84.]
Coram G. filio Petri, etc. [ut in No. 81.]

Inter JOHANNEM FILIUM STEPHANI, petentem, et AMIOTUM DE WODESTOK, tenentem.

De iiij^{or} acris et de una pertica terre cum pertinenciis, in SCELVES.[1]

Unde recognicio de morte antecessoris summonita fuit inter eos in prefata Curia, scilicet quod predictus AMIOTUS recognovit totam predictam terram esse jus et hereditatem ipsius JOHANNIS, et pro hac recognicione, et fine et concordia, predictus JOHANNES concessit predicto AMIOTO totam predictam terram, cum pertinenciis, tenendam tota vita ipsius AMIOTI; et post decessum ipsius AMIOTI, tota predicta terra, cum pertinenciis, revertetur ad ipsum JOHANNEM, et heredibus suis, quieta de heredibus ipsius AMIOTI. Tenenda de WILLELMO FILIO WIDONIS, et heredibus suis, per servicium quod ad terram illam pertinet.

Et hec Concordia facta fuit concessu et voluntate ipsius WILLELMI, et eo presente.

[1] Probably SHELVE in LENHAM.

INDEX TO PEDES FINIUM.

For the convenience of those who may wish to bind up the 'Pedes Finium,' separately, the references in the Index are made, not to the pages, but to the number of the Fine.

The names within brackets show the form of spelling adopted in the original.

INQUISITIONES POST MORTEM.

INQUISITIONES POST MORTEM.

For a complete elucidation of the following Records, a strong temptation presents itself to reprint the fourth and fifth chapters of book ii. of Blackstone's Commentaries, wherein the entire history of ancient English tenures is most lucidly treated; but we must not occupy our pages with information that is readily accessible to all who choose to interest themselves in our early constitutional history. A few quotations with reference to the different kinds of tenure, and specially that by knight-service, will suffice for our present purpose, an explanation, namely, of the origin and nature of the Inquisitions which form the subject of this paper.

"Almost all the real property of this kingdom is by the policy of our laws supposed to be granted by, dependent upon, and *holden* of some superior lord, by and in consideration of certain services to be rendered to the lord by the tenant or possessor of this property. The thing holden is therefore styled a *tenement*, the possessors thereof *tenants*, and the manner of their possession a *tenure*. Thus all the land in the kingdom is supposed to be holden, mediately or immediately, of the king; who is styled the lord *paramount*, or above all. Such tenants as held under the king immediately, when they granted out portions of their lands to inferior persons, became also lords with respect to those inferior persons, just as they themselves were still tenants with respect to the king; and, thus partaking of a middle nature, were called *mesne*, or middle, lords. So that if the king granted a manor to A, and he granted a portion of the land to B, now B was said to hold of A, and A of the king; or in other words, B held his lands immediately of A, but mediately of the king. The king therefore was styled lord paramount; A was both tenant and lord, or was a mesne lord; and B was called tenant *paravail*, or the lowest tenant; being he who was supposed to make avail, or profit, of the land."

"All tenures being thus derived, or supposed to be derived, from the king, those that held immediately under him, in right of his crown and dignity, were called his tenants *in capite*, or in chief; which was the most honourable species of tenure, but at the same subjected the tenants to greater and more burdensome services than inferior tenures did. This distinction ran through all the different sorts of tenure; of which I now proceed to give an account.

"I. There seem to have subsisted among our ancestors four principal species of lay tenures, to which all others may be reduced: the grand criteria of which were the natures of the several services or renders, that were due to the lords from their tenants. The services, in respect of their *quality*, were either *free* or *base* services; in respect of their *quantity* and the time of exacting them, were either *certain* or *uncertain*. *Free* services were such as were not unbecoming the character of a soldier or a freeman to perform; as, to serve under his lord in the wars, to pay a sum of money, and the like. *Base* services were such as were fit only for peasants, or persons of a servile rank; as to plough the lord's land, to make his hedges, or other mean employments. The *certain* services, whether free or base, were such as were stinted in quantity, and could not be exceeded on any pretence; as, to pay a stated annual rent, or to plough such a field for three days. The *uncertain* depended upon unknown contingencies: as, to do military service in person, or pay an assessment in lieu of it, when called upon; or to wind a horn whenever the Scots invaded the realm; which are *free* services: or to do whatever the lord should command; which is a *base* or villein service.

"Where the service was *free*, but *uncertain*, as military service with homage, that tenure was called the tenure in chivalry, *per servitium militare*, or by knight-service. Secondly, where the service was not only *free*, but also *certain*, as by fealty only, by rent and fealty, etc., that tenure was called *liberum socagium*, or free socage.

"The first, most universal, and esteemed the most honourable species of tenure, was that by knight-service, called in Latin *servitium militare*. . . . To make a tenure by knight-service, a determinate quantity of land was necessary, which was called a knight's-fee (*feodum militare*), the measure of which in 3 Edw. I. was estimated at twelve ploughlands, and its value (though it varied with the times) in the reigns of Edw. I. and Edw. II. was stated at £20 per annum. And he who held this proportion of land (or a whole fee) by knight-service, was bound to attend his lord to the wars for forty days in every year, if called upon; which attendance was his *redditus* or return, his rent or service, for the land he claimed to hold. If he held only half a knight's-fee, he was only bound to attend twenty days, and so in proportion."[1]*

There were also—

"Seven fruits and consequences, as inseparably incident to the tenure by knight-service, viz. 1, AIDS; 2, RELIEFS; 3, PRIMER SEISIN; 4, WARDSHIP; 5, MARITAGIUM; 6, FINES FOR ALIENATION; and 7, ESCHEAT."

To each and all of these the King had a claim from tenants *in capite*, *i.e.* from those who held immediately from the Crown by knight-service.[2]

1. By the first, "AIDS," the tenant was bound to ransom the King's person, if taken prisoner; to provide the costs of making his eldest son a knight; and to find a portion for marrying his eldest daughter.

2. By the second, "RELIEF," the tenant had to pay a fine, or "Relief," to the King, on the death of his ancestor, as a composition for taking up his estate; but this was only demandable if the heir was of full age at the time of his succeeding to the estate, when he did his fealty and homage to his lord; that is, he took an oath to be faithful to his lord, and did homage by kneel-

* The notes will be found at p. 313, etc.

ing before him, ungirt, uncovered, and holding up his hands both together between those of his lord, who sate before him, and professing that he did become his "man, from that day forth, of life and limb and earthly honour," and he then received a kiss from his lord. At first the "Relief" was an arbitrary payment, and at the will of the lord, so that if he pleased to demand an exorbitant Relief, it was, in effect, to disinherit the heir, and thus it became one of the greatest grievances of military tenure. After various struggles between the Crown and its tenants, the composition was finally fixed at 100*s.* for every knight's-fee.

3. By the third, "PRIMER SEISIN," the King had a right, when any of his tenants by knight-service *in capite* died, to receive of the heir (if of full age) one year's profits of the lands, if they were in possession; and half a year's profits if they were in reversion, expectant on an estate for life.

4. By the fourth, viz. "WARDSHIP," if the heir were under age of twenty-one, being a male, or fourteen, being a female, the King was entitled to the guardianship, which consisted in having the custody of the body and lands of such heir (without rendering any account of the profits) till the age of twenty-one in males, and sixteen in females.[3] And when the heir thus came of full age, provided he held a knight's-fee *in capite* under the Crown, he was to receive the order of knighthood, and was compellable to take it upon him, or else pay a fine to the King. On arriving at full age, the heir had his writ "de ætate probandâ." A jury was summoned to inquire into his age, returning their verdict on oath; on which, if proved of full age, he obtained livery and seisin of his lands. Occasionally, frauds were attempted on the Crown, by false representations of age, and reinvestigation became necessary. Among the Inquisitions are frequently found the evidences used on these proofs

of age,—an exceedingly interesting class of documents, which we shall print in order as they occur.

5. And during the same period of nonage, the fifth incident, viz. the right of MARRIAGE, "maritagium,"[3] accrued to the King over his tenants. By this, while the infant was in ward, he had the power of tendering him or her a suitable match, without disparagement or inequality, which, if the infants refused, they forfeited to him the value of the marriage, that is, so much as a jury would assess, or any one would *bonâ fide* give for such an alliance; and, if the infants married without his consent, they forfeited double the value.

6. The sixth incident was the "FINE," which the tenant was obliged to pay to the King upon every alienation of his land, which he could not effect without a license from the Crown. If he did, it was in ancient strictness an absolute forfeiture of the land. But this severity was mitigated by the statute 1 Edw. III. cap. 12, which ordained, that in such case the lands should not be forfeited, but a reasonable fine be paid to the King. It was also settled by the same statute that the Crown should not demand more than one-third of the yearly value for a license of alienation.

7. The last incident was "ESCHEAT," whereby, if the tenant died without an heir, or convicted of treason or felony, the estate reverted or "escheated" to the Crown.

The description here given is that of knight-service proper, which was to attend the king in his wars. There was also another species of knight-service of a more honourable nature, but attended with the same fruits and consequences. Such was the tenure by 'grand serjeanty,' *per magnum servitium*, whereby the tenant was bound, instead of serving the King *generally* in his wars, to do him some special honorary service in person, such as to carry his banner, his sword, or the like, or to be his butler, champion, or other officer at his coronation; only a tenant of this kind was not bound to pay aid or escuage; and while the tenant by ordinary knight-service paid five pounds for a "Relief" on each knight's-fee, the tenant by grand serjeanty paid one year's value of the land whether it was much or little.

"These services, both of chivalry and grand serjeanty, were all personal, and uncertain as to their quantity and duration. But the personal attendance in knight's-service growing troublesome and inconvenient in many respects, the tenants found means of compounding for it; by first sending others in their stead, and in process of time making a pecuniary satisfaction to the lord in lieu of it. This pecuniary satisfaction at last came to be levied by assessments, at so much for every knight's-fee, and therefore this kind of tenure was called *scutagium*, *scutum* being then a well known denomination for money.

"By the degenerating of knight-service, or personal military duty, into escuage, or pecuniary assessments, all the advantages (either promised or real) of the feodal constitution were destroyed, and nothing but the hardships remained. Instead of forming a national militia composed of barons, knights, and gentlemen, bound by their interest, their honour, and their oaths, to defend their king and country, the whole of this system of tenures now tended to nothing else but a wretched means of raising money to pay an army of occasional mercenaries. In the meantime the families of all our nobility groaned under the intolerable burdens, which (in consequence of the fiction adopted after the Conquest) were introduced and laid upon them by the subtlety and finesse of the Norman lawyers. For, besides the scutages to which they were liable in defect of personal attendance, which however were assessed by themselves in parliament, they might be called upon by the king or lord paramount for *aids*, whenever his eldest son was to be knighted or his eldest daughter married; not to forget the ransom of his own person. The heir, on the death of his ancestor, if of full age, was plundered of the first emoluments arising from his inheritance, by way of *relief* and *primer seisin*; and, if under age, of the whole of his estate during infancy. And then, as Sir Thomas Smith very feelingly complains, 'when he came to his own, after he was out of *wardship*, his woods decayed, houses fallen down, stock wasted and gone, lands let forth and ploughed to be barren,' to reduce him still further, he was yet to pay half a year's profits as a fine for suing out his *livery*; and also the price or value of his *marriage*, if he refused such wife as his lord and guardian had bartered for, and imposed upon him; or twice that value if he married another woman. Add to this, the untimely and expensive honour of *knighthood*, to make his poverty more completely splendid. And when by these deductions his fortune was so shattered and ruined, that perhaps he was obliged to sell his patrimony, he had not even that poor privilege allowed him, without paying an exorbitant fine for a *license of alienation*.

"A slavery so complicated, and so extensive as this, called aloud for a remedy in a nation that boasted of its freedom. Palliatives were from time to time applied by successive acts of parliament, which assuaged some temporary grievances. Till at length the humanity of King James I. consented, in consideration of a proper equivalent, to abolish them all; though the plan proceeded not to effect.

"At length the military tenures, with all their heavy appendages (having during the usurpation been discontinued) were destroyed at one blow by the statute 12 Car. II. c. 24, which enacts, 'that the court of wards and liveries, and all wardships, liveries, primer seisins, and ousterlemains, values and forfeitures of marriages, by reason of any tenure of the king or others, be totally taken away. And that all fines for alienations, tenures by homage, knight-service, and escuage, and also aids for marrying the daughter or knighting the son, and all tenures of the king *in capite*, be likewise taken away. And that all sorts of tenures, held of the king or others, be turned into free and common socage; save only tenures in frankalmoign, copyholds, and the honorary services (without the slavish part) of grand serjeanty.' A statute, which was a greater acquisition to the civil property of this kingdom than even *Magna Carta* itself: since that only pruned the luxuriances that had grown out of the military tenures, and thereby preserved them in vigour; but the statute of King Charles extirpated the whole, and demolished both root and branches."

Thus far we have cited from Blackstone, somewhat

copiously perhaps, but we have done so in order that we may be spared hereafter the necessity of endless notes and discussions during the progress of our transcripts. Our readers too are thus furnished, at the onset, with a running commentary, elucidating nearly every question that may arise during the examination of these Inquisitions, as necessary to explain the Records before us; for the rest, we would urge our readers, learned or unlearned, to study carefully the fourth and fifth chapters of the second book of Blackstone's Commentaries, and can promise them much enjoyment in the perusal of that luminous writer's history of the origin and nature of the feudal system and its requirements, as specially exemplified in early English Tenures. The study too of these chapters will enable them to appreciate correctly the Records now presented to them.

In order to ensure to the Crown the rights which we have enumerated, when a supposed tenant by knight-service *in capite* died, "Inquisitiones post Mortem" were taken, by virtue of the King's writ, directed to the sheriff or escheator of the county or district in which the party died, requiring the said officer to summon a jury to inquire—if the deceased held *in capite*—of what lands he had died seized,—and by what services the same were held,—who was the next heir,—and of what age he was,—and to make their return upon oath and under seal, in order that the King might ascertain his rights of wardship, marriage, etc., and take the lands into his own hands during the minority of the heir, or permanently if the estate had actually escheated.

These writs and the returns to them,[4] made by the escheator and his jury, are preserved among the public records of the kingdom, from the early part of the reign of Henry III. There are, as might be expected, many deficiencies, especially in the more early periods; but, with these exceptions, a series of them is preserved from that period till the abolition of the Courts of Wards and Liveries by Charles II., when all tenures by knight-service, and of the King *in capite*, were abolished.

The great importance of these records to ordinary county history has long been acknowledged. In the descents of family and property, they are the best evidence that can be produced, and nearly the only one on which we can thoroughly rely. Moreover, if the tenant was convicted of treason or felony, it appears on these Records, which often furnish an actual "extent" or survey of the manors and lands held by the tenant, with their quality and measurement and value, recorded in full detail. Many obsolete customs too are here recorded. But, to *this* county, it is impossible to overrate their value. To us they are not merely interesting items in archæological research, but they are the indispensable evidences, in many instances the only title, which some of us have to our property. Herein are specified what particular estates are held by the custom of Gavelkind, and which are exempt therefrom.

Many an estate has been partitioned among coheirs, on an intestacy, to which the younger brothers had no more right than an utter alien in blood, and the elder son has thus been unconsciously robbed of his inheritance, merely from ignorance of the fact which these Records would have developed, that his estate was originally held by knight-service, and therefore exempt from the operation of Gavelkind. Within the last four years the writer of these lines has himself rescued two important estates from being lost to the elder son, by the evidence supplied from these very documents which we here purpose to print, in regular series, for the use of our county. In the instance of "Pedes Finium," we have printed the Record entire in the original Latin, because a short heading in English suffices, in those Records, to give the whole substance of the document; but in these

Inquisitions, which contain minute details of every particular attaching to the estate in question, no abstract would suffice. In these therefore, for the convenience of the general reader, we have rendered into English all the items of the Record. It will enable him to trace the descent of families and property from a very early period; and ever and anon, in cases of intestacy, the heir, in this county, will here find a clue to save himself from the distribution of his estate among younger brothers, securing thereby, in almost every instance, a result for which the father, had he made a will, would most probably have provided.

The English translation will suffice for general purposes; in every instance we have given the reference to the original Record, so that, in those cases where legal evidence is required, the party needing it can always obtain by this reference a verbatim copy of the original, which will be undeniable evidence in all the Courts of Law in the kingdom.

Literary friends in whose counsel we have great confidence, have, we are free to confess, advised the non-admission of these Records, and the "Pedes Finium," into our Volume; but we have so strong a conviction of their conferring something of much higher benefit to our Members than mere archæological information (which, by the way, is of itself, in these instances, exceedingly interesting), that we have resisted their counsel, and printed them. It rests with our Members to decide whether they approve the step or no. If any strong intimation be given (which we can hardly anticipate) that they are not acceptable, they shall be discontinued. As we descend to the fifteenth and sixteenth centuries, we have in these Inquisitions the most minute particulars, (very often even descending to actual fields,) of the manors and estates of deceased tenants *in capite;* and, after a study of these Records, through their course as it proceeds, the reader will find himself as conversant with the early history of the lands in his parish, as he is of the farms around him in the present day. Connected with the "Pedes Finium," he will trace them through all their alienations, and map them out as readily as though he had lived in the times whose changes they record.

We have given, at page 298, a facsimile of one of the earliest writs, and the return of the Inquisition to it, viz. that of William le Taillur, relating to his estate in Milton, etc.; it is a fair sample of the earliest of these Inquisitions. We have selected it, as an instance where the Jury, in their return, carefully distinguish between the lands held in Gavelkind, divisible among all the brothers, and those held by knight's-service, not so divisible. Having now made our readers acquainted with the nature and history of these Records, we proceed to print them in regular series.

But we must first render our cordial acknowledgments to our old and valued friend, Thomas Duffus Hardy, Esq., and the officers presiding over the different departments of the General Record Office, for their unremittingly kind attentions. To that gentleman, and to the Rev. J. Hunter, H. J. Sharpe, Esq., the Rev. Professor Brewer, W. Nelson, Esq., J. J. Bond, Esq., C. Cole, Esq., J. Burtt, Esq., and W. B. Sanders, Esq., we cannot be sufficiently grateful for the valuable assistance rendered to us in preparing for publication the Records which we have used in this and our former volume; and we cannot refrain from adding our testimony to the great efficiency of the office, and to the uniform courtesy and attention rendered to those literary students who have occasion to consult the Public Records.

The earliest Inquisition for the county of Kent is that relating to the rents of the Prior of MODINDEN, as follows[5]:—

I.

[Esc. No. 13, 20 Hen. III., 1235-6.]

Writ to inquire if the Prior of Modinden was seised of certain rents etc., of the gift and grant of Robert de Rokel, during the life of the said Robert, etc., and for how long the said Prior was in seisin thereof in the time of the said Robert. Tested at Rochester, 18*th January,* 20 *Hen. III.*

The Inquisition was taken by—

Godard de Cilgrave,—William Godeholt,—William de Kingeslond,—Martin de Pirnlee,—Pagan de Wilgare,—Baldewin de Wulgare,—Hamo de Forstalle,—Thomas de Wode,—Henry Beket,—William de Pecke,—Peter de Wilgare,—William Fitz Adam;

Who say upon their oath, that—The PRIOR OF MODINDEN[6] was in seizin of 14*s.* 6*d.* and eight hens rent, of the gift and grant of ROBERT DE ROKEL, in the lifetime of the said ROBERT, out of a tenement which the said ROBERT had in OSPRING, for two years before his death. And likewise of eleven seams of barley, of the gift of the said ROBERT, in his lifetime,—likewise for two years before his death, out of a tenement which the said ROBERT had in PLUMWORTH.[7] But of the entire domain which the said ROBERT had in PLUMWORTH, they say that the PRIOR had no service therefrom before the death of the said ROBERT, as they believe. But the said PRIOR had seisin of the rents, homages, and other pertinencies to the said domain, for two years before the death of the said ROBERT, as above.[8]

II.

[Esc. No. 8, 20 Hen. III., 1236.]

Writ to inquire how much land Richard Noel held of the King in capite, etc.; who is next heir, etc. Tested at Clarendon, 17*th June,* 20 *Hen. III.*

The Inquisition was taken by—

Josceus at Hamme,—Bartholomew de Shyrland,—Hamo the Monk,—Richard Smecok,[9]—Philip Upedune,—Alan de Ryde,

—Hamo Upetune,—Luke de Hornesclyve,—Henry de Shilgrave,—Godard de Sylgrave,—William de Beggynge,—Andred de Trulegh;

Who say upon their oath, that—RICHARD NOEL had in the hundred of MILTON land worth £4. 10*s*. per annum, and a rent of two sieves[10] of Salt, worth 10*s*. per annum; and in the hundred of FAVERSHAM, an annual rent in money, viz. £4. Out of all the above, he paid to our Lord the King one pair of gilt spurs per annum. WILLIAM, son of the said RICHARD, is next heir of the said RICHARD.[11]

III.

[Esc. No. 2, 30 Hen. III., 1245–6.]

Writ to inquire how much land Thomas de Normanvill held in capite, etc.; who is next heir, etc. Tested at Westminster, 14th March, 30 Hen. III.

The Inquisition was taken by—

Sir[12] John de Cryoll,—Sir[12] Simon de Cryoll,—Robert de Gatton,— . . . . . . John de Hukinge,—William de Shamelesforde,—Warin Gernetarius,— . . . . . . de Pecham,[13]—Hamo de la Dune;

Who say upon their oath, that—RALPH DE . . . . NORMANVILE,—and is of full age, and holds of our Lord the King *in capite*, ... of one knight's-fee . . . . and is in all, by the year, £10. 15*s*.[14]

IV.

[Esc. No. 7, 30 Hen. III., 1246.]

Writ to inquire how much land Geffrey de Euerle held of the inheritance of Alice his wife, and of what value. Tested at Faversham, 20th May, 30 Hen. III.

The Inquisition was taken by—

Richard de Gredle,—Joceus Puynant,—William Parcarius,—

Walter Wyse,—Alan Brid,—Simon Grobee,—William de Monte, —John de Holte,—Roger de Luffinton,—Roger Wython,—Geoffry Carpentar,—Roger de Tanilonde;[15]

Who say upon their oath, that—The said GEFFREY holds at SMETH ninety-eight acres of land worth 73*s*. 6*d*. per annum, at 9*d*. the acre. Also, he holds there sixteen acres of meadow, worth 24*s*. per annum, at 18*d*. the acre. He also holds pasture there, worth 6*s*. 8*d*. per annum, and Rent of Assize[16] 14*s*. 8*d*. And in mills, the annual value of 30*s*., and a rent of twenty hens,[17] worth 2*s*. 6*d*. per annum. And that he has a garden worth 9*s*. per annum. And that he has there in average,[18] 6*s*. 8*d*., and in the custom of mowing[19] half an acre, 2*d*. And that he has there, by the year, one hundred eggs worth 3*d*. Sum total thereof £8. 7*s*. 5*d*. of my Lady's dower. They say also, that the marriage of the heir of the said Alice[20] is worth, to sell, ten marks.

V.

[Esc. No. 5, 30 Hen. III., 1246.]

Writ to inquire how much land Isolda de Grey held in capite, etc.; who is next heir, etc. Tested at Beaulieu, 18 *June*, 30 *Hen. III.*

The Inquisition was taken by—

John Fitz Godfrey,—John Malemein,—John Pede,—Stephen de Hallestowe,—Simon de Delham,—Geffrey Salomon,—Philip de Delham,—Osbert de Fonte,—William de la Hoke,—Henry de Ecclâ,[21]—Henry de Bradefeld,—Robert Fitz Alan;

Who say upon their oath, that—ISOLDA DE GREY held half the manor of HOU, by exchange made with her four parceners, by service of half a knight's-fee; they say also, that no more than a fifth part of the entire manor came to her by inheritance. They say also, that half the entire manor is worth per annum, in domains, rents, homages, and all other issues from land, £33. 17*s*. 11*d*. And that RICHARD DE GRAY is her son and next heir.[22]

VI.

[Esc. No. 39, 30 Hen. III., 1246.]

Writ to inquire how much land Jollan de Nevill held of the King in capite, etc.; who is next heir, etc. Tested at Windsor, 5th October, 30 Hen. III.

The Inquisition was taken by—

John de Grene,—John de Dunlege,—William de Tumberwode,—Adam de Puteo,—Roger de Tumberwode,—Philip de Merston,—Henry de Lamare,—Geffrey le Fugel,—Christopher de Sorene,—Henry de la Hoke,—Jordan de Brenne,—Hugh le Sone,—Henry de Sorens,—Thomas Smaleman,—Sefan de Sorene;

Who say on their oath, that—JOLAN DE NEVILL held of our Lord the King, in SORENE,[23] twenty librates[24] of land *in capite*, by service of one knight's-fee. They say also that one JOLAN, son of the said JOLAN,[25] is his next heir, and of the age of twenty-two years and a half.

VII.[26]

[Esc. No. 11, 31 Hen. III., 1247.]

Writ to Henry de Wengeham, the Escheator, to inquire how much land Elyas de Boctun held of the King in capite, etc. Tested at Westminster, 1st Oct., 31 Hen. III.

The Inquisition was taken by—

Richard de Sotinden,—Richard de Bocton,—Stephen atte Lese,—Simon de Eechesdenne,—William de Gatele,—Robert de Golstanstrete,—Richard de Gatele,—Roger de Regisdune,—Richard de Aula,—Andrew de la Redee,—Adam Bedell,—Benedict de Frenchisburne;

Who say upon their oath, that—the said ELYAS held the manor of BOCTON[27] of our Lord the King *in capite*, by service of one knight's-fee. They say also that he had in the same manor £29. 4*s*. 0¼*d*. of rent of assize by the year; and two carucates[28] of land, with one watermill, and a windmill, with meadows and pasture worth £12. per annum. They say also that the customary services of the tenants of the said manor, and the perquisites of Courts,[29] ought to be worth in ordinary years 119*s*. and 7*d*.; and there is due therefrom every year, to the hospital of lepers at Boulogne, £20. The Jury also say that the said ELYAS held a certain land called GRESSIMERE, by the service of half a knight's-fee, of Sir Reginald de Cobbeham; and a mill there, of the fee of the Abbot of St. Augustine's, Canterbury; and that they are worth ten marks per annum. They say also that PETER,[30] eldest son of the said ELYAS, is his next heir, and is twenty-two years old and more.

VIII.

[Esc. No. 17, 31 Hen. III., 1247.]

Writ to inquire how much land Master Odo de Scerington[31] *held of the King in capite, etc.; who is the next heir, etc. Tested at Westminster*, 15*th Oct.*, 31 *Hen. III.*

The Inquisition was taken by—

Simon Potyn,—Henry de Baill,—Richard Clericus,—Gilbert Unwine,—Eustace Fitz Reymer,[32]—Alan le Gey,—Ralph the Forrestar,—John Lacy,—Hugh, son of the Priest,[33]—Arnold Tirlewine,—Ivo Fitz Ralph,—John Tirlewine;

Who say upon their oath, that—Master ODO held *in capite* of our Lord the King the manor of DELCE,[34] by service of one knight's-fee and a half, and ward to Rochester Castle as much as belongs to one knight's-fee and a half, and that the manor is worth £16 per annum. WALRAN DE SCERINTON, brother of the said ODO, is his next heir, and is forty years old and more.

IX.

[Esc. No. 56, 33 Hen. III., 1248-9.]

Writ to H. de Wengeham, and his Co-Eschcator of Kent, to inquire how much land Robert de Seuanz held of the King in capite, etc.; who is the next heir, etc. Tested at Merton, 3rd January, 33 Hen. III.

The Inquisition was taken by—

Wibert Ketiere,—Thomas ate Dune,—Gilbert ate Dune,—Bartholomew ate Wode,—Hugh Gold,—John Brutin,—Godefry Horn,—Ralph de Ysindane,—Nicholas de Wielmeston,—Arnold de Shorne,—Adam de Forstalle,—and Thomas Kix;

Who say upon their oath, that—the said ROBERT held one knight's-fee in ALDINTONE[35] of our Lord the King *in capite*, and has in domain sixty-six acres of arable land and eight acres of pasture, at 6*d*. per acre per annum, Total 37*s*.; and in rent of assize per annum 40*s*. 1½*d*., and thirty hens at 1½*d*. each, Total 3*s*. 9*d*., and three ploughs, 2*s*.,—Total of this, £4. 2*s*. 10½*d*.; and thereout is due to the castle of Rochester for ward, by the year, 14*s*. They also say that the said ROBERT held in MELETON[36] one knight's-fee of the Earl of Gloucester, and had in domain seventy-five acres of arable land and twelve acres of pasture, worth per acre 4*d*.,—Total 29*s*.; and sixteen acres of meadow, worth 16*s*.; and sixteen acres of pasture in the Alders,[37] worth 8*s*.; and he had a mill worth 30*s*. per annum; also he had 40*s*. rent of assize; and thirty-five hens, worth 1½*d*. per hen, total 4*s*. 4½*d*.; and also five ploughs, worth 2*s*. 6*d*.: Total, £5. 19*s*. 10½*d*. They also say that the said ROBERT held in WIELMESTON[38] half a knight's-fee of the Archbishop of Canterbury, and it is all in homages, and it is worth per year in rent of assize in money 38*s*. 4*d*.; and thirteen hens at 1½*d*. each,—total 19½*d*.: Total of this, 39*s*. 11½*d*. Sum total £12. 2*s*. 8½*d*., but thereout is due, as aforesaid, 14*s*. Also they say that the said ROBERT held two knights'-fees in the County of ESSEX of William de Shoford, but they know not the value. And they say that ROBERT DE SEUONT, son of the said ROBERT, is his next heir, and is about forty years old.[39]

X.

[Esc. No. 22, 34 Hen. III., 1249-50.]

[Verbatim transcript of the facsimile, *in extenso*, and a translation.]

Henricus dei gratia Rex Angliæ, Dominus Hybernie, Dux Normannie, Aquitanie, et Comes Andegavie, dilecto clerico suo Henrico de Wengham et coescaetori suo in Comitatu Kancie salutem.

Mandamus vobis, quod per sacramentum proborum et legalium hominum de Comitatu predicto, per quos rei veritas melius sciri poterit, diligenter inquiratis quantum terre Willelmus le Taylur tenuit de nobis in capite in comitatu predicto et alibi, et quantum de aliis et per quod servicium, et quantum terra illa valeat per annum, et quis propinquior heres ejus sit, et cujus etatis. Et inquisicionem inde factam, sub sigillis vestris et sigillis eorum per quos facta fuerit, nobis sine dilacione mittatis et hoc Breve. Teste meipso, apud Westmonasterium, vij die Marcii, anno regni nostri xxxiiij^{to}.

Transmittitur Aluredo de Den, Escaetori Kancie.

Nomina eorum per quos facta fuit inquisicio terrarum que fuerunt Willelmi le Tailur in Comitatu Kancie, scilicet—Robertus de Godiston,—Rogerus de Northwod,—Matheus de Eynton,—Radulphus Salvage,—Petrus Dudeman,—Turtheyn de Bobbing,—Radulphus de Cardeslose,—Radulphus de Barkesore,—Rogerus de Bosco,—Johannes de Codested,—Radulphus de Boldestred,—Radulphus de Chechele;

Qui dicunt per sacramentum suum, quod dictus Willelmus tenuit c solidatas[40] terre, in terris, redditibus, et serviciis, de domino Rege, in capite, per liberum servitium unius sperverii sori,[41] pro omnibus serviciis, per annum, in hundredo de Middelton. Dicunt etiam, quod idem Willelmus tenuit de domino Rege in predicto hundredo de Middelton, xl solidatas terre et redditus, per servicium viij solidorum iiij denariorum, pro omnibus serviciis, et est illa terra partibilis secundum consuetudinem Kancie.[42] Preterea, idem Willelmus tenuit xl solidatas terre, in terris, redditibus, et aliis serviciis, de pluribus dominis, et est similiter partibilis, in eodem comitatu. Dicunt etiam quod idem Willelmus habuit j marcam annui redditus in civitate Wyntonie, de pluribus civibus ejusdem civitatis, et hoc dicunt per auditum. Dicunt etiam quod idem Willelmus habuit v filios,

E. D. gr(aci)a Rex Angl(ie) D(omi)n(u)s Hib(er)n(ie) Dux Aquit(anie) [illegible] dilecto clerico suo Henr(ico) de Bingham escaetori suo in Comitatu Kancie salutem. [illegible] Will(elm)us Le Taylur tenuit de nobis in capite in Com(itatu) pred(icto) [illegible]

Teste me ipso apud Westm(onasterium) [illegible] anno r(egni) n(ostri) xxxiij.

[illegible] per quos facta fuit [illegible] que fuit Willi Le Taylur [illegible]

[illegible]

scilicet, WILLELMUM primogenitum, JOHANNEM, ROBERTUM, BALDEWINUM, et RADULPHUM. Et dicunt quod WILLELMUS filius suus primogenitus est propinquior heres ejus de libero tenemento suo, videlicet de predictis c solidatis terre quas tenuit de domino Rege in capite per liberum servicium unius sperverii, et etatis xxij annorum, et est maritatus tempore patris sui, et quod iste WILLELMUS est heres predicti WILLELMI patris sui cum fratribus suis prenominatis secundum equalem porcionem quemlibet contingentem de terra predicta que est partibilis secundum consuetudinem Kancie.

[Translation.]

Henry, by the grace of God, King of England, Lord of Ireland, Duke of Normandy and Aquitaine, Earl of Anjou, to his beloved Clerk, Henry de Wengham, and his Co-Escheator in Kent, greeting.

We command you, that, by the oath of good and legal men of the foresaid County, by whom the truth of the thing may be better known, you diligently inquire how much land WILLIAM LE TAYLUR held of us *in capite*, in the foresaid county and elsewhere, and how much of others, and by what service, and how much that land is worth per annum, and who is the next heir, and of what age. And that the Inquisition thereof made, under your seals and the seals of those by whom it is made, you send to us without delay, and this Writ. Witness myself at Westminster, the 7th day of March, in the year of our reign the 34th.

It is transmitted to Alured de Den, the Escheator of Kent.

The names of those by whom the Inquisition of the lands which were WILLIAM LE TAILUR's, in the county of Kent, was made, viz.—Robert de Godiston,—Roger de Northwod,—Mathew de Eynton,—Ralph Salvage,—Peter Dudeman,—Turtheyn de Bobbing,—Ralph de Eardeslose,—Ralph de Barkesore,—Roger de Bosco,—John de Codested,—Ralph de Boldestred,—Ralph de Chechele;

Who say upon their oath, that—the said WILLIAM held 100 solidates[40] of land, in lands, rents, and services, of our Lord the King *in capite*, by the free service of one sperver sore[41] by the year, for all services, in the hundred of MILTON. They say also that the said WILLIAM held of our Lord the King, in the said hundred of MILTON, 40 solidates of lands and rents, by service of 8*s*. 4*d*., for all services, and that land is divisible according to the custom of Kent.[42] Further, the same WILLIAM held 40 solidates of land, in lands, rents, and other services, of more lords, in the same county, and it is in like manner divisible. They say also that the said WILLIAM held one mark of annual rent, in the city of WINCHESTER, of many citizens of the said city, and this they say by hearsay. They say also that the said WILLIAM had five sons, viz. WILLIAM the firstborn, JOHN, ROBERT, BALDEWIN, and RALPH. And they say that his eldest son WILLIAM is his next heir of his freehold, viz. of the foresaid hundred solidates of land which he held of our Lord the King *in capite*, by the free service of one sperver sore; and he is twenty-two years of age, and was married in his father's lifetime; and that the said WILLIAM is heir of the said WILLIAM his father, together with his foresaid brothers, according to the equal portion belonging to each, of the foresaid land, which is partible according to the custom of Kent.[43]

XI.

[Esc. No. 5, 34 Hen. III., 1250.]

Writ to inquire whether ten acres, which William Turstan (who has abjured the kingdom[44] for felony) held in Hecham,[45] have been in the King's hands a year and a day, and of whom he held the land. Tested at Westminster, 30th April, 34 Hen. III.

Inquisition taken by—

Adam de Berfeld,—Stonhord de Marisco,—Henry de la Hok,—Reginald de Acle,—Turstan de Cruce,—Adam de Lefwell,—William de Dunleg,—Turstan Fitz Walter,—Turstan Fitz Aleys,—Fulco Winter,—Lambert de Acle,—and John de Regedweya;

Who say upon their oath, that—the said ten acres were in the hands of our Lord the King for a full year and a day and more;[46] and that the said WILLIAM held the said ten acres *in capite* of the Prioress of Hecham.[47]

XII.

[Esc. No. 17, 34 Hen. III., 1250.]

Writ to Henry de Wengham, and his Co-Eschcator in Kent, to inquire what land Aluf de Roking held of the King in capite. Tested at Windsor, 27th Sept., 34 Hen. III.

Inquisition held by—

William Dore,—Adam Hunte,—Turstan le Dykere,—John de Hoddeworth,—William de Parco,—Henry de Stonheld,—Eylword de Holestrete,—Dionisius de Horton,—Theobald de Roking,—William Peyteuin,—Philip de Herring,—William de Brokeshole,—Walter de Stoneheld;

Who say upon their oath, that—the said ALUF held *in capite* of our Lord the King, of the honour of HAGENET,[48] in the ville of Roking, thirty-six acres of land, by service of half a knight's-fee, and it is worth per annum in domains, homages, rents, and other issues of the land, 36*s.* 4*d.* They say also that the same ALULF held, of the fee of Roger de Markeshale, in SUTHENE, twenty-one acres, by service of 14*d.* per annum; and of John Fitz Bernard, twenty-two acres of gavelkind land, by service of 7*s.* per annum in the same ville; and those two lands are worth in domains, rents, and other issues of lands, 37*s.* . . . *d.* per annum. They say also that THOMAS, his eldest son, is his next heir, for all the land which he holds by knight-service, and Sir . . . . and ROGER, brothers of the said THOMAS, are heirs of all the remainder of his land, which he held in gavelkind. And the said THOMAS was twenty-three years old on the Translation of . . . . 34 Hen. III.[49] And this Inquisition was taken on the day . . . . St. Michael in the same year.

XIII.

[Esc. No. 47, 35 Hen. III., 1250.]

Writ to Henry de Wingham to inquire what lands Richard de Wrotham held of the King in capite in Somersetshire and Dorsetshire. Tested at Winchester, 27th December, 35 Hen. III.

Inquisition taken by a Jury, who delare the lands held in those counties by the said RICHARD DE WROTHAM, and that

William de Plessetz, aged thirty, and Constance the wife of John le Blund, aged forty, Geffrey de Skelonde, aged twenty-four, and Christiana, wife of Thomas Pikot, aged thirty, are his next heirs. They say also that the said Richard had in Kent, in the ville of Hegheland, certain land which he held of the Archbishop of Canterbury, worth 16*s*. 8*d*. per annum.[50]

XIV.

[Esc. No. 34, 35 Hen. III., 1250-1.]

The King's Writ to B. de Cryoll, and R. de Cobbeham, his Sheriff ("Vicecomiti suo") of Kent, to take into the King's hands and keep till further precept from the King, the house which was Isabella Goldwin's in Canterbury, about which there is a contention between the Prior and Convent of Christ Church, Canterbury, and the Burgesses of Canterbury; and to hold an Inquisition to inquire if the said Isabella left the said house by will to the said Prior and Convent, and whether the said Prior and Convent were in seisin thereof before the death of the said Isabella, or she herself died in seisin thereof, and if so, what seisin; and if the said Isabella could bequeath the said house, which was of her inheritance as it is said "de perquisito;" and if the said house was in the King's fee or of the fee of the said Church; and what damage the King will sustain, etc. Tested at Woodstock, 6th February, 35 Hen. III.

The Inquisition was taken at Canterbury, on Tuesday next before the feast of St. Peter in Cathedra,[51] by—

Henry le Jay,—Meyner the Dyer,—Nigell Talebot,—William Clericus,—Peter de Malling,—Dionisius le Mercer,—Gregory le Palmer,—Henry Talebot,—William Russel,—John Alex,—Robert Burre,—and Columbinus Clericus;

Who say upon their oath, that—Isabella did not and could not bequeath the said house to the said Prior and Convent, according to the custom of the said town, because it is of her inheritance "super seisinam Prioris et Conventus." They say that the said Isabella, about the feast of St. Nicholas last past, labouring under some illness, made a certain deed of feoffment to the said Prior and Convent; but, after the making of the said deed, the said Isabella remained in seisin for six weeks, and died in the seisin thereof, and with her John le Porter and Maria his wife, daughter and heir of the said ISABELLA; and that the said monks had no seisin of the said house, except by the intrusion which they made therein on the day that the said ISABELLA was buried, and ejected the said John and Maria his wife. They say also that the said house is of the fee of our Lord the King, which if it were given in frankalmoigne[52] it would be to the damage of our Lord the King, etc. etc., because if any laic held it in fee, and forfeited by any misfortune life and limb, our Lord the King would lose felon's chattels and waste[53] of the said tenement; also talliage, when any such might be collected in the said city. They say also that after the making of the said deed, on the same day, the said monks caused the said ISABELLA to be carried to the house of Andrew le Soler, but she immediately perceiving that she was not in her own house, she rose up and returned to her own house aforesaid, and drove out certain monks whom she found there, and remained in the same house as is aforesaid, in which she died. And that she had a husband, by name Robert Tolo [? Telo], who is still living; and that she, during her husband's life, could not make any gift or bequest of any tenement, according to the custom of the said city.[54]

XV.

[Esc. No. 65, 35 Hen. III., 1251.]

Writ to Nicholas de Haulo, Sheriff of Kent, and the Bailiffs of Canterbury, to inquire into the circumstances of a robbery committed on Giles Godintin, servant of John Alverdon, a merchant of Bruges, in Canterbury, of which Henry Baudewin, the host of the said Giles, his wife, and Peter Ruban, a merchant of Boulogne, are suspected. Tested at Woodstock, 6 July, 35 Hen. III.[55]

The Jury are,—

William le Brazur,—William Cokin,—Robert Polre,—John Dodeker,—William le Jay,—Henry Talebot,—Meyner the Dyer [le Tenturer],—Nigell Talebot,—Peter de Meauling,—William de Westgate,—Thomas Malemy,—Arnold the Goldsmith,—Robert Burre,—John Digge,—Alan Pecok,—Robert le Marescall,—Symon Turgis,—Walter Oysel,—Geffrey de Stureya,—and John Alex;

Who say upon their oath, that—they suspect HENRY BAUDEWIN,

the host of the said GILES, and his wife, and PETER RUBEN, merchant of Boulogne, and for this reason,—because the said PETER was commonly, through the whole of the preceding Lent, viz. for three or four days in each week, at the house of the said HENRY, in the company of the said HENRY, and used to take his meals with him at his table, and often afterwards. And they say, that the same PETER lay, the same night in which the theft was committed, on a certain floor joining the floor on which the said GILES lay, so that no one could enter the chamber in which the said GILESl ay without passing by the bed of the said PETER, and without the said PETER's hearing any one who might pass towards the chamber of the said GILES. And they suspect the said HENRY BAUDEWIN and his wife of the said robbery because of the constant companionship which the same PETER and HENRY had together, and because no one could have committed this act without the consent and abetting of others. And they say this, asking for a cessation of further inquiry until our Lord the King shall have declared his will concerning these [parties]. And further, the said Jury testify in their verdict, that the said GILES carried the said money which he seeks into the house of the said HENRY, and that in it it was thus stolen.

Another writ to the Bailiffs of Canterbury, to inquire by good and legal men of the ville of Canterbury, whether Henry Baldewin was taken in clerical habit[56] *or not. Tested at Reading,* 29 *July,* 35 *Hen. III.*

The names of the Jury,—

Meyner the Dyer,—Geffrey de Stureya,—Alexander the Mercer,—John his brother,—Stephen Cissor,—Stephen his brother,—Alan Pecok,—Andrew le Seler, John Ferre,—Gregory le Palmer,—Robert le Fenur,—Robert Burre,—Robert Ferrer;

Who say on their oath, that the said BALDWIN was taken in a lay habit, and not a clerical one, and that he always counted himself among them as a layman. Also there was exhibited the mandate of our Lord the King to the Bailiffs of Canterbury, to hold the said Inquisition on Monday next after the feast of St. Peter ad Vincula, [7 August,] before Sir Nicholas Hadlo, Sheriff of Kent, etc.

Then follows the writ to the Sheriff, ordering him to be at Canterbury on the Monday after the feast of St. Peter ad Vincula, and on that day to cause to come before him and others thereto assigned, twelve out of each of the four neighbouring hundreds, knights as well as others, by whom inquiry may be made concerning crimes in the said city.[57] *Tested at Windsor, 1 August, 35 Hen. III., by Ralph Fitz Nicholas.*

Inquisition taken by,—

The four neighbouring hundreds of the City of Canterbury, concerning crimes committed in the said city, to wit, by the hundreds of Whitstapel, Westgate, Dunhamford, and the half hundred of Blengate.

The Jury of Whitstapel say upon their oath, that—they well understand, and by report know, that GILES DE GODENTYN, servant of JOHN ALUERDON took into the house of HENRY BALDEWYN two wallets, with £200, of which, one with £100 was stolen in the said house. And they say, that they hold no one suspected of the said robbery, but the foresaid HENRY BAUDEWIN and SUSANNA his wife, and NICHOLAS the servant boy of the said HENRY, who is since dead. And they know this, because the said host acknowledges that the said merchant brought the said money into his house. Being required, however, to give verdict concerning PETER RUBIN, merchant of Boulogne, they say that they do not suspect him in any way concerning the said robbery, because he was an unknown man, and having no acquaintance with any one in the said City of Canterbury. The Jurors of all the other hundreds agree in everything with the said Jurors of Whitstapel. And because the said HENRY, as well by this foreign Inquisition,[58] as by the Inquisition formerly taken by the citizens of the Town, was convicted of the said robbery, the Justices thereto assigned were ready to render justice thereon, but, because thereupon came Master Peter Lumbard, official Commissary of the Archbishop of Canterbury, and demands him as a cleric, the foresaid judgment was prorogued until the will of our Lord the King as he shall command. And SUSANNA the wife of the said HENRY comes and says that she is pregnant, and further seeks judgment if she ought to suffer judgment "desicut ei desponš est," and so judgment upon her is likewise deferred. And because PETER RUBEN did not present himself before the Inquisition of the Town by which he was found guilty, and now by this foreign Inquisition is found altogether guiltless, judgment upon him is likewise deferred, till our Lord the King has declared his will thereon. And the Jurors of the City testify in all things the same as before.

XVI.

[Esc. No. 3, 35 Hen. III., 1251.]

Writ to inquire whether the land of Ralph la Weyte, in Benindenn, outlawed for felony, has been in the King's hands for a year and a day, or no, and of whom he held, etc. Tested at Windsor, 10*th August,* 35 *Hen. III.*

The Inquisition was taken by—

Hereword de More,—William Francois and William de Wald,—William de Metelingehame,—William de Hechindenn,—Hubert de Rolande,—Robert de Mehamme,—Thomas de Benindenn,—Richard de Leyne,—Richard Francois,—Robert la Weyte,—William de Mapledrsdenne;

Who say upon their oath, that—the land which was the foresaid Ralph's was in the King's hands for a year and a day, and that the said Ralph held the said land of the Abbot of Robertsbridge and the Convent of the same place.

XVII.

[Esc. No. 82, 36 Hen. III., 1251-2.]

Writ to inquire whether the land of Trehanston, which the brothers of the King's hospital of Ofspring have of the King's bailiwick, be of the King's domain or his escheats, and if his escheat, why? and how much it is worth, and whether the King can grant it to whom he will. Tested at Canterbury, 10 *March,* 36 *Hen. III.*

Inquisition taken by,—

Nicholas Jordan,—William Fitz Robert,—William Fitz Kynoth,—Thomas Jordan,—Simon Warman,—Daniel Prikel,—Robert de Demechirche,—James le Franceis,—Walter Goldwin,—Henry Mody,—William Hermenard,—and Hamo de Ros;

Who say upon their oath, that—the said land of Tryenestone, immediately after the Conquest of England, was given to a certain knight named Tryan, who held it as long as he lived, and, after his decease, Hugh Tryan, his son and heir, retained it, and after the said Hugh, Robert Tryan, son and heir of the said

Hugh, retained it. So that the said Trian, Hugh, and Robert, held the said land without challenge,[59] from the Lord William the King, the Bastard, to the time of King John, who took the said land, together with other lands of the Normans, into his own hands, as his escheats, and expelled the said Robert, the last holder, from his kingdom of England, and held it in his own hand for two years, and afterwards gave it to Alberic de Marinis, to hold at his pleasure, who held it to the time of our Lord the King Henry that now is. And they say, that because the said Alberic ill-treated the tenants of the said manor, the said tenants came to our Lord the King and complained to him of much wrong inflicted upon them by the said Alberic, so that, owing to the said complaint, our Lord the King took away from him the said land, and conferred it on Walter de Burgo; and after Walter de Burgo, our Lord the King gave it to Thomas de Normanvill, to hold during his pleasure; and after the said Thomas, Nicholas de Chandeler held it, of the gift of our Lord the King, during pleasure; and afterwards, our Lord the King conferred it on Jordan de Monte Martini, to hold during pleasure; and after the said Jordan, our Lord the King conferred it on the Brethren of his hospital of OSPRENG,[60] who still hold it. The said land is worth yearly, in rents and other issues of land, 100*s.*, the service of the chief lord reserved.

XVIII.

[Esc. No. 15, 36 Hen. III., 1251-2.]

Writ to inquire whether it will be to the King's injury, or that of neighbouring traders, if the King grants to the Archbishop of Canterbury to hold a Market on every Tuesday at his Manor of Wingham. Tested at Otford, 14 March, 36 Hen. III.

Inquisition taken by,—

Roger de Chilton,—Theobald de Helles,—Sampson de Wenderton,—Walter de Wenderton,—John de Hauking,—William de Dene,—Hamo Attermede,—William Adgar,—William Attemolande,—Richard de la Hale,—Thomas de Rollinge,—and Henry de Pedinge;

Who say upon their oath, that—it will not be to the injury of the King, or of neighbouring traders, but rather to their advantage; that the markets of Canterbury and Sandwich will be improved by the accession of traders coming to the said market of WINGHAM. They say also, that on Tuesday there is no market near WINGHAM which it can possibly hurt, nor any nearer than twenty leagues, which is at Lenham.[61]

XIX.

[Esc. No. 3, 36 Hen. III., 1252.]

Writ to inquire whether two acres and one perch of land in Cumbe,[62] which belonged to John, son of Robert de Cumbe, outlawed for the death of a man, were in the King's hands for a year and a day, and of whom the said John held, etc. etc. Tested at Westminster, 1 May, 36 Hen. III.

Inquisition taken by,—

Richard Fitz Matilda,—Simon Fitz Letice,—Th. Elfrich,—Geffrey Caluel,—Richard de Scalaria,—Swetman de Cherelton,—Robert Biset,—Jordan de Westgrenewich,—Robert de Ponte,—Philip Fitz John,—John Remond,—Geffrey Fitz Peter . . . .

Who say on their oath, that—the said land was in the hands of the King a year and a day, and that two acres of that land are held *in capite* of Sir Edward Albemarle, and the residue, viz. one perch, is held *in capite* of Hamo Brogan.

XX.

[Esc. No. 33, 36 Hen. III., 1252.]

Writ to the Sheriff of Kent, to inquire what lands, etc., the Advocate Bethun and the Count de Gysnes held in your bailiwick, and what fees or parts of fees ought, with justice, to be kept from them, and who now hold them. Tested at Merton, 22 May, 36 Hen. III.

[Unfortunately the Inquisition is lost, only the Writ remains.]

XXI.

[Esc. No. 20, 36 Hen. III., 1252.]

Writ to inquire whether a messuage, with its pertinencies, in Canterbury, which Mathew le Vinetar held of the King's bailiwick for life, is the King's escheat, etc., and how, etc., and what is demandable out of it for the debts of said Mathew, etc. Tested at Westminster, 9 October, 36 Hen. III.

The Inquisition was taken on the Friday before the feast of St. Simon and St. Jude (*i.e.* 25 October) by,—

John Dodeker,—Robert Polre,—Richard Samuel,—William le Brasur,—William Cokin,—William Russel,—Nigel Talebot,—John Digges,—Robert le Enuoise,—John Duraunt,—William de Westgate,—Thomas Malemie,—Henry Talebot;

Who say upon their oath, that—our Lord the King gave to MATHEW VINITAR for life, the house which was Viuard's the Jew, in Canterbury, which MATHEW is dead; whence, they say, that our Lord the King can give it to whom he pleases, without wrong to any one, as his escheat;[63] and it is worth 10*s*. per annum, the services of the Lords of the fee reserved. They say also, that Sir BERTRAND DE CRIOLL, after the death of the said MATHEW, demanded £7. 10*s*. as a debt to the King, to wit, for the Castle of Dover. Item, a certain Gascon named William Alon demanded 40*s*., but who is to pay the foresaid debts they are ignorant.

[*In dorso.*] "Facta fuit presens inquisicio per homines de Civitate, nemine pro Vicecomite Kancie presente, et sicut michi fuit transmissa, ita vobis transmitto per presentem portatorem."

XXII.

[Esc. No. 27, 37 Hen. III., 1252.]

Writ to the Sheriff of Kent, to make an extent[64] *of the land which was Joan de Saunford's, in Dene,*[65] *etc. etc.—You shall also inquire by the same Escheator, who they were who cut down and carried away the wood of Dene, after the death of the said Joan.—Summon also Hamo de Creuecqer that he be before us on the morrow of the Purification, to show why he intruded on the said land of Dene, after the death of the said Joan, whose moiety ought to be in our hands, by reason of Hugh de Plesset, one of the heirs of the said Joan, who ought to hold of us in capite in Melton.*[66] *Tested at Clarendon, 16th December, 37 Hen. III.*

The names of those by whom the extent was made, at Dene, on Friday next after the feast of St. Hillary, 37th year of Hen. III. (*i.e.* 17th January, 1252-3), of the lands which were Joan de Sanford's, in Dene, by their oaths :—

Thomas de Scorne,—Thomas de Dene,—Alexander atte Worde,—Thomas de Cumbe,—William Faukner,—Walter Cupere,—Walter Gerin,—Geoffrey de Wriksling,—Walter le Here, —Gilbert de Weelete,—William Forestar,—Adam de Wixling, —Eylwaker le Pesoner,—Simon le Harpere,—and Herbert Gangi,—the Jury ;

Who say, that JOAN DE SANFORD held 100 acres of land in DENE, and each acre is worth 8*d*. per annum,—Total, 66*s*. 8*d*. The same Joan held in DENE 24 acres of wood, from which nothing can be taken without destruction, beyond what is required for maintaining the manor of DENE. Of rent, they say that the said JOAN held in DENE 18*s*. and 4½*d*; of rent of hens, 26 hens, and they are worth 3*s*. 3*d*., at 1½*d*. per hen. The same Jury say that Henry de Chipenham, John le Boteler, the men of J., Earl of Warwick; John, the man of Mathew le Huse; Richard de la Done, the man of Thomas de Aldenham; and Nigell de Tedesdenn, the man of Sir Hamo de Creuequer, cut and carried away the wood of DENE, after the death of the said JOAN.[67]

[Stitched up with the above is a writ to the Escheator of Bucks to inquire what land the Lady Joan de Sanford held in Missenden, etc., but the Inquisition thereon is lost.]

XXIII.

[Esc. No. 17, 37 Hen. III., 1252-3.]

[The following Inquisition is a mere fragment; only about the first six words of each line remain; it is headed :—]

E. the Abbot of Pershore, to his beloved Sir Anered de Dene, his Co-Escheator in Kent. We have received the King's mandate, etc., to inquire how much land Robert de Seuanz held of him in capite, in your bailiwick. Tested at Windsor, 20 *January,* 37 *Hen. III.*

Jury,—

William Brutin,—John his brother,—. . . . . . . ,—Dru de la Warre,—Ernald . . . .

That the said Robert held of our Lord . . . . and twenty-four acres, 11*s.* 4*d.* . . . . and thirty-six hens of the value of 3*s.* . . . . that the said manor is held by the service of the fee . . . . the Lady Matilda holds the manor in dower . . . . in Meleton thirty-two acres of arable land . . . . and that he held a certain water-mill . . . . 2*s.* 10*d.* And they say, that that manor is held of . . . . by service of half a knight's-fee. In homages, rents, ... and is of the age of four years.

Total of the land, which
Edward Roff. but the wife of Robert de Sewans . . . .

Total of the land which he holds of the Earl of Gloucester . . . . £9. 6*s.* 10*d.*
Total of the land which he holds of the Archbishop . . . . 40*s.*[68]

XXIV.

[Esc. No. 36, 37 Hen. III., 1253.]

Writ to the Abbot of Pershore, the King's Escheator, to inquire how much the manor of Derteford is worth by the year. Tested at Windsor, 12*th June,* 37 *Hen. III.*

Inquisition taken by—

Richard de Gurnay,—Roger de Wilmenton,—Thomas le Vinetar,—William de Wilmenton,—Alexander Fitz Henry,—

Joses de Marisco,—John Ruffus,—Adam de Hamstall,—Robert de Rypa,—Simon de Cumbe,—. . . . . .—Jordan de Sutton,—and Geffry de Marisco;

Who say upon their oath, that—in the manor of DERTEFORD are $3\frac{1}{2}$ acres of meadow in domain, and worth 16*s.* per annum. They say also, that of the said manor are held 28 yokes of land, by service of £28 of rent of assize per annum; and certain other lands, which are called MATHILDELAND, are held of the same manor, by service of 12*s.* of rent of assize per annum. Further, the said land called MATHILDELAND ought to find one horse for the lord of the manor, twice a year, at Winchester or at Dover, to carry the rent of the lord, at the cost of the lord in going, and at his own cost in returning; and be it known, that if the horse die in the service of the lord, the lord is bound to restore the value of the horse, and that service is estimated at 2*s.* per annum. And be it known, that 24 yokes of the said 28 yokes, and the said land which is called MATHILDELAND, render, by the year, 16*s.* 8*d.*, for the ploughing that is due, and that service is called 'Erthselver.' Item, to the said manor pertains 7*s.* of rent, which is called 'Medgavel.' Item, in the said manor is a certain rent, which is called 'Inland,' and is worth 100*s.* per annum. Item, from a certain land, which is called 'Acolt,' 40*s.* per annum are rendered to the said manor. Item, from one watermill and a half, 40*s.* per annum. Item, from burgage,[69] 39*s.* per annum. Item, from a certain liberty in the said manor, which is called 'Gilde,' 23*s.* 4*d.*, and sometimes more, when the number of the brethren increases, and sometimes less, when the number of the brethren decreases. Item, from toll of the bank, and of passage of the town, and of alepeny,[70] and of the market, 10 marks per annum of rent. Item, there are certain members pertaining to the said manor, viz. CRANESTEDE, with its pertinencies, and it renders 66*s.* 3*d.* per annum of rent of assize; and CHISELHERST, 104*s.* 10*d.* of rent of assize; and CUMBE, £6 per annum of rent of assize; and COBBEHAM, £4. 13*s.* 4*d.* per annum of rent of assize. They say also that the perquisites and reliefs of the said court are worth, in ordinary years, according to the estimate of the said Jury, c^{s}.

Sum total of this Extent,—£73. 13*s.* 1*d.*

APPENDIX.

(1.) In Sir Roger Twysden's MS. *Adversaria* to Cowell (*sub voce* "Knight's-fee"), there occurs the following valuable note on the much debated question of the quantity of land contained in a Knight's-fee, the measurement of the Hide, Scutage, etc. etc.:—

"Sciendum quod magnum feodum militare constat de quatuor Hidis, et quælibet Hida de quatuor virgatis, et quælibet Virgata terræ de quatuor Farendellis, et quælibet Farendella ex decem acris arabilibus. Et sciendum, quando dabitur ad Scutum pro magno feodo militari prædicto 40*s.*, tunc pro una virgata 40 acrarum 2*s.* 6*d.*, pro dimidia virgata 15*d.*, pro una farendella $7\frac{1}{2}$*d.*, pro una acra $\frac{3}{4}$*d.*, et sic 160 acræ terræ arabilis, et Hidata faciunt unam Hidam, et 4 Hidæ, quarum quælibet 160 acræ terræ arabilis, et Hidata faciunt unum magnum Feodum militare, quod dat ad Relevium centum solidos; et sciendum, quod quando magnum Feodum dat ad Scutagium 40*s.*, vel Relevium 100*s.*, tunc minus Feodum quod dicitur "de Maritona" dabit ad Scutagium 25*s.*, vel ad Relevium 5 markes, in utroque casu sic sciendum quantitatem. Ex libro Thomæ Fanshaw. Et sic nota quod Feodum militis constat ex quatuor Hidis, i.e. quatuor carucatis.

"By which accompt the fee of a knight being £20, a carve of land, which is the fee of a sokeman or yeoman, is £5; et nota, that hyde is sometime taken for virgata terræ; et nota, that there is virgata terræ major, minor, minima,—major 40 acres, minor 20, minima 4 [sic MSS., quære annon debet esse 5? R. T.], as may be gathered by the Record following:—Anno 19 Willelmi I. 'He raysed a newe kynd of taxe over all England, that is, of every hyde 6*s.*, and every hyde contained 4 yards; every yard (as to that tribut) 4 acres' [quære annon debet esse 5? R. T.]; and so an hyde, according to the least quantity is 20 acres, according to the lesser 80, according to the greatest 160 acres, which is a carve of land, and a knight's-fee is 4 carves.—Ex eodem libro collect. [Sir Edward Coke's Reports, MSS. fol. 361 b.]"*

* This passage is from an interleaved copy of Cowel's Interpreter, very copiously annotated by the learned Baronet. On the fly-leaf he gives a list of the authors and works cited by him. *Inter alia*, "Sir Edward Coke's reports MSS.—It is a great thick booke in fol., having on y[e] leaves CCC. It is now my brother Thom's [*i.e.* Sir Thomas Twisden, Bart., the Judge], and was my uncle Heneage's [*i.e.* Sir Heneage Finch, Serjeant-at-Law, Recorder of London]. S[r] Ed. Cooke, when my uncle had once

(2.) It should be noted here, that all the rights which attached to the King over his tenants by knight's-service *in capite*, belonged also (with the exception of "Primer seisin" and "Fine for alienation") to all feudal lords over their tenants who held of them by knight's-service.

The position of these mesne lords, as intermediate between the Crown, whose tenants they were, and those inferior tenants of whom they themselves were lords, is fully explained at p. 4.

(3.) The wardship and marriage of the heir were fruitful sources of revenue to the Lord; they were saleable as ordinary chattels, and were so treated. "The guardian in chivalry was not accountable for the profits made of the infant's lands during the wardship, but received them for his own private emolument, subject only to the bare maintenance of the infant; and this guardianship being deemed more an interest for the profit of the guardian than a trust for the benefit of the ward, was saleable and transferable, like the ordinary subjects of property, to the best bidder." (Hargrave, cited in a note to Blackstone, vol. ii. p. 70.) And the same remark applies to the right of marriage, "maritagium." This power led to such grievous oppression, that, in Magna Charta, and all the charters of liberties, we have this clause—"Heirs shall be married without disparagement." [In the Great Charter it is further added,—"Ita quod antequam contrahatur matrimonium, ostendatur propinquis de consanguinitate hæredis,"—it was to be announced to the blood relatives.] "Without disparagement,"—that is,—If they were given in marriage before the age of fourteen, which was deemed their age of discretion, they might disagree to the match, if any kind of disparagement existed; and by the Statute of Merton (20 Hen. III.) heirs of any age were not to be compelled to marry at the command of their lord; but then, when they came of age, they were to pay their lord whatever sum might have been given for their marriage. The words of the statute are these:—"Yf any heyre (of what age soever he be) wyll not marrye at the requeste of his Lorde, he shall not be compelled thereto, but, when he commeth to

argued for hym passing well, and saved hym from beeing fyned, in requitall of hys paynes, permitted him to write all ye Reports, y^t he, a long practiser and a Judge, had collected, of wch some were published, but, in my slender judgment, the best remayned only in writing. These, I say, he suffer'd my uncle to copy out. This book is since burnt."

full age, he shall gyve to hys Lorde, and paye him asmoche as any wolde have gyven hym for the maryage before the receyte of his lande, and that whither he wyl marye himself or not. For the maryage of hym that is within age of mere ryghte pertayneth to the lorde of the fee." To enter into the legal cases of disparagement, and all the points relating to the law of "maritagium," would occupy too much of our space here. For the rest we must refer to the lucid chapter on Tenures in Blackstone.

(4.) It is as well to observe here, that among these Records some "Inquisitiones ad quod Damnum" and Pleadings in the King's Court, etc., have been intermingled, probably by accident. We transcribe them, as they occur, because none of them are without their interest to county or even to general history.

(5.) There is, however, an earlier document among these Records. It is not an "Inquisitio post mortem," but belongs properly to an entirely different class of Records, and was not originally calendered with the Escheats. It is tested at Westminster, 22nd January: the regnal year is gone.

"Writ to inquire whether William Briwerr was disseised of one carucate of land, with its pertinencies, in Niweton, by the sentence or will of King John, 'our father;' also to inquire if . . . . de Lucy was disseised of the said carucate of land, with its pertinencies, 'occasione gwerre vel non.'

"Teste Com. W. Mar., rectore nostro et regni nostri, xxij die Januarii, per dominum Wintoniensem et Justič . . . . de Lucy quod intersit inquisitioni illi faciende si voluerit."

[The date of this Writ, then, must have been between January 1216–7 and 1219, the 1st and 3rd Hen. III., because William, Earl Marshall, Governor of the King, died in 1219.]

"Names of the knights by whom the Inquisition of Newinton was taken—

"William de Ceritun,—Albricus de Marines,—Simon de Chelesfeld,—William de Dudintun,—Stephen de Chileh . . . . ford,—Roger de Everinges,—Hugh de Sumesfeld,—Reginald de Waldis,—Robert de . . . . de Dene,—Giles de Badlesmere,—William Puingnent,—William de Barmling,—Alexander . . . . Balestarius—Ralph de Selling,—Philip de Hegham,—Joceus de Eterh . . . . selin de Valuinnes,—Adam de Bendinges,—Bartholemew de Moriston,—. . . . de Campania,—Stephen de Wimundell (?),—Thomas de

Rugeleston,—. . . . Ful . . . .,—Henry de Cobbeham,—. . . . . . . Simon de Maneby.

"They say that certainly William Briwere was disseised . . . . pertinencies in Newintun, by the will of our Lord the King, and on judgment; but they do not know . . . . de Luci was afterwards disseised; but the Court of our Lord the King will know how better than they; and this Inquisition is made 'in pleno comitatu.'

"Witnesses all others there present."

(6.) The Priory of Modinden in Hedcorne was founded by Sir Richard de Rokesle, 9 Hen. III., 1224, for Friars of the Order of the Holy Trinity; being the first house of the order founded in England.—*Hasted.*

(7.) Plumworth, now Plumford,—a farm, formerly a manor, in Ospringe.

(8.) This writ was probably issued in order to secure the King's rights in the rents in question, held of him hitherto *in capite* by the De Rokesles, and now claimed to be exempt from knight's-service, as held in "frank-almoigne" by the Prior of Modinden. The Inquisition was to investigate the truth of the Prior's claim to exemption.

(9.) ? Sinecok,—Siuecok.

(10.) "Syva;"—a sieve of fruit in Kent, in the present day, contains one bushel.

(11.) By an entry on the Fine Roll, 20 Hen. III. m. 7, it appears that Dionisia was widow of this Richard Noel.—"Dionisia que fuit uxor Ricardi Noel, finem fecit cum Rege, per centum solidos, pro habenda custodia terre et heredum prefati Ricardi, una cum maritagio eorundem heredum."—T. R. apud Evesham, 15 Julii, 20 Hen. III.

From this entry, then, and the Inquisition we may conjecture the following descent:—

Richard Noel = Dionisia.
Dead 1236. 1236.

William Noel,
son and heir, 1236.

(12.) "Dominus" in original.

(13.) ? Petham.

(14.) The above is a mere fragment. In the Calendars the

property is cited as at Kenardington, which word, though now gone, was probably extant when the Calendars were made.

(15.) ? Tamlonde.

(16.) "Rent of Assize," or "Assized Rents," were fixed rents to be paid either in money or provisions by the free-holders and ancient copyholders of a manor; the amount was fixed and could not be altered; they are now generally called "quit-rents."

(17.) "Gall."—It may be intended either for "gallos" or "gallinas."

(18.) "Averagium,"—the service of horse and carriage which the tenant owes to the lord.

(19.) "Metandi,"—the service of mowing which the tenant owes to the lord.

(20.) On the Fine Roll, 34 Hen. III. m. 1, there is this entry:—"Geffrey de Everle ('finem fecit') with the King, for twenty marks, for the wardship of the land and heirs of Alice de Gresley, to hold till the legal age of the said heirs, together with their marriage."

By the above entry and the Inquisition, we may conjecture the following pedigree:—

Geffrey de Everle = Alice de Gresley.
1246–1250.

It would seem, therefore, that Alice de Gresley was an heiress, and had had issue by a previous husband.

(21.) Ecclã, for "Ecclesia," *i.e.* Henry of the Church.

(22.) From an entry on the Fine Roll, 9 Hen. III. m. 3, we have—"Our Lord the King took homage of Jordan Foliot, Isolda de Gray, and Ralph Paynel, of the portions which belong to them of the lands which were their uncle's, Robert Bardulf, which he held of our Lord the King *in capite*. The Sheriff to give them seisin, after taking security for their relief. Like security is to be taken of Robert Lupus, in place of his mother, Matilda Bardulf, who is also one of the heirs of the said Robert Bardulf, for her portion. But of the portion of Hugh Poinz, likewise one of the heirs of the said Robert, the Sheriff is to keep custody."

From the above entry on the Fine Roll and the Inquisition, the following conjectural pedigree may be deduced:—

. . . . Bardulf =
dead 1246.

Robert Bardulf ob. s.p. 1246. | . . . . = dau. dead 1246. | . . Foliot = dau. dead 1246. dead 1246. | . . Paynel = dau. dead 1246. dead 1246. | Lupus = Matilda. dead 1246. 1246. | Poinz = dau. dead 1246. dead 1246.

. . . . de Grey dead 1246. = Isolda. 1246. | Jordan Foliot. 1246. | Ralph Paynel. 1246. | Robert Lupus. 1246. | Hugh Poinz, inf. æt. 1246.

Richard de Grey, heir to his mother, 1246.

But this is capable of many variations which may be imagined, and yet none of them contradictory to our Record; indeed, it would seem most probable, from his being under age, that Hugh Poinz was a *grandson* of a sister of Robert Bardulf,—not the *son*.

(23.) Sorene, *i.e.* Shorne.

(24.) "Librata terre," as much land as is worth 20*s*. a year.

(25.) On the Fine Roll, 4 Hen. III. m. 8, we have this entry:—"To the Sheriff of Kent.—John de Nevill, as we have been given to understand, is dead, and we have received the homage and fealty of Jolland, brother and heir of the said John, for one knight's-fee, which the said John held of us in Shornesse."

On Fine Roll, 29 Hen. III. (between 2nd and 10th November, 1244), m. 17, we have:—"Jollan de Nevill gives our Lord the King twenty marks for the royal assent to his marrying Sarah, widow of John Heriz."

On Fine Roll, 30 Hen. III. (19th October, 1246), m. 2,—The King receives the homage of Jollan, son and heir of Jollan de Nevill, for one knight's-fee held of the King *in capite* in Shornes.—19th Oct., 30 Hen. III.

From the Fine Roll and Inquisition together we get the following pedigree:—

. . . . de Nevill =
Dead.

John de Nevill. Dead 1219. | Jollan de Nevill = heir to his brother. Dies 1246. | ? was Sarah (widow of John Hariz), wife to the father or the son?

Jollan de Nevill.
Æt. 22, 1246.

(26.) The next in order of these Records is Esc. No. 52, 31 Hen. III., 1247. The Writ alone is extant; the Inquisition itself is wanting: we therefore omit it from our text. It is a Writ, tested at Windsor 28th August, 31 Hen. III., 1247, to the Sheriff of Kent, that he, together with R. de Chornehille and R. de Sevanz, shall inquire by a Jury whether William Potin of Rochester inhibited the men of the Prior of Rochester, of the city of Rochester, "ne ipsi aliquid contribuerent ad tallagium quod assessum fuit in ipsa civitate pro carta quatuordecim civium posita in judaismo acquietanda, que ibi posita fuit ad instanciam totius communitatis ejusdem ville, et pro communi utilitate; et si per inhibicionem illam carta illa remansit acquietanda, propter quod super cartam illam multe cucurrerunt usure; et quante usure super cartam illam cucurrerunt a tempore quo predictum tallagium debuit fuisse solutum," and to return the said Inquisition under seal. Meanwhile they are not to take the body of the said William, but take security of him for 40*s*.

(27.) This is most probably Boughton-under-Blean.

(28.) Carucate, "ploughlands,"—as much land as one horse could plough in a year, the number of acres necessarily varying according to the nature of the soil; but much uncertainty still exists as to the extent of the carucate. See note 1.

(29.) Perquisites of Court,—profits that came to the Lord of the Manor by casualty and not yearly, as escheats, heriots, reliefs, waifes, estrays, etc. etc.

(30.) On Fine Roll, 31 Hen. III., it appears that the King received the homage of this Peter de Bocton 25th October.

(31.) Sceriton,—generally written "Ciriton."

(32.) Fitz Reymer,—? Fitz Reyner.

(33.) "Filius Sacerdotis."

(34.) *i.e.* Delce, in Rochester.

. . . . de Sceriuton =

Odo de Sceriuton.	Walran de Sceriuton.
Dead 1247.	Æt. 40.
	Heir to his brother.

(35.) This is the manor of Aldington Septvans, in Thurnham; so called from the Septvans family, one of whom, as evidenced by the Pipe Roll, inherited it as one of the coheirs of William

Fitz Helte, temp. Hen. II. As we hope to give in a future volume, in fullest detail, the early history of Thurnham and Aldington, with their owners, Fitz Helte, Septvans, Thurnham, Fitz Bernard, Northwode, etc. etc., we will not prolong this note.

(36.) This is Milton-next-Canterbury.

(37.) "Alneto,"—"an alder-bed," which we usually, in Kent, call "The Alders."

(38.) Wielneston.—We conjecture this to be the manor of Vielston, or Filston, in Shoreham, belonging to the Archbishops of Canterbury, and held of the Archbishops *circiter* 1260 by the Earls of Clare.

(39.) By the Fine Roll, 33 Hen. III. m. 11, we find that Robert de Sevanz did his homage, as tested, January 17th, 33 Hen. III.

By the same Roll, 34 Hen. III. m. 11, the King grants to Robert de Sevanz, that, of the fifty marks which he owes for his relief for the third part of the Barony which was William Fitz Helte's (see an account of the three coheirs of Fitz Helte, p. 30, *supra*), he pay twenty-five marks at Michaelmas, and twenty-five at Easter next. Tested 1st May, 34 Hen. III.

We defer the complete pedigree elicited by the Fine Roll and this Inquisition till we come to the Inquisition on the death of this Robert, *infra*, No. XXIV.

(40.) "Solidata,"—as much land as is worth 1*s*. per annum. "One hundred solidates" of land, therefore, was as much land as is worth £5 per annum.

(41.) "Spervarius,"—a sparrow-hawk. "Sore,"—a young hawk of the first year ("Anniculus et primarum pennarum,"—*Du Cange*).

(42.) *i.e.* Gavelkind.

(43.) From this Inquisition we have the following pedigree:—

William le Taylur =
Dead 1250.

William = eldest, æt. 22.	John.	Robert.	Baldwin.	Ralph.

William's homage (by Fine Roll 34 Hen. III. m. 13) is tested 15th March, and seisin given to him in the lands which he held *in capite*, and to him and his brothers in the gavelkind lands.

(44.) "Abjuravit regnum."—Formerly, in Edward the Confessor's time, and down to 22 Hen. VIII., if a man committed felony, and he could fly to a church or churchyard before his apprehension, he might not be taken thence to be tried for his crime; but, on confession thereof before a Justice, or before the Coroner, he was admitted to swear that he would "abjure" or forsake the realm, during which time any persons might give him meat and drink for his sustenance; but not after, on pain of being guilty of felony.—*Jacob*.

(45.) Hecham, *i.e.* Higham, near Gravesend.

(46.) "A year and a day."—The King's prerogative was, that he should have the profits of lands and tenements, for "a year and a day," of those that are attainted of petit treason or felony, whosoever is lord of the manor whereto the lands or tenements belong. The same prerogative gave him a right to Waste, *i.e.* he might destroy the houses, plough up the meadows, root up the woods, etc., afterwards restoring the land to the lord of the fee. He had also an absolute right to the chattels of felons.—*Jacob*.

(47.) *i.e.* the Prioress of the Priory of Lillechurch in Higham.

(48.) Hagenet, probably Aghne Court, in Romney.

(49.) The Inquisition supplies this pedigree:—

Aluf de Roking =

Thomas de Roking, eldest son and heir, æt. 23, 1250.	A son. 1250.	Sir Roger de Roking. 1250.

(50.) On the Fine Roll, 35 Hen. III. m. 6, we have this entry:—

"The King received the homage of John Blund and Thomas Picot, who had for their wives two sisters and heirs of Richard de Wrotham, and the homage of William Plessiz and Geffrey Shoplond, who are nephews and two heirs of the said Richard, of all the lands and tenements which the said Richard held of the King *in capite*. Tested at Woodstock, 6th February."

The Fine Roll, 35 Hen. III. m. 12, cites William de Plessetis, "qui habet eyniciam hereditatis que fuit Ricardi de Wrotham." Tested at Westminster, 15th May.

On the same Roll, 35 Hen. III., m. 13, we have "Cecilia, who was wife of Richard de Wrotham, pays to the King one mark for an assize of novel disseisin" (Somersetshire). Tested at Reading, 16th May.

From the Fine Roll, then, and Inquisition, we have this pedigree:—

. . . . de Wrotham =

Richard de Wrotham. Dead 1250. = Cecilia. Dead 1251.

. . Plessitz Dead 1250. = eldest dau. Dead 1250.

John le Blund. 1250. = Constance, dau. & coh. to her bro. æt. 40, 1250.

. . . . de Skelonde Dead 1250. = dau. Dead 1250.

Thomas Picot. 1250. = Christiana, dau. & coh. to her bro., æt. 30, 1250.

William de Plessitz, æt. 30, 1250, coheir to his uncle, Richard de Wrotham.

Geffrey de Skelonde, æt. 24, 1250. coheir to his uncle, Richard de Wrotham.

(51.) *i.e.* 21st February.

(52.) "Elemosinata."

(53.) *Vide* above, note 46.

(54.) Robert Tolo 1250-1. = Isabella Goldwin. Dead 1250-1.

John le Porter 1250-1. = Maria, daugh. and heir of her mother, 1250-1, but ? whether by a former husband or by Robert Tolo.

(55.) Though not an "Inquisitio post mortem," yet of too much interest, as illustrating constitutional history, to be omitted.

(56.) "Clericali habitu."—Originally the law held, that no man should be admitted to the privilege of Clergy but such as had the "habitum et tonsuram clericalem." When the Ordinary, by his Commissary, claimed the accused as a cleric, a writ was issued to inquire into the validity of the claim. Such was this writ. With regard to the origin of this privilege it is to be observed that, anciently, Princes converted to Christianity granted great immunities to the Clergy, *inter alia* exemption of their persons from criminal proceedings, even in capital cases, before secular judges. The Privilege of Clergy is said to have had its beginning from an encroachment of the Pope upon the temporal power in behalf of the Clergy, whom he endeavoured to exempt from the jurisdiction of lay judges, in case of life and member;

which the temporal courts would only partly yield to; and, first they would indict clerks of felony as well as others, and proceed thereon, until the Ordinary did demand them, and if the Ordinary would not demand them, the King's Court proceeded to conviction, attainder, and execution: and if the Ordinary claimed clerks before conviction, then an Inquisition was taken whether the party was guilty or not, and if acquitted, he was discharged, but if found guilty, then delivered to the Ordinary, to be dealt with according to the Ecclesiastical Canon. The privilege, thus restrained, was confirmed by Statute of Westminster I. cap. 2:—

"It is provyded also that when a clerke is taken for gylte of Felonye, and is demaunded by the Ordynarye, he shall be delyvered to hym accordyng to the privylege of holy church, in suche paryll as belongeth to it, after the custome afore tymes used. And the Kynge admonyshed the Prelates and enioyned them upon the fayth that they owe hym, and for the commen profyte and peace of the realme, that they whiche be indyted of suche offences by solempne inqueste of lawefull men in the Kynge's courte, in no maner shall be delyvered without due purgacyon, so that the Kynge shall not nede to provyde any other remedye therin."

The Ordinary, when the accused was delivered over to him on his demand, "would not be satisfied with the proofs adduced in the profane Court, but set himself formally to work to make purgation of the offender by a new Canonical trial, although he had been previously convicted by his country, or perhaps by his own confession. This trial was held before the Bishop in person, or his deputy, or by a jury of twelve clerks; and there first the party himself was required to make oath of his own innocence; next there was to be the oath of twelve compurgators, who swore they believed he spoke the truth; then witnesses were to be examined upon oath, but on behalf of the prisoner only; and lastly, the jury were to bring in their verdict upon oath, which usually acquitted the prisoner; otherwise, if a clerk, he was degraded or put to penance."—*Blackstone.*

(57.) This was the Hundred Court Leet. Court Leets could inquire of all offences under treason; but those which were punishable with loss of life or member, were only inquirable and presentable here, and to be certified over to the Justices of

Assize. But, after all, was not this a Writ de Inquirendo, not for trying the parties, but to ascertain the King's title to the forfeiture of the felon's lands and goods? "There is no such nicety required in an 'Inquisition' as in Pleading, because an 'Inquisition' is only to inform the Court how Process shall issue for the King, whose title accrues by the attainder, not by the Inquisition."—*Jacob*.

(58.) Foreign Inquisition.—"Forinceca," *i.e.* not taken from the city, but from without.

(59.) Here we have an unusually clear and unbroken descent of a manor from the Conquest down to days of regular record. It may be questioned however on what evidence the jury had founded their verdict. It seems hardly credible that there should have been only three generations from the time of the Conquest to John.* Still it is possible. If we suppose the Conqueror's grant to have been made to the first Tryan when he was twenty-five years old, as late as 1085, and that at the age of forty-five he had his son Hugh, this would make the date of Hugh's birth 1105. Now, suppose that this Hugh be forty-five years old when his son Robert was born, this would be in the year 1150, and would bring it within the limits of possibility that this Robert lived to be dispossessed by John. The forfeiture of the Norman's lands was about 5 John, *i.e.* about 1203, when (on our supposition) Robert Tryan would have been fifty-three years of age. If we suppose him seventy-three at the period of his expulsion, we shall have sufficient latitude for readily acquiescing in the declaration of the jury, for then his father and grandfather need neither of them have been more than thirty-five when their respective sons were born. On the rebellion in Normandy, by which John lost that province, he seized upon the possessions which any of the rebels happened to have in England, and thus the land in

* According to the pedigree which they give,—

. . . . Tryan =
temp. Wm. I.

Hugh Tryan =

Robert Tryan
temp. Jo.

question, of Robert Tryan, escheated to him. The manor in question is TRIENSTONE, in the parish of BURMARSH. By the aid of this Inquisition we shall be enabled to trace the descent of this manor from the Conquest to the present day.

(60.) The King's hospital, the Maison Dieu, of Ospringe, was founded by Henry III., about fifteen years previous to our Inquisition. The manor was held by the King himself.

(61.) Writs of "ad quod damnum" were always issued before the grant of Letters Patent for a market, in order to secure the King, and more especially the owners of neighbouring markets, from any injury to be sustained by the establishment of a new market in the vicinage.

(62.) ? Whether this be the manor of Combe in Swanscombe, or Combe in Greenwich, see Survey of Dartford, *supra*, p. 312.

Robert de Cumbe =
|
John de Cumbe.

(63.) On the Fine Roll, 37 Hen. III. m. 24, we have—

"The King granted to Adam Maresč (Marescall) the messuage, with its pertinencies, in Canterbury, which Mathew le Vinitor held of the bailiwick of the King, for life, etc. etc. Tested at Windsor, 2nd November."

(64.) "Extendi facias,"—have an extent or survey made.

(65.) This may be Dene manor, in Wingham; but we have not been able to identify it.

(66.) ? Melton.

(67.) On the Fine Roll, 37 Hen. III. m. 21, we have,—John de Plessetis, Earl of Warwick, gives the King two marks for seisin of the mediety of the lands which were Joan de Saunford's, in Messenden (Bucks).

According to Dugdale, this is the pedigree attaching to this John de Plessetis :—

Hugh de Sanford = Joan de Sanford.
|
Margery, sister and heir of Earl of Warwick. =(2) John de Plessetis Earl of Warwick. =(1) Christian, daughter and heir.
|
Hugh de Plessetis.

(68.) On Fine Roll, 37 Hen. III. m. 17, we have—

"The Sheriff of Kent is ordered to take into the King's hands the manor of Meleton, which was Robert de Sevanz, deceased, except the dower of Matilda, who was wife of Robert de Sevanz, father of said Robert, etc."

And on Fine Roll, 37 Hen. III. m. 16, we have—

"The King, for twenty marks, etc., grants to Reginald de Cobeham the wardship of the heirs of Robert de Sevanz, and of all the lands, etc. which he held of the King *in capite*, with all other the lands and tenements which were the said Robert's on the day he died, of whomsoever he held them; to hold to the said Reginald and his heirs and assigns till the lawful age of the heirs of the said Robert; together with the marriage of the said heirs, and of Isabella the widow of the said Robert, if she chooses to marry, etc. etc. Tested at Windsor, 14 February."

From these entries and the Inquisition No. 56, 33 Hen. III., p. 17, *supra*, we gather the following pedigree:—

Robert de Sevanz = Matilda.
Dead 1249. 1253.

Robert de Sevanz = Isabella.
Æt. 40, 1249. 1253.
Dead 1253.

Robert de Sevanz.
Æt. 3 (? 4), 1253.
Son and heir.

(69.) 'Burgage,'—the tenure by which the inhabitants of the town held their lands and tenements.

(70.) 'Alepeny,' or 'alesilver,'—tax paid for the right of selling ale within the manor.

INDEX TO INQUISITIONES.

For the convenience of those who may wish to bind up the 'Inquisitiones post mortem' separately, the references in the Index are made, not to the pages, but to the number of the Fine.

The names within brackets show the form of spelling adopted in the original.

GENERAL INDEX.

W. signifies that the party is witness to a deed.

J. E. TAYLOR, PRINTER, LITTLE QUEEN STREET, LINCOLN'S INN FIELDS.

CPSIA information can be obtained
at www.ICGtesting.com
Printed in the USA
LVHW100733010323
740521LV00002B/130

9 783382 302276